A Butterfly in Paris

Written by Matt Pelicano
Cover by Don Cornue

April Fool Publishing, Inc.

Cover by Don Cornue.
www.DonCornue.com

April Fool Publishing, Inc.
Matt Pelicano
www.mattpelicano.com

Summary: Esmée Délancourt was perfectly happy never to leave her quiet home in Saint-Denis-lès-Chevreuse, France. But when the doors of the commuter train bound for Paris slide closed, trapping her inside, she finds herself an unwilling participant in an adventure through the City of Lights.

As Esmée struggles to find her way home again, the little butterfly meets a cast of characters and witnesses a world of wonders she could never have imagined. Through danger, love, and loss, she comes to understand the meaning of the word *home* and the symbolism hidden in a sculpture tucked away in the Louvre Museum; a sculpture her mother used to teach an important childhood lesson.

1. YOUNG ADULT FICTION / Animals / General
2. YOUNG ADULT FICTION / Travel & Transportation / General
3. YOUNG ADULT FICTION / People & Places / Europe

ISBN/SKU: 9780578667867
ISBN Complete: 978-0-578-66786-7
Publication Date: 4/27/2020

A Butterfly in Paris/Matt Pelicano. -- 1st ed.
ISBN 978-0-578-66786-7

For Cécilia, who inspires far more than mere words.
Tu es ma muse et le centre de tous les désirs de mon cœur.

*"The world is a book and those who do not travel
read only one page."*

-Augustine of Hippo

Table of Contents

Preface

When I was young, I was afraid to fly. The first time I traveled by plane, I was twelve years old. My parents and I flew to the Gulf coast to visit my oldest brother, who was in the military at that time. In the weeks leading up to our departure, I whipped myself up into a frenzied state of dread. When the day finally arrived, I was certain it would be my last on this planet.

I remember the sensation of taking-off and thinking that the tail of the plane was going to drop back and hit the runway. I remember flying into Newark International Airport and seeing the Statue of Liberty covered in scaffolding (it was being renovated in preparation for its centennial celebration). Most of all, I remember getting sick – violently sick – and the look on the flight attendant's face when my father handed her the air-sickness bag as we left the plane. Perhaps I should dedicate this book to her.

The whole time we were at my brother's house, despite the beautiful, white-sand beaches and the enjoyable company, all I could think about – or rather, *worry* about – was the flight home. Wasn't there some other way to get from Alabama back to New York? Flying just seemed to be completely unnatural. Birds never needed air-sickness bags.

Maybe that should be a red flag to us humans. If we'd been meant to fly, the whole experience would be more agreeable.

Needless to say, I survived my first flight -- and every one of the many flights that followed.

I grew up in a small town in Upstate New York that had absolutely nothing in it except family, love and the warmth of a close-knit community. Like Esmée, I didn't know that the world had more to offer than could be found in my small town. Even if it did, I wasn't terribly interested. What we didn't have, wasn't missed. What we did have, was essential. No matter what I see or experience these days, I still value love and family above all else; they'll always be essential, and they'll always be missed.

A few years ago, my whole life changed. As with most major life-changes, it didn't happen by choice. Something I had been afraid of all my life (much like flying) just simply *happened*. After that, nothing frightened me anymore. I guess when you experience the worst, everything else doesn't look so bad. For me, this included flying.

I travel constantly, these days. I almost never return home without having purchased my next airline ticket. In my restless journeying, I've seen and experienced far more than I could have in my hometown. From wiggling my toes in the chilly waters of the English Channel to struggling for breath on top of Europe's highest mountain, the world has opened up into vast vistas of wonder and excitement for me.

Still, home is essential to happiness. Even restlessness must rest once in a while. How else could I process all this movement, except in the stillness of my home? Yet, I've come to understand the idea of home better than ever before. For me, it's not just a place; it's a way of being. Home is where the heart is, to be sure; but it's also where love reaches perfection.

I've also learned that love and the warmth of a close-knit community can be found everywhere. All human beings crave the same things; some aren't allowed to do so openly, but each human heart is both infinitely unique and also formed from the same DNA. I have experienced the warm embrace of family 4,000 miles away from the place of my birth; and I was welcomed as if I'd been returning home. Love creates community. Love is universal; and that's very comforting to know.

This book was born of movement. The idea came to me during a hike in the French Alps (nowhere near a commuter train). It matured among the treasures of the Louvre. It was crowned in my favorite "thinking spot" between *le Pont Neuf* and *le Pont des Arts* in Paris. It's a restless book; but it's also a book about home; what home means; where home abides; and how love is the only way to manage life-changing events -- events that we never chose. This is the most important lesson Esmée and I have learned.

On a side note, it was brought to my attention that the vocabulary and use of French phrases in this book might be a bit challenging for some of my readers. Good. Traveling in a foreign country *is* challenging; and reading should educate, as well as entertain. Though the book is directed toward a middle school-aged audience, the thought that some parents might read this story to their younger children makes the work that much sweeter.

I love language. The idea that we can capture in print something as intangible as the sounds of speech and music fascinates me. I also believe that everyone has something to say; and being able to communicate our hearts and minds is essential to our happiness. So, the vocabulary employed in this book is meant to lift and elevate the articulation of my more youthful readers to a height worthy of their own thoughts and feelings. Where the French phrases are concerned, many of them are translated into English in the same sentence. Nonetheless, I've also included a glossary of my own composition at the end of the book.

I would like to thank those who helped make this book a reality; those who shaped my love for France by opening their hearts and homes to me; and those who introduced me, village by village and cheese by wine, to their beautiful country. I tried to recreate Paris within the pages of this book. If I've failed to do so, it was because of my own limitations and no other reason. These good people spared no expense and overlooked no generous act in making sure I experienced it all.

Special thanks to Marysou Hauguel whose loving kindness always made me feel at home in the warm embrace of family; to Nicolas Hauguel who taught me the proper way to exchange a toast and the dire consequences of breaking eye contact; to Xavier, Cécile and Adrien Brissard for opening their home and extending their friendship to me time and time again; and to the three older French couples with whom I had the privilege of sharing meals in a bed and breakfast in Normandy. You made a deeper impact on me than you will ever know.

I have seen so much of France and experienced it all thanks to one person. She invested almost as much of herself in this book as she inspired. Without her, there would have been no dinner cruise down the Seine, no castles in Dordogne, and no Mont Saint-Michel. Indeed, without her there would not be much at all. Thank you, Cécilia Saurel, for loving this book into existence. Finally, thanks are due to my children: Megan, Andy and Joey. You listened, you suggested, you contributed, and you never fail to support your father in every possible way. Truly, I have the best children a man could hope for – and the best friends.

Today, I ventured into Paris in order to use its name in the signature of this preface (a shameless act), and to follow Esmée's path one more time. As I sit in my favorite Parisian restaurant, with its cliched, tourist-pleasing food and indifferent waitstaff (quintessentially and delightfully French in every regard), I write this introduction surrounded by the chaos of city life. Esmée found herself in similar circumstances. Unlike me, though, she found adventure here in the City of Lights. I find only those things I have always found in Paris: endless inspiration and a thousand years-worth of imagination. Adventure can be found *everywhere*.

I hope this book engenders the same love of Paris that Esmée discovered. I also hope it will inspire us to read more than just our own *one page* in the book of life; for, *"the world is a book and those who do not travel read only one page."*

Bonne aventure, mes amis!

M.R.P.

Paris, France
March 6, 2020

CHAPTER ONE

Leaving Saint-Denis

There is a quaint, little town in France called Saint-Denis-lès-Chevreuse. It's a vibrant village, filled with young and old alike. On any given day, at any given time, one can see all the hustle and bustle of daily life on display.

Children – in varying degrees of squirminess and distraction - accompany their parents on errands; while savvy businesspeople sell their wares from street-side shops. Elder citizens -- long-since retired – look on from park benches and verandas with hard-earned satisfaction and the occasional wry smile. Everywhere you turn, snapshots of a simple, quiet life present themselves. In fact, the pace of life in Saint-Denis-lès-Chevreuse is much the same as it has always been.

Winding streets, lined with yellow stone cottages -- each displaying a well-manicured flowerbox -- wander through the town, without much regard for distance or travel time. The shortest distance between *here-and-there* might very well be a straight line; but curves, it would seem, are much more interesting to the local street planners.

As the sun traces its course in the afternoon sky, warming the walls and windowpanes of the buildings, the air grows heavy with the scent of flowers. The gardenias of Saint-Denis-lès-Chevreuse rival the scents of the finest

Parisian *parfumier*. Roses, especially those in the churchyard gardens, breathe their delicate fragrance and lighten the hearts of all who pass nearby.

An ever-present breeze drifts up from the cool ripples of the Yvette River, which plods its path all the way from the town of Rambouillet in the south. Thanks to the Yvette, the whole region always maintains a comfortable temperature, even in the heat of summer. Of course, by the time the long, narrow river waters the fields of the Chevreuse Valley, it is little more than a stream. It's quite easy to miss the slender ribbon of water flowing through town; but all would agree, she's been the lifeblood of the village for a thousand years.

Strewn throughout, clinging to hills and riverbanks, tiny towns exist in near perfect isolation from one another; the smallest of these being Saint-Denis-lès-Chevreuse. All who have the good fortune to live there -- people and animals alike – know that they share something special. Few of them have ever traveled abroad -- even so far as the neighboring villages. Those who have "gone visiting" (as they call it), come home convinced of the fact that they really do have everything they need right there in Saint-Denis-lès-Chevreuse. The outside world just doesn't compare. They all know that their valley is as pleasant a place to live as could be dreamed of or found in all of France.

Idyllic, though it may be, it should be pointed out – in all honesty -- that the town itself really is much too small to accommodate a name as long as Saint-Denis-lès-Chevreuse. For years and years, visitors and villagers alike have had great difficulty trying to fit such a long name onto everything from postage stamps and postcards to placards and Peugeots. Nowadays, most people simply shorten it to Saint-Denis, and they find that it fits everything so much better that way.

Even though people have made a habit of

dispensing with lès-Chevreuse, strictly speaking it *is* still part of the town's name. Therefore, it's important to know where it came from, and so to appreciate the long history (not *just* the long name) of Saint-Denis-lès-Chevreuse. It's important to the townsfolk, most especially.

Everyone familiar with the French language knows that *chèvre* is the word for goat. What is not so widely known, however, is the crucial role goats have played in the history and naming of this particular village.

So, the story of Saint-Denis-lès-Chevreuse begins with a goat; like all great stories do.

Centuries ago, there lived an entrepreneurial goatherder and *fromager* (what we would call a *cheesemaker*) named Nicolas Méchant. He was famously possessed of great talent and insight into the subtle secrets of cheesemaking. His goat cheese was as sublime as the finest wines, filled with the character of the valley's pasturelands. Creamier than silk -- when creamy was the desired outcome; more perfectly crumbly than the tumbled-down walls of fabled Jericho; nothing of its kind had ever been experienced in the long, noble history of the cheesemaking craft.

Word spread, throughout the valley and surrounding villages, of the quality of Nicolas Méchant's cheese; and his name soon came to the attention of every king and commoner in Europe. Had he been content to practice his artistry with humble dedication to the craft, the history (and undoubtedly, the name) of Saint-Denis-lès-Chevreuse would have been much different. For, though blessed with many gifts, humility and a healthy conscience were not among them.

The *fromager's* ambition for success, renown and riches grew unbridled, alongside his fame. He became increasingly withdrawn, brooding deep in that cheese-cavernous heart of his how best to possess what he was convinced was his by right: namely, the grandest cheese empire the world would ever know.

His dark scheming soon led him to fall in with the wrong sort of people; and over time, he came to make the acquaintance of the worst of their lot. The people of that region had long whispered of the existence of the Wizard of the Valley. Whether myth or mere mystery, the shadowy figure of the wizard became a byword among the people.

If a hailstorm destroyed the summer harvest, the meddling wizard was to blame. If a spotted lamb was born in Monsieur Berger's sheep paddock beneath a blood moon, the wizard was at work. Few people had ever seen him; but all believed in his existence and feared him.

Nicolas Méchant sought out the friendship – if *friendship* it can be called – of the wizard and began to meet regularly with him, slowly advancing Méchant's cheese-dynasty agenda. After many late-night rendezvous in the dark corners of a seedy pub known as *L'âme Perdue*, Méchant concocted a way to increase his herd and his fortune.

"My friend," Méchant began one night, over a pint of bitter beer, "surely the fates have brought us together. Do you not see the unique opportunity before us?"

The wizard trusted no one, least of all his friends; but he was willing to hear what the manipulative *fromager* had to say. He leaned in closer, his dark eyes flickering in the firelight cast by a solitary candle. An ember of soot and the stiff reek of burning hair rose up like a demon, as the wizard pushed the candle out of reach of his grizzled beard. His mouth, though partially hidden by a thicket of gray, greasy hair, bore a permanent sneer. There was cold cruelty and disdainful condescension in the wizard's every word; but Méchant was unable to see it -- blinded as much by greed as he was by the shadows in his own heart.

The wizard's eyes pierced the darkness, as he spoke with oily prodding in his voice, "Go on, Méchant. Tell me about this *unique* opportunity."

Encouraged by the wizard's show of interest, Méchant continued, "I have been heralded – and rightly so -- as the world's greatest *fromager*; an artist among cheesemakers; I might even say, a genius. I'm sure you'd agree."

The wizard smiled the kind of smile a hunter might employ moments before pulling the trigger; his face barely moved, so as not to startle his prey. He had long despised and harassed the people of the valley. They were sheep to be herded, nothing more. Méchant may have spent weeks working up to this conversation, but the wizard knew very well who the real genius was and who was merely the fool.

With a long draw on the tiny stump of a carved-bone pipe he held clenched in his teeth, the wizard said, without the slightest urgency, "Go on."

"This valley will be the seat of my empire. From here, I will produce legendary cheese and distribute it to all the world. The story of my fame and fortune will grow unparalleled in the history of my craft. All I require is a supply of goat's milk vast enough to meet the demand. At present, my ambitions are limited by my ability to find the amount of goat's milk I need. This is where you'd be wise to play a role; for, rest assured, my gratitude would be significant."

Méchant took a drink from his glass; set it down without a sound; then wiped the foam from his lips with his shirt sleeve. He sat as if waiting to receive the wizard's request to be included in such an exciting business proposal. He felt that his vision of a global cheese empire was all the reason he needed in order to do whatever he liked. It was his destiny to build a business endeavor that would eliminate all competition and leave him to reap the vast rewards. Anyone who failed to see this was an obstacle to be removed, a stone in his path. When the wizard finally did respond, it was not at all what Méchant expected.

"Let me guess," he said between outbursts of uncomfortably-exaggerated laughter, "you want me to milk your goats for you? Ah Méchant, yours is a singular wit. Truly the fates *have* brought us together."

His disdain now hardened, as his eyes narrowed. The whole reason he had allowed the foolish *fromager* to befriend him in the first place was now about to be revealed.

"What exactly is it that you want from me, Méchant? Be clear," the wizard commanded, with harsh anger barely restrained behind each word.

Méchant's moment had arrived. He drew himself upright in his chair, leaned forward on his elbows -- hands joined in front of himself -- and delivered his sales pitch.

"Multiply my herd," he said. "Give them long life, comparable to the lifespan of a man. Bless them with unrivaled productivity, and your cheese caves will never go empty. I will give you the best of the batch -- as much as you can store. Forever."

The cheesemaker sat back in his chair. Having delivered his speech, he now awaited the wizard's hearty agreement. Méchant knew the old conjurer had the power to multiply his goat herd, but the wizard had something much darker in mind; something Méchant never imagined. If the old wizard could bring harm to the people of the valley, while seeing to it that the blame fell on Méchant, well, this would be an ideal arrangement.

The wizard's eyes shifted from one side to the other, then came to rest on the *fromager* with such weight that Méchant's shoulders sagged beneath the evil stare. Sparks leapt from the bowl of the wizard's pipe, and smoldered in his beard, as he inhaled. Blowing acrid smoke in Méchant's face, the wizard whispered to himself, "…the lifespan of a man," then smiled with hateful delight.

"I accept your proposal, Méchant. I will multiply your goat herd and give them each…" he sneered and chuckled, savoring the irony, "a lifespan comparable to that of a man. You shall have more goats than there are people in this valley. This very night, in the 3 o'clock hour, it shall be done.

"Tomorrow, you will gather your herd together from every street and sidewalk, every cottage and farmhouse for miles around. I will expect the first delivery of goat cheese – enough to fill my lower caverns – within the fortnight; and monthly deliveries thereafter. I will specify the amount by messenger pigeon on the first of every month and take delivery no later than the fifteenth. This concludes our business dealings."

With that, the wizard seemed to fold-up like a piece of sinister origami -- smaller and smaller -- then disappear in a sigh of smoke and soot. Méchant's mouth dropped open, as a sense of foreboding flooded in on his mind. Beneath his arrogance, fear now grew. The whole transaction seemed to conclude much too quickly. He had received assurance of everything he'd wanted at the price he'd named; so, why did he feel that, somehow, he'd paid too much?

Méchant walked home from the pub in the dark, not realizing that it would be the people of the valley who'd pay so dearly for his greed and treachery. For, deep in the festering bowels of his ancient stronghold -- surrounded by twisted herbs and loathsome potions -- the wizard worked away into the small hours of the night. Hammering with mortar and pestle, sparks flew in a mist of green vapor, like lightning in a thunderhead. A pestilent cloud of alchemy and hatred surrounded the old man, until his labors brought forth a potent sorcery.

Tying tiny sacks to the rat-like feet of his army of enslaved bats, he sent them out into the night. Flying the length and breadth of the valley, avoiding only the house of the cheesemaker and his wife, the bats released the contents of their baggage into the air. The dark sky grew thick with a pale, green dust which descended everywhere and coated the valley in silent despair; while its inhabitants slept unaware.

It was now 3 am -- the hour in which ghouls and goblins, phantoms and shadows walk unhindered among the living. But throughout the valley, the living were nowhere to be found; at least, none belonging to the race of mankind.

Inside bedrooms, goats now slept, their heads resting upon pillows; some could be found snoring in armchairs beside flickering fireplaces, their feet supported by footstools. All around the village and surrounding area, goats assumed human positions; wore human clothing; and occupied places in which goats simply should not be. The Chevreuse Valley was now a valley of *chèvres*; and no one knew why, except the Wizard of the Valley.

The next day, the scene was a desperate one. People... or rather, goats awoke to find everything entirely changed. Where once children could be found playing on the shores of *l'Yvette*, now kid-goats congregated in the shallows, drinking in the heat of the summer sun.

Farmers in the fields had been replaced by grazing herds of goats. There was endless gnawing and munching in every garden and flowerbed in town. The quaint, little village was overrun with goats as far as a greedy goatherder could see. The townspeople were nowhere to be found.

A great cry of lament went up from the poor souls who were now enslaved within the cloven-hooved bodies of lesser beasts -- their minds unmercifully aware of their unfortunate predicament. They recognized, behind the confused eyes of their neighbors, shadowy hints of once-familiar friends. Opening their mouths in anguish, they struggled to form their thoughts into sound; but their "Why?" and "How?" came out merely as bleating. Try as they might, intelligent communication was impossible; and no comfort could be found among them. Only two villagers seemed to have escaped the wizard's villainy.

Nicolas Méchant awoke that morning to the panicked sound of bleating goats; more goats than he had ever heard before. His first thought was of the promise made by the old wizard the night before: *"You shall have more goats than there are people in the valley."* He did not yet know just how true those words now were. As he prepared himself to go gather goats into his pastures, his wife entered the room -- white as curdled goat's milk -- carefully positioning herself between her husband and their young son.

"What is it, woman?"

"What have you done?" she asked, with accusation in her voice.

"I have no idea what you're talking about. What have I done, where?"

He was in no mood for his wife's cryptic question. In fact, the darker and more withdrawn he became, the less interest he took in her at all. For years, his craft had gradually become his obsession. Cheesemaking now filled the places in his heart where, once, he'd held his wife so dear. There was a time when she had been his partner and confidant; but now he had no time for her -- or their son -- at all.

"The wizard," the woman said, realization now dawning on her. "The wizard... you made your foolish little deal with that wizard, didn't you?"

"How is that any of your business?" Méchant

replied, an uneasiness now growing in his black heart.

"You fool, you made it *everyone's* business. The wizard tricked you, and now *you're* to blame. Look what you've done. Look!"

She threw open the window curtains, revealing a sight stranger than Méchant could have ever imagined. Everywhere his astonished eyes looked, he saw goats wearing clothing, wrinkled from a restless night's sleep. There were goats with shoes; goats with straw hats; even a goat walking upright, leaning on a wheelbarrow it was pushing down a garden path. In an astonished instant, Méchant understood the wicked tragedy of what had happened.

Turning to his horrified wife, he said, "Close the curtains, woman. I have goats to collect."

With that, he took his hat, left the house, and began the grim task of herding his former neighbors into his goat paddock. His wife stood at the open door of their cottage, weeping with shame; their young boy at her side.

Where once there was brilliance in her husband's mind, darkness now snuffed out all reason. Where kindness had grown and blossomed in his heart, coldness now withered even the roots. She had watched the man she once loved fester and die, until all that remained was one twisted purpose. Now that one purpose preyed upon the good people of the village, and she could bear it no more.

For the goat-people of the valley, hope grew thin with the passage of time; as years upon years of prayerful bleating echoed unanswered throughout the valley. Without human care, the abandoned town crumbled into decay. The townspeople now lived as goats among the ruins of their old homes. Seeing and remembering -- but being unable to prevent the destruction of their neglected homes -- only added to their despair.

The people's experience had become that of farm

animals. All that they kept of their human existence was the length of their lives and the sadness of their dim memories. Without words to express their pain, many retreated deep into themselves; too deep for even hope to reach.

Without the rituals and routines of their former human lives, many began to forget – or try to forget – that they had ever been human at all. Sometimes it's easier to just let go and slip deeper down into the well, than to cling painfully to the eroding walls. Many were tempted to do just that: let go and let the blackness swallow them whole. If they'd lost their human lives, perhaps it was best just to give up and be goats. There was no reason to hope for anything more.

Until at last, a stranger came to town.

He was like the *fromager*, in that he walked upright on his two hind legs. Unlike the wicked cheesemaker, though, his soothing voice had a magical quality. His eyes shown bright with unfathomed intelligence; and there was a kindness in his smile. He made his way, walking the length and breadth of the valley, laying a hand upon the head of every goat he met – whether by chance encounter or purposeful charity -- and he whispered words of comfort to encourage them in their suffering. Somehow, he seemed to understand. Somehow, he knew all that had happened.

Memories – feelings really – from decades past, and long-since regarded as mere myth, stirred deep within the hairy hearts of billies, nannies and kids alike. A fire was kindled in their darkening minds; and *les chèvres* began to recall a time when they had been so much more. They remembered speaking in words and weaving rhymes into poetry. They remembered the joyous sounds of music and the mystical freedom of dance. They had once been human; and they longed to be human once more.

The stranger strode the streets of the little French town, fanning the sparks of remembrance into resolute flames of rebellion by his kind encouragement and reminders of a happier time. It was clear that he recognized in the goats of the valley something much more than *goat-likeness*. His words were hopeful; and he spoke of the past as if it could really be theirs once more.

"People of the valley, remember! A great injustice has been done to you; but it is not too late to reclaim your true selves!"

The charismatic stranger used words the goats could understand; words they could relate to; evocative words, like *"gnawing through the ropes which bind you"* and *"leaping toward freedom once more!"*

Thoughts of taking back what had been stolen from them now turned to action. Uniting behind their new leader and beneath the banner of *Le Faune Sautant* (*The Leaping Faun*), the herd of goats resolved to march with common purpose on the walls of the fiendish *fromagerie*.

In one great herd of bleating and bellowing goat-people, they approached the outer defenses of the cheesemaker's fortress. Locking horns against stone, the massive flock pushed with the might of a million goats, until the walls buckled and gave way.

As they flooded the halls and passageways of the breached *fromagerie*, the goat-people sought and soon found their enemy. With hearts aflame, they lifted and carried the cornered goatherder to the brow of a nearby cliff. Far below, the thirsty river reached its long, white fingers toward the shore, as it roiled a rocky path to the sea.

The pious and kindly stranger - now known by his name, Denis - was unwilling to allow the hysterical herd to throw their captor headlong into the river below. Denis begged and pleaded with them for mercy; but his efforts did not succeed. For just then, in mid-sentence, he caught sight of an old woman running toward the perilous edge. She grabbed the goatherder from the midst of the angry mob and threw him, bodily, over the brink and into the torrent below.

She'd lived with her infernal husband for decades, since long before he made the monstrous agreement which laid waste to the town and all of its inhabitants. She'd endured his cruelty and scheming. She could endure it no longer. Brushing the filth of her husband from her hands, she turned from the edge of the cliff and walked over to where Denis stood in silent disbelief.

"Of everyone here, surely you recall most clearly," she said to the young man, laying a hand on Denis' arm. "His was the blackest of hearts, and I vowed to undo the evil he'd done. I kept my vow, this day. The rest is up to you, my son."

The old woman managed a sad and mournful smile at Denis, then turned and walked through the astonished herd of goat-people, back to her home. Closing the door behind her, she sat beside the fire and wept as she had done many times before.

Blinking his eyes in the midday sun, Denis at last turned his gaze toward the highest house on the loneliest hill. This vile and menacing citadel belonged to the villainous Wizard of the Valley. Rarely seen by the unfortunate inhabitants of the town, the wizard kept to himself - and with good reason.

The goat-men and -women knew who it was who held their fate in his hands. With the snap of his fingers, he could restore them all to human form. He had long since received payment of all the goat cheese he could store in his overstocked caverns. He had no further reason -- other than spite and a corrupt contract with the goatherder -- to continue holding the people in bondage to their bitter bleating.

Denis led the four-legged herd to the steps of the

stone cottage. Knocking on the door, he commanded, "Wizard, come forth and face the wrath of those you've enslaved!"

There was no reply from within. Knowing that the wizard must surely be home, Denis knocked once more; but there was still no answer. Denis turned back to the goats accompanying him and said, with sober gravity, "He leaves me no choice."

Picking up a vegetable from the wizard's garden, Denis tossed it into the air while speaking these words, *"Que le geôlier soit emprisonné!"*

Catching the purple vegetable in his right hand, he threw it with great force, smashing it against the door of the wizard's home. In a flash of lightning from a clear blue sky, the house disappeared with a thunderclap! In its place was left the most grotesquely shaped, hideously ugly eggplant anyone had ever seen.

Moments before, there had stood a great herd of goats beside Denis. Now there stood a crowd of townspeople, all in human form once more; their mouths open and confusion in their eyes.

A loud cry of jubilation swelled and burst forth from their hearts and lips! At long last, the villagers were free from their unfortunate condition. The greedy goatherder was gone, thanks to his unhappy wife, Yvette. The wizard had been turned into an eggplant, which, of course, is the most wicked of vegetables; and all of this had been brought about by the wondrous stranger who came to town.

A great party was held for many days, celebrating the people's release from bondage. The good people of the valley stretched their limbs and danced upright for the first time in decades. A tremendous noise of endless conversation filled the town, as people once again spoke in words and animated hand gestures about their experience as mute, four-legged creatures.

It may be that -- grateful for their deliverance -- the townspeople decided, then and there, to name the river after the woman who appeared out of nowhere; wove a path through the crowd; and washed the grimy goatherder from their village. Whatever the reason, the River Yvette still weaves her path through the town to this very day.

Denis was heralded as a saint by the townsfolk, who chose to name their village in his honor. Statues were erected, pictures painted, and stories told of the "Blessed Stranger who came to town one day."

Amid all the celebrations and festivities -- after bidding his mother farewell -- Denis simply vanished without a trace. This certainly added to his mystique and may have contributed greatly to his status as a saint. Down through the centuries, songs would be sung, and tales told of the Dark Ages when the light of humanity was swallowed up in shadow and restored again by the hands of Yvette the Cheese-Slayer and her son, Saint-Denis-of-the-Goat-People: *Saint-Denis-lès-Chevreuse*.

Nowadays, the villagers are unlikely to discuss their Goat Period or *Le Temps des Chèvres*. Perhaps this, more than its lengthiness, explains why the people dispense with *lès Chevreuse* altogether. It's too painful a reminder and, frankly, somewhat embarrassing. Whatever the explanation might be, the good people of the Valley of Goats remember well the *Tale of Saint-Denis*. They never *forgoat...* or rather, *forgot* his mighty deeds.

The whole experience also served to soften the people's treatment of goats. Not quite held in reverence, the goats of the Chevreuse Valley do, however, enjoy a high regard and a life of relative leisure. It's no secret that the local ducks, in particular, feel ill-used compared to the goats of the valley. Undoubtedly, a wide-spread love of *foie gras* has a great deal to do with this.

Incidentally, the people of the Chevreuse Valley

still refuse to eat eggplant - which, of course, *continues to be* the most wicked of vegetables and will likely always be regarded as such. The few who do eat eggplant are looked upon with deep misgivings and suspicion.

As is true with most stories that begin with a goat, the story of the naming of *Saint-Denis-lès-Chevreuse* is composed of both happy and sad elements, to be sure. But all would agree that the people of Saint-Denis share a proud history and a very beautiful home.

Returning now from the mists of myth and legend to walk the streets of modern-day Saint-Denis, we find (as with every French town) a *boulangerie*, a *boucherie*, an *église*, and a *rond-point*. But there is one other feature of the village that must also be mentioned; for it is here that our story truly begins. In this little corner of *les Yvelines*, Saint-Denis is also known for its train station.

The B line of the RER train begins and ends in Saint-Denis; and every morning, bleary-eyed travelers -- descendants of the Goat-People of the Chevreuse Valley -- shuffle aboard the sleepy railcars. Patiently, they wait for the commuter train to carry them to -- among many other stops -- *Gare du Nord* in Paris. By the time the train reaches *la gare*, the once-empty cars are bursting with crammed and crowded (and often very crabby) commuters. From there, most will leave the RER and ride the metro to destinations all throughout the city.

From the moment they awaken until the minute their heads hit their pillows at night, many of these good people barely notice the faces of those around them. This should not be thought of as rudeness, though. In a country of so many different faces, it can be very tiring trying to recognize and put a name to each one -- even the ones you see *tous les jours*. Instead, the French tend to keep to themselves, and spend their energies creating such wonders as the Eiffel Tower, Sainte-Chapelle, and (most especially) Roquefort cheese.

On this particular day, as the train stood waiting on the tracks, a curious thing happened.

Inside carriage #9, a young woman sat looking out the window. In her lap lay a large bouquet of assorted flowers. Her mother phoned the day before to report that she had, *"a head cold with a sinus infection."* As anyone can tell you, *"a head cold with a sinus infection"* is a thing *no one* wants to have. Those who do have it invariably try to get rid of it as soon as is convenient.

Hoping to cheer her mother and brighten her day, the young woman got up early; put on her walking shoes; bought an impressive bouquet of her mother's favorite flowers; and hopped aboard the RER B bound for Paris. She placed the bouquet on the seat next to her; opened a crinkly, brown paper bag; and began eating the croissant she had purchased for her *petit déjeuner*.

She would need all the strength she could muster for the train ride; followed by the metro ride; followed by the 5-block walk to her mother's Paris apartment. She would then daydream, thinking back to the delightfully flaky croissant she enjoyed on the train, while her mother complained for hours about her *"head cold with a sinus infection."*

Indeed, there's nothing curious about a croissant being eaten by a French woman -- except maybe the mysterious secret of the croissant's melt-in-your-mouth, buttery, flakiness. What *was* curious was what happened next.

Through the open door of carriage #9 flitted a beautiful butterfly, which landed with delicate softness upon the bouquet of flowers. Its wings of golden orange, flecked with flame and moonbeams, framed the butterfly's wide, brown body in finery fit for a queen. In flight, she was as graceful as sunlight. Enthroned upon the petals of a rose, she appeared as fragile as eggshell porcelain.

Her name was Esmée Délancourt, and she'd never been on a train before. In fact, she hadn't really meant to board the RER B at all; but butterflies find flowers hard to resist and the woman's bouquet was exceptionally alluring.

The young woman was engrossed in her croissant and took no notice of the tiny stow-away. Instead, Esmée tip-toed from petal to petal and stem to stem, sampling the nectar of roses, carnations, lilies and straw flowers with great delight. Her long, curled-up tongue extended to probe the folds and recesses of each bud in the bouquet.

It's true that she'd never been on a train; and like most people and animals who call Saint-Denis their home, Esmée had never even ventured beyond the streets and fields of her village. The quaint, little town was all Esmée knew; and she knew it quite well.

There were the roses in the churchyard of *l'église Saint-Denis*, and the wildflowers in the pastures of Monsieur Deschamps' farm. There were the wisteria vines hanging from the pergolas of Monsieur Beaulieu's vineyard, and the gladiolas in Madame Laurent's flowerbeds. Most of all, there was the enormous butterfly bush in the backyard of Madame Legrand's *grande maison* astride the Yvette River.

It was here at the butterfly bush -- known to the locals as *l'arbuste à papillons* -- that Esmée met with her friends each morning. In between sips of nectar, *les papillons* would discuss the news of the day; catch up on each other's lives; and share the location of the latest, newly planted flowerbeds and rosebushes. It was a pleasant place, and Esmée loved it very much.

Although she had never before left Saint-Denis, Esmée couldn't imagine she was missing much. She had everything she needed to be happy right there; and the world beyond was a complete and utter mystery to her -- filled with rumors and tales of darkness; none of which, of course, held any interest for her. She was quite happy never to leave her beautiful, peaceful and idyllic home.

While Esmée enjoyed her breakfast-bouquet and the young woman enjoyed her croissant, an announcement was heard on the train's loudspeaker. *"...pour Gare du Nord Paris,"* was all that Esmée could understand of the rushed and garbled message. She barely had time to react, when the very next thing Esmée heard was, "Doors closing."

With that, the doors of carriage #9 slid shut, the train lunged forward, and Esmée was trapped aboard the RER B bound for Paris and the dark, ominous world beyond Saint- Denis.

CHAPTER TWO

Aboard the RER B

Esmée was startled by the unexpected lurch of the train and leapt into flight the moment she sensed danger. Fluttering toward the doors through which she'd entered the carriage, she encountered a distressing peculiarity. She'd experienced something similar to this before, when attempting to sample the nectar from Madame Lafleur's greenhouse orchids. The result of that confrontation was a bruised antenna and a bewildering headache. The same sorcery was at work aboard the RER B.

From her place onboard the train, she could see the station, the town, and the fields beyond; but try as she might, she could not reach them. Over and over again, she flapped her tiny wings and flew with full force in the direction of freedom. Each time, she was stopped by some invisible wall of wizardry; some unseen barrier of black magic. Hurling herself against the transparent obstacle of the windowpane with exhausting desperation, Esmée was becoming flustered.

Deciding to try another approach, she landed on the back of a seat, and began beating her wings as hard as she could. Like an airplane, she revved her engine to build-up momentum. Finally reaching her maximum *beats-per-minute,* Esmée jumped off the seat and flew toward the window. Crash! Just like before, the unseen barrier stopped her midflight. She slid down the face of the window in a flattened sheet of dazed butterfly, landing in a heap on the floor.

All around her, pairs of facing seats -- upholstered in grey and blue patterns of stained and faded fabric – lined the aisle. The musty odor of stagnant air gripped Esmée's senses. She couldn't draw a breath deep enough to satisfy her need for fresh air. Within sight, the world of clean, country breezes stared back at her from the other side of the windowpane. She had to break out and breathe freely, or she just knew that she'd end up suffocating in the stuffy train car.

As the commuter train gained speed, everything Esmée had ever known receded into the distance. Trees flew by in blurry splotches of green; homes and businesses rushed past at varying speeds, depending on how far away they were from the train. The pulsing rhythm of steel wheels on cold tracks, and the occasional screech of metal on metal set Esmée on edge. She was already much farther from home than she had ever been before and getting farther by the minute.

Tired and sore from her fight with the windowpane, Esmée gave up in despair. Picking herself up from the floor, she flew up toward the ceiling and landed on top of a high handrail, resting her bruised and crumpled wings.

Down below, seated beside her bouquet of flowers, the young woman neatly folded the crinkly, brown paper bag that had held her croissant. Tucking it into the pocket of her backpack, she wiped the flaky goodness from her lap; straightened the dark-rimmed glasses on her slender nose; and turned to enjoy the scenery as it sped by.

Esmée found herself staring out the window over the young woman's shoulder. The flashes of sunlight through the scratched windowpanes had a lullaby effect on passengers, many of whom sat motionless. A few read newspapers or paperback novels; others played word games on their phones. Esmée just gazed in bewilderment, trying to make sense of her situation, and wanting more than anything just to go home.

After about five minutes, the train slowed and came to rest at the first station along the way. Courcelle-sur-Yvette was the name written in large white letters against the navy blue of the sign. Esmée recognized the word, Yvette. She had seen it many times along the riverbanks in Saint-Denis.

Perhaps she wasn't as far from home as she'd thought. She had only been on the train for a short while. If the "Yvette" on the sign referred to the river that ran through Saint-Denis, then this was her chance to follow it home. She would try again to break through the forcefield of the windowpane, in the hope that it might just give way this time. She could then follow the Yvette River back to Saint-Denis and her beloved butterfly bush in Madame Legrand's backyard.

The recorded announcement played, saying *"Courcelle-sur-Yvette. Attention à la marche en descendant du train,"* and the doors slid open, clearing all barriers – seen and unseen -- between Esmée and freedom. Flapping her delicate wings, she jumped from her perch above the young woman's seat; pointed herself in the direction of the door; and flew with all her might toward the outside world.

As she neared the open door, Esmée was greeted by a stiff breeze rising up from the platform below. Readjusting her pitch, she began to tack like an expert yachtsman, riding the wave of wind down and to the right. Feeling it lessen its force against her, Esmée turned herself windward, sailing toward the sky once more.

She was less than a foot from the open doorway, when a surge of commuters began pushing and herding themselves -- like ill-mannered goat-people of old -- up from the platform and into carriage #9.

The wind and the turbulence caused by the crowd of people created a little swirling tornado in the entryway which carried Esmée high up to the ceiling of the train car. Spinning out of control, she managed to grab hold of the handrail, just as the doors of the carriage slid closed. With uncalled-for rudeness, the train jumped forward -- feeling the weight of the additional passengers -- and continued along its course toward Paris and away from Saint-Denis.

Esmée's eyes swelled, as a look of terror broke across her face. She reached out her wings toward the station sign on the receding platform; but it was no use. Surely *that* had been her last chance of reaching the river and finding her way home. The tiniest tear fell from her eye all the way down to the floor, making a sound too small to be heard. If Esmée had been human (or even a goat), her tears would not have gone unobserved. As a little butterfly, though, her sorrow was completely unnoticed.

The handrail upon which she now sat was warm with the heat of a dozen filthy hands. Smears and smudges from grimy fingers turned the stainless-steel surface into a slippery and revolting place to rest. All around her, commuters sat with expressionless faces.

A messy, wrinkled old man had boarded the train, just before the doors slid closed, and made an announcement to the disinterested passengers. He then walked the length of the railcar with his hand outstretched. A few people dropped a coin or two into his open hand; but most just looked away, hoping he wouldn't speak to them.

Esmée felt sorry for the man. Whether truly in need or not, her heart was moved with pity for him. She watched him hobble to the front of the carriage, where he sat down and began counting his few meager coins -- waiting for the next stop and hoping his luck would improve.

Sadness softened her heart, until everything around her seemed to disappear -- leaving only Esmée and the poor man. She wondered what these coins might buy him. Would they be enough to fill his empty stomach? Would they buy the ticket that would carry him to his home? Would they purchase decent clothing or even just a blanket against the night's chill. With sudden awareness, she was awakened from her thoughts by a realization. It wasn't just the man she was thinking about; it was her own hunger and homesickness, too. She turned her face back toward the outside world.

Through the carriage window, another station sign came into view: Gif-sur-Yvette. A second chance, perhaps! The train must be following the course of the Yvette River, and that meant Esmée's path home! Jumping to her feet, she stretched out her wings, and prepared herself for a second dash toward freedom.

This time, she would wait until the commotion in the doorway settled down. She'd tried before to fight the breeze and the crowd, with no success; but now she would save her energy for just the right moment and just the right conditions.

The recording announced, *"Gif-sur-Yvette. Attention à la marche en descendant du train."* The doors slid open. The breeze rushed in from the platform below and fluttered Esmée's golden orange wings. A group of grumpy travelers pushed their way aboard the train -- careful not to make eye contact with one another – and crowded into the doorway.

One man, deciding he'd rather remain standing, stepped out of the way of the jostling crowd and reached up to take hold of the handrail above his head. As he did, the smallest part of his little finger came to rest across

Esmée's foot. Had he placed his hand one inch further to the right, Esmée would have been crushed. As it was, she was in no pain; but she was completely unable to fly away. The doors slid closed; the train eased forward; and Esmée's fragile hope of following the Yvette River home slipped away yet again.

Esmée fluttered her wings, straining toward the ceiling, and hoping to free herself from beneath the man's finger. It was no use. That one finger alone weighed 100 times what Esmée weighed. Deciding to try another approach, she bent over and began tickling the man's finger with her antennae. At first, the muscle of his chubby pinky twitched. Then the neighboring finger arched up, scratching and rubbing the offended pinky.

Esmée flapped a flutter of tingly tickling all up and down the stubby finger. The movement of the train made vibrations all along the handrail, disguising the tiny butterfly's efforts. Still, the feel of her wings on his knuckles should have been enough to get his attention. Had it been anyone else's pinky, they would have been utterly alarmed! But not this man. He simply readjusted his grip and directed his eyes back to his smartphone.

Esmée was desperate to be free. In one wild burst of flailing legs and wings, she poured all her energy into raising the man's attention and his finger at the same time. At last, becoming aware of the assault taking place on his pudgy pinky, the man finally withdrew his hand.

Inspecting it with horror, he thought for sure he had interrupted the path of some hairy spider. He was relieved to see Esmée flit past his face, taking up her new position high out of reach of clumsy hands and misplaced pinkies. Folding her wings and stroking her antennae one against the other, Esmée raised one eyebrow in the direction of the clueless passenger and let out a long, irritated sigh.

She was now in a good position to examine the map of the RER B trainline, displayed just below where she was sitting. The next stop would be La Hacquinière, then after that, Bures-sur-Yvette. Looking down the map at the next twenty-three stations before Gare du Nord, Esmée saw no more mention of *l'Yvette*. That confirmed it; this was her last chance to escape and follow the narrow river all the way back to Saint-Denis. She had to get out at Bures-sur-Yvette, or she'd certainly never make it home again.

Flying from her seat up near the ceiling, Esmée landed on a large advertisement sign located right beside the door. She wanted to be sure she was ready when the train stopped, and the doors opened. She had one more stop before they arrived at her station; she was entirely focused.

Looking out the window, she saw the blue sign for La Hacquinière approaching. The train pulled to a halt, the doors opened, and Esmée watched with hopefulness when no one boarded the train. If the next stop was like this one, she'd have no competition for the doorway.

As the train pulled away from the station, Esmée played the scenario over and over again in her mind. Her plan was foolproof. The train would stop once more, this time at Bures-sur-Yvette – her exit. The doors would open, and no one would be waiting on the empty platform. She'd be free to fly through the doors and out into the fresh, clean summer air. It might take her a day or so to fly back to Saint-Denis, but her path would be an easy one to follow. She'd find *l'Yvette* and let it guide her all the way to Madame Legrand's *grande maison*; the butterfly bush; and her friends.

Esmée was ready. Her position was perfect. The plan had been rehearsed in her mind. She was well out of reach of any grasping hands or meaty fingers. All she needed now was the next station stop. Excitement and anticipation rose in her heart.

There it was, the sign for Bures-sur-Yvette. The train was rapidly approaching the station. Esmée spread her wings, readying herself to spring into flight. She could see the station up ahead. The platform was clear; there was no one standing around waiting for the train. She now knew that her plan would work. With no one crowding and tussling at the door, she'd have a clear flight path to the outside world and home. The train sped on toward *le gare*, as Esmée took a deep breath and waited for the usual recorded message announcing the station name.

The train accelerated, then accelerated again. No announcement came. The platform approached then sped past, as the RER B continued down the line toward Gare du Nord in the heart of Paris.

Esmée turned in panicked confusion to examine the map once more. She saw it clearly. Bures-sur-Yvette, right after La Hacquinière. Why hadn't they stopped? Then it occurred to her. The little round light marking the location of the station on the B line map wasn't illuminated. The station *was* on their route, but unless the light on the map is lit the train does not stop.

Esmée stood atop the sign, her wings outstretched in stifled readiness; her back straight and rigid; and her heart in her throat. The train accelerated down the tracks, screaming as it rounded a long curve. She was rapidly being carried into the largest city in France; and she never wanted to leave Saint-Denis in the first place. Warmth rose in her face, blushing her cheeks with fear and distress.

The names of the stations on the map were all strange to her, from here on. There was no more mention of Yvette; no more echo of home. The faces all around her were unknown and unfriendly. Even the countryside laid out around her, and flying by in a muddle of dizziness, was completely foreign and unwelcoming. From the window she caught the sharp glint of sunlight off the surface of a distant river. She knew it was *l'Yvette*, and she knew she'd never see it again. Esmée hid her face in her wings and cried.

CHAPTER THREE

The Warrior Butterfly

A steady stream of unfamiliar station names flew past the window of the train in quick succession. Orsay-Ville, Le Guichet, Lozère, Palaiseau-Villebon; none of them meant a thing to the baffled butterfly. Indeed, she could barely pronounce them (much like you're struggling to do, right now). At every station stop, more and more people boarded the train, until soon it was standing room only. Esmée found a light fixture on the ceiling upon which to rest and sort out the events of the day.

The growing ache in her head made thinking a painful, throbbing ordeal. On top of that, her foot was still sore from bearing the weight of the careless passenger's pinky finger. She was exhausted, hungry and moving deeper into the unknown – and, what was worse, farther away from home. If there had been an emergency brake in sight, Esmée would have found a way to throw it and bring the train to a sudden stop. As it was, all she could do was sit on the light fixture and consider all of her options.

She thought about changing trains; but she had no way of knowing exactly which train would carry her back home. Looking at the map, all she knew for sure was the order in which the stations occurred -- and at which stations the train would actually stop. She'd learned that much in the last twenty minutes; unfortunately, she'd learned it the hard way.

Below each station name were listed any number of connecting lines in various colors and with different letters and numbers. The map stretched out in a long line of stations, then forked into two optional lines at either end -- looking much like a tuning fork. There were trains, *gares,* metro stations, and airports represented – none of which made much sense to Esmée; and none offered any clear path home. It was mind-boggling for a human-sized brain to navigate. For a tiny butterfly, it was all too much to take in.

She realized that the train track itself was just as good a guide to follow as the Yvette River; but she'd have to follow it high enough to avoid the rail traffic below. She was worried about the wild winds stirred up by the trains and the difficulties they would present to a butterfly's stable flightpath.

If she flew too close to the tracks, the winds in the wake of a passing train might blow her miles off course or cast her out of the sky and into harm's way. If she flew too high, she ran the risk of losing the tracks altogether or becoming an open-air target for a hungry owl or crow. Even in the safety of her home, she'd learned about the dangers of remaining out in the open for too long.

She yearned for home. Her whole heart was bent on escaping her moving cage and fleeing from the fearful world. Opening up before her at 55 miles per hour was a universe of unknowns. She took no enjoyment in watching the countryside fly by outside the window. She had no interest in what wonders might await her at such train stops as Massy-Palaiseau or Fontaine-Michalon. She was distracted and consumed by one thought alone: escaping her situation and finding her way home.

Maybe if she just stayed in carriage #9 long enough it would eventually make its way back to Saint-Denis; but how long might that take? Would her train return to Saint-Denis that evening, or would it take weeks to travel the entire circuit of all the RER routes?

If she stayed with the young woman and her bouquet of flowers, might they lead her home again? The woman appeared to be kind -- the type to help a lost and homesick butterfly -- and her bouquet *was* irresistibly beautiful. Maybe if Esmée flew down and hid herself among the sweet-smelling buds of the woman's bouquet, she would be safely delivered back to Saint-Denis at the end of the day. There were just too many unknowns; and she couldn't risk making the wrong decision.

Eventually, she would need nectar; and right now, the only source lay in the lap of the young woman seated below. The more crowded the train became, the more dangerous it would be for Esmée to risk flying. If she left her safe area, she might be picked out of the air by an over-curious child or swatted to the floor by a nervous adult mistaking her for a less-friendly insect. She just couldn't take the chance. The bouquet was effectively out of reach. Her situation was becoming impossible, and there seemed to be no hope of it improving.

La Croix de Berny, Parc de Sceaux, Cité Universitaire and Denfert-Rochereau flew by in a flash of white lettering, blue signs, half-empty stations and sullen commuters. At each stop, the monotonous repetition of *"Attention à la marche en descendant du train"* served only to measure out the miles and the station stops between there and home.

Desperate to find whatever hope she could, Esmée examined the map once more. She read the next three station names: Port-Royal, Luxembourg, and Saint-Michel-Notre-Dame. Then an idea flashed across her mind.

Back in Saint-Denis, whenever she was visiting the home of her best friend, Lisette Cueilleur -- near the Rue François Chesneau -- and needed a quick drink of nectar, she'd head north toward the river to find *l'église Saint-Denis*. The roses in the churchyard were heavenly, blessed with the best rosewater in the valley.

In the lush, green church garden -- surrounded by red, white and yellow roses heavy with nectar -- there was a statue of a great warrior-butterfly, clad in armor breastplate and greaves. His enormous wings were outstretched in commanding grandeur, as he kept watch over a seashell-shaped birdbath. With a flaming sword in his hand, the god-like butterfly clamped one foot across the throat of a writhing serpent -- a pose that was very reassuring to *un petit papillon* such as Esmée.

At the base of the statue were inscribed the words: Saint-Michel. In her mind, Saint-Michel meant safety and a place to find refreshment. She always trusted the kindly warrior-butterfly to guide her to nectar; and he never let her down. Whenever she followed Saint-Michel, she found everything she needed.

Maybe if she summoned the courage to leave the RER train at the Saint-Michel-Notre-Dame station, her faith in her patron would be rewarded in a similar way. She had no better choices and no more familiar name to entrust herself to. At the moment, this was her best option. If only she could make it past the throng of pushing passengers; off the train; and out of the station, she just might find Saint-Michel and everything she needed along with him. She resolved to try.

Esmée watched the map carefully. She was determined not to miss her exit-opportunity. She only had three more stops to go; and all three stations were illuminated on the map. They would surely be stopping at them all.

The train slowed; then came to a crawl; then made a full stop. The announcement played, *"Port-Royal. Attention à la marche en descendant du train."* She nodded in agreement, then surveyed the map once more.

Two more stops. Esmée spread her wings, beating them against the stagnant air, in preparation for her upcoming flight. The train car was still packed, but a pathway to the door was left open; and Esmée plotted her course through the air.

The train bucked, then started back down the tracks -- careening around tight curves and screeching like sharp fingernails on a dry chalkboard. Passengers shifted their weight from side to side, back and forth; some holding onto the handrail above; others staggering and stumbling with the lurching train. A few minutes later, slowing with a sudden jerk, the train drifted into the next station, *"Luxembourg. Attention à la marche en descendant du train."*

Esmée glanced once more at the B line map, confirming what she already knew. Next stop: Saint-Michel-Notre-Dame. That was her goal, her departure point; and all of her hopes clung to her ability to reach the exit door. At every station the train entered, the previous station's map-light would go out -- ticking off each stop along the way and bringing her closer to Saint-Michel. Esmée flapped her wings, hovering over the light fixture for a moment, then settled back down again. There was electric anticipation pulsing through her wings.

This time, her escape plan was entirely different; no more would she cautiously weave her way through the herd of commuters. Esmée was determined to simply flap with all her might and blitz the door. He would channel all the strength of her willpower into one, fierce effort.

She couldn't afford to fail this time. She was ready. She would not be deterred. Every ounce of strength, every drop of passion she felt for home, was now called up from the depths of her heart. She was only a very small butterfly -- shy and reserved – but her formidable heart would not be restrained. She had faith in Saint-Michel, the warrior-butterfly; but it was Esmée who would have to deliver the victory.

"Saint-Michel-Notre-Dame. Attention à la marche en descendant du train." Moments before the doors of carriage #9 flew open, Esmée leapt to her wings -- hurling herself directly at the door handles, full tilt. With no wind to offer resistance, she was falling more than flying.

In a frenzy of desperate flight, Esmée tucked her wings in close to her body and pierced a hole through the air. She was a dart, an arrow of aerodynamic genius. If someone had had the misfortune of stepping between her and the exit, they might have found a butterfly stuck in their forehead like a thumbtack in a corkboard. A split second before hitting them at a dizzying speed, the doors opened to let Esmée pass.

Everyone onboard, who had gathered around the doorway of carriage #9 in anticipation of exiting the train, looked up in astonishment at the little golden winged butterfly who seemed to drop like a needle from the ceiling. As soon as the doors opened, the pushing and shoving began; and the passengers quickly lost interest in anything except finding their next station.

At the same time, the people standing on the platform below, waiting to board the train, stepped back with alarm as Esmée extended her tucked-in wings and flew straight for their noses. A surprised exclamation of, "Oh!" went up from the chorus of commuters, but then fizzled away like bubbles in a shaken-up soda. This may have been the only moment during that day when any of them were roused from their own thoughts. Many even let their smartphones drop from eye-level long enough to realize that it was *"only* a butterfly," and so, "not *really* worth seeing."

The moment Esmée was gone, all eyes locked back onto cellphone screens and a glazed look returned to the commuters' faces. Like sleep-deprived zombies, they made their way onto the train; into a seat; and through their workday.

Esmée beat her wings -- flying like a fighter jet being chased by a nightmare -- and didn't let up until she was out of sight of that train. Over the heads of distracted commuters; through turnstiles and ticket-takers; up the escalator shaft toward daylight; and high above the crowded city streets, she sailed on a breath of summer breeze.

For the first time in a long time, Esmée felt the warmth of a *sunshine-blanket* spreading itself across her shoulders. Smiling down from its seat in the cloudless blue above, the life-giving sun was all the encouragement she needed to keep flapping to safety.

A few minutes later, from the top of a signpost around the corner, Esmée felt the swirling wind of the departing RER B train; and she knew she was on her own. Her plan to escape the train car had worked; but now she faced a new challenge.

There wasn't a face in sight that reminded her of Saint-Denis. There wasn't a single field or meadow within miles; nothing that brought her comfort. She sat there breathless, each muscle burning from the exertion, and wishing more than ever that she were back among the flowers of Madame Legrand's *arbuste à papillons.* How different was her current view!

All around the little butterfly, Paris spread out in radial magnificence. The City of Lights glistened in the golden sunlight like an alabaster sculpture. White stone buildings -- made brighter in contrast with the coral sky -- wore lace lattices of wrought iron with elegant sophistication. There were no skyscrapers to block the view; no concrete canyons or valleys of steel and shadow. Everywhere Esmée looked, her view extended to the horizon; and all the buildings were arranged in picture-postcard precision.

Lining the sidewalks, sycamore trees stood tall and broad; their giant leaves -- like elephant ears -- shivering in the breeze. In the buildings and landmarks; in the parks and gardens, a mixture of old and new presented itself. The ancient city's memory stretched back into ages unknown; while its confidence defined the latest trends. Paris stood at every intersection of history; and she was quite certain she had seen it all.

The city streets were designed to draw you deeper into the marvelous architecture and hidden treasures they housed. Wandering from wonder to wonder, an explorer might lose himself and never be seen or heard from again -- and he'd be perfectly fine with that. Paris offers something for everyone, and disappointment for no one.

Esmée was enchanted by the beauty of the city and overwhelmed by the cramped commotion pressing in from every side. She saw motorcycles and scooters parked in herds on the sidewalks; tiny cars, shaped like baby booties with training wheels, vying for any available inch of space in the *rues* and *routes*; boats and barges ducking beneath an endless parade of bridges straddling the river; and people… oh, so many people.

There were tourists taking selfies in front of *any*- and *every*- thing they thought might be vaguely historic -- content to see the sights later, when they reviewed the day's photos on their phones.

There were street vendors selling five-cent, plastic Eiffel Towers for one euro each. There were carefully collected groups of schoolchildren, all dressed in the same brightly colored t-shirts for easy identification. And of course, there were Parisians going about their day -- betraying no clue of how they were feeling or what they were thinking. The Parisians know they live in an exceptional place, but they try in vain to keep it a secret from the tourists of the world.

Esmée was no tourist, though. She had left the

familiarity of her quaint little village and the safety of carriage #9; and now she found herself in the middle of Paris with no idea of which direction to fly. The train station sign read, "Saint-Michel-Notre-Dame," but where was Saint-Michel?

Esmée decided her best bet was to get up above street-level and take a look around. If she couldn't find him, maybe Saint-Michel would see her. Mounting the warm breeze, she was soon high above the rooftops of the surrounding buildings. From there, she could better see the river which fractured the circular city in two. Not far from her, an enormous island sat bobbing in the water like the hull of a great ship. The river formed an *eye-of-a-needle*, casting its arms around the island in a protective embrace. The site of the ancient walled city of Paris, the *Île de la Cité* still commands the river and sits shimmering like a diamond in its watery setting.

As she broke free from the walls and chimneys blocking her view of the ground, Esmée spied -- in the middle of the intersection of four streets -- a large statue, at the base of which stood a fountain. The statue rose up to the full height of the nearby buildings and was set within an alcove of a massive stone wall. On either side of the statue, a pair of marble columns supported the heavens themselves. Esmée flew closer to inspect this wonder.

Approaching the statue, she crossed the wide intersection and spotted a sign reading, "Place Saint-Michel." Street cafes with lines of tables facing the river, straddled the Boulevard Saint-Michel and guided the eye to the magnificent statue nearby.

The busy intersection below proved to be an obstacle to pedestrians, but not to the curious butterfly. Esmée flew across the noisy street and glided without effort down to the railing of a stairwell leading deep into a subterranean metro station very close to the fountain.

There, she was able to see the enormous statue more clearly.

It was him! The great warrior-butterfly with his flaming sword held high! There he stood, tall and proud, one foot planted firmly on the back of a writhing demon. He was majestic, powerful and a welcome sight to Esmée's weary eyes.

Leaving her vantage point, Esmée flew closer to the valiant saint. As she drew near, she noticed that his left arm was outstretched above his head. The index finger of his left hand was extended, as if he were pointing to something. Esmée landed on top of the finger.

From her place high above the city, she could survey the surrounding area for blocks in every direction. She saw rooftops with terra cotta chimneys; diverging streets and intersecting avenues; tablecloths flapping in the lazy breeze; black-tied waiters and plump, pink women with fluffy white lapdogs. But there were no rosebushes or gardens anywhere in sight.

She could see the river, of course, forded by bridge after beautiful bridge. She saw endless marches of sycamore trees with sagging rolls of skin; and spires vaulting suddenly upward toward heaven. But there was no rose trellis; no flower petals; no nectar. Of all the wonder and beauty surrounding her, none offered what she needed most of all.

Saint-Michel had never disappointed her before. At home, in the gardens of *l'église Saint-Denis*, Saint-Michel always led Esmée to refreshing rosewater. He always pointed her way to nectar; but this was Paris, not Saint-Denis. Esmée rested her chin on her knees, drawn up beneath her folded wings. Maybe it had been a mistake to trust to faith and leave carriage #9; but it was much too late for such thoughts now.

If only she could find some nectar, she just might have the energy to begin the long and uncertain search for home. Without nectar, though, home might just as well not exist at all. She'd never see her family or friends again. She'd be lost in Paris, where even Saint-Michel had abandoned her to fate.

Out of the corner of her eye, she caught sight of the tall, slender spire of a two-towered cathedral -- just across the river and up the island from Saint-Michel. Between the two massive towers, an enormous round window of stained-glass petals shone like a rosebud in the summer sun. Esmée became aware that it was toward this very cathedral, and its glorious rose window, that Saint-Michel was pointing - with the same finger upon which she now sat.

Esmée looked up at the face of the statue and smiled. She would trust her patron once more; she would follow his direction. What else could she do? Bending down to kiss the outstretched finger of the beneficent, warrior-butterfly, she said in a tiny wisp of a voice, "*Merci, Saint-Michel*," then turned and leapt into the wind.

Esmée quickly crossed the Place Saint-Michel on her way to the Seine. Riding the upward thrust of thermals rising from the warm pavement below, she landed in a sycamore tree beside the swift, brown river. Taking a short break to muster her strength before crossing *le fleuve*, she fixed her eyes on the majestic spire -- then once again took to flight.

The Seine, just inches beneath her, flowed with determination to the sea. On its back, tour boats and pleasure vessels cruised -- churning up a wake of white foam. Driftwood meandered by and paused along the steep, stone banks -- caught up in the eddies and propwash of passing traffic.

Along the broad sidewalks and over bridges soaked-through with long, unbroken memory, lovers walked hand-in-hand -- sharing secrets between themselves and the Seine alone. Esmée opened her wings wide, letting the cool breeze billow them out like sails on a sailboat. Stepping off the tree limb, she rose on a cushion of air -- leaving the secretive Seine and its lovers far below.

Over river and *rue*, rooftop and *route*, Esmée held to the course indicated by Saint-Michel's index finger; until at last, she had crossed the water, streets and courtyards of the *Île de la Cité* and set foot upon the prickly spire of Notre-Dame Cathedral. From such a height, the air was clean and refreshing. It was peaceful and quiet, high above the noisy streets; and the absence of distractions sharpened her sight.

Exhausted, yet hopeful and trusting in her warrior-friend, Esmée rested atop the sharp point of the spire. She could see into the green, rectangular grounds behind the cathedral. There in the garden, framed and flanked by flying buttresses of ancient stone, she spied the grandest, most breathtaking roses she had ever seen.

CHAPTER FOUR

Brother Apius and the Honeybees

The moment she saw the rosebushes behind the cathedral, Esmée jumped down from the high spire and headed straight for the garden. Landing with reverential care upon the stone buttresses which jut out like grasshopper legs on either side of the ancient church, she inspected the whole scene carefully.

Billowing up from the lawn – like green, leafy storm clouds – a gathering of dome-shaped shrubs dominated the landscape. Rivulets of tulips and streams of snapdragons flowed in wandering beds among the trees that shade the gravel paths. Birds nested in every nook and hollow of the cathedral walls, while chipmunks ducked in and out of holes in the ground like puffy-cheeked jacks-in-the-box.

From her seat upon the buttress, Esmée could see a steady stream of honeybees buzzing busily back and forth between the flowers below and a collection of beehives on the sacristy rooftop. Moving in two lanes of traffic – one down to the gardens and another back toward the roof – the bees formed an endlessly looping conveyor belt. Any tourists who may have been tempted to pick a rose from the cathedral gardens quickly changed their minds when they saw the patrolling swarm of honeybees.

Looking very much like wooden filing cabinets with slanted tin roofs, the beehives that sat upon the sacristy rooftop appeared entirely out of place one-hundred and fifteen feet above the garden floor. Their multi-colored hive-bodies were stacked one on top of the other -- each sporting a tiny square hole in the front just big enough for two or three bees to pass shoulder-to-shoulder.

Inside, a constant hum of tireless wings was proof of the sweet labors underway. Collecting nectar from the flowers strewn throughout the garden, the bees occupied themselves day and night with spinning it into honey.

Apart from the odd pigeon, the honeybees were the only living things to make their home so high atop the cathedral. Unlike many other buildings in Paris, there were no flowers or trees growing on the roof of Notre-Dame. Instead, without any cover to shade or shelter their hives from the pelting rain, the bees lived beneath the naked sky; and they were completely surrounded by the city.

But the *Ignifuge* (pronounced: in-ee-foo-*jsh*) bees of Notre-Dame Cathedral wouldn't have had it any other way. Theirs is a proud place, a celestial setting, a noble history. Still, the bees of Notre-Dame haven't *always* lived in such lofty places. Like many tales of a rise from humble beginnings, theirs was anything but a beeline to the top.

Many years ago, over field and hedgerow; beyond the cliffs of Étretat; and across *la Manche* to England; there lived a monk named Brother Apius.

I'm afraid that - even *this* early in the story – the facts start to get fuzzy (much like the bees, themselves). So, we will have to weave them together with threads of fancy; which is perhaps where the phrase "spin a yarn" comes from.

Nonetheless, *our* thread picks up in Devonshire, England -- the home of Brother Apius -- along the banks of the River Dart.

In those days, the people of Glowermouth-on-Dart suffered from a rare condition, a singular affliction. They were completely unable to smile. Try as they might, they simply could not bring themselves to laugh, grin, or even smirk.

It wasn't because their hearts were heavy with sorrow. It wasn't a lack of humor in their homes or businesses. Life in Glowermouth had the potential to be just as mirthful as any other village along the River Dart. But the sad truth of it was that the people of Glowermouth were stricken with a raging case of *malevolum puckerfacie* (pronounced mal-*ev*-o-lum pucker-*fatch*-ee); commonly known as Grumpy Pucker Face.

There is widespread confusion between *malevolum **pokerfacie*** and *malevolum **puckerfacie**;* but the two conditions couldn't be more different. The first is a highly cultivated and essential skill possessed by any successful poker player. It is absolutely key to concealing the contents of one's cards by means of a studied lack of emotion in the eyes and facial expression. The second, however, is a most unpleasant condition.

*Malevolum **puckerfacie*** is a hardening of the muscles of the face. Without the ability to curl the corners of the mouth into bow-like, stress-releasing, joy-giving smiles, the patient (also known as the Pucker Face) is completely unable to express the happiness within. As a result, a sullen sadness eventually sets in and the victim becomes inconsolably miserable. It was this wretched affliction that plagued the people of Glowermouth-on-Dart.

In those days, a taste for foreign delicacies among the Glowermouthians gave way to a heavy influx of imported foods. Spices from the Orient; cured meats from the Iberian Peninsula; and *foie gras* and cheese from Gallic lands all flooded the markets and shops of Glowermouth. One French cheese, in particular, became widely sought-after and, indeed, famous the world over: *Méchant's Fromage de Chèvre.*

At first, the delicious goat cheese was sold only by a select few merchants in all of Devonshire. Though somewhat expensive due to its scarcity, the people gladly dug deep into their meager resources to purchase this exquisite cheese. The versatile goat cheese could be used to stuff a chicken breast; crown a tenderloin; or cover a cracker for *apéro.* Suitable for savory as well as sweet cooking, the cheese found its way into *crêpes* and pastries as well.

Soon, ravenous demand outstripped supplies and the price of *Méchant's Fromage de Chèvre* skyrocketed well out of reach of the average Glowermouthian. No longer able to afford their beloved French import, the people complained to their local merchants and distributors. They demanded that greater supplies of the cheese be found; original prices be restored; and that the growing demand be met -- and soon -- or rioting would surely erupt, casting all of Devonshire into chaos.

The people even went so far as to send a flood of letters to Méchant himself. They were convinced that the sudden cheese shortage and drastic increase in cost were part of a scheme on the part of the cheesemaker to extort greater profit at the expense of the people of Glowermouth. Anger flared up and threats were made to sail to France, find the *fromager,* and make him pay for his price-fixing. The Glowermouthians smashed storefront windows and burned cheese merchants in effigy, just to make their point. The merchants got the message loud and clear, and passed it on up the supply chain.

Word soon reached the *fromager,* Nicolas Méchant, back in France. The situation was getting out of hand, across *la Manche.* The English merchants were tired of being blamed for the cheese shortage. They begged Méchant to take action. However, when the cheesemaker heard the threats that had been made against him, his heart hardened; and cold cruelty awoke deep within him. He did not appreciate the accusations leveled by the people of Glowermouth; and he would not forgive their angry threats.

The truth was that demand for his goat cheese had far exceeded his own resources. He could not produce cheese fast enough, and he lacked the quantity of goat's milk required to keep up. Threats of violence aside, something needed to be done soon. Méchant was facing the prospect of missing his one chance at acquiring a vast fortune; building a global cheese empire; and becoming the most famous *fromager* in history. All he needed was an enormous supply of goat's milk; that's all that stood in the way of his fame and fortune. He was determined that nothing would snatch this opportunity from his hands.

But the blindness of greed is the blackest of nights. Groping in the darkness of ambition, Méchant reached too far and took hold of more than he'd intended. A deal struck with the Wizard of the Valley turned all the townspeople into goats, as you well know; and when it came to light that the foul wizard had played a fiendish trick upon the cheesemaker, Méchant simply gathered the goat-people into his paddocks and shut his eyes to the fate of his neighbors. So be it. Nothing would steal this opportunity from his hands. Nothing.

Thanks to his ill-gotten goat herd, *Méchant's Fromage de Chèvre* filled the shops of Glowermouth-on-Dart once more. The townspeople were quite pleased with the reasonable prices and inexhaustible supply. Life in Glowermouth was as it should be again.

Except, as he had vowed to himself, Méchant refused to forget the threats and accusations made by the people of Glowermouth-on-Dart. He rarely forgave any slight. Rather, he chose to bury his hatred deep in his black heart where he could feed and cultivate it like a toadstool in a compost pile. It was now time for this particular grudge to be harvested. Méchant had plans for the people of Glowermouth; plans to repay their former anger with his own brand of revenge.

The *fromager* was a brilliant chemist, having perfected his goat cheese scientifically. He understood how milk curdles to become cheese; he knew the name of every enzyme and bacteria; but, above all else, he knew how to twist good into bad.

Searching scroll after scroll, he came across the name of a little-known germ called *malevolum.* Extracted from the stump of a rotten hemlock tree, the germ thrived in darkness, much like the *fromager.* Adding it to a sample of goat's milk, Méchant curdled nature itself and created a new bacterium called *malevolum puckerfacie.*

Eager to see the results of his treachery, the spiteful cheesemaker tested his foul concoction on his own dog, until the once-playful puppy lost all desire to play. Trapped in a sullen world of his master's making, the poor animal spent the rest of his days without ever again knowing the joy of fetching, digging, or chewing on a bone.

To his satisfaction, Méchant discovered that his creation had, indeed, achieved the desired effect. Over time, the condition would worsen; and it would be nearly impossible to trace back to the cheesemaker. Mixing the cheese destined for Glowermouth-on-Dart with *malevolum puckerfacie*, Méchant exacted his revenge on the town without anyone suspecting.

At first, the townspeople felt a mild soreness in their cheeks, as if from too much grinning. Then a sluggishness weighed heavy on the facial muscles, making them slow to respond. Finally, a somber stare nudged out all hope of ever making any other expression. It now became clear; the poor people of Glowermouth were doomed to wander through their days, meeting each other with faces as hard as if hidden by lifeless masks.

At first, fear gripped the villagers. What was happening among them? Were they cursed? Was this a punishment from above? Then, panic took root in their hearts. There was no clear explanation and no hopeful solution. There was only desperation.

As their condition worsened, panic gave way to sad submission and then despair. The light of joy had been extinguished in Glowermouth. The things in which the people had once delighted no longer brought them any happiness. Family, friendship, food: it all turned to dust. Even their beloved *fromage de chévre* had lost its appeal. All of life had become a grey rag draped over the hearts of the townsfolk.

Toiling day and night within his silent cloister on Buckfast hill, the monk-turned-scientist, Brother Apius, sought a cure for the dismal disorder. Gathering every plant and herb, salve and balm possessed of the power of merriment, Brother Apius bravely tested their efficacy on himself.

Solutions of saffron and cinnamon; poultices of plum and persimmon; and wine after heady wine were taken; tasted; tweaked and tinkered-with, but to no lasting effect. Desperation grew with the dimming of his cloister's candles, as the old monk labored and prayed without rest for a breakthrough.

A lover of goat cheese, himself, Brother Apius had long since suffered the effects of the bacteria without realizing its connection to the cheese. This, plus his natural talent for scientific studies and his dedication to finding a cure for his fellow villagers, made him the ideal person to study the condition. Cataloging plants; identifying insects; and interviewing townspeople about everything from the amount of sun they took each day to how much raw honey they put in their tea, Brother Apius had compiled a vast library of scientific data.

One fateful day, in a flash of inspiration, Brother Apius stumbled upon a promising discovery. He had been recording the eating habits of the townspeople for months and was poring over the data when he noted something interesting. Among the inhabitants of Glowermouth-on-Dart who regularly ate goat cheese, those who also ate honey from two specific types of bees displayed a resistance to the disease. Instead of wearing the telltale Pucker Face, the slightest hint of a smirk could be seen on their lips.

He also determined that the amount of goat cheese the people consumed on a daily basis had a direct connection to the seriousness of their condition. The more goat cheese they ate, the worse were their symptoms.

He sampled goat cheese from every merchant in town, cultured them, and grew whatever bacteria he could find. The good brother grew everything from beer yeast to athlete's foot in his Petri dishes -- and crossed a good many goat cheeses off his regular grocery list in the process. He discovered that the samples taken from *Méchant's Fromage de Chèvre* all contained the rare *malevolum* bacteria. Moreover, Brother Apius determined that the townspeople who ate more of *Méchant's Fromage de Chèvre* had the most advanced cases of the condition. There was no doubt in Brother Apius' mind, the town had been poisoned by the wicked cheesemaker.

Remembering the good effects of the daily dose of honey in some of the townspeople's tea, Brother Apius worked to identify and isolate the beneficial elements within the beneficial honey made by the two species of bee. Combining them together, he successfully engineered a new strain of bee now known as the *Ignifuge* bee.

Brother Apius also discovered that the healing

properties of *Ignifuge* bees could be further improved upon by a regular diet of rosewater, lily nectar, and the occasional sip of red wine taken by the bees themselves. He also noted that a sip of wine, every now and then, did wonders for his own disposition, too.

Within a year of his discovery, Brother Apius' *Ignifuge* bees were producing enough honey to support their own thriving colony and to share a good amount with the clever monk, too. He began a daily practice of taking one teaspoon of honey in his morning tea; and in a matter of days, the effects of the *malevolum puckerfacie* began to fade from his face. In the space of a month, the condition had been reversed and entirely erased. The cure had worked. It was time for Brother Apius to share his discovery with the people of Glowermouth-on-Dart.

At first, the villagers were skeptical. If the cause of their condition was in *Méchant's Fromage de Chèvre*, why was the condition to be found only in Glowermouth and not all throughout Europe? Why would Méchant want to poison them? How could a little bit of sweetness every day cure the sadness among them?

Still, the results could be seen in Brother Apius, himself. It was impossible to argue with; the monk had found a cure and tested it on himself with perfect success. The villagers formed a line which stretched from the door of the monk's cloister, down the garden path, around the abbey, and all the way through the streets of town. Everyone arrived with an empty jar and left with a month's supply of honey. Thirty days later, there was laughter in the streets of Glowermouth-on-Dart once more.

Brother Apius soon began to enjoy the success of his life's work and became widely known as the Mirthful Monk. The constant glow of joy and happiness shining from his angelic face was the perfect advertisement for what the happy villagers called *The Mirthful Monk's*

Miraculous Miel.

News of the breakthrough spread far and wide, as people soon discovered its healthy effects. Even those who were fortunate enough to have escaped the Pucker Face Plague found that honey from the *Ignifuge* bees brought a deeper joy than they had ever known. Pleasant moods became permanent; happiness became joy; the amazing honey made good things twice as good and bad things half as bad. The bees were now in high demand across all of Europe.

Unhappy people traveled great distances, like pilgrims on a quest, to steal joy itself from the *Ignifuge* bees. Brother Apius and his magical honeybees were hounded by visitors, night and day. Not even the sanctity of the cloister's walls could protect them any longer. The townspeople began sneaking into the apiary late at night, braving the inevitable stings, for just one swollen handful of sticky combs. The searing burn of a few stings was a small price to pay for the promise of lasting happiness.

Like tiny darts aimed at thieving intruders, the bees unleashed their stingers in an attempt to defend their honey. Many villagers would run screaming from the abbey, swiping wildly at the cloud of pursuing bees. There in the cool comfort of the nearby river, the stinging darts from the poor oppressed bees were washed from the hands and limbs of the wicked townspeople. Legend has it, this is how the River Dart may have gotten its name.

Brother Apius felt a grateful responsibility toward his bees and was resolved to rescue them from a life of unwanted attention and unending harassment. It was his hope that, kept well out of reach of unfriendly hands, the bees would be allowed to live a life of freedom and peaceful coexistence. It must be understood that the bees were not miserly with their honey; they merely craved a quiet life of solitude. Brother Apius was determined to give them just that. Willing to share their honey in reasonable measure, the bees agreed to an arrangement of the monk's own devising.

One night, under the cover of a moonless sky, Brother Apius packed up his hives, sandaled his feet, and set out for the River Dart. He was reluctant to trust the darkness alone to conceal his movements from the ever-watchful eyes of greedy townspeople. So, creaking his way down hidden and forgotten pathways -- overgrown with disuse -- the rickety mule-drawn wagon crept along toward the river, unseen. The thick brush and undergrowth muffled the sounds of mule and wagon alike. Clutched in the old monk's hand, a box-shaped lantern hung at the end of a wooden pole. Dangling above the head of the mule, it cast a faint orange flicker on the unfamiliar footpath; barely bright enough to light their way.

Silent as the night sky, they proceeded. The mule seemed to tip-toe with such caution that not even a snapping twig betrayed their presence. After nearly an hour spent feeling their way along a path that could have been traveled in minutes by daylight, they arrived at the dock where a small boat awaited them. One of the younger brothers from the abbey, Brother Zephyrinus, stood holding the mooring rope. He had set out from the abbey 30 minutes before Brother Apius, so as to avoid the attention of curious eyes. There, he waited for his confrere to arrive.

Loading the hives into a dingy tied to the back of the boat, Brother Apius took his small sack of worldly possessions, bid his friend farewell, and set foot inside the wooden barque bound for the English Channel. Brother Zephyrinus waved goodbye, then mounted the mule cart and rode silently back to Buckfast. The townsfolk all lay sleeping in their beds, none the wiser.

From Glowermouth to the coast of France, the crossing was perilous. Wind and wave, darkness and doubt assaulted the tiny fleet as if they were merely sticks on the surface of the great salt sea. Brother Apius sat in the main boat -- manning the tiller and sail as best he could -- as the restless waves rolled beneath them.

Without the moon to light their way, starlight was all they could hope for. The reflection of the sky in the water made it feel as if all the world was a watery, starlit sphere and they were awash within it; above and below, sky and sea were one and the same.

The wind battered the boats, threatening to tear the sail from the oaken mast and fling it far out to sea. All around, the night was wild with the sounds of the howling wind. The bees, no strangers to a brisk breeze, popped out of their hives to weather the passage on the shoulders and beneath the hood of their protector. Brother Apius reassured them as best he could; but being so far from dry land and a solid footing is terrifying, even if you are a winged creature.

Heading for the Cherbourg peninsula, across the Channel to France, they turned southeast toward Le Havre. Navigating by flickering stars and faltering faith, Brother Apius pointed the small flotilla into the white-capped waves, with frozen fingers wrapped tightly around the tiller. If only they could cross the open expanse of the English Channel, their hopes would be shored-up by the French coastline.

Hours passed, as they fought the fickle wind and waves -- soaked to the bone and shivering with cold. When at last, the monk and his precious cargo finally experienced a turn of good fortune. Having been forced to tack an indirect course against unhelpful winds, the breeze now shifted to their backs and began pushing them with great speed directly southeast. They were now within sight of the French coastline, and greatly heartened by its approach. Brother Apius could see the waterway that would take them deep into the heart of the country.

Leaving the open waters of the English Channel, they were soon in the relative calm of the *Crique de Rouen*. From there, the glassy harbor gave way to the estuary of the Seine River at Honfleur; the worst of their journey was now behind them. For miles upon miles, and through endless hours into the pale morning's light, they rode the back of the serpentine Seine as it slithered its course toward Paris. Past farmland and villages, they sailed in silence; while all the world around them lay sleeping.

Brother Apius' mother was French, and he often visited her in the little Norman town in which she'd grown up. After the death of her husband, she returned to the land of her birth, to live out her days among familiar sights, sounds and memories. The pastoral landscape of Normandy, organized by hedgerows and thickets; the floral sounds of her native language; and the food, taken from field to table with such skill and devotion, brought comfort and perspective to her lengthening days. Brother Apius thought about his beloved mother now, as the boats crept past the docks of her village en route to their destination.

For hours, the river looped and crawled along its path. On its shoulders, a dingy full of beehives -- tied to a barely seaworthy sailboat – made its way, with great effort, inland. Now manning the oars, a threadbare monk -- his back covered in honeybees -- worked away in silence. Digging deep into the brown water, Brother Apius prayed quietly to the rhythm of his rowing. It had been a long and arduous night; but the sun lay just below the horizon -- their journey was drawing to an end.

With salt-crusted lips -- aches in their joints, and eyes held open by willpower alone -- the exhausted company rounded the last loop of the broad-backed Seine, and finally entered the city of their destination. All at once, the landscape changed from farmland to metropolis. White stone walls caught the first rays of the faint morning sunrise and bounced it from building to building before casting it like a skipping stone across the surface of the river.

Sailing beneath *les ponts de Paris*, they reached a point where the river split, straddling the *Île de la Cité*. Here, at the leading prow of the island, a solitary weeping willow draped its long hair down to the lapping water below. Choosing the righthand branch of the river, the exhausted travelers passed the willow tree, and crept along the stone wall which shored-up the island against the water's edge.

A series of large, iron rings could be seen attached to the banks of the limestone quay. Brother Apius leaned over and took hold of a mooring rope -- looped through the great rings -- and secured both boats to the dock. Standing, with some difficulty, he stretched his limbs, then slowly disembarked and began loading the beehives into a horse cart that had been sent to meet them.

Shifting and shimmying up cobblestone streets beneath ghostly gas streetlights -- still flickering in the morning sunrise -- a vision broke upon them like the noonday sun. Rising up between heaven and earth, Notre-Dame Cathedral stood with welcoming arms, guiding the tired travelers to their new home.

Helped by the hands of the cardinal-archbishop himself, the hives were taken from the cart and carried through the sacred space of the cathedral's interior. Past statues and paintings, votive lights and sanctuary lamp, the hives were secreted away inside the walls of the ancient church.

Higher and higher, up winding stone staircases -- as if ascending to their eternal reward -- the *Ignifuge* bees were installed at last atop the sacristy roof where no hand could assault them, and no thief could pillage their stores. It was a brilliant hiding place, in sight of no one but the angels.

Weeks prior, Brother Apius had written to seek the help of the archbishop of Paris, who proposed an arrangement of mutual benefit. The bees would live atop the safety of the cathedral's summit, in exchange for a small share of their exceptional honey. The archbishop would distribute the honey to the poor of the city, keeping only a modest portion for his own use. Brother Apius could remain with his beloved bees as their beekeeper and live out his long years in their service. The good monk presented the plan to the bees, who agreed without reservation.

Thus, began a new chapter for bees and brother, alike. Thanks to the research done by Brother Apius, the *Ignifuge* bees were born and their healing honey dispensed to the unfortunate people of Glowermouth-on-Dart. Because of the hospitality of the archbishop of Paris, the bees continue to share their honey with the poor of the city -- all the while living in safe seclusion atop the world's most elegant cathedral.

Brother Apius lived and died in the service of his beloved bees. The last taste to pass his lips -- this side of eternity -- was the taste of honey. Slipping away into blissful sleep, he left behind nothing more than a half-dozen hives, a worn-out pair of sandals, a legacy of love and a sweet smile. On his tombstone, one single line is etched in simple limestone: *The Mirthful Monk of the Miraculous Miel.*

Over time, the *Ignifuge* bees found their living arrangements so satisfactory that their gratitude literally bloomed and blossomed into the most spectacular rose garden in France. It was here in the gardens of *Notre-Dame de Paris* that Esmée now found herself -- watching the descendants of this noble line of *Ignifuge* bees tend to the rosebushes their ancestors once cared for with the same dedication and devotion.

There was a meticulous method to the bees' movements throughout the garden. With heads down and antennae forward, the fuzzy, gold and black worker-bees flew a tight pattern; never missing a single bud. Attached to their hips, like yellow saddlebags, were sacks filled with pollen collected from every flower they'd visited.

Like cargo helicopters, they buzzed in from above; collected nectar in their mouths; stored it in their extra stomach (yes, bees really do have two!); and carried it back to the hive. Along the way, tiny grains of pollen attached themselves to the bees' legs like foxtail burrs, hitching a ride from flower to flower, pollinating as they went.

Back at the hive, the worker-bees poured their nectar into hexagonal wax honeycombs. Hive-bees then fanned the liquid with their wings, until just enough moisture had evaporated, leaving behind the gooey, golden honey for which bees have become so deservedly famous.

It was an impressive operation, and Esmée delighted in watching the thousands of bees at work; but it only reminded her of her own gnawing hunger. Saint-Michel had shown her the way to rosewater nectar, and she was grateful to him for having literally pointed it out. But she was more than ready to sample some and compare it to the nectar from back home.

The air around her was thick with bees and making her way down to the rose garden would be much like merging onto the *Périphérique* -- the highway which rings the city of Paris. Esmée hopped off her stone buttress and glided down into a gentle descent. A straight-line flight would have carried her directly into oncoming bee-traffic. Unwilling to risk a merge, Esmée stayed close to the giant buttress, and made her way directly to ground-level.

Landing on a lily, she surveyed the traffic patterns

around the bushes and decided to stay below the radar and close to the ground. Flying below the bees, Esmée approached an immense rosebush, strewn with fragrant flowers. She settled on a bud, extended her curled-up tongue, and enjoyed the longest and most refreshing drink she could remember.

Hovering just overhead in a holding pattern, a honeybee patiently waited her turn.

"Zzz… zzz… zzz… take your time, *mademoizelle*. You look like you could uze a good drink. *Je suiz content d'attendre*. I wait."

Esmée looked up in astonishment. The bee's voice was much larger than she would have expected from such a tiny creature. Her accent was difficult to place. Although her French was *impeccable*, there was a mixture of muddled influences in her pronunciation as if she'd done a lot of travelling and collected accents - as well as pollen - along the way.

The look on her face was one of singular purpose. She was all business; yet there was patient kindness in her eyes. On her back, her four wings meshed together, forming one large flying surface attached to either side of her body. Her black and yellow bee-fuzz was well-groomed; and her flight was a picture of masterful movement. Esmée always admired the industrious beauty of a honeybee; and this bee was no exception.

"*Merci, madame*," Esmée replied with a polite nod of her head, then returned to drinking.

"Heaven knowz I could uze a break. Back and forz, up and down, all day long. It'z exhauzting, for sure. My name is Ztéphanie. What'z yourz? You're not from Paree, are you?"

"*Je m'appelle Esmée. Et, non madame*," she said between sips, "*Je suis de Saint-Denis.*"

"Zaint-Denis," Stéphanie replied with a surprised buzz and another misplaced Z. "I zpent a little time zere in my younger dayz. Exzellent rozez. You're a long way from home! What bringz you here?"

"C'est une longue histoire," Esmée said, with a hint of sadness and more than a little fatigue.

"A long ztory, indeed. I'm sure you're here to zee zhe zightz around Paree! What have you zeen zo far?"

Stéphanie failed to notice Esmée's sadness, she was too busy gathering nectar from a neighboring flower.

"Rien, pour le moment," Esmée responded, somewhat evasively.

She didn't want to admit she was lost. Not just yet. She was hesitant even to think of her homesick situation, for fear she might cry.

"Nozhing yet!? Oh well, let me tell you what you need to zee!" Stéphanie rubbed her front feet together with delight.

"Zince you're here, you have to ztart with zhe cazhedral. I've lived here all my life, and it nevair getz old. I have travelled far and wide, but zhis iz my favorite plaze. You will nevair forget it."

Growing animated, Stéphanie continued. "Zhen… ah well, zhen… just follow zhe Zeine! Zhe river, she will guide you to many breaztaking zightz, and she will alwayz lead you home again."

"Ma maison…" Esmée sighed, whispering under her breath.

A droop settled into her wings as she thought about her home. How could she visit the sights in Paris, when her one desire was to find her way home? The thought of spending one single moment longer than necessary away from home was an impossibility. She would never willingly delay her return.

"Az I zaid, begin wizh zhe cazhedral. Zhe entranze iz on zhe ozher zide. I've got to be off! Zo glad to have met you! Enjoy your time in Paree! *À bientôt!* Zzz… zzz… zzz…"

With that, the little honeybee rejoined her friends busily ferrying nectar to the *Ignifuge* hives on the rooftop of the cathedral. Esmée sat amid the rosebuds awhile, watching the show, still sipping sweet nectar.

For those few moments, she forgot her predicament. The refreshment of the much-needed and most-delicious nectar; the hypnotic motion of the buzzing bees; and the beauty of the backdrop of the cathedral garden distracted her heart and mind for a while. She even found herself enjoying all of the sights and sounds of the city around her – at least what she'd seen so far. She was, perhaps, becoming curious to explore her surroundings – maybe just a little bit.

Had she noticed the change that was stealing its way into her heart, she would surely have been alarmed; but, Esmée was falling victim – unaware and unwilling, like so many before her – to the charms of Paris. It had begun back at the statue of Saint-Michel; and the enchantment of her surroundings now made it inevitable. She was falling in love with the City of Lights; and it was unlikely she would ever recover.

The leaves on the trees above glowed like emeralds in the sunlight. A million different shades of green cast shapes and shadows on the cool grass. The low hedges enclosing the gardens were alive with birds and beetles, moths and ladybugs; all going about their day amid the sweet sighs of a gentle breeze.

Esmée inhaled deeply, letting the fresh air clear her mind of worries. A smile crept onto her face, as she closed her eyes and opened her wings to the docile wind. Her heart grew light and her cares, caught up in a breath from heaven, floated away.

Perhaps it was the nectar, or maybe the kindly confidence of her new acquaintance, but for the first time since the doors of the RER B train slid closed that morning, Esmée felt hopeful that she would find her way home. How could a moment of peaceful joy like this *not* lead her home?

She also wondered what Stéphanie had meant when she said that the river would always lead her home again. An expectant faith began to take root in her heart, and it gave her the strength of growing certainty. She could do this. She could find home once more. All around her was wonder! It sang to her heart; it whispered from her memories; there was something to be discovered here.

In a world filled with rumors and tales of darkness, Esmée had already found kindness in a stranger and growing happiness in a strange place. New hope was born in the rose garden of *Notre-Dame de Paris*.

After taking one last sip of nectar, Esmée fluttered her graceful wings and began to fly. As she left the rosebush and turned toward the other side of the cathedral, a voice was heard from within the swarming cloud of bees calling, "*Au revoir, mademoizelle!* Enjoy your vizit to Paree!"

"*Merci, mon amie! Profitez de votre miel!*"

CHAPTER FIVE

Notre-Dame Cathedral

Flapping her wings with deep thrusts, Esmée swam through a tranquil sea of glistening light and winsome waves. Over stone and stained-glass, she pirouetted with playful joy until she had cleared the cathedral's two towers. On the opposite side of the church, Esmée landed on a second-story stone railing running just in front of the enormous rose window. Below her, twenty-eight statues of saints stood guard over the three double-doored entrances to the cathedral.

A queue of tourists stretched out into the stone courtyard in front of the historic building. People were caught up in trying to fit the massive structure within the lens of their cameras. Their attempts were futile, of course. No camera can capture awe. No lens can take hold of wonder. The best they could manage were selfies of oversized heads against a backdrop of blurry beauty. Some resorted to taking photos of pigeons to pass the time, while they awaited their chance to go inside.

Esmée flitted down and stood upon the intricate engravings surrounding the doors. Seven layers of rounded arches, each set deeper into the living stone of the façade, framed dozens of statues stacked one upon the other. Esmée sat there marveling at the stonework and the hands that brought it to life. Every detail was cut with hammer and chisel but appeared as fine as if it had been drawn by the point of a pin.

Like the tourists in the courtyard below, Esmée tried to wrap her mind around it all. She flew out into the square to observe the structure as a whole. She flitted from statue to statue, ledge to lintel in an attempt to see it all in detail. Her eyes failed to encompass what only the heart can take in.

She felt tiny, and yet she understood -- without knowing -- that she, too, was a beautiful detail in the enormity of creation. She felt small, but not insignificant. Wrapping her golden orange wings of flame and moonlight around her long brown body, Esmée sighed with awe at this new sight. So far, the world had been more filled with grandeur and light than she'd ever anticipated; but Esmée had seen nothing yet.

Waiting for a break in the line of distracted tourists, Esmée snuck quickly through the large door of the cathedral and emerged inside a world of celestial light and soaring stone. Her eyes widened against the sheer vastness of the cathedral's interior. She felt the heat of a thousand beeswax candles and understood yet another detail of the ancient agreement between the hardworking rooftop bees and the archbishop.

The scent of beeswax and the resin from the incense of a million thuribles filled Esmée's heart and mind with a deep sense of veneration. Somehow, the interior of the cathedral was more immense than nature herself.

Graceful columns supported a parade of arches marching up the main aisle. The endless nave of the church blended seamlessly with the vaulted apse above the altar which was bathed in the warmth of blue, copper and purple tones. The entire cathedral was awash in enormous waves and pools of light. Esmée sat on the sill of a second-story arch, frozen with reverence.

The golden copper luminance of the cathedral

mixed with the flickering glow of candleflame and danced on Esmée's iridescent wings. She felt like Saint-Michel in all his splendor. Spreading her wings, like a magnificent warrior-butterfly, she cast herself into the pearl-white light of heaven itself. She flew high above the heads of tourists, high above the banners and pews. She rode thermals breathed by candleflame, and mounted heights only accessible beneath the sheltering ceiling of Notre-Dame.

Esmée was an angel in flight; a wisp of wind; a ballerina of the basilica; and her heart was full. She flew along the vaults of the ceiling and through the multi-colored brilliance of the stained-glass windows. She felt like she was bathing in a rainbow and soaking in moonbeams. Never before had she felt so perfectly free, while still enclosed within four walls. She agreed with the little honeybee; this was her new favorite place.

Below her, in front of a statue of a woman in flowing robes, a spray of red roses burst forth from a crystal vase. Stepping with perfect weightlessness among the sweet buds, Esmée drank nectar from the roses of Notre-Dame once again. Overcome with emotion, she flew to the feet of the woman and whispered in prayerful awe, *"Merci, gentille dame. Merci."*

What began with a bouquet of flowers in carriage #9 in Saint-Denis-lès-Chevreuse had led Esmée to a bouquet at the feet of *Notre-Dame de Paris* herself. In the course of a few hours, her world had opened up into unimaginable vistas. No longer was she simply trying to get home at all cost. Whether she chose to be or not, she was now on an adventure. Her destination *was* home, to be sure; but her path had led her astray into unforgettable wonders. Delivered, for a while, from her homesick yearning by the splendor around her, she was content to sit in silence in this sacred space.

Esmée spent hours inside Notre-Dame Cathedral,

just resting her wings and mind in perfect quiet. When the time to leave finally arrived, she felt keenly the contrast between the cathedral and the outside world. Inside it was quiet and still. There was profound depth, as if she had wandered into the deepest valley hidden between soaring mountains. The light inside the cathedral was vibrant, and new as the world's first morning.

Outside, she was back in the perpetual motion of city life. Noise and commotion now reigned where, only the width of a stone wall away, silence and peace held sway. Her heart longed to return to her new favorite place, but the world lay outside; and beyond that, home awaited her. It was time to move on.

She remembered what Stéphanie the bee told her about following the Seine; that the river would be her guide. Esmée was surprised to find herself excited by what the river held in store for her. She wondered how it might lead her home, as her new friend had assured her it would. She was beginning to feel that the world was planted thick with bewildering riddles.

Rising on the wind, she headed toward the river surrounding the *Île de la Cité*, upon which Notre-Dame sat immovable. At the bow of the ship-shaped island was a bridge. Actually, comprised of two separate and slightly angled spans, the Pont Neuf joins the Right and Left Banks of the Seine to the *Île de la Cité*.

Esmée fluttered down low over the swift tan-colored water, dipping the tips of her toes in the cool river. She then rode the breeze up to the face of the bridge, landing upon one of the 381 *mascarons* which adorn the stonework. These masks represent satyrs and sylvains of ancient mythology. Esmée felt right at home with these lesser gods of field, flower and forest. Once again, she marveled at the skill with which these sculptures were coaxed from the reluctant stone.

Flying up to the level of street and sidewalk,

Esmée landed on one of the black iron lampposts which recur every few feet across the deck of the bridge. Down below, she noticed the many "lovers locks" fixed eternally to the lamppost bases: romantic reminders of never-ending love. It's true, of course, that the butterfly is nature's most romantic creature, and so the symbolic beauty of the locks was not lost on Esmée. She rested her chin on her arm, propped up on one knee, and sighed.

The Pont Neuf is the oldest bridge in Paris, even though its name means *New Bridge*. In 1578, when construction began, it was new in design and grandeur. To Esmée, it was the most beautiful bridge she'd ever seen. In her eyes, the bridge spanned more than just the Seine: it spanned the ages; it reached back through centuries of romantic dreams, joining them to her own. She sat there on the lamppost letting the romance and history of the bridge inspire poetry in her mind.

> *Un pont pour traverser les profondeurs de l'amour,*
> *et rapprocher deux cœurs...*
> *A bridge to cross the depths of love,*
> *and bring two hearts together...*

Walking hand-in-hand across the bridge, lovers - young and old - wore far distant faces of lovestruck joy. Esmée watched them pass beneath her, and the echo of every sunset she'd ever seen filled her heart.

"Excusay moi, madam wozzle."

The voice roused Esmée from her romantic daydream, like the rude bell of an alarm clock.

"Je sweez desolay de voos de ranger."

"*Oh, pardon,*" Esmée replied, looking around for the source of the voice. "*Qui est là?*"

Down below on the sidewalk stood a man holding a worn and wrinkled map. At his side, a little girl of 5 or 6 was tethered to a pink balloon. Her mother stood nervously scrutinizing and zooming-in on virtual maps of the Paris metro on her phone. Esmée could immediately tell the man and his family were tourists; mostly because of the man's atrocious pronunciation.

"Parlay voos onglay, sill voos plate?"

The look in his round, dark eyes was desperate and plaintive.

"Please? Parlay voos?"

"*Oui monsieur, un peu.* I speak a *lee-tell*," said a young woman passing by on her lunch break.

She slowed down long enough to respond to the lost and confused tourist, but everything about her body language indicated her desire to continue on her way. The man took no notice of the woman's haste and kept right on talking.

"Oh, thank goodness! I can't find a single American in all of Paris, and the only English I've heard was some kind of British or Australian or I don't *know* what!

"My friends told me I'd be fine… '*English is the universal language,*' they said. '*Everybody speaks enough to get by.*' Well, here I am standin' on the Pont Nerf and ain't nobody speakin' the '*universal language*' within earshot! I ain't '*gettin' by*' so well!"

The young woman's "*un peu*" had just been used up in one, big firehose-blast of American English. Her legs, hips, and shoulders were turned in the direction she'd been walking; only her increasingly alarmed face remained fixed on the gabby American. Up above, Esmée sat on top of her lamppost still trying to figure out what "*gettin' by*" could possibly mean, when it started again.

"I'm just tryin' to find the closest subway. Ya know, in New York there's a sign on every corner, but here in 'The City O' Light" well, I guess they can't spare any of that light for a flashing signpost, or a neon arrow, or… heck, I'd be happy with a smoke signal, right about now!

"How do they expect a guy to get from Point A to Point B without some directions? Or maybe I shoulda said, from *Pont* A to *Pont* B... ha ha, get it? Anyhow, I just need the subway and I'll be on my way. Can ya help a guy out?"

The young woman was lost; left in the dust; still stuck on "smoke signal," with no hope of catching up. Her eyes dilated like two camera shutters in the dark; and that's what she was, completely *in the dark,* with no idea what the talkative American was going on about.

"I am sorry, monsieur. Subway?" she inquired, not yet entirely willing to leave him to his fate – but getting there, and quickly.

"Yeah subway. Underground. The el. The tram. The train. The metro."

"*Ah le métro! Oui*! I know *le métro*."

"Now we're cookin' with gas!" the man said, without explanation. The woman decided not to ask for clarification. "Where's the closest metro?"

"*Oui*, yes. *Le métro n'est pas loin*. It is very near. *C'est ici*." she said, pointing in the direction she'd just come from.

Obviously feeling she'd endured more than her fair share of Americanisms -- while being of definite service to the man -- the young woman turned and bolted across the bridge to freedom.

"Hot dog! Lead the way!" the man said, looking down as he fumbled with his misshapen map -- not realizing he'd just been left alone.

When he finally did look up to find the young woman gone, he turned to his wife with exasperated disbelief. She was still zooming and scrolling on her phone, having paid no attention to what had been going on around her.

Smacking himself squarely in the middle of the forehead, the man exclaimed, "Wow! Just great! Where'd she go? Did she fall off the bridge or somethin'? Now what are we gonna do?!"

During this whole time, the man's daughter had been playing with her pink balloon. Pulling it down to the level of her face, she would then let go of the balloon and watch it float upward until the string was almost out of reach. Grabbing it at the last moment, she'd then repeat the game over and over again.

At the height of one of its ascents, the balloon passed within inches of Esmée who was still seated on top of the lamppost overhead. As the little girl jumped to grab the string, she caught sight of Esmée.

"Hello," the girl said, wrapping the string around her hand. "What's your name?"

Folding and extending her wings in the warm sunlight, Esmée looked down at the child below. Her parents were now both busy zooming and scrolling on their respective phones; no closer to finding the nearby metro station.

"Mommy and Daddy are lost," she said without concern. "But I know where we are. We're right *here*." She pointed to the ground at her feet and giggled.

Esmée fluttered down from her lamppost and landed on the little girl's shoulder. Folding her wings, then extending them, Esmée looked like a brooch on the girl's sweater. The little girl smiled with delight. Esmée returned the smile (though much too small for the child to see), then continued to fan her wings again and again.

"They can't find the metro," the girl said, with a matter-of-fact tone. "Have you ever been on a train?"

If only she knew!

Esmée lifted off the girl's shoulder, flew two or three jittery circles above her head, then began flying toward the Pont Neuf metro station not far from where they now stood -- in the direction the young woman had pointed just before running off.

Esmée flew forward a bit then circled, waiting for the little girl to catch up. After a few moments of forward-circle-circle, forward-circle-circle, they finally arrived at the entrance to the subterranean metro station located near the end of the bridge.

Again, Esmée landed on the little girl's shoulder, fluttering her wings.

"Mommy, mommy!" the girl called from only a few feet away. "Look at the pretty butterfly!"

Her parents looked up from their phones and saw their daughter standing beneath the metro sign for the Pont Neuf station. Their eyes popped and their mouths dropped open, as they turned toward each other in amazement. The man pushed his phone into his back pocket, stowed the weather-worn map in his front pocket, and started walking toward his daughter -- complaining all the way.

"I've seen signs for everything from Noter Dame to Saint Michael to the Loover, but no metro signs. Would it kill 'em to put up a few more metro signs and actually help people out? Unbelievable."

"*Le Louvre?*" Esmée thought to herself. "*Le Louvre est loin?*"

The man was still complaining to his wife, when they both reached their daughter.

"They had some decent stuff at the Loover, don't get me wrong; but I don't see what all the fuss is over that Mona Lisa picture. I could barely see it over the crowd. It looked like a postage stamp at twenty feet. Big let-down, if ya ask me. Anyway, I was about to suggest we walk back down the river and find the station for the Loover, the one we took yesterday. Lucky, I found this one, instead."

His wife just said, "Yes, dear," and left it at that.

"Down the river," Esmée thought. "*Le Louvre* is just down the river! It is *très loin.*"

The little girl knew the truth. She knew that without Esmée, they wouldn't have found the Pont Neuf metro station. She turned her face toward the butterfly on her shoulder and whispered, "Thank you, beautiful butterfly." Then she kissed Esmée's wing and turned to join her parents.

Esmée also knew that without this chance encounter, she would have had no idea just how close she was to the Louvre Museum. Excitement now swelled inside her heart.

"Hey look, a butterfly," the man said as Esmée flitted off the little girl's shoulder and onto the metro sign overhead.

Taking his daughter's hand, the man followed his wife down the stairs, into the metro station, and out of sight.

Resting on the signpost, Esmée thought back to when she was a child. She remembered that her mother would often tell her stories of *le Palais du Louvre* and the treasures it contained. Paintings of flowers of the most exquisite colors, and sculptures of butterflies as fine and fragile as a snowflake filled her imagination and captured her heart.

Most wondrous of all, her mother told her about a beautiful sculpture of Cupid bending his knee to present a rose to a butterfly. As her mother described the milky white of the supple marble, the look on the young god's face, and the gift he made to the beautiful butterfly, Esmée imagined *herself* as the recipient of the divine rose. How it stirred her romantic heart, and how she longed to witness the graceful beauty of this poignant scene with her own eyes.

Esmée always dreamed of one day seeing these things in person; but she never expected the hopes of a tiny butterfly could really ever come true. Now here she was, beside the Seine, and only a few flaps of her delicate wings away from the Louvre Museum and her chance at a dream-come-true.

CHAPTER SIX

Queen of the Louvre

Le Musée du Louvre is enormous; so enormous, in fact, that it's impossible to view the entire collection in one day. It is *not* so enormous, however, that anyone could just sneak in unnoticed. Access to the treasures within is strictly controlled.

The security at the Louvre is designed to protect the collection from those who would harm or destroy it; but it isn't just from people that potential threats might arise. With priceless collections of cloth tapestries, canvas paintings, and fragile antiquities of all kinds, one family of hungry moths could chew their way through hundreds of years-worth of invaluable art and culture in no time.

Although some would (correctly) say that it's just a rumor, it's been reported that there's a small sign hanging above the main entrance to the Louvre; a sign meant for a very specific audience. Difficult to decipher by the millions of human visitors to the museum, the almost imperceptible little sign and its message of warning are clear as day to moths, butterflies, and other insects.

"Pas de Mâcheurs!" are the words printed in red ink on the sign above the main door to the museum. Beneath the warning, an illustration of a winged insect sits at the center of a circle struck through by a red line.

The curators of the Louvre mean business: *No Chewers Allowed!*

Now, you might be thinking, "Butterflies don't chew. They live on only what they can drink. So, it's not right to punish *them* for the behavior of their cousin, the moth."

And I'd agree with you!

Moths are the goats of the insect world (and may, in fact, have had a small role to play in the history of the Goat-People of the Chevreuse Valley… but that, too, is questionable).

What is undeniable is that moths love to chew. They chew their way through wool; they chew their way through linen. They gnaw on canvas, cotton and cornflowers; and when they aren't chewing holes in useful things, they keep their chompers finetuned by chewing on less useful things.

Moths have ruined the reputation of every flittery, fluttery, flying insect in nature. But what can be done about it? Who could hope to unravel millions of years-worth of evolution? And who can readily distinguish a moth from a harmless butterfly?

The problem is, most people don't know that moths rest with their wings closed; while butterflies keep them open. Moths have short feathery antennae; while butterflies' antennae are long and slender. Moths are also more active in the moonlight; while butterflies prefer the sun.

But debunking moth myth and misunderstanding is an exercise in futility. In a world full of litigation lawyers, it would be dangerous to let butterflies enter while keeping moths out. The Louvre simply didn't want to risk being sued by a moth who felt he'd been wronged.

The bottom line is that, to the untrained eye, Esmée was a chewer and so she would definitely not be allowed inside the museum. This would have broken her heart; but as it happened, she didn't have to worry about it. Esmée would not be kept out of the Louvre and away from her dream-come-true because of an unfortunate resemblance to a moth. No, she would not be kept out by ignorance or prejudice; not today she wouldn't.

Today was a Tuesday, and every Parisian knows that the Louvre is closed on Tuesdays for maintenance and renovation work. That was enough to keep *everyone* out for the day, Esmée included.

She arrived at the very museum she'd always wanted to visit, expecting to find a line of tourists shuffling through the entrance to the inner courtyard off the *Rue du Louvre*. What she found, after her hopeful flight from the Pont Neuf, was a sign by the entrance with the museum's hours of operation. *Mardi: Fermé*, it read. *Tuesday: Closed.* Her one hope of seeing her sculpture had been dashed.

Esmée flew a short distance and landed on a gaslight just inside the inner courtyard, crestfallen. All her life she dreamed of her chance to flit down the endless hallways and over the wide expanse of the world's largest museum. She always dreamed of admiring the thoughtful Cupid and his gift to the little butterfly. She always dreamed it all took place on a *weekend*, though; never on a Tuesday.

She'd come too far to be turned away by a Tuesday, of all things! She'd flown too hard with too much hope to be disappointed in such a way. But disappointment didn't begin to describe her heartbreak. She would never get this chance again. Her one consolation was that the vast inner courtyard of the museum, and the great outer courtyard beyond, were open *every* day. That was small consolation; but then she was a very small butterfly in need of consolation. It would have to do.

Beyond the inner courtyard, through the gate in

the opposite wall, the famous glass pyramid crowned the outer plaza in controversial grandeur. You see, the Parisians are very picky about their pyramids. Most of them believe pyramids belong either in Egypt or Las Vegas, depending on their level of culture.

Many Parisians believe that the great glass pyramid of the Louvre is an eyesore, and stands in the way of an unbroken line of sight from the gates of the Louvre; through the Arc de Triomphe du Carrousel; down the Tuileries Garden; past the Place de la Concorde with its ancient obelisk; and all the way to the centerpiece of the city: the famous Arc de Triomphe.

As I'm sure you've experienced when trying to enjoy a pleasant view or watch a good movie, there's nothing more irritating than having someone's big pointy head in your way. Well, that's how many Parisians feel about the Louvre Pyramid.

Not Esmée, though. She was drawn to it. Flitting and flying past statue after sculpture, Esmée finally crossed the inner courtyard - bigger than a city block – and ducked beneath the stone ceiling of the gateway adjoining the inner and outer courtyards. There below her, taking advantage of the wonderful acoustical properties of the arched and echoing entryway, a string quartet played Bach in the summer breeze.

The fugue was brooding and as intricate as a timepiece. The instruments seemed to speak with one another, carrying on a serious conversation about a topic known only to them. As the piece continued, it took on shades and textures of worlds long past.

Esmée never experienced such sounds of celestial enchantment. Every note rose from bowed strings to tickle the feet of the tiny butterfly. She felt that she might find her footing on a B flat or ride the ascent of C major all the way to the heavens, before lilting back to earth in the moody arms of G minor.

The vibrations of the strings resonated in her outstretched wings (because butterflies hold their wings *apart* when at rest, unlike the chewing moths). Along the length of her antennae, music pulsed like radio waves through a wire. She'd heard the skylarks singing in the meadows back home; but this was unlike any music she could have imagined.

She wondered if such things were ever performed in places like Notre-Dame Cathedral, where one might bathe a while in the light-drenched music. What heights she might explore beneath the echoing ceiling of the cathedral. Her heart strayed out of all time in that arched entryway.

The musicians drew their performance to a close to the sound of applause and clinking coins tossed in an open cello case. Esmée jumped to her feet and clapped her four front legs in the quietest and most enthusiastic ovation the performers ever received.

Though disappointed to have had the misfortune of getting lost in Paris on a Tuesday, the unexpected concert went a long way toward making up for it. Esmée once again felt ready to continue her journey of discovery.

As soon as she stooped beneath the lintel of the gateway and flew out into the courtyard beyond, her eyes were greeted by the great glass pyramid which forms the central feature. Standing on marble stools positioned in perfect photo-op alignment, tourists posed with one hand outstretched and fingers pointed down. By a trick of perspective, they appeared to be holding the tip of the pyramid in their pinched fingers.

As she neared the enormous geometric structure, Esmée saw young women posing in front of the pyramid like models on the cover of Vogue magazine. She flew to the tip-top and landed on the transparent intersection of the three sides. Looking down through the glass and into the mirror-image of an inverted triangle below the pavement, she marveled at its magnificence.

She spread her wings wide in the afternoon sun, closed her eyes and turned her face toward the sky. Basking in the breeze, she let the wind fill her wings. The iridescent brilliance of her colors cast flecks of golden light down on the shiny surface beneath her feet. Magnified by the glass of the pyramid, her colors danced in the ancient courtyard. Esmée felt the immensity and history of her surroundings overflow in her mind. Set at the center of a blizzard of light, the colors of her wings burned like fire among jewels.

Opening her eyes again, she looked out at the dozens of photogenic tourists with arms outstretched. Rather than holding their fingers down in a pinching pose, they were all holding their index finger out as if waiting for a bird to land.

All around her, Esmée heard people saying, *"Regarde le papillon,"* or, *"Le papillon reine du Louvre!"* It appeared that the light show reflected by the glimmering pyramid's glass had drawn the attention of everyone in the courtyard to Esmée.

Instead of grasping the top of the pyramid in their pinched fingers, people were being photographed in perspective with Esmée on their index finger! Even the Vogue models asked their friends to snap pictures of them with *le papillon reine du Louvre*. Esmée felt like a supermodel.

Batting her eyelashes and tossing her head over one shoulder, Esmée made the most of her ten minutes of fame. With one wing drawn up like a fan in front of her face, she flirted with the camera. She fluttered her wings, kicked one foot out from beneath their golden orange radiance, and smiled coyly for her admirers. She ate up the attention, much to her own surprise, and basked in the white-hot spotlight for very nearly a quarter of an hour.

After everyone had taken their share of selfies and forced-perspective photos with *the Butterfly Queen of the Louvre*, the whole crowd of tourists broke out in spontaneous applause. Lifting off and catching the wind as it rushed up one side of the pyramid, Esmée twirled around in midair and took a bow. The crowd went wild with excitement, applauding all the more loudly and crying, *"Hourra!"* and *"C'est magnifique!"*

The little butterfly from Saint-Denis had won the hearts of tourists and conquered the City of Lights. It's true that Paris is famous the world over for its beauty, and Parisians are known for their style. But this day, Parisians and tourists from all over the world recognized and applauded the beauty and style of one little butterfly from the country town of Saint-Denis-lès-Chevreuse.

Among the many people in the crowded courtyard that afternoon, a photographer from the newspaper, *Le Journal*, caught the scene on camera. He was amazed by the spontaneous reaction of the people to the glamorous butterfly atop the *Pyramide du Louvre*. He thought this would make a great feature story for tomorrow's early edition.

Walking home that evening, he composed his tagline:

La nouvelle exposition du Louvre capture le cœur des touristes!

The new exhibition at the Louvre captures the hearts of tourists!

As the sun sank behind the walls of the *Palais du Louvre*, Esmée crossed the street from the outer courtyard and landed in a tree -- not far from the Arc de Triomphe du Carrousel in the Tuileries Garden. Nightfall was approaching and with it the reminder that Esmée was still far from home. The sights and sounds and short-lived fame of the day had distracted her from her dire situation, but now it all returned with the lengthening of the shadows.

She was alone and the emptiness of nighttime has a way of magnifying your loneliness. Taking a sip of nectar from a nearby cherry blossom, Esmée pulled her wings around her body as protection against the damp chill of the settling dew.

All around her, down below, people walked home for the evening. Warmth, familiarity, family or friends, food and rest awaited them in their homes. For Esmée, only fear awaited her in the dark of night. This would be the longest nighttime she ever passed, and who could say what the morning would bring?

CHAPTER SEVEN

A Night in the Tuileries

Fog from the river crept up the pathways of the Tuileries Garden and hung heavy in the night air. Beneath the small tree in which Esmée huddled against the invading cold, a sea of mist now spread out in every direction. Where once there were flowerbeds and sidewalks, a featureless moonscape was all Esmée could see. She felt isolated, like a single vibrant color against a canvas of drab grey.

Back home, Esmée had her favorite trees in which to pass the night; trees in which she felt safe, high above the ground. There was the sycamore tree in Monsieur Caron's backyard. This was popular with many butterflies, and so she often had company through the long night.

The black walnut in Madame Morel's sheep pasture was located conveniently close to Esmée's favorite wildflowers. Then, of course, the Beauplan Forest offered varieties of trees and flowers beyond count. Tonight, in this strange place far from all familiarity, Esmée was forced to find shelter in a scrawny cherry tree -- without ample cover, and without the safety of height.

The open spaces of the Tuileries echoed with an unnerving mix of forest and city noises. Esmée felt uneasy with the animal sounds around her. City animals were unlike those she knew from the Chevreuse Valley.

They were wilder, in unwholesome ways -- she could sense it. She was certain that they were dangerous and untrustworthy. Fear exaggerated every misgiving and made her forget those she had met earlier in the day. Perhaps remembering the *Ignifuge* bees of Notre-Dame would have given her more faith in city animals, but it would have been short-lived.

For in the cold darkness, Esmée now felt the weight of two eyes come to rest on the back of her neck. A chill ran up her long back to the tips of her antennae, leaving a shudder in its wake. Something was watching her closely.

In that moment, the black night pushed in upon her with the weight of terror. Her mind was surrounded by what felt like a million needles; each one pricking her heightened awareness. She held her breath; only her eyes moved, scanning the black curtain which hung all around her.

Maybe this was an animal that could see her only if she moved. Maybe it was an animal that could sense her location only by sound. If it was one of those animals that could see in the dark -- well, those were the deadliest kind. She would remain still and as silent as a stare.

"Who… who… who do we have here?"

The words echoed, round and resonant, in the emptiness of the night. From the branch just above her own -- alarmingly close and well within grabbing-distance -- two luminous eyes looked down at Esmée. They neither blinked nor shifted; instead, their sickly-yellow glow held the frightened Esmée as tight as if they'd been talons. Still hoping this was an animal that could only sense movement, she remained perfectly motionless.

"Come now, we mustn't be rude. Do tell me your name."

Esmée mustered every ounce of willpower she

could find to turn her face in the direction of the taunting voice. When she saw the big, circular eyes shining back at her, she let out a tiny gasp. She could feel the heat from its foul breath on her face. She sensed the great size of the creature and trembled in its shadow. How had it gotten so close to her without Esmée noticing?

At last, the two eyes blinked, but not in unison like yours or mine do. A fraction of a second elapsed between the left and the right eye's heavy blink. In the brief moment when both eyes were closed, it was as if the light of the moon had gone out.

"Yes, I can see you quite well," the voice assured her without sympathy. "Now, what is your name?"

"Esmée," came the softest and most reluctant, fearful reply.

"Pleased to meet you, Esmée."

She shuddered to hear her name spoken by such a sinister voice. There was no kindness in it, only cold lifelessness.

"Now tell me, what are you doing in my tree?"

There was a noticeable change in its tone. It was now clearly threatening, menacing. What had merely been a warning in Esmée's heart now became alarm. She knew she was in grave danger.

"I am sorry, *Monsieur*. I did not mean… I did not… *Je ne savais pas…* I did not know that this was your… *votre arbre*."

Esmée was trembling and stuttering with dread. Terror stole the words from her mouth, and the breath from her chest.

A shaft of moonlight fell upon the branch between Esmée and the threatening creature, at last revealing the identity of her unwelcome companion. Only inches away, the round, white, expressionless mask of an English barn owl scowled in the dreary light. Its beak formed the sharp point of a prominent V-shaped nose. Its eyes betrayed no hint of compassion.

"What you *meant* to do, matters not at all. The fact is, you are in my tree, uninvited. I have no tolerance for bad manners and even less for tourists and country-folk. I can tell that *you* are both."

The owl took one step closer to Esmée, putting it within striking distance. Leaning in toward her, its ghostly face was now fully illuminated by the moonlight. Esmée took one step backward; but an owl's step and a butterfly's step are quite different in size and length. She was still far too close.

The barn owl shot out its neck, catching Esmée in its mouth. Fluttering wildly to break free, Esmée felt the bonelike beak tighten around her fragile body. The owl let a hideous chuckle roil up from deep within its chest. There was no question what it intended to do with Esmée. She'd made the mistake of choosing the wrong tree and the owl would see to it that she never made that mistake again. Dropping her onto the branch upon which he stood, the villainous owl clamped his sharp talons around Esmée's body and held her tightly against the wood of the tree.

"Please, please *monsieur* owl," Esmée pleaded for her life. "I am sorry. I did not know. Please…"

Her heart pounded against her chest; her wings lay flat on the tree branch. She knew she had no hope of flying to freedom; pleading was her only option. But how could she appeal to the heart of a heartless creature? Her pleas served only to amuse the cruel predator. Esmée was tired and worn thin with fear. Lacking the strength to fight, and feeling as if she might faint, she began to resign herself to her fate.

"I am sorry, *monsieur*. I am *so* sorry…" Esmée began to cry.

The owl dropped his head and opened his ravenous beak -- ready to parse out the weeping butterfly into courses for his evening meal -- when another voice called out in the darkness from a few branches away.

"In fact, this is *my* tree."

"Whoo said that?" the old bully demanded, with a ferocity meant to terrify.

"I'm afraid, you've got your trees mistaken. This is Cherry Tree #3, Tuileries Lane, Paris, France."

The new voice was engaging in a dangerous game by mocking the deadly owl. There was a playful confidence in the way it challenged the owl's authority. Of course, confidence can also be foolhardiness, when taken too far.

"Show yourself!"

The barn owl was in no mood for such foolishness. He knew very well that this *was* his tree. There was no Cherry Tree #3. There was no Tuileries Lane. This was nonsense, and he had no patience for such things. He was hungry and dinner lay squirming between his toes. He would get rid of the stranger and then dispatch Esmée.

"You are wasting my time, sir. Depart now or I will deal with you accordingly."

Out of the shadows, two more yellow eyes now appeared. Their shape and size were familiar to Esmée and brought her no comfort. Just like the barn owl, these eyes neither blinked nor shifted; instead, they stared with unflinching attention at the wretched predator and his unfortunate prey.

Yet there was something different and altogether eerier about *these* eyes. There was no life in them, no feeling. They were similar to those of the barn owl, but more unnerving. There was no question about it; the second voice must be that of another owl who had come to fight over the privilege of eating poor Esmée.

"I will not leave *my* tree," the second owl said, this time without the playful confidence. "You are trespassing, and I will have justice before the sun is up.”

Esmée sensed a change come over the old barn owl, as the newcomer was speaking. He began to loosen his grip and nervously shift his stance. There was something less resolute and more hesitant in his demeanor. As with all bullies, once confronted, he began to buckle-under and back down. All bullies are cowards beneath their big talk and bravado; the wretched barn owl was no exception.

The unseen stranger pressed his luck a bit further, “As payment for your crime, you will leave the butterfly for me. Now, go before my patience runs out.”

The barn owl felt fierce and powerful when up against a tiny butterfly, but his ferocity was little more than a show. His cruelty was real, but his cowardice always got the better of him. No butterfly was worth risking injury in a fight with another owl. Besides, there were plenty of mice and rats in Paris to go around; and a rodent felt better in the stomach than a butterfly, any day.

“Fine,” the barn owl growled, through a clenched beak. “Have your tree, *and* your worthless butterfly.”

He flung Esmée at the newcomer, like an old dish rag. She landed on a branch in front of the mysterious creature and rolled into a tumbled heap. Peering at the shadow looming over her, she could only see its two lifeless eyes. She began to fear this new threat just as much as she had feared the barn owl.

“Pfft. Neither of you are worth the trouble.”

With that, the wicked old owl spread its enormous wings and flapped a fuss of feathers and fury. Rising into the air, it flew off into the darkness with a sound like a hurricane -- leaving Esmée alone with the unknown.

As soon as the barn owl was out of sight, Esmée heard the stranger breathe a long sigh of relief. A moment of tense silence then passed, during which Esmée weighed her chances of escaping the situation. She was cold and tired, and the barn owl's grip had been cruel. She wasn't sure she'd be able to fly at all, let alone with enough speed to flee the unseen stranger. Morning was approaching, she could feel it drawing near. How she longed for sleep in the safety of her own home.

"Are you alright?" the voice asked her.

Esmée hardly knew what to say. Was this question just the taunt of her new captor? Was he making fun of her or sizing her up? She decided to proceed cautiously and avoid aggravating him.

"Yes, I am well," she said, thinking it best not to reveal any weakness or injury that the stranger might take advantage of.

"Good. For a while there, I wasn't sure how things were going to turn out. But the miserable old bully bought it."

"Bought it?" Esmée didn't understand the phrase.

"Fell for it, I mean. If he hadn't, I have no idea what I would have done next. Fly straight for his eyeballs and poke him with *all six* of my legs, I guess!" He laughed.

Now Esmée was really confused. Six legs? What kind of owl has six legs?

"*Monsieur*, may I ask, what *are* you?"

Stepping out of the shadows and into the cold light of the moon, Esmée now saw her rescuer clearly. She could not believe her eyes.

"I'm an owl moth," he said. "My name's Baxter, but my friends call me Norman. Don't ask me why; I'm sure I couldn't tell you. What's your name?"

Esmée was stunned. There before her stood a large moth, twice her size. Its brown, black, rust and yellow markings were exactly the same as those of a woodland owl. What was most striking were its eyes – or rather the large spots on its wings designed to look like the eyes of an owl. Lifeless, but for the "blinking" caused by the slow hinge-like movement of its wings, the eye spots were eerily haunting in the dark of night. Indeed, the barn owl *had* fallen for it and he'd been completely unnerved by the clever camouflage of a moth.

"*Monsieur, vous êtes merveilleux!* You saved my life. I thank you so very much, *oui, merci beaucoup!*"

"Don't mention it, miss. I never liked owls much anyway. No sense of humor."

Norman winked an eye (his real eye) at Esmée, then wiped one wing across his forehead. He was relieved things had turned out so well for them both.

"Whew! If he'd gotten wise to me, we would've been in trouble. I guess it just debunks the old myth about 'wise old owls.' Not so wise, after all, was he?"

"Happily, *non,*" Esmée agreed, with a sudden burst of nervous laughter.

Grabbing a leaf, Norman began munching on it, as he started to take an interest in the butterfly.

"Where are you headed, miss; if I might ask?"

"I must stay with *le fleuve,*" Esmée said with assurance. "She will lead me home again."

"Where's home?" the moth asked.

"Saint-Denis-lès-Chevreuse," Esmée replied with wistful sadness in her voice.

"Oh, I see. Hm, well, I hate to tell you this, but the Seine won't take you to Saint-Denis. It just doesn't flow anywhere near there. You're a long way off. But, why not stay here in the City of Lights for a while? Enjoy the sights! You could do worse, you know."

The kindly owl moth smiled in an attempt to reassure the crestfallen Esmée, but it was no use. Esmée sat there in disbelief. She just felt like rolling up into a little ball. Why had the honeybee told her that the river would always lead her home again if it wasn't true? Was it just another act of cruelty at the hands of a city animal? She couldn't believe it. She wouldn't believe it. The promise of following the Seine back to Saint-Denis was all the hope she had left. Without it – well, she didn't even want to think about it.

"You should fly down to the Place de la Concorde or even over to the Arc de Triomphe. Have an adventure. It would be a shame not to."

"*Non merci, monsieur.* I want to go home now. I have had enough adventure. Adventure is not for me."

"I understand." The moth was helpless to bring Esmée any encouragement. "Well, the morning is here and it's time for this moth to get some rest."

Norman finished munching on leaf and stem, then wiped the crumbs from his mouth, before saying, "Best of luck to you, miss. Just remember, there are more friends in this world than there are strangers. *Au revoir, gentille mademoiselle.*"

"*Merci monsieur.* Thank you so very much. *Au revoir.*"

Norman tipped his head to Esmée, bowing with kind courtesy, then flew off toward the river. Esmée was alone again, but she wasn't entirely sad to see her new friend go. She couldn't look at the eye spots on his wings without being reminded of her ordeal with the barn owl. These were strange creatures, and Esmée wasn't sure she could ever feel at home in such a place.

The long and frightful night had hardened her resolve. She was focused on one goal and one goal alone: finding her way back home. The ancient city which had, just the day before, held such wondrous enchantments, no longer interested her at all. She'd set her sights too high; she had allowed herself to forget that she was just a very small country butterfly in a big world filled with rumors and tales of darkness. She would never let herself forget again.

CHAPTER EIGHT

Lisette

Lisette Cueilleur had been Esmée's best friend since the day she emerged from her chrysalis. The two butterflies had much in common. They shared a deep appreciation of rosewater nectar. They shared an interest in sculpture, thanks to the stories Esmée's mother told of the treasures of the Louvre. They even had the same smiley-face-shaped birthmark on the underside of their right wing, which was truly remarkable! Most significant of all, having broken free from their cocoons within minutes of each other, they shared the same BB-Day.

In a way, butterflies are born twice: once when they hatch as caterpillars; then again when they leave their chrysalis as butterflies. The first, they call their birthday, or just B-Day. The second, they refer to as their Becoming Butterflies Day or BB-Day. The best thing about being a butterfly is that you get to observe both days as gift-giving occasions! Twice the birthdays, means twice the gifts. Esmée and Lisette were very proud of the fact that they shared a BB-Day, and they would often sit and sip from the red roses in the churchyard, reminiscing about that momentous day.

It was summertime then, and the green hills of the Chevreuse Valley rolled with lazy daydreams down to the banks of *l'Yvette*. Carefully threading its toes between the smooth stones in its path, the river cast cool breezes up through the trees and tall grass of the nearby pastures.

On that particular day, the farmland-fields surrounding Saint-Denis stood poised between the early and late summer harvests. It was amid this idyllic setting that a solitary milkweed could be found, carefully hidden among the yellow flowers of Farmer Jacques Ghislaine's canola crop.

Up until about a week before, two chubby caterpillars had been busily cutting and consuming endless snacks of juicy, green leaves. Chance had led the two of them to the same milkweed plant, but they were far too busy spinning chrysalises to notice one another. A week later, Esmée and Lisette emerged from their transformations from caterpillar to *belle dame* butterflies and stretched out their golden wings in the summer sun for the very first time.

How beautiful the two young butterflies were, fanning their wings in the fresh breezes running up from the valley below. Their colors were bright and new; their broad, delicate wings were dusted in powder and shone with sparkling brilliance. They were stunning to behold, against the green of the milkweed; so very much like the monarch butterfly of North America.

It's true that people in France, and indeed the world over, often mistake *la belle dame* (or the *painted lady*) for the monarch butterfly. Who can blame them? The two are very similar in appearance. However, it's common knowledge that there are no monarch butterflies in France. Careful consideration reveals that a monarch is an historical impossibility in France. The reason for this is somewhat complicated, but I'll do my best to unravel the yarn for you.

Before the Revolution of 1789, there was a lesser-known event which often goes unnoticed in the history books. This somewhat obscure (and even mythical) occurrence is known as The Slip of '77. This event is often entirely forgotten, for it was soon completely overshadowed by the French Revolution.

Nonetheless, the tale of The Slip of '77 deserves to be told; for two animals received particularly uncomfortable attention -- although in very different ways. Allow me to explain.

The first was the housecat. Prior to the late seventeen-hundreds, the housecat occupied a highly respected position in French society. From prince to pauper, everyone owned a housecat.

Those of high social standing spoiled and pampered their preening felines. It was not uncommon to find, among the upper crust of society, fluffy cat pillows strewn throughout the marble-columned halls of wealthy homes. Sitting on silken cushions, these privileged kitties knew nothing of the lives of less fortunate cats.

The cats belonging to the peasants were strangers to kitty cushions and marble columns. These poor souls, forced to live a bit closer to the earth, were employed to keep the rat population in check. Since there were, in those days, plenty of rats, the country cats usually didn't go hungry; but their lives were poor and paltry, nonetheless. With no cushions to cuddle, the country cats were forced to sleep on the hard floor. Without proper shelter, they knew many a cold night and damp, rainy day. They could not imagine the idea of a free meal; they knew only skimpy snacks caught by their own cunning.

Still, whatever their station in life - whether royal courtier or rat controller - the housecat was found everywhere and was reasonably happy wherever they were found... except in the district of *Nullepart*.

Nullepart was remote and backward, cut off from all that made the rest of France civilized and cultured. Famous for their simple ways, age-old farming lifestyle, and exceptional talent for baking, *Nullepart* had few resources, apart from their timeless skills.

So, when the winds turned southerly and the clouds withered, the resulting drought and famine was felt most dreadfully by the impoverished and ill-prepared people of *Nullepart*. Hunger spread like a blaze of despair across the fields and forests of this lonesome backwater.

Drought brought ruin to crops, and without hay or barley the livestock suffered brutally. Farmers were utterly unable to coax milk from their cows. Goats and ducks, pigs and poultry stopped producing and simply faded away.

With no wheat in the fields, *boulangeries* ran low on flour. People began to starve; and a scrawny rat population brought acute suffering to droves of hungry housecats. There was precious little food and even less hope in the hearts and homes of the good people of *Nullepart*.

The dire situation was soon brought to the attention of *le duc de Nullepart*. He was alarmed to learn of the great suffering of his people. Eager to offer an alternative source of sustenance to the starving population of his district, the duke put quill to parchment and issued a hasty decree.

A man of high education and refinement, the duke spoke several languages, including French, German and Spanish. As any polyglot will tell you…

Wait, what was that?

Oh, polyglot.

Well, polyglot (pronounced: *polly-glot*) is not only a very useful word meaning "someone who speaks many languages," but it's also a word that will impress others if you can work it into conversation.

Now, as I was saying…

As any polyglot will tell you, in the heat of excited decree-writing, mistakes and substitutions are bound to occur. In a truly epic case of linguistic substitution (which means using entirely the wrong word in entirely the wrong way), *le duc de Nullepart* included a fateful typo in his decree -- a typo that changed the course of history: *Nullepart*'s history; the duke's history; and very nearly the history of housecats in this little corner of France.

Without thought for the nutritional needs or waistlines of his subjects, the duke meant to suggest a diet of junk food as an alternative to starvation, but mistakenly recommended something far worse.

Hurriedly jotting down the words, *"Qu'ils mangent du gato!"* the duke accidentally wrote the Spanish word for *cat (gato)*, rather than *gâteau* – which is the French word for *cake* -- of which *Nullepart* still had ample, though dwindling, supplies.

The hasty decree read, "Let them eat cats," rather than the intended "Let them eat cake," which is far more humane, though arguably less nutritious. This was a slip-up of mythical proportions!

Before the error was pointed out to the duke, many cats came dangerously close to becoming the main course. Correcting his slip, the duke reissued his decree; but by then famine had turned to rioting and panicked meowing in the streets.

Not only did the people believe that their duke was out of touch with reality (thanks to his innocent slip-up), but after the Let Them Eat Cats Incident (which came to be called The Slip of '77), they were quite certain that *le duc de Nullepart* was mad. A change of leadership was given wide and passionate support by people and cats alike.

I know what you're thinking. You were taught that it was Marie-Antoinette who said, "Let them eat cake," but this is a widespread error. In reality, Marie-Antoinette said, "Let them eat brioche," which is a sweet bread and not cake at all. Similar to the duke, her suggestion cost her the crown, but that was well over a decade later. Unlike the infamous duke and his epic slip,

Marie-Antoinette was also famous for actually having existed.

But, back to our story…

The fact that this one innocent typo cost the duke his crown (precisely because it was sitting on top of his head when he was led to the guillotine), is enough to emphasize the importance of proofreading. So, please, by all means, proofread your text messages, emails, letters, and important decrees before clicking "Send." So much is riding on your accuracy.

Fortunately, the housecat fared far better than the duke; but the second species impacted by The Slip of '77 wasn't so lucky.

In the wake of *le duc de Nullepart's* outrageous suggestion, the people grew increasingly wary of anything that reminded them of royalty. Anything which even hinted at the monarchy was rounded up, removed, repurposed or renamed.

The duke was arrested, and his palace was turned into yet another museum closed for cleaning every Tuesday. The fires of revolution had been stoked by one haphazard slip, and the monarchy was in trouble. Unfortunately, this included the monarch butterfly, as well.

In the second recorded case of a decree gone wrong, the revolutionaries voted unanimously to outlaw all monarchs. Surely, the intention was the outlawing of kings, queens, dukes and the like; but as with most *brand-new things*, the people hadn't had time to learn how to "do democracy" very well, yet. So, their first democratic action, though unanimous, was not as well-worded as perhaps it should have been. But the law is the law and enforcing the law is a serious business.

Up and down the country, the *gendarmerie* arrested and detained monarch butterflies, careful to gather the caterpillars as well. Distrustful of these *agents of the old order*, the authorities put the hapless butterflies on a ship bound for the New World. This was a great injustice, and a terrible pity, too, for the monarch butterfly is *trop beau*. Now, they would never again be seen in France.

Weeks later, The *SS Papillon* arrived in New York Harbor, its stores of nectar nearly exhausted. When the cargo hold was opened, a storm-cloud of butterflies darkened the sky for the better part of the afternoon. Hundreds of thousands of monarchs descended upon the fields and flowers, meadows and milkweed of America. The people of the New World were very happy to welcome them. It is said that the monarch butterfly is the *only* monarch ever to be invited to make its home in *the land of the free*. It's likely this will never change.

There is a saying: *imitation is the highest form of flattery.* If so, then *la belle dame* butterfly flatters the monarch like no other. The same was certainly true of our two *belles dames* in particular. They weren't monarchs, but they certainly looked like princesses.

On that breezy summer day in Jacques Ghislaine's canola field, dangling like emerald earrings from the same milkweed branch, Esmée and Lisette began their lives as *belles dames*, together. They have seldom been seen apart, ever since.

This is why, when Esmée failed to show up at Madame Legrand's butterfly bush that Tuesday morning, Lisette immediately became concerned. They had been sharing breakfast together since their old milkweed days. Every morning, without fail, they met and sipped and shared the news of the day.

Esmée's absence that morning kindled concern in Lisette's heart. Her best friend was in trouble; she could sense it. Lisette was about to discover just how far Esmée had wandered away from home; and her discovery would forever change the way she saw her best friend.

CHAPTER NINE

Audrey Loriot

Every morning, the butterflies of Saint-Denis gather in the garden of Madame Legrand's *grande maison.* Her large, yellow stone house is framed with shrubberies and hedges which form a maze of garden paths. Grapevines and fig trees, apple trees and berry brambles all provide an ample selection of blossoms from which to drink. At the center of the big backyard, near a collection of wooden birdfeeders, stands the famed Butterfly Bush of Madame Legrand.

It is here among the tiny, purple teacup flowers that a thousand colorful butterflies congregate for their daily breakfast -- much to the delight of Madame Legrand. Esmée and Lisette were always among these regular visitors. On this particular Tuesday, Lisette was more eager to see her best friend than usual. She had news that simply would not keep.

She'd learned that Sylvie de Clément, while attempting to reach the orchids in Madame Lafleur's greenhouse, had discovered the secret of *the unseen barrier.* Sylvie had been flinging herself, over and over again, against the greenhouse glass, when out of nowhere a goldfinch descended at full speed from the sky and hit the window with great force.

Lying spread-eagle on the ground and shaking his head in dazed amazement (more economically described as "damazement"), the goldfinch and Sylvie both looked up in time to see a crack form in the glass -- in the very place where the finch's beak had struck. The crack began as a divot in the face of the windowpane. Then, a single hairline ventured slowly outward, dividing and branching into veins in the pane.

Startling butterfly and bird alike, the window at last shattered into a shower of tinkling shards, which fell to the ground all around them. The unseen barrier had fallen. The greenhouse defenses were down. Jumping to their feet, Sylvie and the clever goldfinch rushed through the breach and began feasting on nectar and greenhouse strawberries to their hearts' content.

You must understand. This was monumental news! The discovery of the weakness of the unseen barrier would have serious implications for both finches and butterflies for years to come. A mutually beneficial partnership was in the making. Lisette couldn't wait to tell Esmée all the details.

Resting on their favorite butterfly bush branch, Lisette impatiently awaited Esmée's arrival. Where was she? Did she sleep in? Of all the days to be late to breakfast! What was the hold-up? Lisette's impatience boiled into irritation. She flapped her wings indignantly, rising a few inches off the branch then settling back down in a flurry of frustration.

"Hmph! There'd better be a good explanation," she said with a sassy stomp of her forefoot. Lisette paced the branch, awaiting her friend's arrival, and growing more impatient by the minute.

Minutes mounted to hours, and still there was no sign of Esmée. No one would have guessed she was aboard the RER B bound for Paris at that very moment. Lisette knew her friend well; she knew Esmée was no adventurer. Wherever she was, it couldn't be far.

So, after waiting; and pacing; and fuming; Lisette

at last took to the wing, determined to cover every inch of ground between there and each one of their favorite places. She was quite sure Esmée would turn up; she'd better, anyhow, or Esmée would be in big trouble! Lisette was almost the polar opposite of her calm, sweet-natured and shy best friend. The two of them balanced each other well.

Lisette's search began right there in the backyard of Madame Legrand's *grande maison* on the banks of *l'Yvette*. Flitting from branch to branch, Lisette inquired of every butterfly she met whether they had seen Esmée since the day before. Amid gulps and gossip, sips and swallows, she determined that no one knew of Esmée's whereabouts. She took stock once more of all the branches on the bush. She had visited each one of them, she was quite certain.

Satisfied that she had exhausted the news at the butterfly bush, Lisette fluttered off to visit every other bush, tree, and shrub in Madame Legrand's backyard; but it was the same result at every stop: no one had heard news of Esmée. Lisette would have to broaden her search.

She now made her way to the center of town. It was now 8:42 am and the morning Mass attendees at *l'église Saint-Denis* were just leaving the church, when Lisette arrived. Landing with exhaustion on the rim of the holy water font, Lisette helped herself to a long drink. Her eyes scanned the churchyard, as her antennae twitched and trembled in the morning air. There was neither sight nor scent of Esmée anywhere nearby. She needed a better vantagepoint if she was to survey the entire churchyard to her satisfaction.

Lisette leapt from her perch and rode the rising breeze to the top of the church steeple. From there, she looked out over the rose garden. The rosewater nectar of the churchyard was the only thing Lisette could think of that would be more tempting than Madame Legrand's butterfly bush. Her eyes scoured the surrounding area. Surely Esmée would be *here*.

Spotting a flicker of orange among the green leaves of a fig tree below, Lisette dropped from the steeple and headed in that direction. When she was only a few feet away, she called out, hopeful she'd found her friend.

"Esmée? *C'est toi?*"

As she approached, the flicker of orange raised her head and immediately recognized Lisette.

"*Bonjour*, Lisette! *Comment ça va?*"

"*Oh non, c'est toi, Audrey. Je pensais que tu étais Esmée.* I have been looking for her all morning."

The flicker of orange in the fig tree was a butterfly by the name of Audrey Loriot. A bookworm among butterflies, Audrey spent much of her day – everyday – just reading in the churchyard.

Of course, butterflies do not have books; so, you can put that image right out of your mind. Even if they did have books, they wouldn't be able to carry them, since they don't have thumbs. If you've ever tried to carry something without using your thumb, you understand my point.

But Audrey loved to read absolutely anything she could find -- or rather, anything that found her. Scraps of paper, flyers, brochures, and people's discarded mail comprised her regular reading material. If she was lucky, an edition of the daily newspaper would blow into the churchyard. There she would learn about everything happening in the world beyond Saint-Denis. She was especially interested in the news from Paris and, of course, international politics.

Mostly, however, she read Père Lamoine's daily sermon which the exiting churchgoers would discreetly discard in the recycle bin outside. Invariably, the wind would carry one of the under-appreciated and crumpled sermons out of the bin and deposit it in the shade of a fig tree. Audrey would then be able to spend hours learning the ins and outs of ancient church doctrine. She was undeniably the leading expert on religion in all the Chevreuse Valley.

"Je suis désolée, Lisette. I am not, in fact, Esmée. So sorry."

Audrey wasn't at all hurt by Lisette's obvious disappointment in finding her. She was too engrossed in this morning's sermon. Not that it would bother her much. She was used to Lisette being disinterested in her. Audrey always seemed to understand reading-material much better than she understood people, anyway. People weren't nearly as interesting, and they required far more work than reading did.

"Sorry, Audrey. I'm completely beside myself. I can't find Esmée anywhere and she wasn't at breakfast this morning. Have you seen her today?"

"Non, I have not. Have you tried *l'arbuste*? That's where I would begin. In fact, statistically speaking, that would be the most likely place to find Esmée. Of course, we must also factor in an appropriate margin of error, to account for any eventualities…"

Lisette's face began to turn more and more red with every word Audrey worked into her reply. Patience was wearing disastrously thin and Lisette had a reputation for blowing her fiery stack; more like a dragon than a butterfly.

"I haven't got time, Audrey. I'm in a hurry. If you haven't seen Esmée, then tell me and I'll be on my way."

Lisette was eager to be going, not only because she was anxious to locate her best friend, but also because she knew that Audrey had a way of slowing all progress to a dead stop.

Like many intellectuals, Audrey lacked some basic people-skills. She was sure that everyone she met was just as interested in international politics and ancient church doctrine as she was. She was also sure that everyone she spoke with understood big, long words filled with -isms and -ologies, theories and -osophies.

She never seemed to want to arrive at her point, rather she enjoyed wandering around it for hours. Her motto was, *"Why use 10 little words when 1,000 big ones will do?"* Audrey's heart was in the right place, but her mind was always bogged down in books, big words and complicated things; and those she cornered always got tangled up in it all, too.

Audrey also had a way of simply picking up where she had left off in conversation, even if she hadn't seen you in days. This was very confusing for those she met, since most butterflies simply want to exchange pleasantries and be on their way. Audrey ignored the pleasantries and dove right into deep discussion.

Lisette was afraid to get tangled up in a slow, tedious conversation. In fact, every conversation with Audrey Loriot was a chore, in Lisette's opinion. Poor Audrey was blessed with a marvelous mind in a world of busy, distracted, and less-intellectual butterflies.

"I could certainly be of great help to you in your search, since I've read extensively on the subject of *search and rescue.* Your timing is optimal, too. I just started reading today's sermon, which is coincidentally on a subject that would be of interest to you. In fact, it might very well form a sort of rallying cry for you and your efforts…"

Audrey offered her assistance then leapt the tracks and lost the topic altogether -- slowly, wordily, but with sincerity. Lisette had no interest in learning today's topic or in finding her "rallying cry." She had more pressing business.

"I wouldn't dream of interrupting your reading," Lisette said; which was absolutely true since it would mean having to speak with Audrey for hours. "Besides, I'm sure Esmée's just fine;" which was *not* strictly true, since Lisette had begun to worry. "Thanks for offering, though. I'm off to Monsieur Deschamps' farm!"

Lisette was already fluttering away as fast as her weary wings would carry her, as she thanked Audrey. She knew that if Audrey joined her, the search would come to a crawl. She'd cover more ground more quickly if she were on her own.

"Remember, *those who seek shall fi...*"

Audrey's voice trailed off behind Lisette who was already halfway to the steeple in a quarter of the time it had taken her to descend in the first place. She saw her chance to escape, and she took it. Without a doubt, that was a close call; but Lisette had successfully avoided taking on a partner and was now free to turn her attention elsewhere.

This time, she headed straight for Monsieur Deschamps' farm and the wildflower pastures so popular with the butterflies of the valley. *La Ferme Deschamps* held a commanding view of the Chevreuse Valley and the Yvette River, below. Situated atop the rich, tumbling hills which cradle the town of Saint-Denis, the farm had been in the Deschamps family since long before the Revolution. Seven generations of Deschamps had tilled, tended and tamed the wild pasturelands of the Chevreuse Valley.

It's true that the best farmer knows how to balance the needs of his family with the needs of the earth. Monsieur Deschamps was just such a soul. He loved the land and respected each and every creature that made its home there. Strewn among the grazing herds of cows, hand-painted birdhouses were affixed to every tree. Tied in bundles of threes and fours, ears of corn hung above the chicken coops for squirrels to nibble on. Even the pig pen had an extra trough just for the field mice to share.

The crowning jewel of Monsieur Deschamps' farm were the wildflower pastures. Each season, the fields left fallow would grow thick and vibrant with a kaleidoscope of colors. Butterflies and honeybees, bunnies and hummingbirds came from all across the Chevreuse Valley to flit and flutter, gather and sample its wealth of pollen, bud and nectar. From afar, the pastures shown in the sunlight like facets in the glittering face of a diamond.

Lisette and Esmée loved to spend days on end discovering one flower after another. While emerald-green hummingbirds hovered over honeysuckle, the butterflies would drink nectar and laugh at the latest impersonations performed by their friend the mockingbird. The wildflower pastures of Monsieur Deschamps were always filled with friendship, which is why Lisette was hopeful she'd find her friend there today.

What she found, however, was news of Esmée she simply could not believe.

CHAPTER TEN

Pica Pica

Lisette landed on a clover bud pom-pom and drank until the heat of the afternoon and the long ache in her back dissolved into relaxation. The long distance she'd already flown that morning, plus the tension and stress of her growing concerns, had stiffened her wings and given her a pounding headache. She was glad for the chance to rest a while.

The fallow fields of Monsieur Deschamps' farm were alive with activity. Looking out over the clover patch in which she now rested, Lisette could see butterflies moving from flower to flower in unpredictably jittery flight. Dragonflies flew with perfect posture, back and forth and side to side, just inches above the blossoms.

Like fairies in the sunlight, tiny white wisps of dandelion fuzz descended with silent delicacy. All around, the air was abuzz with the sounds of insects and birds, as barn swallows -- dive-bombing unsuspecting grasshoppers -- crisscrossed the open sky in every direction. In Monsieur Deschamps' fields, it was easy to forget the world outside.

In the center of this particular field there stood a solitary oak tree. The tree was enormous, -- at least forty feet tall (like a four-story building)– and sprawled out like a vast, multilayered umbrella. In it, birds made their downy nests and woodland squirrels stashed their stores of food for the winter months.

Beneath the tree, tan, baby-faced Aubrac cows sat in the shade of lobed leaves. The Aubracs chewed and chewed with disinterested nonchalance, and never seemed to take a bite of grass. It was easier to think they were chewing gum, as it was to believe they were eating grass. On a branch of the oak tree, high above the gum-chewing cows, there sat a magpie.

Lisette spotted the black and white of the magpie's feathers, at a distance, and immediately recognized her friend, Pica (pronounced *pee*-kah).

It might be strange to say, but it wasn't clear precisely what Pica's name really was. You might think that the best way to find out would be to simply ask him, but if you asked him his name, he always responded, "Pica Pica."

If you tried to clarify further by asking, "Then your first name is Pica?"

He'd respond, *"Oui! Oui!"*

Which didn't really clarify anything at all, since by now you were beginning to suspect that Pica just liked to repeat himself.

Trying once more to get a clear answer, you might ask, "So, your full name is…?"

To which he always replied, "Pica Pica," bringing you right back to the beginning again, without having learned anything at all -- and feeling just a little bit annoyed.

Everyone decided to just call him Pica, which seemed to work just fine in all the ways names are expected to work. Still, it was impossible to deny that Pica liked to say things more often than was strictly necessary.

Each time he spoke, he would repeat himself exactly twice, and always with two little hops in the air for added emphasis. But he was a gentle soul, so everyone was inclined to overlook his eccentricity; some more than others; Lisette less than most.

She was sure that if anyone had seen Esmée in Monsieur Deschamps' fields that day, it would've been Pica. She fluttered over from the clover patch, up above the baby-faced cows, and landed on a branch beside the magpie.

"Bonjour, Pica. Comment vas-tu aujourd'hui?"

"Bien! Bien!" the redundant bird replied, with two hops for good measure.

"Have you seen Esmée today? She wasn't at breakfast and I've been looking for her ever since."

"Oui, oui."

Pica's response caught Lisette by surprise. She had been hopeful to hear news of Esmée, but she'd also begun to lose heart and expected to find only disappointment. Now that Pica said he'd seen Esmée, she was impatient for details

"You saw her? Where? When? Was she alright? What was she doing? Tell me everything you know! Come on, Pica!"

Poor Pica was overwhelmed with questions and -- somewhat excitable to begin with -- didn't know exactly where to begin. The truth is, he had only seen her briefly and had no idea what she was doing or where she was going. All he knew was that she was at the train station first thing that morning. His reply to Lisette's barrage of questioning left her even more disappointed and dangerously annoyed with him.

"À la gare, à la gare!"

"At the train station? You saw Esmée at the train station?! What was she doing there? Did you talk to her? What did she say? Why didn't you tell me? Why would she be at the train station?"

"Je ne sais pas, je ne sais pas."

Lisette, who was infamous for her explosive

temper, was becoming very displeased with Pica and his unhelpful repetitions. He was the only one to have seen Esmée that day and, rather than giving Lisette helpful details, all he could do was repeat, *"À la gare, à la gare."*

If Esmée was at the train station that morning, she could be anywhere by now. That was over 8 hours ago. Maybe she left the station and visited the nearby churchyard, leaving there before Audrey arrived. Maybe they just barely missed one another. Perhaps, from the church, she visited Monsieur Deschamps' pasture, but left before Pica got to the oak tree. There were just too many possibilities.

The one possibility that never crossed Lisette's mind, however, was that Esmée had actually boarded a train and headed down the tracks away from the station and out of Saint-Denis. Since Pica hadn't stuck around long enough to witness it, nobody knew that that's precisely what she *had* done.

Lisette was no closer to finding her friend than she had been that morning. She still had no idea where Esmée was right now. She was irritated that Pica hadn't bothered to find out what Esmée was doing at the station, which of course was unfair to Pica. Her irritation boiled up out of her like scalding steam from a tea kettle.

"Quel oiseau pénible! Quel oiseau pénible!" she said, mocking his habit of repeating things.

Pica didn't know what to say, let alone what to say *twice*. He just sat looking at his feet; shuffling back and forth; his face blushing beneath his black and white feathers.

Lisette wasn't sure if she could even believe him. Anyone who felt the need to repeat himself all the time could easily be mistaken for an exaggerator, or worse. She was inclined to dismiss the whole train station sighting as being highly suspect.

Lisette was in despair. No one at Madame

Legrand's butterfly bush, or in the whole of her backyard, had seen Esmée. Audrey Loriot at *l'église Saint-Denis* hadn't seen her; and no one in Monsieur Deschamps' pastures had seen or heard anything, either. Lisette was running out of places to look. Of all the places Esmée could go, why would she choose the train station? No. Lisette was certain this could not be true. She would not believe it. Pica was mistaken.

She had a decision to make. She could continue searching the rest of Saint-Denis and run the risk of missing Esmée if she turned up at Monsieur Deschamps', or she could stay-put in the field and wait for Esmée to arrive. Lisette was tired and becoming increasingly afraid for her friend's well-being.

Maybe they'd been missing each other all morning. Or maybe Esmée was in real trouble. She just didn't know what to think. She decided that the best thing to do right now was to pass the afternoon and night in the pasture. That would give her time to think things through; and just maybe Esmée would turn up, in the meantime.

She would also spend the remaining hours before sundown spreading the word among the other butterflies, moths, dragonflies, bees and birds in the field and surrounding area. With their help, maybe more ground could be covered, and word would spread throughout the valley. The morning might just bring more hopeful news. Most of all, Lisette would put Pica to work helping her. She felt that it was the least he could do after his failure to provide any useful information.

"I want you to fly around to *every inch* of this field and tell *everyone you meet* that Esmée is lost and that we *all need* to be looking for her. If anyone sees her or hears anything about her, they are to find me, you, or Audrey Loriot and let us know – *without delay*. Better yet, they should find *me or Audrey*."

Pica dropped his head like a crestfallen puppy.

Noticing Pica's dejection, and softening her tone a bit, Lisette added, "I'm counting on you, Pica. And I'm glad for your help. Now get going!"

Pica's mood brightened with the trust Lisette had decided to place in him.

"J'y vais! J'y vais!" Pica was happy to help, but even happier to be back in Lisette's good graces again.

Off he flew to the four corners of the field, passing along Lisette's message to everyone he met along the way – and repeating it for emphasis, as only Pica could. Meanwhile, Lisette spent the late afternoon flitting and fluttering to every bush and flower, telling everyone to be on the lookout for Esmée. She was determined to enlist the help of every creature in the valley, without exception.

The sun began to set, and the evening dew grew heavy on the delicate wings of butterfly and bird, alike. Everyone snuggled down into nests and cozy places -- wherever they could be found -- to sleep away the night in warm comfort. The fallow fields of Monsieur Deschamps' farm were filled with safe and quiet places to spend the night.

Many miles away, a frightened Esmée was about to face the terrors of a barn owl's beak in a lonely cherry tree in the Tuileries Garden. She had no idea what lay ahead of her on her long, hopeless journey home. Her thoughts strayed to her friends, and she wondered if they were worried about her at all. With a heavy heart, she watched the people walk past her cherry tree on their way home to their loved ones. If she ever found her way back to the valley, she intended to never leave it again.

Back home in Monsieur Deschamps' pasture, in the cuddly comfort of a dandelion's mane, Lisette slept in safety. She had spent the entire day searching for her friend with increasing desperation. Rather than calm her fears, Pica's sighting at the train station had only filled Lisette with questions. She needed answers; but few could be found. The next day was Wednesday and Lisette would at last receive news of her friend, but from a most unlikely source.

C H A P T E R   E L E V E N

Le Journal

Audrey Loriot lived in a purple lilac tree belonging to a young woman named Penelope Porcher. The lilac was situated in the eastern corner of Penelope's yard and was the first of her trees to receive the sun's early morning rays. Any bird or butterfly asleep in this particular lilac would awaken first, snuggling softly in the sun's first embrace.

It was by choice that Audrey had always been an early riser. The moment the morning dew evaporated from her gossamer wings she'd be off, headed for the churchyard located just one block away. But it wasn't just her love of reading that made her fly off to the churchyard at first light every morning. Audrey also loved solitude, and as the oldest of a family of seventeen butterflies, solitude was hard to come by. If she didn't get up early, she'd find herself stuck babysitting her little sister, Amélie; or showing her brothers, François and Antony, where to find the best nectar. Audrey was an intellectual who craved quiet reading time above all else.

The best reading material she could usually hope for was one of Père Lamoine's discarded daily sermons. Though not a bad writer, *le bon père* was an absolutely terrible public speaker. He hemmed and hummed, stammered and *ummed* his way through every tortured sentence; making his captive flock most uncomfortable and painfully antsy.

For this reason, they all assumed that the printed version of his sermon was just as bad as the spoken. So, every last one of them crumpled and tossed the bulletin into the trash on the way out of church. Little did Père Lamoine know, but the only person reading his daily sermon was Audrey Loriot, *le papillon.*

However, that Wednesday morning, Audrey was in luck. When she arrived at the church, the early edition of *Le Journal* lay on the front step of the rectory. Père Lamoine was running late for morning Mass and hadn't yet brought the newspaper in from outside. While he was busy attending to his duties, Audrey would have plenty of time to catch up on current events.

She flew over and landed on top of the front page, which was folded to display the upper half only. Running across the top, in big, bold letters, read the headline, *"La nouvelle exposition du Louvre capture le cœur des touristes!"*

Beneath the headline was a photograph of the *Pyramide du Louvre.* Sitting proudly atop the pyramid's point, was a tiny butterfly. Below the main photograph, Audrey could see another picture, which began above the fold of the newspaper, but extended below the crease and out of sight. As she read the story, her curiosity about the subject of this second photograph grew -- as did the suspicion that she just might know this *"nouvelle exposition du Louvre."*

The newspaper story read as follows:

La nouvelle exposition du Louvre capture le cœur des touristes!

Les touristes ont eu droit à une nouvelle exposition au Louvre, hier, lorsqu'un papillon belle dame s'est posé sur le sommet de la Pyramide. Brillant de couleur jaune orangée au soleil, le papillon posait pour des photos sous les acclamations spontanées de ses admirateurs. Il était clair que cette visiteuse unique était une touriste elle-même, de par son intérêt pour la monstruosité controversée du verre. Pendant quelques minutes, cette œuvre d'art naturelle éclipsa toutes les autres au Louvre. Bravo petit papillon!

The new exhibition of the Louvre captures the hearts of tourists!

Tourists were treated to a new exhibit at the Louvre, yesterday, when a painted lady butterfly landed on the pinnacle of la Pyramide. Shining in golden orange in the sunlight, the butterfly posed for pictures amid the spontaneous cheers of her affectionate admirers. It was clear that this unique visitor was a tourist herself, by the interest she took in the controversial glass monstrosity. For a few brief minutes, though, this natural work of art eclipsed all others in the Louvre. Bravo, little butterfly!

Audrey examined the photo as best she could, but the butterfly on top of *la Pyramide* was too small to be identified. She could tell, by what she could see of the second photo, that it was a closeup. She needed to find a way to open the newspaper. Her suspicions were growing, and she had to learn whatever this second photo could tell her.

Wasting no time, Audrey fluttered as fast as she could in the direction of Monsieur Deschamps' farm. She had to let Lisette know of her suspicions about what she'd seen in *Le Journal*. Most of all, Audrey needed Pica's help. Time was against her. Mass would be over in 30 minutes and Père Lamoine would be wanting his newspaper. She had to find her friends and get back in time to show them the article.

Audrey flew with all her might, the morning breeze at her back. As she flew, the sun broke through the mist, burning off the fog and lifting the weight of the dew drops from her wings. With a strong tailwind and serious determination, Audrey flew with the might of five butterflies.

The most direct path took her high above rooftops and across the narrow, white footbridge spanning the Yvette River. She was laser-focused on speed, aware of her rapidly closing window of opportunity; and crossed the town in record time, arriving at Monsieur Deschamps' farm in under ten minutes.

From the edge of the fallow field, she spotted the great oak tree rising out of the shredded remnants of morning fog. Upon his usual branch sat Pica the magpie, grooming his feathers in the warmth of the sun. Audrey flew right for Pica -- relieved to have found him in his usual place -- and landed with a trip and a tumble beside the startled bird.

"Tu vas bien, tu vas bien?" Pica said, with his usual hop, hop and repeat.

Audrey was out of breath and could barely speak. While she took a moment to compose herself, Pica sensed the urgency of her errand and called down to Lisette, who was just finishing her breakfast in the clover patch beneath the oak.

"Weet-weet-weet. Weet-weet-weet," the magpie tweeted.

Lisette flew up to the branch to see what the matter was. There, she found Audrey -- thoroughly exhausted -- panting and straightening her bent antennae.

"I flew… as fast as I could," Audrey began. "We don't have much time. I think…" She was still trying to catch her breath. "Esmée… I think… I think I found Esmée. Quickly, before it's too late."

Lisette and Pica had no idea what all this could mean. Clearly, there was no time for questions. Without hesitation, the two friends began flying, following Audrey's lead. This time, the wind was in their faces. Like fish swimming against the current, the two butterflies and solitary magpie fought their way back over field and farm; over rooftops and garden walls; and through the tangled streets of the city to the tiny, stone church.

Nearing the churchyard, they heard the bells chime the half hour. They only had a few minutes before Mass would be over. Flapping and fluttering with great effort, Audrey at last led them to the front steps of the rectory -- landing beside the folded newspaper

"There! Pica open the paper. Make haste! Quickly, now!"

Pica hopped over to the newspaper and, grabbing it with his beak, shook it until it fell open. He then laid it back down on the doorstep for all to see. Audrey quickly read the story aloud to the other two, then pointed to the second photo.

The new exhibition of the Louvre captures the hearts of tourists!

Tourists were treated to a new exhibit at the Louvre, yesterday, when a painted lady butterfly landed on the pinnacle of la Pyramide. Shining in golden orange in the sunlight, the butterfly posed for pictures amid the spontaneous cheers of her affectionate admirers. It was clear that this unique visitor was a tourist herself, by the interest she took in the controversial glass monstrosity. For a few brief minutes, though, this natural work of art eclipsed all others in the Louvre. Bravo, little butterfly!

"Look! I knew it," she said in triumph, "I just

knew it. That *has* to be Esmée! I couldn't be sure until I saw the second picture; but that must be her! Look closely."

Lisette flew over and landed on the face of the newspaper's front page, just beneath the second photograph, and inspected it with intense interest. The picture was a closeup of a butterfly. With wings outstretched in the sunlight, the butterfly stood smiling on the pointy tip of *la Pyramide du Louvre*. All around, tourists stood applauding, snapping pictures, and pointing with amazement on their up-turned faces. The butterfly – a *belle dame* – posed like a supermodel, basking in the attention of an adoring audience. Beneath her right wing -- as clear as day to anyone who knew where to find it – there was a smiley-face-shaped birthmark.

"It *is* Esmée!" Lisette said. "But what is she… how did she… why didn't she tell… *me*?"

Lisette was puzzled. Ever since their BB-Day, they had never been apart for longer than a few hours. Now, there she was -- her best friend – on the front page of *Le Journal*. Esmée was in Paris, and she hadn't even bothered to tell Lisette she was going. She was at the Louvre, and she hadn't invited Lisette. Esmée had never shown any interest in leaving the valley before. She'd always been happy in Saint-Denis. What could have possibly made her want to visit Paris alone, without her best friend? None of it made any sense.

Then it hit her.

"The Louvre," Lisette thought. "Of course!"

Lisette had heard the stories Esmée's mother told about the treasures of the Louvre; about the statue of Cupid presenting a rose to the tiny butterfly. She'd heard Esmée's mother talk about how the rose represented love and the butterfly symbolized the heart. The young god, Cupid, is awakening the heart to love by the scent of the rose.

But she also understood the warnings Esmée's mother had shared with them. Warnings about being tempted by beautiful things; of being taken captive — caught in a butterfly net; warnings about the dangers in the world; warnings about heartbreak. Lisette understood it all; but Esmée always seemed to focus on the romance of the sculpture. She was always more interested in such *dreamy* things; much more so than in warnings.

Lisette knew how badly Esmée had wanted to see the statue in person and wander through the galleries of the greatest museum in the world. Little by little, it started to become clear. The prospect of visiting the Louvre was the only thing Lisette could think of that would draw Esmée away from Saint-Denis; but why hadn't she told Lisette? Why did she simply leave without a word? Was the promise of seeing this sculpture more important than their friendship?

Everything she ever knew about her friend was now called into question.

The two of them had been inseparable; but now Esmée had left Lisette behind.

Esmée had always been afraid to wander too far from home; but now she was miles away, in Paris. Esmée was shy and reserved -- she had always been careful to avoid the attention of unpredictable humans; but now there she was on the front page of *Le Journal*, posing for the camera.

Lisette was hurt. She felt abandoned. She was relieved to see that her friend was safe; but now she wondered if she'd ever see Esmée again. Had she left the valley for good? Had she outgrown the little town and cast it off like an old chrysalis that had served its purpose? Had it been too hard for her to say goodbye, and so she simply… didn't?

On top of it all, Lisette felt like she'd been made a fool of. She'd been in a panic since yesterday morning.

She'd searched the town all day for news of her friend. She had spread the word far and wide, putting the entire valley on alert. All the while, Esmée was busy playing the supermodel at the Louvre. Lisette didn't know *how* to react to it all. She just felt… lonely.

After a long silence, she said, "I'm going home."

"But we found her!" Audrey said in confusion. "We found Esmée!"

"Yeah, good job, Audrey."

Lisette's voice was cold and numb; there was no feeling, no sincerity in her words. Her face was distant; her eyes, expressionless.

No one knew what to say. Audrey and Pica were still trying to understand Lisette's reaction when, without another word, she simply flew away. Her friends stood staring at each other, utterly dumbfounded.

"Lisette?" Pica said, as she disappeared from sight; and Audrey didn't even notice that he only said it once.

CHAPTER TWELVE

Pierre Cardui

Esmée sat in the cherry tree of the Tuileries Garden, in the heart of Paris, watching the kind and clever owl moth fly away toward the river. She was grateful to her protector for coming to her rescue; and she wished she had been more enthusiastic in her thanks. The truth is, she was still in shock over all that had happened during the night. She knew just how close she'd come to being… well, she shuddered to think of it.

The sun had just begun to paint the morning sky pink; the city was still wrapped in drowsy silence. Off to the west, beyond the trees and green grass of the Tuileries Garden, a graceful structure of iron lace stood firm and surefooted in the sunlight -- a nightgown of morning mist gathered loosely around its feet.

The horrific moments spent in the beak of the barn owl had hardened Esmée's resolve. She was no longer distracted by the beauty and wonder of the city. Yesterday, she'd actually begun to forget her homesickness and enjoy her adventure through Paris; but the terrors of the night had driven all excitement back into fearful hiding. She desperately wanted to go home, but she didn't know how; and she didn't know the way.

As warmth returned to her legs and wings, the words of Stéphanie, the *Ignifuge* bee of Notre-Dame Cathedral, returned to her thoughts: "Follow the river, it will always lead you home again."

If she was to have any hope of finding her way back to Saint-Denis, she had to put her trust in someone. Even if she didn't quite understand what the bee had meant, Esmée felt that Stéphanie was certainly trustworthy. Her promise about the river was the closest thing Esmée had to hope. She had little choice but to hold on to it with all her might.

This much was certain: all thoughts would become less cloudy, and all hopes would appear more certain once she'd had a good breakfast. Esmée just happened to be surrounded by more flowerbeds than she'd realized in the half-light of the previous evening. If she had to face another day of tiresome uncertainty, at least she could do it on a full belly. So, Esmée began the long process of *petit déjeuner*, sampling the nectar of kings, while flitting from flower to flower among the royal flowerbeds of the Tuileries Garden.

By the time she'd had her fill, the sun was already climbing high in the eastern sky and the fog from the river had been replaced by glints and sparkles of sunlight on the Seine. From the top of a lamppost near the entrance to the gardens, Esmée could see the river on her left.

Stretching out in front of her, a broad tree-lined avenue ran undeterred for a mile and a half, before passing through the center of a great traffic circle. At the center of the circle, a thick-stoned, massive arch stood astride the avenue; and formed a hub for twelve spoke-like streets, radiating outward in every direction. The perfection of its symmetry was mesmerizing.

Still, Esmée resisted the temptation to explore. She had to stay close to the Seine; the river would lead her home. Somehow, it would. Esmée left the lamppost she'd been resting on and flew the short distance down to the river. Alighting in a sycamore tree on the bank, she collected her thoughts for a while.

If the river was to be her guide home, surely, she'd find a sign or a clue as to how it would accomplish its task. She looked around. Nothing. Flitting from tree to lamppost, and lamppost to street sign, Esmée searched the area for a hint. She couldn't find a single familiar name. No mention of *l'Yvette*. No sign mentioning Saint-Denis. There were streets and metros, trains and buses; but there was nothing to strengthen her flagging hope.

Flying back to the high safety of the sycamore tree, Esmée stared out in despair at the sprawling city. She could see for miles in every direction, but it was no use; she could see no wildflower fields, no farmland, no butterfly bush, no friends or family. She was surrounded by everything unfamiliar. Whatever the bee had meant, it could not help her now. The Seine was silent.

Down the river to her left, Esmée saw the Eiffel Tower stretching up to touch the sky. Behind her, she looked back toward the long straight sidewalk that ran through the Tuileries and all the way to the Arc du Carrousel. Beyond that, was the Louvre.

To her right, she saw bridge after bridge and the hint of an island in the middle of the Seine. She knew that Saint-Michel stood astride that island, his finger outstretched, motioning toward Notre-Dame. In front of her, down the broad avenue, the steadfast *Arc de Triomphe* sat brave and unmoved in the eye of a hurricane of traffic. Esmée had seen so much already; but her eyes ached only to see her home again.

"It is beautee-ful, *non*?"

Esmée turned with a start in the direction of the voice. She'd had more than enough of strangers creeping up on her unannounced. She was still a bit jumpy and on edge, so her reaction was sharp and far less than friendly.

"*Qui êtes vous*?!" she snapped, nearly falling off her branch with alarm.

"Pardon me, *mademoiselle*. I did not mean to

startle you. *Je suis désolé.* My name is Pierre Cardui. *Enchanté.*"

The stranger bowed, drawing his right wing across his chest as he did. When he drew himself upright again, the sight that met Esmée's eyes was that of the most handsome butterfly she had ever seen. His markings were similar to hers; with wings of golden orange and flickering fire; but his eyes were uniquely his own. She was enchanted, indeed.

"The river, it is beautee-ful, *non*? Often, I will fly to the top of the grand obelisk… there, in *la Place de la Concorde…* just to lose myself in the splendor all around me."

As Pierre spoke, Esmée found herself paying more attention to the way his words expressed themselves in his soft eyes than to what he was actually saying. She noticed, in particular, the subtle way his smile seemed to blossom and fade with the heat of his passion. His was a deep and resonant heart, and it echoed with every word. Esmée was riveted; she could not coax her gaze away from his face

"But I forget myself, *mademoiselle. Pardon.* Surely, I have interrupted you in your own thoughts and in the stirring of your heart. May I, perhaps, have the privilege of your name?"

Esmée was falling way behind. Pierre's voice was the most soothing of any music; and she let each note soak into her mind slowly. Unfortunately, Pierre spoke faster than words could slowly soak into the mind of a lovestruck butterfly. Esmée reached the question mark at the end of Pierre's sentence so late that he interpreted her tardiness as an unwillingness to share her name with him.

"Forgive my impertinence, *mademoiselle.* Of course, you are right. I am a stranger. Please accept my apologies for disturbing you on this glorious morning. I wish you all the joy of discovery. *Bonne journée, mademoiselle.*"

With the slightest tilt of his head, Pierre expressed his delicate deference; straightened his back once more; then smiled with a kindness Esmée would never forget.

"*Au rev...*"

"Esmée," she interrupted. "*Je m'appelle Esmée.*"

Pierre left his "*au revoir*" unfinished, then paused a moment, beaming at the sound of Esmée's name.

Closing his eyes briefly, and bobbing his head slowly, he said, "*Merci, mademoiselle. Enchanté.* I am honored to make your acquaintance. Will you, I wonder, be visiting the Arc de Triomphe, today, *mademoiselle?*"

He motioned with one wing in the direction of the Arc.

Esmée didn't know what to say; she scarcely knew where she was. Pierre's "*enchanté*" was more thrilling a sound than she had ever heard. This one word swept through her like the first breeze of spring, lifting away the last fallen leaves of fear that had been shaken loose by the barn owl the night before. In their place, new things now grew.

Before, Esmée had been reluctant to leave her watery guide; always keeping the river within sight. Now, at Pierre's suggestion – and at his side, she hoped – Esmée found herself willing to venture deeper into the city and away from the Seine. Her reason and reluctance had been swept away by his gentle demeanor.

"I would be honored if you would allow me to accompany you, *mademoiselle*. The Arc, it is a wonder to behold."

With great difficulty, warmth in her cheeks, and a lump in her throat, Esmée whispered her reply.

"*Oui, monsieur,* I would like to visit the Arc... *avec vous.*"

"*S'il vous plait, mademoiselle, 'avec toi,'*" Pierre said with a smile, inviting Esmée to address him with greater familiarity – using the *tu* instead of the *vous* for "you."

"*Oui, monsieur, avec toi...* it would be my pleasure. *Merci.*"

Esmée dropped her antennae over her eyes. She was afraid she had revealed too much by saying, "it would be my pleasure." She felt the rose-red of her warm cheeks; she sensed the trembling in her own voice. How she wished to hide it all from Pierre. Still, she was both relieved and terrified that she'd found the courage to accept his offer.

"*Puis-je?*" Pierre said, extending his upper-most leg in a gesture, most gentlemanly. "Allow me?"

Esmée reached out to take his hand, averting her eyes in a last attempt to conceal the flowers now blooming in her heart. As her hand met Pierre's, Esmée felt a surge of electricity pulse through her arm all the way to the tips of her wings. She took a deep breath, then turned her face, until her eyes met Pierre's. A smile spread like waves on the surface of a pond; her face was now aglow with expectation.

Turning toward the center of the city, the two butterflies flew – hand-in-hand – in the direction of the Arc de Triomphe. Below them, wandering the paths of the Tuileries Garden, lovers held hands and whispered secret somethings, one to the other, as the sun slipped from its noonday height in the sky.

Crossing the Place de la Concorde, Esmée and Pierre paused atop the ancient obelisk. Shading her against the heat of the summer sun, Pierre extended his right wing over Esmée's head. Using his left wing, he pointed in the direction of the Eiffel Tower.

"*C'est magnifique, non?* Ah, but she plays a game of hide and seek from every point in the city. Just when you've forgotten she's there, she peeks her face from behind a building. But when you seek her, the tower, she hides from sight. Ah, *oui*, she knows she is the star of the show; but she's a prima donna, *oui*, a prima donna, *certainement.*"

Pierre laughed with admiration at the noble tower. His laugh was wrapped in kindness, and Esmée smiled at the warmth of his voice.

"Have you ever seen the great tower at night, *mademoiselle*? Have you ever seen the sparkle in her eyes? *C'est fantastique.*"

"*Non, monsieur,* I have never seen the Eiffel Tower at all."

Esmée's voice blushed with embarrassment. She was, after all, a simple, country butterfly. She expected Pierre to emphasize her simplicity by his surprised reaction; but his response caught her off guard.

"I hope you will permit me to introduce you, *mademoiselle*. It would be an honor."

Pierre's sincerity chased away all of Esmée's embarrassment. She was beginning to think that, after the worst night of her life, she just might be embarking on what would be the most wonderful day she'd ever known.

"Shall we continue, *mademoiselle*? The Arc, he awaits us."

Taking Esmée's hand once again, Pierre guided her to flight by his side. Together they made their way from the Place de la Concorde, down the Champs-Élysées, toward the Arc de Triomphe.

Below them, the wide, treelined avenue passed beneath their wings. Endless lines of cars inched along like accordions – slowing down in great jumbles, then spreading out again in thin lines. Pedestrians poured into intersections jammed with stopped cars; like cement between stones, they filled every space, then leaked out onto the sidewalks on the opposite side of the street. All of Paris was in motion; and Esmée marveled at the spectacle.

The two butterflies rode a cushion of fast flowing air, whipped up and carried along by the cars on the street below. Like body surfers on an ocean wave, they moved through the city with no more effort than it took to extend their wings. Bobbing up and down, weaving side to side, they laughed and played on the rushing breeze. Hand-in-hand, Pierre supported Esmée as she danced in the wind above the busy street below.

At one point, Esmée let go of Pierre's hand and pirouetted out into midair. She imagined herself flying through the warm, white light of Notre-Dame Cathedral once again. Her wings, like two kites, held her -- weightless and free – upon the billowing breeze. She closed her eyes and smiled in the swirling sunlight.

At that moment, a bus filled with tourists pulled into the stream of traffic beneath the butterflies, interrupting the flow of air they'd been riding. Like closing a door in a drafty room, there was suddenly no breeze, and no support under Esmée's wings. She began to fall.

Flapping her wings wildly, she struggled to gather together enough air to halt her descent. The swoosh and whirl of wind, stirred up by the cars below, created turbulence which picked Esmée up and threw her -- full force -- into the path of oncoming traffic. The situation had taken an unexpected turn, and Esmée was helpless -- unable to avoid the grimy windshield of the tourist bus barreling toward her.

From inside the chaos, Esmée saw the scene move in slow motion. She felt the panicked sensation of falling without the smallest foothold of calm air against which to brace herself. The wolfpack of cars circling all around her was an endless blur of shapes, colors and honking horns. She could feel the heat rising up off the pavement; and she smelled the acrid sweat of the asphalt. A single thought kept repeating itself in her mind: she'd never get to share the story of her adventure in Paris with her best friend, Lisette. This was her one regret.

The bus approached at full speed, showing no concern for the tiny butterfly in its path. Esmée made one last attempt to mount the tornado which snaked its way in and out, above and between the stampeding cars which were now overwhelming and engulfing the falling butterfly. Gaining a few inches of altitude, the wind was pulled out from under her struggling wings without warning, and she began to fall with newfound momentum. Esmée felt the surge of oncoming air as it tried and failed to outrun the tourist bus; she knew she'd be the next to feel the bus's deadly impact.

The unexpected sensation of upward flight now grabbed hold of Esmée and jerked her out of the path of the tourist bus. She was rising with such force; she thought her wings would be ripped from her body. A stabbing pain shot through her strained limbs, as the tip of her hindmost feet grazed the windshield of the speeding bus. Her head was spinning, throbbing with a burning ache which threatened to pull her eyes from their sockets. She wasn't sure if she'd been struck by the barreling bus or by some other vehicle; she was certain only of the agony now invading her entire body.

As quickly as it had all begun, the chaos disappeared; the confusion dissolved; and the anguish of the attack was replaced by a sudden calm. Esmée found herself lying on her side on cold, hard stone -- one wing crushed beneath her, the other draped over her bruised body.

Slowly, she became aware that she was sobbing; warm tears pooled beneath her face. Down below where she now lay, traffic revolved around her in a broad circle. Twelve streets fed the roundabout with a steady glut of cars from all directions. The noise of horns and choking mufflers pressed outward from inside Esmée's bursting head. She felt as if she might faint.

"*Mademoiselle... mademoiselle...* Esmée, can you hear me?"

The voice was soft and soothing. A familiar feeling now stole into Esmée's heart, and she opened her eyes to find Pierre standing over her.

"Are you well?" he asked with great concern. "I do hope I did not hurt you."

"*Oui*, Pierre... I am well."

Esmée wasn't sure what had happened or whether she was really unhurt; but somehow the sound of Pierre's voice made her feel that all would be well.

"I am relieved, sweet one."

Pierre reached out a trembling hand and brushed the road dust from Esmée's wing. His brow was wrinkled with worry and hung heavy above his eyes.

"What happened? How did I get up here?"

"You fell, *mademoiselle.* And I... caught you." His voice broke with emotion, as he finished wiping Esmée's wing clean -- straightening it with care.

"But I felt... the bus... the pain."

"I'm afraid that was me, *mademoiselle.* I had to catch you anyway I could. Your wings were easiest to grab hold of... I have no doubt, it was painful. *Je suis désolé...* I am so very sorry. "

Pierre was downcast. His words came slowly and with heartfelt emotion; his eyes were full of sadness. When he first saw Esmée begin to fall, he raced to reach her side in time. The constant rush of traffic threw obstacles in his path, through which he navigated as quickly as he could. What Esmée experienced in slow motion, Pierre moved through at twice the speed of the tourist bus -- desperate to save her life.

Maneuvering to within arms-reach just before the bus's windshield struck her, Pierre grabbed Esmée's wings and yanked her up and out of the path of danger as fast as his powerful wings could carry them. The pain of being dragged through the air by her wings was excruciating; but being struck by the bus would have been too much for Esmée to bear.

"*Merci,* Pierre. But *merci* is too little to say. Far too little."

Esmée began to cry again, but it was not from the pain in her body that her tears now came.

"*Mademoiselle*, your *merci* is more than I could have ever hoped to earn. *Merci à toi.*"

Pierre leaned down and kissed Esmée on the forehead, with a tenderness to heal all of her ills.

"Welcome to the Arc de Triomphe, *mademoiselle.*"

CHAPTER THIRTEEN

Crows!

Audrey and Pica were still trying to make sense of Lisette's reaction to learning of Esmée's whereabouts. It was not at all what they'd expected. After spending a frantic day searching for her friend, Lisette might have been expected to react with joyful relief upon learning that Esmée was at the Louvre Museum. Seeing her safe and sound (and astonishingly famous!) on the cover of *Le Journal*, should certainly have set Lisette's worries at ease and replaced her burden of fear with happiness; but that's not what Audrey and Pica had witnessed. Why had Lisette reacted with such coldness and then simply flown away? They could find no explanation; but there were bigger questions to be answered at present.

Audrey sat thinking to herself, as she often did. Stroking her antennae with her right, upper leg, she stared off into the distance. She was troubled, and she couldn't put her finger on exactly why. There was something about the whole situation that just didn't sit right with her. None of it seemed to add up.

"I don't like this, Pica. It doesn't make sense. This is not like Esmée at all."

Pica stood by and listened to Audrey puzzle it out. He was content to let her do the thinking. Pica was a bird of action, not an intellectual like Audrey. Anytime there was someone around to think and make decisions, Pica gladly stepped aside and let them do their thing.

"I don't care what the photo in *Le Journal* showed; something's just not right here. We need to *know* that Esmée's ok. We need to be sure of it. And we can't just wait around. I think we need to find her ourselves; and I'm afraid it won't be easy."

"*Comment? Comment?*"

"I don't know *how*; I haven't gotten that far, yet," she said, somewhat annoyed that Pica would press her for details this early in her thinking.

Standing up and straitening her antennae with resolve, she continued, "Père Lamoine always says, '*a good start will often show the way*'. We just need to make a good start."

"Lisette? Lisette?" Pica asked, with his usual overemphasis.

"We don't have time to figure her out, Pica. Heaven knows, I *never* understood her. And now's not the time to try. If we go looking for Esmée and find out nothing's wrong, then Lisette won't even know we left. That means she won't be able to make fun of us for "freaking out" and heading out on a needless *search and rescue*.

"But if we're right, and Esmée *is* in trouble, then Lisette might just end up thanking us. Either way, my redundant friend, it's up to us to find out -- one way or another."

Audrey noted the direction of the wind, then checked the position of the sun in the sky.

"It's a little before noon and our destination is many miles in that direction." She pointed to the east. "*Paris* is that way, Pica. The big city. Esmée is that way, too. And there's a whole lot of *unknown* in between. But, deciding which way to go is the hardest part of making a good start. Everything after that should be pretty easy."

Pica smiled and nodded his head in hearty

agreement. Audrey's assurance bred confidence in the little magpie. He was ready to follow her and be of help any way he could. He always was. That was Pica's greatest quality.

"Time to be on our way. Bid the fallow field farewell, my friend. We won't see anything like it in Paris. *Allons!*"

Audrey took to flight, and Pica followed. What a sight these two misfits were: the awkward, black and white magpie following the brainy butterfly through the air. Anyone might be mistaken in thinking the bird meant to sneak up on the unsuspecting butterfly. Little would they believe that the two friends were really on a mission.

Armed with no more than the certainty of the general direction in which Paris lay, Audrey and Pica set out with the sole purpose of confirming whether or not their friend was alright; and to bring whatever help Esmée might need, however they might bring it.

Neither had ever been outside of Saint-Denis; although Audrey had traveled far and wide in her reading. Neither of them had ever had the slightest desire to leave the valley: Audrey preferred the solitude of the churchyard, and Pica preferred his oak tree in the fallow field.

There were never a pair of less likely adventurers than these. Still, Père Lamoine was right; a good start will often show the way; and Audrey and Pica's path would reveal itself at the rate of 60 minutes per hour. They would have gladly sped their way, if only they could.

As Audrey and Pica flew northeast toward Paris, a very grumpy Lisette sat alone on the same branch of the milkweed in Monsieur Deschamps' pasture from which she and Esmée had emerged as butterflies. She stared motionless at the golden carpet of canola flowers swaying in the breeze all around her. With her knees drawn up beneath her chin, she hugged her legs with both arms and began to sob.

Lisette rarely cried; she simply would not permit it. But in the few moments when she did break down, it was always more out of anger with herself for falling apart than out of sadness. Today was no different.

She was angry for letting Esmée's trip to Paris bother her so much. She was mad at Esmée for causing her to worry and spend all day searching high and low. But, most of all, she was angry with Esmée for having fun without her. Realizing this -- admitting it to herself -- made her resentful. When it all became too hot to hold inside, the warm tears began to flow.

The more she thought about Esmée posing for *Le Journal* on the peak of the *Pyramide du Louvre*, the more bitterness she felt. Sitting there alone, she wrapped herself up in emotion. There was just no good explanation for what Esmée had done. None at all.

Of the two of them, Lisette was the adventurer, not Esmée; and Esmée knew it. Was this some sort of competition? Did Esmée hope to prove something to Lisette by going off alone? There had always been a gentle sort of rivalry between them, but neither took it very seriously -- or so Lisette had thought. Confusion, doubt and indignation mixed together inside her heart, like a poisonous cocktail. Her bruised pride led her down pathways that ended up in dead ends crammed full of wrong conclusions.

Minutes passed, perhaps an hour, until at last, she just grew tired of being upset. It was a waste of time, she thought; a waste of energy. Her embarrassment with herself about crying had grown stronger than anger, and her tears abruptly stopped.

She stood up; wiped her eyes dry with her wings; snorted at herself in disgust; and left the milkweed in Monsieur Deschamps' canola pasture. It was time for a new beginning. Her first beginning just hadn't turned out the way she thought it would. This time, she wouldn't let herself need anyone. This time, she was on her own -- the way she liked it.

Overhead, unnoticed by the brooding Lisette, Audrey Loriot and Pica the magpie flew along their way to find Esmée. Without a thought for themselves, the two had set off into the strange, unknown. It didn't take them long to encounter the first reminder of just how dangerous the world outside Saint-Denis could be.

Crossing the river, not far from the last house on the outskirts of town, the pair were met by a flock of black crows rising up from the ruins of an abandoned cornfield. Crows have a reputation for taking whatever they can get their beaks around; and they're no friends to magpies or butterflies – especially butterflies.

"Corbeaux! Corbeaux!"

Pica was alarmed at the sight of a dozen or so crows flying straight at them like a ragged pirate flag caught in a hurricane. Any one of the crows was much bigger than the little magpie; and they were all more cunning, by far.

"Just stay close to me, Pica. I know how to handle their sort."

This time, Audrey's assurance failed to ignite any confidence in the little bird. A butterfly isn't much to hide behind, for a magpie facing a murder of treacherous crows. He had serious doubts that Audrey could really "handle their sort," as she put it. His doubts only grew as the crows approached.

Like an ink splotch on the crystal blue canvas of the sky, the gang of birds cast an ominous shadow from overhead. Their endless cawing made the feathers stand up on the back of Pica's neck. It was deafening, and all the countryside seemed to echo with alarm. Swooping down uncomfortably close to Audrey and Pica, the dreaded flock began to circle them tighter and tighter beneath the hot sun.

"Stupid magpie. Just eat the wretched butterfly and be done with it," the leader taunted, as he flew in and out of the encircling bullies.

Bigger than the others, the leader pierced the ring of crows -- flying straight at the two helpless friends -- before flying out the other side again. It was clear that he meant to scare Pica away, to ensure the magpie couldn't defend his little butterfly friend. Swirling all around them in a dizzying shadow of endless motion, the hateful crows drew their circle as tight as a knot.

"*Non, non!*" Pica yelled back in disgust.

The idea of eating a fellow creature, especially his friend, was as foreign to the gentle magpie as any other act of unkindness. If the crows wanted to, they could certainly knock Pica out of the air and snatch up Audrey. They were just cruel enough to do it, too. There was nothing Pica could do to stop them. He was frightened and becoming more uneasy by the minute. The longer the wicked crows made fun of the timid magpie, the more likely he was to get flustered; and that's exactly what they were counting on.

"*Non? Non?*" the lead crow taunted. "*Pourquoi? Pourquoi?* This muddled magpie has a skip in his speech, boys. Well, maybe if *he* won't eat the little fly, I will."

Pica began to stammer and stutter with fear. What could he do against so many crows? They were all around him now; circling and flying just above his head, too. The bullying birds now began to fly lower and lower overtop of Pica, forcing him closer to the ground, until he found himself entangled in the upper limbs of a forest.

With no way to fly upward through the pressing ceiling of crows, Pica had no choice but to flop down on the branch of a tall sycamore tree. Like chocolate chips scattered throughout a lump of cookie dough, the crows now spread to every branch of the same sycamore, cackling-up a murderous storm.

Some of them continued teasing the terrified magpie, with calls of, "Muddled magpie got caught in a tree," and "Stupid bird can't fly!" The noise was maddening and set Pica's nerves on edge. He could see no way of escaping the swarm of crows surrounding him and Audrey.

But where *was* Audrey? Pica couldn't see her anywhere. In the chaos of rustling leaves and cawing crows, he'd lost track of his little friend.

Pica flapped his wings and tried to fly off the branch he'd landed on; but the moment he was in the air a big bully of a crow flew right for him, knocking him back down onto the branch. He was desperate to search for Audrey; but every time he tried to leap into flight, he was battered down again.

Hopping back and forth and turning this way and that, Pica did his best to look around his surroundings for Audrey. She'd been right by his side when the crows approached and started flying circles around the two travelers. She'd told him to keep close to her and Pica was sure he'd done just that. But somehow, he'd lost her in the commotion and now he feared the worst.

The leader of the gang was the biggest and cruelest of them all. He now flapped down and landed atop the branch Pica was cowering on. Hopping uncomfortably close to Pica, he began shooting his neck out, poking Pica in the chest with his sharp beak.

"Are you frightened, muddled magpie? Are you scared?"

Pica backed away from the bully, bumping into another crow that had landed right behind him. He was now trapped on the same branch between two enormous birds. The leader continued prodding Pica with his beak. Each time he did, Pica lost a feather; and it was beginning to hurt badly. A tear now came to poor Pica's eye and he started to shake with fear.

"Stupid magpie, are you going to cry?"

The hateful leader delivered a sharp peck of his beak to Pica's forehead, scraping the skin and drawing a drop of blood in the process. A great noise of cruel laughter went up from the crowd of crows surrounding the little magpie. They were all enjoying the show.

"Didn't like that, did you, stupid magpie?" the leader sneered. "Maybe you'll like this one better…"

As the huge crow reared his head back to deliver another painful peck to Pica's bruised and bloodied forehead, a sound was heard that cut through the cloud of vicious laughter like a siren in the night. Every bird in that tree fell quiet and froze in terror, listening with ears and eyes wide open. Not a feather moved, not a wing flapped. All was tense silence.

Then they heard it again, sharp and shrill as a cold knifepoint. There was no question; it was the screech of a hawk echoing overhead. Hawks are brilliant predators and will make a meal out of mice and squirrels, when they're able; but eating other birds will do just fine, too. A crow is no match for the might of a hungry hawk; and this one sounded close enough to strike at any moment.

Not a single crow in that tree waited for another warning. Like a thick puff of diesel smoke, they all darkened the sky at the same time. No taunting caws were heard; only the sound of frightened wings pounding the air with muffled panic. In a matter of seconds, the whole flock was gone from sight and Pica was alone.

At first, he wasn't sure what to do. He dared not risk a flight into open air. One lonely magpie would surely attract the attention of a hawk on the prowl. His best bet was to find shelter on the forest floor below and find it quickly.

Jumping off the branch on which he'd been standing, Pica glided down through the tree limbs and landed on the soft and leaf-covered ground. Chalk-white boulders -- carpeted in thick, spongy moss -- stood like the bones of ancient ruins, all around him. Close by, a stream flowed -- clear and cool -- and chattered over round stones in its way.

Across the stream from where he stood, Pica spied a small opening in the rocks. This would be perfect shelter from the hawk. Wasting no time, he flew over the water and into the dripping mouth of the cave. Finding a drifted pile of leaves inside, Pica nestled deep down into them -- hiding himself from the sharp eyes of the prowling predator.

Now that he was safe from the hawk, and the menacing crows were gone, Pica's thoughts turned to his friend, Audrey. His heart was heavy, and a lump now formed itself in his throat, as he thought about how the crows must have simply gobbled her up in midair. How horrible. If only he hadn't lost track of her. If only... His thoughts were overwhelmed with sorrow and Pica burst into tears, sobbing loudly. The whole cave echoed with the sound of Pica's sadness.

"Hush, you silly bird," came a voice from deep inside the cave. "Do you want those crows to come back?"

Jumping with a start, the little pile of Pica-leaves rustled with astonishment. Turning his head and popping up out of his cover, Pica saw a familiar face. It was Audrey, back from the dead; or so he thought.

"Audrey! Audrey! Audrey!" he said, hopping up and down and breaking his habit of mere repetition. It was a special occasion, after all.

"Tu vas bien! Tu vas bien!"

"I'm just fine. I told you I knew how to handle crows." Brushing some moss from her antennae, she said, with mild indignation, "Maybe you'll actually *listen* to me, from now on."

"Mais le faucon, le faucon..."

"You mean *this* hawk?"

Audrey turned to face the back of the cave and made an absolutely blood-curdling imitation of a hawk's cry, which bounced around the cave like a scream in a megaphone. Pica covered his ears with his wings and winced.

Through the forest all around, the screech traveled until it reached the crows who were holed up in a tree half a mile away. They all hunkered down low and trembled with terror on their branches; reminded of the danger that had driven them into hiding. The hawk was still out there; there was no doubt about it.

"C'est fantastique! C'est fantastique!" Pica was truly impressed, and so very relieved.

"When those odious crows were circling and picking on you, I saw my chance. Just what I'd been hoping to find: a cave; something to make my voice bigger and louder. *Attenborough's Guide to the Birds of Northern Europe*, or at least page 42 – which blew into the churchyard one fortuitous spring morning -- says that crows are terrified of hawks. I've heard enough hawks in the Chevreuse Valley to know what they sound like, so I thought I'd give it a try. Pretty convincing, no?"

Pica just hopped up and down with excitement, glad that his friend was alright. Audrey's endless reading had saved them both from the crows, and he would never doubt her again.

CHAPTER FOURTEEN

Making the Right Choice

Their run-in with the flock of bullying birds had pushed Audrey and Pica way off course. The whole experience had been a tornado of fast flight and circling terror, followed by a maze of tree limbs. They had no idea exactly where they were or how far they'd travelled. All they knew was that they were surrounded by forest as far as they could see. Audrey needed to get up above the trees and take a look around; but she was still wary of the crows returning. She didn't want to risk being seen.

"We need to get back on track, Pica. That means finding northeast again. The good news is we're in a forest, and every tree is a compass."

The young magpie raised one bewildered eyebrow in the direction of his butterfly friend.

"Bark on the north side of a tree is often darker than bark on the other sides. And, of course, everyone knows that moss and lichens grow on that side, too. If we follow the trees, and head just a little bit to the right, we should end up going northeast... more or less. Once we've left the forest, and we're further away from those crows, we should be able to fly up and get the lay of the land."

The two began examining every tree along their path. Some were better compasses than others; but they began to get a general feel for which direction was north.

At first, they moved slowly, careful to avoid losing their bearings. Neither of them had ever done this sort of thing before; Audrey had only ever read about it on the missing page of some book or other. So, they took their time, feeling their way from compass-tree to compass-tree.

The forest was dense, which made flying for any distance nearly impossible. Instead, Audrey and Pica flew in short, quick bursts from one tree trunk to the next; landing, examining, then moving forward cautiously. With every tree that confirmed their direction, the travelers' confidence increased -- along with their speed.

Soon, the forest began to thin out. Fewer trees with more space between them, allowed shafts of light to filter down to the forest floor. Suspended in the air, tiny specks of dust swam in slow motion through the sunlight -- like scuba divers in an ocean of molten gold. The soothing scent of leaves and pine needles rose up from the ground and lightened the hearts of the weary travelers. There was something comforting about the forest, something not unlike the warm, aromatic space within the walls of a cathedral.

Audrey and Pica stopped at the place where thinning trees gave way to open fields. They were still reluctant to leave the cover of the forest and venture out under the attentive eyes of the sky. The trauma of the crow attack was too near; Pica still felt the soreness in his forehead, and the loss of precious feathers from his chest.

Through the trees on the edge of the forest, Audrey could clearly see the sun in the western sky. Her intuition had been perfect; they now stood at the northeastern borders of the Meudon Forest; about halfway to Paris from Saint-Denis.

"Before we leave the forest, let's fly up to the rooftop and take a look around. Come on, Pica."

Audrey fluttered up to the top of the highest tree on the edge of the woods, with Pica close behind. He was determined to keep her in his sight; not only for her protection, but because he never wanted to hear her frightful hawk imitation ever again.

Landing on the uppermost branch and shading her eyes with her wings, Audrey looked out over the open fields; across the approaching villages; and beyond, to the northeast. At the limits of her sight she could just make out the lazy loop of a great river.

"Perfect!" she said, clasping her hands together in front of her chest. "We really must go back and find those crows."

Pica looked at her with horrified disbelief. Why on earth would they want to do *that*? Audrey chuckled.

"They deserve our thanks, my friend. They drove us hard and fast, halfway to Paris. Do you know what river that is, there?"

"*L'Yvette. L'Yvette.*" the magpie said, with certainty.

"No, sir. *L'Yvette* would be swallowed up without a trace by *le fleuve*. That's the Seine, Pica. And beyond that, Paris. We're almost there."

Emboldened by the nearness of their destination, the two now left the safety of the forest behind them and began to fly freely. They were glad to be rid of the nudging elbows of the pine trees' boney arms. Pica kept glancing back over his shoulder, expecting to find a flock of crows in pursuit; but none ever came. The more ground they covered, the more his fears subsided.

Down below, a quick succession of small towns gave way to bigger and denser gatherings of limestone cottages. All of France seemed to push and shove its way toward Paris. The houses, cars, and even the landscape itself, slowed to a jumbled stop at the edge of the river which skirts the city.

Thanks to the easterly wind pushing them along, Audrey and Pica gained speed as they drew nearer to

Paris. From a short distance away, they could see the Seine. In it, they saw a crescent-shaped island that appeared to have broken free from shore and drifted out into the center of the river. Every inch of space, on land and over water, was occupied with everything from buildings to bridges to begonias. There were so many places in which a lost butterfly might hide; so many places to search.

Thinking it best to have a plan before entering the city, Audrey pulled up short of the river and landed in a small tree. Pica followed.

"It's a big world, isn't it, Pica? And we only flew over a tiny part of it today."

Pica sat catching his breath on the branch beside her, as Audrey continued her pep talk.

"Across the river is an even bigger world. And *that* one is crammed into less space than we covered today!"

Pica tried to wrap his understanding around what Audrey had just said but decided just to take her word for it. Anything bigger than Monsieur Deschamps' fallow field felt like another universe to the little magpie.

"We need a plan. Like Julius Caesar said on page 81 of *The Conquest of Gaul,* we need to divide and conquer. It worked for him; it will work for us, too."

At this point, Pica was totally lost and had no idea who or what she was talking about. He often felt this way around others; but Audrey always had a way of explaining herself when it was clear Pica didn't understand. No one else ever took the time.

"Think of it this way, Pica… It's like when you're looking for berries in Monsieur Deschamps' bramble patch; it's best to take it one bush at a time. You divide the bushes up and conquer them one by one."

Pica's eyes lit up and he began flapping his wings with understanding. He readily understood everything in terms of berries.

"That's better," Audrey continued. "So, we need a plan. Paris is a big bramble patch! Just as important as a plan, though, we also need a *backup* plan."

Audrey enjoyed this sort of thing. Planning, talking, giving directions, and putting her knowledge to good use were all just as much fun as reading itself. She was a natural leader, and Pica was happy to follow.

"We should stay together at all times; but if we happen to get separated, let's plan to meet at the northern end of that crescent-shaped island."

She pointed with her wing to the tip of the island, which was crowned by a large, circular building with windows that looked like the scales of a great, coiled snake.

"That's *la Seine Musicale*; the auditorium, there. You can't miss it. That's our backup plan, our meeting place. If we get lost or separated, we make for *la Seine Musicale*."

The magpie was doing better at keeping up, now. He didn't want to think about getting lost or separated; but it was comforting to know what to do if it happened.

"Now for the main plan of attack… Hmm… Since the island is our emergency meeting spot, maybe we should start our search for Esmée along the river which divides the city. The only question is, do we begin by following the river to the left or to the right?"

Pica shrugged his shoulders twice, in keeping with his custom of doing and saying everything in pairs – especially when he had no idea what to say. To the left they could see green forests beyond the city sprawl. The crowded buildings seemed to end in beautiful, green patches of trees, perfect for a butterfly. Surely this is where Esmée would be.

To the right, the city stretched on for miles beyond their sight. Of course, they had no way of knowing that the Louvre and its famous pyramid lay in this direction. All they could tell was that their search would be much more difficult and filled with chaotic and congested city streets, if they chose to follow the river up the righthand side of the island. Yet, that is precisely the direction in which Esmée could be found at that very moment -- sitting on top the Arc de Triomphe, recovering from her close scrape with the tourist bus. As with most things, much depended upon them making the right choice of path to follow.

"If we head to the left, we could cross off a smaller part of the city and then be free to focus on *'conquering'* the other side. But we might get caught up in searching the vast forest and lose precious time. Plus, without street names and landmarks, it might be difficult to search among the nameless trees in an organized way. Still, it's always best to begin with small bites."

Audrey rubbed her antennae with her right front leg, the way she always did when she was thinking extra hard about a problem. If she made the wrong choice, it would mean wasting days searching that side of the city; they'd miss finding Esmée altogether. If only she *knew* which side of the river the Louvre was on.

"I read it once, on page 73 of the driver's manual, *le Code de la Route:* at intersections, the 'right-of-way' is given priority. I don't know exactly what that means," which was something Audrey rarely admitted, "since page 74 never blew into the churchyard, but I think it means that, when in doubt, the right side is the way to go. Well, we're in doubt right now! It's best to follow the rules of the road, I always say; so, I think we should follow the river up the righthand side. What do you think, Pica?"

Pica was just relieved that she'd made a decision. He liked it when someone else made all the decisions; and Audrey excelled at deciding things. After the incident with the crows, he'd promised himself never to doubt her again. He had complete confidence in her and wanted her to know it.

"*À droite. À droite.*" Pica agreed, then added without repetition, "*Avec toi.*"

For Pica, the way was clear: follow Audrey. If that meant following her to the right, then that's what he'd do.

"Very well," she agreed. "We'll head up the river to the right. If we get separated, the river will guide us back here to the orchestra house. The Seine should give us plenty to see and search. Let's just hope that Esmée stayed near the river, too. Either way, it's a good start, and *'a good start will often show the way.'*"

After a long drink of nectar from a nearby flower and a beak-full of berries from an elderberry bush, the two were ready to enter Paris and follow the Seine wherever it might lead them. Pica hoped that they were leaving the worst of their journey behind them along with the crows; but Audrey knew better. She'd read more than enough newspapers in the churchyard to know that the city held dangers Pica's innocent mind couldn't even imagine.

He intended to stay close by her side to protect her, but Audrey knew that it just might be she who did the protecting -- like she'd done in the forest cave. Pica was naïve enough to be blissfully confident of their chances of finding Esmée. Audrey was wise enough to know just how slim those chances really were. Searching the city for one small butterfly was like hoping to find one raindrop in the big, blue sea; but this was their task.

There was one more concern that had not yet occurred to Pica, but which weighed heavy on Audrey's mind: the crows' assault had begun near the village of Jouy-en-Josas, not far from Saint-Denis. The road from Saint-Denis to Jouy-en-Josas was clear; but their course from Jouy-en-Josas to the Meudon Forest had been a stressful blur. They'd been chased with such speed and confusion that there's no way they would remember their way back to Jouy-en-Josas from the forest. They had no idea how to get home.

Audrey decided not to worry about that yet. There was no guarantee they'd find Esmée, and none that they'd even make it back to where they now stood. Only one thing was certain: Esmée was in Paris right now, at that very moment. She might very well be in need of help; and that's what Audrey and Pica intended to do.

The sun broke through the clouds that had gathered in the western sky, casting what looked like the ray from a giant flashlight across the city landscape stretched out before them. Audrey and Pica stood a moment, admiring the white stone buildings now drenched in shades of rosy pink.

Across the river in a small café an accordion could be heard playing *La Vie en Rose*. Audrey looked at Pica whose eyes had never gazed upon anything so big and wide and grand as Paris before. Behind his wide eyes, she sensed a hint of fear. The impossibility of their mission was beginning to sink in at last, and Pica was scared. Resting one wing on his shoulder, Audrey smiled.

"We'll find her, Pica," she said. "I know we will."

Drawing his attention back to the city painted pink by the setting sun, she added, "Our chances are as rosy as those buildings over there."

…and just as much of an illusion; but she didn't mention that to the little magpie. She just patted his wing and smiled.

CHAPTER FIFTEEN

Les Ponts de Paris

Miles away, upriver from Audrey and Pica, Esmée sat in the lengthening shadows of the late afternoon. She was sore all over from being yanked out of the path of the tourist bus by Pierre. Weary and still in shock from her ordeal, she rested her limbs and gathered her strength.

Pierre had flown down from the top of the Arc de Triomphe to collect a tiny flower blossom growing in a nearby window box. He now returned with it held tightly in his two uppermost legs and presented it to Esmée. She drank every drop of its nectar with gratitude.

"*Merci*, Pierre. *Tu es très gentil.* I am feeling much better now. I do not want you to waste this beautiful afternoon by waiting on me."

"An afternoon spent with you could not possibly be a waste, *ma petite.* Besides, we've arrived here at the Arc de Triomphe at last -- just as we'd planned."

Pierre smiled and Esmée felt what remained of her pain and fatigue drain away. She was surprised to find within herself not the slightest hint of homesickness. It was as if she'd always lived in Paris, always spent time in Pierre's company. Her homesickness seemed to have been silently replaced by awe: awe over the beauties all around her; awe over the happiness blossoming inside her heart, too. For the first time in her life, Esmée felt like maybe home wasn't *only* to be found in Saint-Denis.

Maybe home was something she carried within her.

"Pas exactement. This isn't *exactly* how we'd planned it," Esmée laughed, "but it has been unforgettable."

"Oui, and the view *c'est magnifique, non?"*

Esmée stood up and walked over to the edge of the platform upon which she had been sitting. From the top of the Arc de Triomphe, she looked down each of the twelve streets which join to form a bustling traffic circle around the Arc. The city sprawl appeared to be both expertly planned *and* alive and throbbing with organic growth.

As the roads sped away from the Arc, the city was carved into increasingly wider wedges, separated by the diverging streets and crisscrossed by *rues* and *routes.* Esmée felt as if she were at the heart of it all -- like Napoleon, to whose honor the monument had been constructed. She imagined herself as the great warrior butterfly, standing triumphant atop her Arc. The height, the encircling traffic, and the grandeur of it all was positively dizzying.

"Oui, Pierre, it is magnificent."

"There is much more I would like to show you of my city, but it would take months to even scratch the surface. I have an idea, though… an idea that just might provide a good sample. And it would end with the most spectacular view of them all. I wonder, would you permit me the honor of showing you?"

"I cannot imagine anything more dazzling than what I have already seen; but I would be delighted to follow you. *Merci, mon ami.* Please, lead the way."

With that, Esmée spread wide her wings to the late afternoon breeze and threw her head back in the sunshine. She felt the excitement all around her and she was eager to see more. Mostly, she was eager to spend more time with Pierre. Whatever he had in mind, she had no doubt that it would be spectacular, indeed.

"We must fly back to the river then. We have a boat to catch," he said with a raise of his eyebrows.

Pierre extended his hand to Esmée, and they both took to the air. Flying southeast in the direction of the river, they headed back toward the Tuileries Garden and the Louvre. Beneath them, the broad, tree-lined boulevard led straight into the Place de la Concorde -- where their flight had begun earlier that morning.

As she flew over the Tuileries Garden and the site of her encounter with the barn owl, Esmée was surprised by the lack of fear or dread in her heart. Maybe it was the time spent on top of the triumphal Arc, or maybe it was the sense of confidence she felt at Pierre's side, but she almost hoped they'd meet the wicked barn owl on their way to the river. She'd kick him in the knee, she thought. Esmée had seen and experienced too much to ever let an old barn owl get the better of her again.

Just beyond the Louvre, near the Pont des Arts, Pierre led Esmée down to a quay on the river. Moored at the dock was an elegant, dinner boat. The two-storied boat had an enclosed dining room below decks in which a three-course gourmet dinner would be served to the guests.

Up above, an open-air deck with tables and chairs created the perfect setting to enjoy *les ponts de Paris* and the other sights, as they drifted downstream. A photographer charmed and coaxed the guests into posing against a backdrop of the Pont Neuf with Notre-Dame Cathedral in the distance; while the restless river carried the cruise boat west and then south toward a crescent-shaped island at a bend in the lower Seine.

"Here we are, *mademoiselle*."

"This?" Esmée asked, her eyes filled with excitement. "This is for *us*?"

"*Oui*. This is for *you*. Allow me…"

Taking her hand once more, Pierre guided Esmée as they flew over the water from the quay and onto the upper deck of the cruise boat where they landed on top of a handrail. Just then, the ship's crew cast the mooring lines off the boat and onto the dock. The captain maneuvered them away from the shore and into the steady current of khaki water. They were away, and Esmée was aboard her very first dinner cruise.

The sun was low in the western sky, casting long shadows across the river. The sky was a blaze of rose-red and blood-orange, which painted every building and framed every silhouette. On the water, the world was silent; the only sounds that could be heard were the whisper of the wind and gentle slap of the river against the hull. It was soothing as slumber, and Esmée felt it might all be just a dream.

Sprinkled across the upper deck of the boat, small, circular tables -- each with two chairs – provided comfortable places to sit, relax and enjoy the view. In a small crystal vase on each table, a bouquet of flowers breathed its perfume into the evening air. Pierre led Esmée to an empty table where they landed in the lap of a red rosebud.

"Après toi," Pierre said, offering Esmée the first drink of rosewater.

As she sipped, Pierre pointed out the spire of Notre-Dame Cathedral off in the distance.

"There, upon the *Île de la Cité*, sits the grand cathedral. Inside you will find a sacred space like none other. I will take you there someday; and we must meet *Frére* Apius' rooftop bees. Oh yes, it's true, *ma petite,* there *are* beehives on the roof of the cathedral."

Esmée shot an apologetic smile back at Pierre.

"What is it?" he asked.

"I believe you," she said with sheepish eyes. "I've met them already. And I have sailed through the light of heaven itself inside the walls of the cathedral."

"*Non.* You have? Then all of my surprises are discovered!" Pierre shook his head with playful defeat. "But have you tasted the famous honey, the Miraculous *Miel* of the *Ignifuge* bees?"

"That, I have not yet done. I was hoping we might do so together." Esmée took another sip of rosewater, smiling out from under her drooping antennae which concealed her blushing cheeks.

"That would be sweeter still," Pierre said with a slight bow. "Look," he pointed downstream, "our first bridge approaches: the *Pont du Carrousel.* There, off to the right, is the Louvre with its great, glass pyramid. This, you must see, *mademoiselle!"*

Esmée just smiled. She knew the *Pyramide du Louvre* quite well; but that was a story for another day.

"And there, just beyond the bridge and to the right, is the Arc de Triomphe du Carrousel. *C'est magnifique,* though much smaller than *your* Arc de Triomphe."

The *Pont du Carrousel* was a tan stone bridge spanning the river in three shallow arches. Esmée was concerned that the boat might not be able to duck beneath the low ceiling. As they passed under the bridge, Pierre flew up and touched the cold stone before landing again at Esmée's side.

"It is a tight squeeze, *non?* There. Do you see the four statues -- two at either entrance to the bridge's roadway? They are like guardians."

Pierre was happy to point out every detail, like an expert tour guide.

Esmée loved the sound the boat made as it echoed underneath the concrete spans. The sounds of splashing waves and gurgling water bounced from river to stone and back again. All of a sudden, the wide-open spaces of *Paris-beneath-a-clear-blue-sky* were confined to the space of a tiny room no bigger than the bridge's archway. As the boat emerged on the other side, leaving the bridge behind, all the world grew large again and spread itself out before them.

The upper deck of the boat was now empty of people; only Esmée and Pierre remained. Below, the dinner guests were beginning their first course of wine and cheese. Fine china, polished silverware, crystal wine glasses and starched white napkins set tables fit for a king and queen. Up above, two butterflies felt just as regal, drinking from Parisian roses and watching the sun set over the City of Lights.

Esmée sat looking out over the starboard side. Her eyes wore a smile and her face was aglow with a drowsy happiness. Pierre was struck by the quiet charm of this little butterfly from Saint-Denis. There was something timeless about her, something noble and strong. His mind took a photo of the moment and filed it away in a box of keepsakes in his heart. He would never forget this experience, forever frozen in time.

The boat now approached the *Pont Royal*. Similar in shape and color to the *Pont du Carrousel*, the *Pont Royal* spanned the Seine in five arches. Distinguished by the turrets embedded in its stone face, this was a taller structure with higher archways than the previous bridge. Esmée did not have the sensation of being in a small, confining room while underneath the *Pont Royal*.

Off to the right, the Tuileries Garden drew near. Esmée had spent a harrowing time there only the night before. Still, something had erased the darkness of that experience from her mind. Sailing past the wide, green space -- onboard the cruise boat with Pierre -- her heart was so full that no room could be found for anything else. She turned her eyes to the opposite side of the river, and away from the past.

There, the *Musée d'Orsay* occupied a building

that had once been a train station. Now, it housed the paintings of such artists as Claude Monet and Vincent Van Gogh. The enormous clock on the front of the museum was unmistakable. Inside, visitors could look out over the city from behind the transparent face of the clock. People have been looking out over the unchanging city for countless ages. The huge clock-window was a symbol of this; and Esmée smiled at the idea of being a part of the timelessness of it all.

The boat now floated toward a single arch joining right and left bank high above the brown water. The *Passerelle Léopold-Sédar-Senghor* is a metal footbridge with a name nearly as long as the bridge's span. Along with the *Pont des Arts,* from which Esmée and Pierre's cruise began, this bridge is also known for its *love locks.*

In a gesture of eternal commitment, lovers write their names on a padlock and secure it to the bridge's mesh walls. As with the love locks on the *Pont des Arts,* city officials regularly remove the heavy padlocks to prevent the bridges from being pulled down into the river below by the added weight. Nevertheless, new locks always appear within hours of removing the old.

The sky had darkened to a deep purple. Small, yellow bulbs now illuminated the upper deck of the boat, like strings of Christmas lights strung along the railings. As they continued down the river, the dim glow of the boat's lighting gave the approaching bridge an eerily medieval feel.

The *Pont de la Concorde* is a bulky, solid structure that looks more like an ancient castle with battlements than it does a bridge. Esmée thought that it appeared so heavy and immovable that the river itself might be prevented from flowing any further, should the bridge have a mind to stop it.

Off to the right was the entrance to the Tuileries Garden, where she had first met Pierre earlier in the day, and the *Place de la Concorde* with its Egyptian obelisk. The scenery was familiar, but their viewpoint was altogether new.

"We have come full circle, *mademoiselle*." Pierre whispered, in the light of a thousand tiny bulbs. "If our story is ever written," he winked with a grin, "it must begin in a sycamore tree in the Tuileries Garden, there." Pierre pointed off the starboard side of the boat.

"Not yet one day old, but what a story we have lived already, eh, *ma petite? Ah, the Pont Alexandre III...*"

Pierre interrupted himself and motioned with both wings in the direction of the next bridge on their way.

The *Pont Alexandre III* is perhaps the most splendid of all the bridges in Paris. Its white stone is trimmed in gold decorations, and its deck is illuminated by a parade of black, iron lampposts. The bridge spans the river in one spry leap, then gracefully blends in with the city around it.

Now, in the dark of this perfect night, Esmée saw the white of the *Pont Alexandre III* stained in the warm, orange glow from its lampposts. Pairs of golden, winged horses stood high atop granite pillars on either end of the bridge. Like a polished marble sculpture draped in precious jewels, silver and gold, the bridge captivated Esmée's attention.

"It is so beautiful," she said in hushed admiration. "I didn't know such things existed."

"Mais oui," Pierre replied, "and they are all here in Paris."

As the cruise boat continued its course down the river, and the guests below continued their *third* course – a dessert in the shape of a lattice-work tower – they passed beneath two more bridges. The boat then gradually slowed to a stop in the middle of the river.

"Is everything alright?" Esmée asked with

concern. She had not expected the cruise to end here.

"*Oui, mademoiselle,* everything is as it should be. We have arrived."

"Arrived?"

"At the *grand finale.* The boat will eventually return to where it started its journey, but not before... well, you will see."

Esmée was filled with anticipation. Pierre had done his best to keep the secret of their destination from her; and now that his waiting was over, he was bursting with excitement.

As the boat cleared the second bridge, Esmée saw it. Rising up from the banks of the Seine, like a giant of myth and mystery, the silhouette of a towering creature stood staring at the tiny boat. In the dark, it appeared to have its feet firmly planted at shoulder width. Tall and slender, there was an elegance about the way it walked down to meet the river. The two were soulmates; they were made to be together.

If the dinner cruise had been one, long, spectacularly unforgettable moment, this encounter was to be its crowning achievement.

Pierre leaned over and whispered in Esmée's ear, "The Eiffel Tower, *mademoiselle.* Like I said, the tower, she plays a game of hide and seek... but we have found her at last."

Esmée just stared up at the giant structure. The tower was so enormous that Esmée felt like the boat was caught between its feet. There was nothing nearby to compare it with; all other buildings disappeared in its shadow. Only the river was mighty enough for comparison. Despite the elegance of its bridges, the Seine preferred the company of the steel tower to that of anything else in Paris.

"Our timing, it is perfect, I think. The captain, he knows. Soon, everyone will come upstairs for a better view. We must choose our place before the deck is too crowded. Here, *ma petite;* over here is best, perhaps."

Pierre led the way up to the top of a flagpole at the back of the boat. There, Esmée landed beside him and shuddered in the cool night air. The flagpole was an excellent location from which to view the Eiffel Tower; but it left the butterflies exposed to the cold breezes coming up from the water.

"May I, *mademoiselle?*" Pierre offered one of his broad, soft wings to Esmée.

"*Oui, merci mon ami,*" she replied, drawing herself up under Pierre's wing.

The two butterflies now sat gazing up at the Eiffel Tower; snuggled up against the chill of the river with Pierre's wings to keep them warm. Dinner guests now filed up the stairs from the dining room to choose their own viewing locations. Beneath them all, the Seine flowed in silence to the sea; while all around, Paris gleamed in the faint flicker of gaslights. Esmée was in love; and where better to fall in love than in Paris?

"It is time," Pierre whispered.

As if obeying Pierre's cue, the tower -- which peeks its face out from behind buildings and flirts with the tourist's camera from every point in the city -- was now illuminated by 20,000 bulbs. Across its surface, white lights -- like strobes of fireflies chasing one another -- added movement to the great immovable structure.

The moment the Eiffel Tower burst into flame a choir of "oohs" and "ahs" went up from the mouths of every person aboard that boat. Some began recording the spectacle with their phones; some took photographs; some just held their loved ones close.

"*Oui,*" Pierre said with a chuckle, "As I said, the tower, she knows she is the star of the show; but she's a prima donna, *certainement. Mais oui,* she does love the attention."

Esmée turned and looked into Pierre's eyes. Deep happiness was flooding her heart, but she could not find the words to give it voice. She just sat there, wrapped in his wings, and smiled in silence. Leaning over, Pierre kissed Esmée's forehead with tenderness.

"The pleasure is mine, *ma petite.*"

CHAPTER SIXTEEN

Meet Marmot

Thursday morning dawned as rosy as the previous night's sunset. Audrey and Pica had spent the night just inside the city limits, hidden among a thicket of honeysuckle beside the river. Their excitement with the marauding crows the day before gave way to a night of deep sleep. When they awoke with the sun, they felt as if they'd only fallen asleep a few minutes before. The noise from the streets all around reminded them that they were far from Saint-Denis. But they had things to do; it was time to get moving.

Audrey and Pica had decided to follow the river up toward the right, into the heart of the city. They were convinced they'd have a much better chance of finding Esmée if they started their search in the busier, more crowded parts of Paris. The city was wide and sprawling, with densely packed streets and thousands of trees in which to hide. It was far too much for a tiny butterfly and a repetitive magpie to search on their own. If they were to be successful, they'd need some help.

Despite all of her reading, Audrey knew very little about how to find her way around Paris. She knew more about its ancient history and modern-day politics than about its layout. Though interesting topics, neither ancient history nor stuffy politics would be of much use to them in their search. Had a map of Paris blown into the churchyard in Saint-Denis one morning, Audrey would certainly have studied it and learned that the Louvre Museum was, in fact, located up the righthand branch of the river. As it was, they'd made the right choice, but purely by chance.

They needed much more than a good map, though. They needed some way to get the word out. Just like Lisette had done back in the fallow field of Monsieur Deschamps, Audrey and Pica needed to spread the word to friendly ears that Esmée was missing and possibly in danger. Even better, they needed some way to let Esmée know that they were looking for her; some way to assure her they were on their way. Maybe then, she'd be able to look for them, too.

Something Audrey had read about now came to mind. With luck, she just might be able to put this little bit of knowledge to work for them. Landing on the wrought iron terrace of a third story apartment -- not far from their honeysuckle bush -- Audrey took a sip of nectar from a curled-up morning glory bloom then began relating her story to Pica.

"It was a particularly warm Saturday morning, as I recall. Père Lamoine had decided to open a few windows in the parish library to let in the breeze. The air in that musty old room hadn't been replaced in ages; but not that many people would have noticed. Only Père Lamoine ever visited the library. With the windows open, I saw my chance. I didn't even care if I got locked inside; this was a real library filled with books that would never just blow into the churchyard -- no matter how windy it got. If there had been a steady supply of nectar, I would have been happy to be stuck inside forever with nothing to do but read!

"Anyway, as soon as the windows were open and Père Lamoine had left for Morning Prayer, I ducked inside. It was like a leather-bound heaven! The smell of binder's glue and printer's ink crowded into every inch and corner of that glorious room. The combination of mahogany tables, wood-paneled walls, and oak bookcases made me feel like I'd wandered into a prehistoric forest. Everywhere I looked, there were books on shelves, books on tables, stacks of books on countertops and windowsills. The comforting scent of tight-bound pages and loose-leaf parchment -- like the smell of leaves kicked up on an autumn day – made me feel like I'd finally found my home.

"Even though there were books piled high on every available surface, Père Lamoine's orderly mind had made its mark on the little library. The system of organizing the books on the shelves spilled over into the books stacked in other places, too.

"So, when the collection of *Reference Books* pertaining to *Animals*, specifically *Mammals*, native to *France*, with a focus on the city of *Paris* outgrew the shelves, the collection continued in an unbroken line onto the floor beside the bookcases. The A to Z reference books then snaked their way around the wall; up onto the windowsill; down the steps of a nearby footstool; and ended with *Zoology and the Art of Rosa Bonheur* which was leaned up against a water fountain near the back door of the library! It was in this collection that I found a most useful volume.

"On the first shelf, near the beginning of the collection, I spotted an old leather-bound edition with gold-foil lettering. It was a handsome book and it bore a unique maker's mark: a hooded monk, smiling, holding honeybees in his right hand. When I read the title and the author's name, it all made sense: *A Complete Guide to the Wildlife of Paris by Brother Apius of Glowermouth-on-Dart*.

"Of course, I'd heard the legend of the bees of Notre-Dame, and I knew that Brother Apius passed his final years studying the animals living in and around Paris. I had no idea he had written a book on the subject. Given his reputation for scientific studies and high learning, this was certainly a must-read.

"Enlisting the help of Père Lamoine's golden retriever, Orly -- who was kind enough to take the book down from the shelf and open the heavy cover for me – I spent the afternoon inside the mind of one of the greatest animal experts of all time. Brother Apius' research was painstakingly precise and catalogued every species of animal to be found within the city of Paris. One species, in particular, caught my interest."

Pica listened with great attention. He may have been the *only* one of Audrey's friends to enjoy her long, wordy stories. When others might summarize a story such as this, Audrey enjoyed giving the background and every detail along the way.

Pica found that he learned a lot by listening to Audrey. Maybe it was his humble heart that made learning possible. Some, like Lisette, might not take the time to listen; or if they did, they listened only with their ears and not with their brains. But Pica listened with his whole heart and that made all the difference. Audrey continued her tale.

"Brother Apius wrote two whole chapters about the groundhogs that live in the Bois de Boulogne forest. Over there."

Audrey pointed out over the river to the northwest where the city came to an abrupt end and a vast, green forest sprouted up. To their left, the Seine sagged south and then west, skirting its way around the crescent-shaped island that served as Audrey and Pica's rendezvous point should they get separated. As the river looped north again, it backed up against the Bois de Boulogne -- holding the forest on its right before leaving Paris behind and following its course to the sea.

"The learned monk said that the Boulogne groundhogs are exceptional for the system of tunnels they construct. These tunnels far exceed the Paris metro system in their length and coverage. Brother Apius estimated that there were hundreds of thousands of miles worth of groundhog tunnels crisscrossing the old city. He referred to it as an *interconnected network,* or *inter-net,* for short. He even stated that these clever groundhogs had found a way to extend the *internet* they invented across the river; though he was never able to find out exactly how they did so.

"If we can find one of these Boulogne groundhogs, just maybe they can put out a message across their internet and help us find Esmée. The more I think about the task ahead, the more I'm convinced that gaining the help of the groundhogs of Bois de Boulogne is our best bet. What do you think, Pica?"

This was the second time that anyone had ever asked Pica what he thought. He was quite sure of this fact, because the first time anyone ever asked him what he thought was earlier that same day. Audrey had asked his opinion on which branch of the river to follow; and now she was asking what he thought about her suggestion that they find a groundhog. No one but Audrey had ever taken much of an interest in Pica's thoughts. No one ever paid him much heed at all. Maybe that's why he repeated himself all the time, just to get someone's attention.

"Oui, oui!" he replied, excited to be able to share his opinion and thinking it was smartest just to go along with Audrey's idea.

"Very good," Audrey said, with conviction. "According to Brother Apius' book, groundhogs can most easily be found along the riverbank. Their network of tunnels often has openings near sources of water; these openings, Brother Apius referred to as *inter-net access points.* I think we should fly along the riverbank looking for *inter-net access points,* and hopefully we'll find a groundhog nearby. *Allons!*"

When Audrey made up her mind, action was never far behind. She was a unique sort of intellectual. She knew that reading about things and increasing her knowledge was always best when she then put it to good use. Although she could happily lose herself in a book for an entire afternoon without noticing the passage of time, she couldn't think of a better reason to do so than to help a friend in need.

Leaving their scenic perch on the third story terrace, Audrey and Pica flew down close to the surface of the river. It had been decided that Pica would take the righthand bank and Audrey would fly over the left. This way, they could cover twice as much ground in the same amount of time.

Pica stopped frequently, allowing Audrey time to catch up. He didn't mind, though, since it meant that he could take a drink from the river or pluck a berry or two (or three, or four, or more) from a briar patch. What felt like work to Audrey, felt very much like a leisurely day by the Yvette River back home, to Pica.

The two searchers scoured the riverbank, careful not to overlook any possible sign of groundhog activity. Every stick of driftwood, every rock or piece of debris was closely examined. Anywhere the overgrowth looked like it might be hiding a groundhog hole, Audrey and Pica flew in for a more detailed inspection.

As they neared the end of a second, larger, crescent-shaped island, Audrey spotted a cemetery off to the left. A street ran up the bank, between the cemetery and a line of trees. Between the line of trees and the water, there was what appeared to be a very small beach. It was, in fact, only visible when the river ran low and receded away from its banks.

There, on the muddy bank above the tidal beach,

Audrey spied a hole big enough for a groundhog. Calling to Pica from across the river -- where he was stuffing his cheeks with elderberries -- she landed in a tree overlooking the hole. Pica soon joined her, purple berry juice running down his beak and into his breast feathers.

"Look, Pica. Do you see them?"

"Quoi? Quoi?"

"Those are groundhog tracks, leading from the hole down to the river and back again. Some groundhog must have been drinking or fishing for catfish there. We found our hole; now we just need a groundhog to go with it. Maybe we can *make* one appear."

Flying down to the hole, Audrey landed without leaving a single print in the soft mud. Pica, on the other hand, flew down and landed beside her -- leaving four-toed tracks everywhere he tromped. Audrey ducked inside the groundhog hole, then paused.

"Faucon? Faucon?" Pica asked, confident he had figured out her plan.

"Oh no, my friend," she said. "The screech of a hawk worked well for us with the crows; but I'm afraid the groundhogs would just run and hide even deeper within their tunnels. I have another idea in mind."

Turning back toward the long, dark tunnel, Audrey cupped her wings around her mouth and started making a whistling sound. Her whistling was not at all like whistling a song or whistling for attention. Audrey's whistling sounded more like she was *speaking* in whistles.

She'd whistle a series of fast, choppy, high-pitched sounds; then she'd throw in a few lower, longer, more drawn-out ones. There was no detectable pattern. It was more like she was looking for the right words to say, or rather, whistle.

This went on for close to twenty minutes, but no groundhog appeared. Still, Audrey continued. She was undeterred; she had no choice, really. So much relied upon their success in finding a Boulogne groundhog to help spread the word about Esmée.

"I'm sure that I'm doing it right," she said to herself.

"Brother Apius was quite clear. The whistles he describes in his book are exactly like this and unique to this species. In fact," she now turned to Pica who was looking on, not sure if she was speaking to him or to herself, "in the United States -- specifically the Appalachian Mountains -- groundhogs are even *called* whistle-pigs. It's what they do!"

"Cochon? Cochon?"

"Not exactly, Pica; but that's not the point. The point is, I'm quite certain I'm speaking their language properly."

"Well, you are, I guess; but it's a bit outdated and a little like gibberish," came a voice from the riverbank above. "You're speaking version 2.0. There've been several upgrades since."

Beneath the trees, just above where Audrey and Pica now stood, there sat a furry, brown animal with buckteeth. He was not quite as big as a beaver; but there were many similarities, to be sure.

"As with most upgrades, I think you'll find version 5.1 much more efficient. Of course, when 5.0 came out there was that bug that resulted in a good bit of confusion. *'Tout droit'* and *'à droite'* sound similar enough; but the fact that they're used when giving directions, that caused some headaches. How many needless righthand turns were made, when 'straight ahead' was all that was intended? Building a tunnel is hard work. Building a tunnel twice because of shoddy directions, well, what can I say? All of that was corrected in the latest release. Yep, 5.1 is the way to go. My name's Marmot. Who are you folks?"

The little groundhog now stood up on his hind legs, in order to get a good look at Audrey and Pica. He was actually quite tall and the fur on his underside was somewhat lighter than the rest of him. There was a restless quirkiness to his quick, twitching movements; but his big, brown eyes were full of obvious intelligence. It was easy to see the characteristic Brother Apius described as "technical genius." This groundhog knew his stuff.

Audrey flew up to the lip of the riverbank and landed in front of Marmot.

"My name is Audrey Loriot, and this is Pica..." she hesitated, never knowing exactly how to introduce Pica; mostly because she wasn't sure if the second 'Pica' was his last name or just a repetition of the first. "This is Pica the magpie." She decided this was a safe option.

"Nice to meet you both. When I heard a choppy 2.0 at the riverbank *access point*, I couldn't help but come check it out. Of course, our *internet* has multiple *access points*, so I popped up over there, just to be safe. I gotta ask, though, where did you learn to speak Groundhog?"

With a matter-of-fact shrug of her shoulders, Audrey replied, "From a book by Brother Apius called *A Complete Guide to...*"

"*...the Wildlife of Paris!*" Marmot interrupted, without apology.

"Sure, everybody knows about Brother Apius and his research. He wrote some very complimentary things about Bois de Boulogne groundhogs. He's kind of a national hero among us, ever since he credited groundhogs with inventing the *internet*. And rightfully so. Our *interconnected network* of tunnels is second to none."

Marmot was clearly proud of his heritage; but a look of concern now crept across his clever face.

"Like I said, 2.0 is kind of outdated -- plus you were hashing it up pretty viciously -- so I might have misunderstood you; but it sounded like you were asking for help. Something about a lost friend?"

"Esmée! Esmée!" Pica blurted out, hopping twice in the air.

"Alright, Pica, I'll tell him," Audrey said, overlooking Marmot's comments about her inability to properly speak Groundhog 2.0.

"We're on a search and rescue mission. Our friend disappeared from Saint-Denis a few days ago without a word of warning. She was last seen at the Louvre Museum. The truth is, we're not sure if she's in any danger or not. All we know is what we've told you. It's just not like her to leave home let alone to go on an adventure. We're very worried, and eager to find her -- or at least hear for certain that she's alright."

"Saint-Denis?! That's no short hike. How in the world did you find your way here? Well, you can tell me all about *that* later. Right now, we have work to do. How can I help?"

"Oh, thank you!" Audrey was relieved. "What we really need is a way to get the word out about Esmée, so that if anyone has seen her or heard anything about her, they can let us know. Somehow, we also need to let Esmée know that we're looking for her. If she's in trouble, it might give her hope. If she's alright, then maybe it will help her find *us*. I know I'm asking a lot, but…"

Marmot held up one paw, interrupting Audrey in midsentence.

"That's no problem at all. You just happen to be talking to a *network manager*. I can connect you to the Boulogne *internet* and we'll start making things happen in no time. Describe Esmée to me; we'll send a description of her out across the *net*."

Audrey described Esmée to Marmot, from her fuzzy, brown antennae to the smiley-face-shaped birthmark under her right wing. Not a detail was left out. She told him about how Pica had been the last to see her at the train station in Saint-Denis, and how Lisette, Pica and she had seen the photo of Esmée in *Le Journal*.

"Lisette?" Marmot interrupted, once again. "Who's she?"

"She's Esmée's best friend from birth. She's the one who mounted a search for her back home," Audrey replied.

"Where is she now? Is she lost, too?"

Audrey paused, hesitant to answer Marmot's question. She didn't know how to answer without sounding like she was faulting or judging Lisette for staying home. In fact, she was afraid to even think about the situation with Lisette. She knew it would only make her angry.

"Pica and I left without her," she said, with caution in her voice.

Marmot sensed that there was something more to it, but he decided not to press the matter.

"This photo from *Le Journal*, where was it taken?" Marmot's tone changed. He sounded like he might already know the answer to his own question.

"On top of the *Pyramide du Louvre*. She appeared to be… posing for the camera. I know how crazy that…"

Marmot interrupted yet again, which was becoming a habit and just seemed to be "his thing."

"It's not crazy at all. I've seen the picture. It was all over the *internet*. Every groundhog in the Bois de Boulogne must have seen '*le papillon reine du Louvre.*' She's kind of famous. Well, that'll make our job easier. Turns out, we don't need a description anymore. We have a photo; and that's even better. We'll just need to copy it and distribute it with a message asking if anyone has seen or heard anything of your friend… uh, Esmée, right? Well, something's bound to turn up if we do that."

Audrey and Pica looked at each other. Their friend was *famous* in Paris? Could it be they were talking about a different butterfly altogether? This couldn't be Esmée. *Their* friend was shy, reserved, never wanted to leave home, and certainly wouldn't be interested in posing for cameras on top of the *Pyramide du Louvre*. But they'd seen the photo with their own eyes. They'd seen the birthmark beneath her right wing. It *was* Esmée, just not the Esmée they knew from… well, a few days ago.

"I'll send this out over the network straight away. We'll send the photo as soon as we can get it copied. Do you two have somewhere to spend the night? It's getting dark and there's not much more we can do until morning. Besides, I expect we'll start getting some data back on all of this pretty quick. Why not spend the night at my place? I'd be happy to have you."

Audrey turned to Pica, "It *is* getting late, my friend. What do you think?"

That made three times in one day. Pica was feeling pretty good about himself. What started out with Lisette blaming him for "losing" Esmée at the train station, ended up with Audrey asking for his opinion three times in one day. In Lisette's eyes, he was part of the problem. To Audrey, he was a partner.

"Oui! Oui!" he replied, without hesitation.

"We'd be delighted to join you for the night. Thank you, *monsieur* Marmot," Audrey said, with relief.

"Fantastic!" Marmot said, rubbing his paws together. "I haven't had guests in ages. Right this way!"

Leading them to a hole in the ground a few feet away from where Audrey had been whistling in "outdated Groundhog," Marmot motioned for Pica and Audrey to go first.

Pulling Audrey aside, Marmot inquired, "Your friend, he likes to repeat himself a lot, doesn't he?"

"Yes," came Audrey's reply, "but he never

interrupts."
Marmot got the point.

CHAPTER SEVENTEEN

The Internet

Neither Audrey nor Pica had ever been in a groundhog tunnel before. They were both creatures of the sky; they'd never gone *underground*. At first, they didn't know what to make of it all. Instead of blue sky and green fields, they were surrounded by cold, damp dirt. Instead of brisk breezes, they were greeted by warm, stagnant air. Wide-open spaces shrunk down into cramped darkness. It was the exact opposite of everything they'd ever known. To a flying animal, a hole in the ground can feel very much like a prison cell. Still, the newness of the experience was curiously interesting to them both.

The opening of the tunnel was barely wide enough for Marmot to squeeze through. Audrey figured that was on purpose. Any creature small enough to get in would pose very little threat to a groundhog. Any creature too big to fit through the door was also much too big for a groundhog to fight off. Luckily, the real dangers – foxes, dogs, and bobcats – were more likely to get stuck in the entryway.

Once inside, anyone without a map or a personal guide would soon be hopelessly lost. But Marmot was an expert guide. He moved without hesitation, always sure of his way. Though he started out giving directions from just behind Pica and Audrey (mostly because he wanted to ask Audrey about Pica's habit of repeating himself),

Marmot soon found himself in the front of the group. It was much easier to encourage Audrey and Pica to keep up through the sharp turns and complicated intersections than to continually call out, "Left. Right. Straight ahead. Right, again. Now, left."

How Marmot managed to navigate the network of tunnels with such flawless confidence, Audrey couldn't begin to explain. He was like an expert sailor reading subtle hints on the surface of the sea. The shape of the tunnel walls, the smell of the earth, even the specific bugs and worms living in the muddy dirt, all seemed to communicate some meaning to the young groundhog. Marmot reminded them, "I *am* a *network manager*, after all. I spend a lot of time just surfing the *interconnected network*. Too much, really."

Inside the first dozen yards or so of tunnel, it was tight and wet. The hole was too near the riverbank and it was obvious from the puddles and watermarks that it flooded whenever the river ran high. Its nearness to the water was most likely a security feature, designed to keep out would-be predators. It worked quite well.

A heavy odor of damp ground hung in the stale air. It wasn't unpleasant, just overpowering; and it coated the inside of Pica's nose. After half an hour underground, the oozy smell of decaying plants and worms was all he'd be able to smell for the rest of the day. Strange creatures peeked out from the walls and ceiling; creepy, crawly creatures with more eyes and legs than Audrey or Pica thought necessary. As they walked along, squirmy tails of worms and grubs burrowed their way into the packed soil all around them.

The farther they walked, the steeper their path became; the tunnel was climbing up and away from the river toward street level. In fact, Audrey and Pica could feel the rumbling of cars and trucks, just overhead. Every now and then, when an especially big truck bounced along the road above, a little clump of dirt would break free from the roots of plants hanging down into the tunnel. This was especially disheartening to the two inexperienced visitors, who worried that the roof might give way and the road come tumbling down on their heads.

All along their route, holes opened up to the left and right, revealing more and more tunnels identical to their own. There were no signs, no arrows, no mile markers by which to navigate. Still, Marmot proceeded at great speed, taking each turn with assurance. Pica hopped along as fast as he could; leaping forward in low, cramped flight, whenever the width of the passageway permitted. Audrey flitted full steam ahead without any trouble at all.

Every few feet, a pale light – just bright enough to light their path – shown from a rectangular panel on the wall. The panel was flat and thin, and appeared to be embedded in the earth itself. Running along between the panels, a black wire connected them each to the other like a string of pearls. Audrey stopped a moment in front of one of the glowing screens.

"They're tablets," Marmot said, noticing her interest in the mysterious rectangle. "iPads and such. We find them discarded all over the city in trash cans and dumpsters. We bring them down here and use them as path lights. They're solar-powered, too. With a little aluminum foil, a couple of lenses from old eyeglasses and some blueberry juice, you can make a very effective solar panel."

"I've read about things like that, but never seen it done. Fascinating." Audrey was geeking out just a little, as her eyes followed the string of tablets, trying to learn more about how they worked.

"Oh yeah, we're totally off the grid down here! 'Self-sufficient and green, that's the way to be,' we always say! Come on, we're almost to my place." Marmot continued the tour.

Big, cement walls now appeared in their path. Some of them formed the sides of the tunnel, while others stood squarely in the middle of the path. In these instances, the tunnel would split into two branches which then forked around the concrete obstruction before rejoining again as one tunnel on the other side.

Some of the cement walls had large chunks of concrete missing from them. Marmot knocked on the side of the wall with his paw as he passed by, and the ragged opening echoed like an empty concert hall. Approaching the damaged concrete, Pica peered inside the hole. Aside from cobwebs and a few hairy spiders, he was unable to see anything at all. It was just as well that he couldn't. An uneasiness began to unhinge their hearts.

The wet earthiness of the tunnel had been replaced by a musty odor of uncertain origin. There appeared to be far fewer insects living in this part of the tunnel, only spiders and scurrying millipedes. Most unnerving, however, was the fact that the tunnel now echoed for no obvious reason. It was the same width and size as it had been since they entered; but the presence of these concrete boxes added an echoing infinity to their surroundings. Coldness now seeped into their bones.

"What are these?" Audrey asked with apprehension. "They're not…"

"Vaults, yep!" Marmot cut in, with his matter-of-fact way. "We've crossed the street. We're now in the middle of the cemetery."

"Oh," Audrey felt a chill run up her long back which shook her antennae with icy trembling. "Then these are…"

"Yep," interrupted Marmot.

"And inside, there are…"

"Sure are!" (He did it again) "Inside every one of them. Vault, casket, and owner!"

Marmot seemed to enjoy the look of grave discomfort on Audrey and Pica's faces. He kept glancing at them out of the corner of his eye, gauging their level of wariness and fear. Truth be told, most groundhogs didn't like to travel the length of the *Cimetière Pierre Grenier,* let alone live in the middle of it like Marmot did.

"Is your house nearby?" Audrey was suddenly very eager to be done with their journey.

"Sure is. Not far now!"

"*Bon…bon,*" said Pica, under his breath.

Walking through a cemetery is scary enough but tunneling through one in the dark is downright terrifying. Back home, in Saint-Denis, the only animals that spent time in such places were crows. Pica had no love for crows and he *always* avoided the cemetery.

Being *underground* in a cemetery didn't make him feel much safer, even if the crows couldn't reach him down there. It just wasn't natural, he decided; none of it was. Birds had no business tunneling through the dirt. He began to feel the walls closing in on him; and he was eager to see the blue sky again.

The tunnel began to widen, at last giving way to a great empty chamber with a high, rounded ceiling. Around the outside of the room, a succession of openings now appeared. This was an intersection point for dozens of tunnels.

The circular room was much brighter than what they'd grown accustomed to. Light from the surrounding tunnels spilled into the chamber, filling it with a brilliant, warm glow. Above each of the entryways a rectangular sign hung, displaying the name of each tunnel. In white lettering against a blue background, not unlike the RER train station signs, Audrey and Pica read the various route names: *Cat3, Cat5, Cat5e* (an easterly branch), and *Cat6* were among the names.

Marmot explained further, "At regular points

along the network, the different routes all come together in what we call *routers*. From here you can choose a new route to take or continue along the same route. We've been on the *Cat5*. It stands for *Cemetery and Tidewater #5*, since it runs from the tidewater beach where you were whistling 2.0, (Audrey rolled her eyes) all the way to the cemetery we just passed through. It's one of several such routes. But now we'll take that one over there."

Marmot pointed across the *router* to another tunnel opening, identical in every way to all the others.

"That's the *T1*, because it runs from this *router* all the way to the *Tennis Club de Paris*. But we're not going that far. My house is very near. Straight ahead!" And Marmot was off again.

The *T1* tunnel was different from the *Cat5* they'd been on ever since leaving the river. The *T1* felt like a road less traveled. Whereas, the *Cat5* was smooth and made level by the traffic of many feet, the *T1* was bumpy. Audrey wondered why this might be, until she noticed the way in which Marmot moved through the tunnel. He walked on all four legs, but his belly bounced along the bumpy ground like a motorboat on the surface of a wavy lake. Up and down his tummy went, as if he were bodysurfing his way through the tunnel. As a result, his round stomach made waves in the soft, earthen floor.

"Here we are," Marmot declared, turning a sharp corner to the right. "Apartment 4G, Route T1, Bois de Boulogne, Paris, France. Come on in!"

Pushing open a small, round, wooden door, Marmot led his guests inside his home and closed the door behind them. What they saw was completely unexpected. The tunnel outside had been small, muddy and cramped. The only light available to guide their steps had been the dull glow of a thousand tablet screens. Inside Marmot's apartment, it was another story altogether.

The front door opened onto a wide entryway.

From the ceiling, there hung a great chandelier; and immediately to the left, half a dozen coat hooks lined the wall. If it seems odd to you that a Bois de Boulogne groundhog should ever have need of an overcoat, then you've certainly never visited Paris in the winter.

The chandelier was very peculiar and immediately captured Audrey and Pica's attention. Much like the tablets strewn along the walls of the tunnel outside, the chandelier was constructed entirely of old smartphones. There must have been forty or fifty phones hanging amid a collection of glass shards and quartz pebbles, each secured to the ceiling and held in place by an old fisherman's net. Every phone in the chandelier displayed the same screensaver: a flickering fireplace. The overall effect was that of a cloud of flame and ice crystals which cast a warm and inviting light on the entryway of Marmot's home.

Beneath the coat hooks affixed to the wall, a long, narrow bench with a hinged seat provided an excellent place to sit as well as to store one's shoes. Of course, no matter how cold it gets in Paris, groundhogs never actually wear shoes; that would be entirely unseemly. But they often entertain badgers who are known to wear boots from time to time, especially when coordinated with a jacket and a smart waistcoat. However, badgers are also known for their general grumpiness. So, a nice, relaxing bench upon which to sit while removing one's shoes is an absolute must.

Above the long, wooden bench, a rectangular mirror hung on the wall. On either side of the mirror, three oval picture frames -- each bearing the engraved image of a groundhog -- were displayed with pride. Marmot directed Audrey and Pica's attention to the photos.

"This is my grandmother on my father's side," he said, pointing at the photo on the upper left.

"She was one of the inventors of *Binary Groundhog*. Her generation used it to create a much easier way to communicate across the *interconnected network* of tunnels. Pretty cool, really. In those days, the network was much smaller than it is today. It hadn't even crossed the river yet. The invention of the *Binary* language meant that messages could be shared much faster than by *snail mail*."

Pica looked at Marmot, scratching his head with one wing. It was obvious he'd never heard of *snail mail* before.

"Let me explain." Marmot continued, addressing Pica's confused stare.

"Everybody knows that snails are natural postmen; they're built for delivering the mail. They have excellent memories and can remember long messages really well. If the message is written down, they just strap it right onboard their shell; if it's small enough, they can carry it inside. But it takes them forever to travel any distance at all! Poor little guys just skate along on that one slimy foot of theirs. A better way had to be found and Grandma Gallien found it!

"Thanks to the invention of the *Binary Groundhog* language, snails were no longer needed to deliver the mail. They were able to retire early and many of them moved to the surface to live among the fallen logs and rocky streams of the Bois de Boulogne forest. With our new language, we groundhogs were able to pass along *longer* messages using fewer words. It was a huge breakthrough!"

Marmot flicked a tiny speck of dust off the picture frame, straitened it with care, then motioned toward the photograph hanging just below.

"This is my dad, Edmund Gallien. Of course, you've heard of *him*."

Marmot paused and looked at Audrey and Pica,

waiting for confirmation. Instead, the two wore blank stares, having never really heard of Marmot's father.

"Ah well, he's quite famous among the groundhogs of *le Bois de Boulogne,* too. Dad invented the *Groundhog 2.0* language, which you were struggling with pretty badly when we met."

Marmot snorted with laughter. Audrey just scowled and straightened her wings with a huff.

"Without the much more efficient *Groundhog 2.0,* we'd still be sending messages along the internet using *Binary*! Can you imagine?"

Neither Audrey nor Pica could imagine. Truth be told, they had no idea what in the world Marmot was talking about.

"Anyway, 2.0 was twice as fast as *Binary*. Without it and the upgrades that have come ever since its invention, we'd all be whistling like the whistle-pigs of the American Appalachians! We'd be no better than woodchucks! Those poor guys. All they ever do is answer the question about how much wood they could chuck. Embarrassing, really. And don't even get me started on that Punxsutawney Phil character. Crazy Americans. Not our best spokesman, if you ask me. Well, enough about that. Come in, please. Make yourselves at home."

Marmot led them out of the entryway and down a hall which opened out onto a large room, at the center of which was a circular fireplace. A bundle of twigs sat in a pile on the floor beside a hearth made of river stone. Marmot picked up a poker and began uncovering the glowing embers, adding a few twigs to encourage the fire. A funnel-shaped chimney hung above the open flames. Made of a mosaic of brick, limestone, quartz, and river rock, the chimney glistened in the flickering light of the fireplace.

Marmot's living room was perfectly round, and the fireplace was located in the exact center of the room.

Around the hearth, semicircular benches, rocking chairs, and chaise lounges sat with their various pillows arranged with care. The floor was comprised of multicolored river stone, packed into a hard, level surface. It was as clean and dry as any tile or wood flooring. Braided rugs lay beneath the benches, chairs and lounges; organizing them into groups by the color of the rug upon which they sat.

Just to the left of the fireplace, occupying a quarter of the room, the gnarled and tangled roots of a great tree exited the floor and entered the ceiling above in a massive jumble of twisted limbs. Hidden among the knots and spaces of the enormous mesh of wood, bird nests and squirrel dens could be seen by an observant eye. Potted plants sat cradled in the arms of tree roots, while climbing ivy and flowering vines wove their way in and out, up and around the living structure. It was a jungle of lush green leaves and colorful flowers right there in the middle of Marmot's underground apartment.

After a long journey through the cold, damp tunnel, the fireplace was a welcome change for Audrey and Pica. The weary magpie flew over and landed on the hearth in front of the glowing coals, stretching out his wings and letting the heat soak into his limbs. After a moment, Pica flopped down on his tailfeathers. Pointing his four-toed feet straight at the crackling fire, he wiggled them with delight. He had decided that he would stay right there just as long as he was allowed.

Audrey flitted past the fireplace and landed on the back of one of the rocking chairs. Glancing up at the high ceiling of the living room, she felt like she was outside beneath a starlit sky once more. Similar to the floor of Marmot's spacious apartment, the ceiling was a glimmering collection of stone and glass embedded in the velvet blue earth above. Her eyes followed the great dome back down toward the fireplace where Pica sat soaking in the soft glow of the firelight. She smiled.

"Rest beside the fire, while I gather something for your dinner. The sooner you eat, the sooner you can sleep."

Marmot left the room, while Pica grew sleepy by the fire. Audrey rocked back and forth on the rocking chair, looking around the living room as she did. Apart from the tree roots and fireplace, the room was quite simple. Tidy, clean and uncluttered, Audrey could see that Marmot lived alone and liked things just so. There was a place for everything, and everything was in its place.

There was no noise from the busy streets above; no heavy scent of stagnant air from the tunnel outside. The room smelled of woodsmoke and hominess, candlewax, oil lamps and homecooked food. As with Pica, Audrey felt the comfort of Marmot's apartment soak into her like warm water into a dry sponge. She was tired, and she'd only just realized it. Bedtime couldn't come soon enough. Even food failed to appeal to her quite so much as sleep. Her eyes began to blink more slowly; her head began to bob.

Marmot was in the kitchen busily gathering together a bowlful of hazelnuts and blueberries. Just as Audrey and Pica began drifting off, Marmot entered the living room again. Beside the screen of tree roots, a tiny spring bubbled up from the earthen floor and trickled down a waterfall of limestone before pooling in a basin. It was here that Marmot set the bowl of nuts and berries, inviting Pica to eat, drink and refresh himself before giving in to his fatigue.

"There's nothing I can offer you that's more delicious than this," Marmot said to Audrey, motioning to the cascade of flowers dripping down the giant roots of the unseen tree. "Please, help yourself, my little friend."

Audrey thanked Marmot politely then flew from the back of the rocking chair and landed upon the tangle of polished tree roots, drinking deeply from a purple blossom she found growing there. She drank for what must have been fifteen or twenty minutes. The fireside nectar coursed through her tired body, putting her worries to rest and laying a comforting drowsiness upon her eyelids. Curling up among the leaves and flowers of the sheltering roots, Audrey could resist no more, and soon drifted off to sleep.

Finishing his bowl of berries and hazelnuts, Pica hopped over to the tinkling waterfall and quenched his thirst in the cool spring water. Flapping up to a branch high above where Audrey now rested, Pica found a readymade nest that was just his size. Snuggling down into it, he buried his beak in the fluffy feathers of his chest; pulled his wings in close; and quickly fell asleep.

Marmot picked up the empty bowl with great care, so as not to awaken his sleeping guests. He placed it in the wash basin beside the waterfall, then stoked the fire with a few more twigs. Tiptoeing across the living room floor, Marmot paused and turned before leaving the room.

"Sleep well, my new friends," he whispered. "Goodnight."

He walked through a small door near the hallway that led to the main entrance, then closed the door behind him without a sound.

Within the safety and warmth of Marmot's home, they had both found an unexpected friend and a much-needed rest. A few yards above their sleeping heads, Paris hummed with activity. Trucks grumbled down narrow side streets, delivering goods to shops and restaurants. Taxis and buses ferried tourists from one selfie-opportunity to the next. Car horns honked and police sirens blared, as pedestrians flooded into overcrowded intersections and streamed down the streets of the ancient city.

Somewhere amid the chaos and commotion, one

tiny butterfly escaped the notice of everyone who passed by. In the fears of Audrey and Pica, Esmée was lost and alone, miles from home, and surrounded by unfriendly faces and strange, lonely places. Little could they imagine that at that very moment Esmée was happier than she'd ever been before. She'd found something entirely unforeseen in the City of Lights. She'd found love.

CHAPTER EIGHTEEN

Megalina the Field Mouse

What was this new scent? This smell of sweet delight? This aroma of happiness? Like warm blueberries on a bright, blue summer day. Like hazelnuts turned soft and sweet by the heat of the afternoon. But wait, there was also something altogether unfamiliar hidden in this new smell. Like the scent of fluffy-cloud pastries made of cream and sugar. Was it a dream? Could it be real?

Becoming aware, sleep began to shuffle off of Pica's head and shoulders like bedsheets; until at last, he was able to open one eye, then two. Bleary and blurry, the room now came into focus. He recognized the nest in which he had spent a restful night, and the enormous wall of tree roots that had held him cupped and close. He saw the fireplace in the center of the room, its red and orange flames throbbing beneath the funnel-shaped chimney. His eyes were drawn to the nearby spring with its waterfall of river stones. This was a pleasant place to awaken from a good night's sleep.

The scent now pushed its way past all he was seeing and made itself the focus of Pica's attention. It was the smell of perfect happiness.

"Good morning," Marmot said, as he entered the room with a plate in his hands. "Who's hungry?"

"Moi! Moi!" Pica called from his nest in the tree roots.

Audrey stretched her arms and legs. This may have been the first time in her life that she'd slept-in past sunrise. Of course, she didn't have any little brothers or sisters to try and escape from, in Marmot's apartment. It was *safe* for her to sleep-in *here*.

"*Moi aussi,*" Audrey said, through a slow yawn.

"I hope you like blueberry-Nutella crêpes, Pica. I made them just for you."

Marmot was speaking Pica's language! This explained the heavenly aroma that had tickled his nose and roused him from sleep. Blueberries were his favorite, and Nutella – as you know – is made from hazelnuts. Pica loved hazelnuts. He'd never had a crêpe before, but surely it must be the sweet, fluffy cloud he'd been smelling. With blueberries and hazelnuts, you just couldn't go wrong.

"*Merci! Merci!*"

The hungry magpie flew down from his nest and landed right next to a plate prepared just for him. Without delay, he bit into the folded crêpe -- stuffed full of blueberries and drizzled with Nutella; his mouth exploded with pleasure. He ate every crumb in three skillful gulps, then turned with hopeful eyes toward Marmot.

"Plenty more where that came from, my friend!" Marmot loaded Pica's plate with another crêpe then patted him on the back. "I'll keep 'em coming. Don't you worry."

Pica was reassured and dove right into his second-ever crêpe, having no doubt that a third and fourth awaited him. Audrey flitted over to the low table and landed beside a saucer Marmot had laid out for her.

"And for the lady, honeysuckle dew." Marmot said, with a dishtowel draped over his arm like a waiter in a fine restaurant. "Enjoy, my friends. For me, I'll have my usual: salted catfish, straight from the Seine."

Just as Marmot was opening his mouth to enjoy his salted catfish, a tiny bell rang from somewhere inside the apartment. Everyone looked up from their breakfast at the sound; though, of the three of them, only Marmot did not look surprised.

"That figures. The moment I sit down to a meal, the *internet* perks up to interrupt me. Ah well, let's see what it has to say."

Getting up from the table, Marmot walked over to the door near the hallway leading to the front entrance; the same door he had taken the night before.

Pausing a moment, he turned back toward the table and said, "This might interest you both. Come on in."

He then walked through the door and out of sight. Audrey and Pica left their breakfast with great reluctance and followed Marmot. Beyond the door, they encountered a mind-boggling display.

The room in which they now found themselves was very different from the living room. The floor appeared to be made of mismatched planks of sanded driftwood, rescued from the river. The boards were all different shapes, sizes and colors; but they were skillfully fitted together into a smooth and level surface. The ceiling was held in place by several thick wooden beams, which formed a grid much like a tic-tac-toe board. Between the beams, the ceiling was covered over in white plaster, which reflected what light there was and brightened the room.

Unlike the living room, this space was rectangular. In each of the four corners, an oil lamp sat upon a shelf, behind which a mirror had been attached to the walls on each side of the corner. The mirrors cast the flickering light from the lamps toward the center of the room. Despite having no fireplace, it was just as warm and bright as in the living room.

What caught Audrey and Pica's attention was the long side of the rectangular room, directly opposite the doorway. From ceiling to floor and corner to corner, the wall was lined with rows and columns of tiny doors, no bigger than a letterbox. Each door had a brass knob in the middle and what appeared to be a name plate, overtop of which was a sliding toggle switch. On a few of the doors, the switch was showing a green label; on the majority, a red one. There must have been over a thousand of these tiny doors.

Hanging from the ceiling above the entrance to the room, a polished silver bell still echoed with its recent chime. Marmot reached up and silenced it with one paw.

"Wow! Wow!"

Pica was nearly speechless. Still riding high on the excitement from his very first crêpe experience, he was completely overwhelmed by what he now saw.

"What is this place?" asked Audrey.

She was the last to enter the room and landed on top of the bell to take it all in.

"This is the *server room*," Marmot replied, while inspecting the huge collection of tiny doors; obviously searching for one in particular.

"This is where all the messages traveling across the *interconnected network* of tunnels come in, get sorted, and are then either stored or sent back out again. As a *network manager*, it's my job to decide which messages go where and how fast. Ah, here it is."

Marmot's eye was drawn to a new, green label on one of the thousand tiny doors. Walking over to its place on the wall, he pulled on the brass knob, and the wooden door flipped open. Marmot reached a paw inside the opening and pulled out a folded piece of paper. Swinging the door up on the two hinges attached to its bottom edge, he shut it tight and walked back to where Audrey and Pica stood waiting.

"Just what I was hoping to find," he said, opening the folded piece of paper. "A reply."

"A reply to what?" Audrey asked, still rubbing the sleep from her eyes and trying to make sense of everything she was seeing.

"Last night, after you both fell asleep, I sent a message out across the *internet*, asking if anyone had seen or heard anything about Esmée. I was hoping to have news this morning; I just didn't expect it would be this early."

Marmot opened the message and started to read it to himself. Audrey and Pica were rivetted to Marmot's facial expression, trying to decipher what the message could say.

"Ah," Marmot began, in his usual way, "I see. Yes. Excellent idea. Any minute, then. We should finish our breakfast first. Very good."

Walking over to a desk pushed up against the wall, he took a pencil from the center drawer, and scribbled a quick response on the bottom of the piece of paper. Walking back to the tiny door from which he had taken the message, he opened it; put the paper back inside; closed the door; and slid the toggle switch from green to red. He then turned the knob clockwise one-half turn, without explanation. Audrey and Pica were bursting with curiosity.

"She'll be here soon, most likely. So, we should finish our breakfast."

"Esmée? Esmée?" Pica asked with excitement.

"Has she been found?" Audrey could not believe their good fortune. She was impatient to know the details. "Where is…"

"I'm sorry," Marmot began, cutting Audrey off. "I meant to say that *Megalina* will be here shortly. The message was from her. Nothing has been received about Esmée yet."

Audrey and Pica's hearts sank like two, cold lumps of lead. In the quiet comfort of Marmot's home, they had almost begun to forget the urgency of their errand. Now, the dreadful concern and fear about their friend's wellbeing settled back into their hearts and minds. They even started to feel guilty for having allowed themselves to take a break for the night.

Marmot continued, "She received my message from last night and responded, suggesting we copy the photo from *Le Journal* and distribute it out along the network. Excellent idea, I think. Megalina's just the one to do it for us, too."

"We have to get going," Audrey said, irritated with herself and filling up with anxiety. "I should never have waited this long. We've spent too much time here..."

"But where will you go?" Marmot interrupted. "I'm sure that if we send the photo out and wait just a little bit longer for a response, something useful will come in. Otherwise, you're just running out into the dark without a plan. A little patience always pays off."

Audrey knew he was right. She and Pica had wanted to find the groundhogs because they needed their help. Now, they just needed to wait for that help to reach them. But restlessness was becoming rampant inside her heart. She had to do *something*, even if only to feel like she was making progress.

"I can't just wait around while Esmée wanders lost and in danger. I can give you one hour more, but then we *must* leave." Audrey looked at Pica, who voiced his agreement.

"Fair enough," Marmot said. "Let's finish breakfast quickly then. You won't get far if you're hungry; and even three crêpes won't last a magpie very long." He smiled with understanding at Pica.

As they were finishing their hasty breakfast and clearing the dishes from the table, a knock came at

Marmot's front door. Putting the dishes down, he scurried over and eagerly opened the door. Standing in the doorway, Audrey and Pica could see… no one at all.

"Good morning!" Marmot said to no one. "I got your message. Come on in."

Stepping aside, Marmot held the door open long enough for no one to enter, then closed it, and led the way into the living room. Audrey and Pica still couldn't see any cause of the knock at the door. They were beginning to worry about Marmot's sanity. Was he imaging things? Too much time spent on the *internet* was beginning to take its toll on the little groundhog.

"Audrey. Pica. Allow me to introduce you to Megalina."

Marmot turned and motioned toward the floor behind him. Audrey flitted down from the table to take a closer look. Pica hopped off the bench and joined her. There, standing just behind Marmot, was Megalina the field mouse.

"Good morning everyone!" she squeaked. "It'*th* a plea*th*ure to meet you."

The word "tiny" didn't begin to describe Megalina. If she'd had wings, she could have passed for a butterfly. Even her ears were uncommonly small for a field mouse. One physical feature, however, stood out. Megalina had exceptionally, incredibly, impressively large teeth; the two front top teeth, to be precise.

"I under*th*tand we have a photo that need*th* copying."

Megalina's big, beautiful teeth got in the way of every "S" her tiny tongue tried to say. Instead of a clear, sharp "S," her teeth chopped it up into a short, breathy "th." She didn't mind, though. She knew that her teeth were meant for greater things than just saying "S-es." She knew very well that what might appear to be a shortcoming, is often a strength in disguise; and

Megalina's teeth were a strength, to be sure. She knew just how to use them.

Climbing up the bench and onto the table, Megalina produced a newspaper clipping from a bag she had slung over her shoulder. Straightening it out and smoothing the wrinkles, Audrey and Pica recognized it as the photo of Esmée from *Le Journal*.

"We'll need *th*ome paper," she said to Marmot. "And a lot of it."

"Right!" Marmot responded and headed straight for the *server room* desk. Returning with arms stacked high with paper, he set it all down on the table next to Megalina.

"Perhap*th* a gla*th* of water, too," she added as an afterthought. "Thi*th* much copying tend*th* to dry me out."

"Of course," and Marmot was off again, returning without delay, carrying a field mouse-sized thimble of water which he put down on the table.

"Ok, here we go," Megalina took a sip of water, then straightened the photo once more before picking up the first sheet of paper.

Using her two front teeth, Megalina began biting the sheet of paper in a rapid-fire whirlwind of activity. She held the sheet in both hands, turning and tilting it like a seamstress guiding fabric through a sewing machine. All the while, her eyes darted from the *Le Journal* photo, to the paper she was holding in her hands, and back again.

She had a look of intense concentration in her eyes, like a painter who studies her subject then rushes toward the canvas -- capturing what she sees in a series of quick brushstrokes. This went on for maybe two minutes; until at last, she put the sheet of paper down on the table next to the newspaper clipping.

Audrey and Pica could hardly believe their eyes. There on the table in front of them sat the photo of Esmée from *Le Journal*. Beside it, a perfect copy of the picture had been made by Megalina and her talented teeth.

Just like a newspaper photo is made up of thousands of tiny dots, Megalina had reproduced the photo using hundreds of tiny bite marks. In the areas where the photo was darker, there were more bite marks. Where the photo was lighter in color, there were fewer marks. Megalina was a living copy machine; a toothjet printer; an artist of exceptional skill.

"Hm," she said, comparing the copy with the original, "I can do better than that. *Th*till too big. If my counting wa*th* accurate, thi*th* i*th* 597MB. The nex*tht* one will be *th*maller."

"597MB?" Audrey asked Marmot.

"That's how many bites it took her to copy the photo. 597 Megabites. Named after Megalina, since she invented the process. Amazing, isn't she?"

Marmot handed Megalina another sheet of paper, then stood back at a safe distance.

"I'd like to send one picture out across each of the 1,250 tunnels. Are you up for the challenge?" Marmot already knew the answer to his question.

"Am I?" Megalina replied with a confident snort and a playful wink. "You ju*tht* keep the paper coming, I'll do the re*tht*."

With that, the world's tiniest artist began feeding a second sheet of paper across her exceptional teeth, piercing pinholes into pictures as she went. Audrey and Pica looked on in amazement. Pica picked up the first copy, holding it up to the light of the fireplace. It was perfect. He kept turning it, viewing it from every angle. He looked closer, then closer again; his eyes growing wider with each inspection.

Audrey watched Megalina closely. There was great skill in every motion of her hands and teeth. Each piece of paper was ten times the size of the little field mouse, yet she was clearly in command; a master at work.

The second copy was soon completed, and Audrey flew over, landing on top of the sheet of paper. She realized that this was not only a masterpiece of visual art and precision copying; this was also a copy of a photograph that could be seen by those who *could not see at all*. The bumps and indentations made by Megalina's teeth formed a photo in Braille – the fingertip language invented to be read by the blind. Megalina was a genius, there was no doubt.

The morning passed in a flurry of teeth, paper, and picture copying. Audrey realized that Marmot was right. This *was* the best use of her time. This was the most effective way for her and Pica to look for Esmée. The groundhog had delivered more valuable help than Audrey had hoped to receive.

She'd agreed to spend just one hour more in Marmot's apartment; but now she gladly spent all morning and much of the early afternoon watching Megalina copy the newspaper photo and helping Marmot fold and place each copy inside a mailbox on the *server room* wall. As a copy was finished, it was immediately distributed out along the groundhog *internet*. Not a moment was wasted. Word was spreading, and now the message included a photo of Esmée.

By the time Megalina had finished the one-thousand two-hundred and fiftieth copy, she'd succeeded in getting her "bite count" down to 256MB per copy. It had taken her about four hours to finish the job. Exhausted, thirsty, and suffering from sore cheek muscles, Megalina flopped down on the dining room bench. Laying there on her back, her big teeth pointing toward the ceiling, she felt like a wrung-out washcloth.

Returning to the living room after sending out the last picture, Marmot collapsed in his favorite chair, his feet resting on the fireplace hearth. Breathing a long sigh, he said, "Come and relax, friends. We deserve it. Well done, everyone."

Megalina pulled herself up, grabbed her thimble of water, and joined Marmot by the fireplace -- choosing a plump cushion for her seat. She sunk down into the plushy pillow and stared at the fire. Audrey and Pica took up their usual places in the tree roots. Everyone was worn-through with fatigue. No one spoke. No one moved. Hardly an eye blinked. Still, hopes ran high, even if energies were low. They'd distributed 1,250 pictures of Esmée over the *internet*; and something good was bound to come of it.

At last, Marmot found the strength to speak, "After a bit of a rest, I'm sure we can scrounge up something for a late lunch."

No sooner had the words left Marmot's lips, than the *server room* bell started to ring. Swinging his legs off the hearth and back onto the cold, hard floor, Marmot struggled to his feet again with a long sigh like a steam train.

"I shouldn't have mentioned the word 'rest,'" he said, with an ironic smile. "Fine. Rest will have to wait."

Marmot shuffled to the *server room*, silencing the echoing bell with his paw as he passed through the doorway, stopping in front of the wall of mailboxes.

"Where is it?" he said, scanning the wall with his eyes. "Ah! Yes, there it is."

Reaching up, Marmot opened the hinged door of a green-labeled mailbox. Taking the folded message from inside, he closed the door and unfolded the sheet of paper.

"Ah, now this is what we've been waiting for."

Audrey, Pica and Megalina had followed him into the *server room* and were eager to hear the news.

"Let me read it to you."

Pulling a pair of black-rimmed spectacles from the middle drawer of his desk, Marmot rested them on his short, stubby nose; he then cleared his throat and began to read the message aloud.

"It's from Barthélemy Courrier. He's the *network manager* for the *Notre-Dame server station*. Ha! Oh, this is hilarious."

Marmot kept the joke to himself, much to Audrey and Pica's annoyance. They were antsy to know what the message had to say and were not at all pleased with being kept waiting. It's funny how laughter and humor can be so irritating when one is wrapped in impatience – or rather, it's not so funny. They glared at the chuckling Marmot, until at last, he got the point.

"Ahem… Right. Where was I? Oh, yes. He says that on Tuesday there were complaints from a lot of tourists in his area about some butterfly who was ruining their selfies. Many of them even reported it to police officers on the streets around St. Michel. How crazy is that? Anyway, some of his groundhog *data collectors* – you know, groundhogs who keep tabs on human events and report it all to the *internet* -- picked up the story and sent it in to his *server room*."

Audrey didn't make the connection right away. She was now getting very grumpy with Marmot for sharing what she thought was only worthless *internet* chatter.

"But does he say anything about Esmée?" Audrey demanded, her exasperation mounting.

"Well, yeah," Marmot replied, wondering why a butterfly of such high intelligence was missing his point so completely. "It's *all* about Esmée!"

Audrey was still in the dark, and in no mood for riddles.

"There's more. Listen to this. Barthélemy says that the offending butterfly was sitting on St. Michel's outstretched pointer-finger while tourists were trying to take pictures of the great statue. The butterfly was photo-bombing their selfies, which I think is pretty funny."

Audrey disagreed and rolled her eyes with a snort. Marmot just laughed, took a handkerchief from his desk, blew his nose, then continued reading.

"People were so annoyed they wanted the police to chase the butterfly away. Really, people? Come on! How silly. Well anyway, the point is that the butterfly in question was a *belle dame* who had been seen leaving the RER B from Saint-Denis- lès-Chevreuse right there at the St. Michel train station."

"Esmée! Esmée!" Pica was certain it *had* to be her.

"It *is* Esmée," Audrey said slowly. "But this was *before* her photo shoot at the Louvre. This doesn't really help us locate her *now*." Audrey showed no sign of excitement, and Pica's excitement was short-lived, as a result.

"Maybe so, but you're forgetting something important," Marmot said, with a knowing grin.

"Esmée is now the focus of the *Bois de Boulogne Interconnected Network*, and ours is a *social network*. When groundhogs start talking, things start happening. Wait and see."

Before Marmot finished his sentence, the little bell above the doorway began to ring again, and it wouldn't be the last time it rang that afternoon.

CHAPTER NINETEEN

News of Esmée

The exhaustion of nearly four hours-worth of copying, folding, and mailing precisely 1,250 photos out across the *internet* was soon replaced by the exhilaration of results. Audrey and Pica had hoped to have more up-to-date news about Esmée, but Marmot understood how the *internet* worked. He knew what to expect. These things take time, he thought. He was very soon surprised, however, by the speed at which the long-awaited news started coming in.

Megalina's expert photocopying allowed Marmot to flood the internet with pictures of Esmée; and pictures are more interesting than a paragraph of words, any day. Groundhogs are always more likely to look at photos than they are to read a long description on the *internet*.

Plus, with popular social media apps like InstaHog, SnapChuck and ChatterPig (an app that seems to have been designed to allow groundhogs to say things without thinking first – which is never a good idea), Bois de Boulogne groundhogs could now easily share photos over and over again in wider and wider networks. In no time, Esmée's photo would be seen by every groundhog, woodchuck, whistle pig and field mouse in Paris.

Marmot walked over to the *server room* wall of mailboxes and searched for the latest green label indicating the arrival of a new message. Before he was able to find the cause of the most recent ringing, the bell rang again… then again… then again… then once more.

"It's going to be a long day," Marmot said, scratching his head and still trying to find the first of the five new messages. "Ah, here it is. We'll take them one at a time. I always find that's best. Now then, let's see what it has to say."

Taking the folded message out of the mailbox and shutting the door again, Marmot turned toward Audrey, Pica and Megalina and began to read.

"I got up for *this*? Ugh. Spam. Are some groundhogs really so bored that they have to send out nonsense across the *internet* and disturb my rest? If I had a catfish for every spam message I received, I'd be bigger than Boswell Badger – and that's saying something! The recycle bin is too good for this one. I'll stoke the fire with it."

Heading back toward the mailboxes, Marmot removed the second message.

"It's a b-mail message," he said, "From one of the *Ignifuge* bees of Notre-Dame Cathedral. Wow! That's really kinda cool. We hardly ever hear from them."

Marmot appreciated all things techy. He was a bit of a nerd and very proud of it.

"They have their own network, you know. Older than ours even. Totally different, too. They communicate not only by buzzing their buzzy bee-words, but also by complicated dances and subtle body language. Amazing stuff! Not even Brother Apius was able to figure all that out. Anyway, the b-mail is from a honeybee named Stéphanie."

Marmot adjusted his glasses on his nose.

"She says she met Esmée! On Tuesday at Notre-Dame Cathedral. She's certain it was her because they exchanged names. Also, Esmée told her she was from Saint-Denis. Oh, this is good stuff!"

Marmot seemed to see more value in the message

than Audrey did. To her, it sounded like old news. But Audrey had learned to trust her new friend. If it hadn't been for Marmot, she and Pica would surely have headed out first thing that morning and would be wandering aimlessly around Paris by now. His advice to wait a while had paid off. She had every reason to believe her patience and trust in him would continue to do so.

"Listen to this," Marmot went on. "Stéphanie says she could tell Esmée was homesick, although the little bee kept her suspicions to herself. She says she urged Esmée to stay close to the river. Excellent advice," Marmot said to himself, "When in doubt, stick to the river. Otherwise, you risk getting more and more lost!"

Marmot folded the message and laid it down on the desk. Then he turned to the other three who stood looking on.

"Don't you see what this means?"

He waited for the lightbulbs to turn on above their heads, but none came. They didn't understand why Marmot was so enthusiastic.

"It means we now know where Esmée is. Think about it. If she was lost and she got good advice from the honeybee about how to avoid getting *more* lost, don't you think Esmée would follow the bee's advice?"

Audrey knew Esmée well. Esmée was a smart butterfly, no question about it. "You're right. She'd listen to the honeybee. She'd stick to the river. She'd follow it as far as she could."

Then the long-awaited lightbulb…

"Esmée is on the river!" Audrey exclaimed. "Somewhere in Paris, Esmée is on the river!"

"*Exactement!* Thanks to Stéphanie, the clever *Ignifuge* bee, we now know that Esmée is on the Seine somewhere between Notre-Dame Cathedral and us. She hasn't had time to pass our current location. Not yet, anyway. I'd say this was pretty good news." Marmot took his glasses off and smiled with confidence.

"But what if she went the other way after vi*th*iting the cathedral? What if she went north in*th*tead of *th*outh toward u*th*?" Megalina raised an important question.

"But she didn't," Marmot said, replacing his glasses and turning around to face the wall. "*Le Journal* proves it. After leaving Notre-Dame, she was photographed at the Louvre. The Louvre is south of Notre-Dame. And we're *souther* still. She's on her way to us!"

Walking back over to the wall of mailboxes, Marmot quickly found the three-remaining green-labeled boxes and retrieved their messages. Wasting no time, he opened them all and began reading.

"Ha! Yeah, this is to be expected," he said, snorting a disdainful chuckle. "You can't be too willing to believe everything you find on the *internet*. Here's a message from someone claiming to have seen Esmée at the Palais Garnier last Monday. It says she was attending the opera!"

Crumpling the message up in one hand, he tossed it into the recycle bin.

"Who'd believe *anyone* would willingly attend the opera?"

Marmot had only ever seen one opera before, but it was more than enough for the groundhog. He had no appreciation for what he considered to be silly human hobbies.

"It just sounds like a lot of people yawning," he complained. "And yawning loudly! Nobody would spend good money to hear *that*. Pfft. Now, let's see what *this* message has to say."

He was happy to move on. Opening the next message, Marmot read it with careful skepticism.

"Now this is interesting," he said, distracted by the contents of the message.

Audrey, Pica and Megalina drew closer, sensing that Marmot was trying to determine if this message was authentic or not. They watched his reaction closely, as his eyes swept back and forth across the page, reading each sentence with great attention.

"I honestly don't know what to make of this one," he said, scratching his chin. "It's kind of odd; mysterious, even. Listen."

Marmot cleaned his glasses using a tissue from his desk, then started reading the message aloud, word for word.

"I have no doubt that I met your friend this past Tuesday night... or rather, early Wednesday morning, before sunrise. She found herself in grave peril in the Tuileries Garden, and I stumbled upon her just in time it would seem. I have no idea where she went from there, but she made it clear that she was trying to get back to Saint-Denis. Poor kid. I do hope you find her safe and sound. Signed, Norman the Owl Moth."

Audrey, Pica and Megalina just stared at Marmot, motionless. One word hung heavy in the air above everyone's head: peril. Esmée *was* in danger. Grave danger. Their worst fears and the source of all of their anxiety had just been confirmed. Their friend was in need, and still the only news they had of her whereabouts was days old.

Peril. The word froze their hearts.

Without a sound, Marmot opened the final scrap of paper he'd been holding in his hand. He was afraid to read any more messages. The last one had struck fear into everyone's heart. The good news about Esmée's escape from harm was all but buried beneath the word *peril*. She'd gotten lucky once; would she be so lucky the next time? Concern for Esmée's safety was rising to the surface of everyone's heart and mind, like white-hot panic.

Examining the final message, Marmot began to read. His face dropped; his eyes grew hard. Emotion bristled all across his soft, shiny coat. Shaking his head in disgust, Marmot folded the message in half and tore it into tiny pieces; throwing them all in the recycle bin beside his desk. Audrey, Pica and Megalina looked with surprise at their friend, who, finally, acknowledged the concern on their faces.

"Never trust the word of a barn owl," he said with thinly veiled anger. "They're treacherous, every last one of them. They shouldn't be allowed to send messages across our network, the miserable trolls."

No one asked Marmot for an explanation. It was clear that the fifth and final message was an unfriendly, taunting one. If Marmot thought it wasn't worth bothering about or sharing with everyone, that was good enough for his friends.

"Let's not let our fears overshadow hope," he said, changing his mood. "Esmée escaped danger in the Tuileries Garden. It would seem we have Norman the Owl Moth to thank for it, if ever we meet him. She's sticking to the path laid out for her by the river, following it south toward us. We need a plan. It's time to head out and meet her."

"*Oui! Oui!*" Pica was impatient to get moving. He was eager to find Esmée, most of all.

"Someone should stay here, in case messages continue to come in," Audrey suggested.

"I'm happy to *th*tay," Megalina volunteered. "I know thi*th* network ju*tht* a*th* well a*th* Marmot doe*th*."

"It's true," Marmot confirmed, "Megalina's a pro. She'll know which messages to act on and what needs to be done. There's no one I'd more willingly entrust my *server room* to than her."

"Excellent. Thank you, Megalina. Now for a plan. I think the plan should obviously be to stick to the river, like the honeybee told Esmée to do." Audrey asserted. "But our goal is the Tuileries Garden. This is the last place she was seen, so this is where we should go. Hopefully, our paths will cross somewhere in between. But if not, perhaps we'll hear word of her along the way."

"There's one stop we need to make. Trust me, it will be worth our time; and any plan to find Esmée will be more successful because of it."

Audrey wasn't sure what Marmot had in mind.

"There's someone we need to ask for help; although it won't be easy," Marmot explained. "He can be a bit of a grump. But, if we can win him over, he'll be a useful ally, for sure. If the plan is to head toward the Tuileries, our path will take us right past him. No time will be wasted."

Marmot took a sheet of paper from his desk drawer and scribbled a note on it in haste. Folding the piece of paper, he walked over to the wall of mailboxes, opened the one labeled *CM-TE*, and placed the message inside. Rotating the doorknob one-half turn clockwise, he marked the letter as ready for pick-up.

On the tunnel side of the mailbox, a tiny orange flag now popped up. As you know, a green label meant there was a message waiting inside; and when Marmot's side of the box showed a red label, the tunnel side was green. By turning the doorknob, Marmot also raised the little orange flag, indicating there was an urgent message ready to be delivered without delay.

Every groundhog in the *interconnected network* knew what an orange flag on a mailbox meant. Every single groundhog who passed by was expected to pick the message up, if it was addressed to a place they were heading. If they were not headed in that direction, they should leave it for the next passing groundhog. If they *were* bound for that destination, however, they should deliver the message as fast as possible.

If a groundhog was traveling in the direction of a message's destination, but was not going all the way, he could drop the message off at a *server room* along his route. The message would then be marked with an orange flag for the next groundhog who passed by. So many groundhogs passed through the *internet* tunnels every day that messages rarely had to wait longer than a few minutes before being picked up. The emphasis was on moving messages as fast as possible; and everyone viewed it as a sacred responsibility. With every groundhog doing his or her part, this was a very efficient and speedy system of communication.

"It's always best to give him plenty of notice before visiting," Marmot cautioned. "Nothing worse than dropping-in unannounced. Especially before lunchtime. All set?"

"*Prêt! Prêt!*" Pacing anxiously back and forth, Pica had been ready to go for quite some time. He wasn't very good at waiting… even less so at standing still.

"By the time we make it to the river, it will be getting late," Audrey noted. "Where will we spend the night? Where will we sleep…"

"I have an idea," Marmot interrupted, with a hint of a smile spreading across his up-curled lips. "And it just might remind you of home."

"Home? In the middle of Paris? Impossible."

When Audrey thought of Saint-Denis, she thought of wildflower fields, great shady trees, manicured gardens, friendly birds and busy honeybees. Apart from the *Ignifuge* bees of Notre-Dame and a few stuck-up city pigeons, she had seen nothing at all in Paris that even came close to reminding her of home.

"Hm," Marmot chuckled. "We'll see. Anyway, we must be off. Megalina, the *server room* is all yours. If we hear anything, we'll send word over the *internet.* Farewell."

Stepping back into the tunnel after spending a day within the cozy hominess of Marmot's *below-ground* apartment was just like the sensation Audrey and Pica experienced when they first left the *above-ground* world. His apartment was so wide and spacious, they'd forgotten that Marmot lived underground; but the tunnel reminded them in no time. Closing the door behind them, the warm, orange glow of Marmot's fireplace was again replaced by the cold, damp darkness of earthen walls. It took several minutes for their eyes to adjust to the pale light of the iPads and tablets which lined the tunnel.

As he had done before, Marmot took up his position in front, navigating the turns and blind corners without hesitation. It soon became apparent that they were not taking the same route back to the river. This was a consolation to Audrey and Pica who had been dreading the notion of traveling back through the cemetery. Instead, it felt as if they were traveling north and a little bit east.

"We'll head toward the Périphérique," Marmot shouted from up ahead. "Then turn due east and follow the *network* across the river."

Audrey perked up at the mention of crossing the river. She recalled that Brother Apius, in all of his research, had been unable to figure out exactly how the Bois de Boulogne groundhogs extended their *network* over water. Ever since, it had been a closely guarded mystery. Humans who have read the works of Brother Apius (and apart from Père Lamoine, there aren't very many who have) speculated and concocted myths and legends about the topic for ages.

Some have said that the groundhogs tunneled through the bedrock beneath the river itself; which of course is highly unlikely, since it would certainly require dynamite to punch a hole in solid granite. Early on in the development of the *internet,* the groundhogs didn't have dynamite or access to heavy machinery yet. Nowadays, maybe; but back then, not a chance.

Some people have suggested that the industrious groundhogs built a series of cleverly hidden bridges; but this, too, is unlikely. The Seine is well traveled and every inch of the river – throughout the city of Paris, at least – is visible and frequently visited by humans. If such bridges existed, they would be impossible to hide. Plus, they'd need to be high enough to allow boats to pass underneath. Groundhogs are known for their short, stubby legs and fear of heights; so, it would be quite impossible for them to build anything much taller than themselves.

There are even a few people who have proposed that the groundhogs make use of boats to cross the wide river. Some think they use boats of their own construction; but groundhogs do not possess the skill to build boats, let alone to navigate flowing water like their cousin the beaver. They prefer to tunnel through the ground not float on the water, otherwise they would be called *waterhogs* or *riverchucks* or even *whistle fish*. Of course, this is ridiculous.

Those who think the groundhogs simply hitch a ride on human-owned boats, crossing the river in this manner, overlook one important fact. Human-owned boats depart from and return to the same dock on the same side of the river. The boats rarely travel from side to side. For a groundhog hoping to cross the river, it would be faster to swim across. Which brings us to the final theory, popular among speculators.

Perhaps it's the similarity in appearance between a groundhog and a beaver -- or even a groundhog and an otter – that makes people think groundhogs are expert swimmers. The truth is, they *can* swim; but they avoid it whenever possible. It's not that they dislike swimming or feel it's beneath their dignity as expert tunnellers. It's not even that they find it to be an inefficient and slow way of carrying messages across the river.

Groundhogs avoid swimming for one reason and one reason alone: mud. Despite living underground in the dirt, they are actually very tidy creatures -- as you could tell from Marmot's apartment. But introduce ten-thousand wet, soggy, dripping groundhogs -- fresh from a swim in the Seine – into the *interconnected network* of earthen tunnels, and you have a whole lot of mud on your hands -- and on your feet, in your hair, all over your face, up your nose and under your fingernails. No. Groundhogs avoid swimming because they prefer their tunnels to be as clean and dry as possible.

Anyway, here at last was Audrey's chance to find out how the Bois de Boulogne groundhogs extended their *network* across the river. She paid close attention to every turn they made, every identifying characteristic of the tunnels through which they now sped. She spent more time admiring the workmanship all around her and less time fearing the collapse of the ceiling, until…

A rumbling growl echoed through the passageway. Like a grizzly bear snoring in the depths of his lair, the tunnel vibrated with warning. Running from ceiling to floor, long cracks in the walls did little to calm their fears.

"What is it?" Audrey whispered, afraid to awaken the sleeping bear. Her eyes were frozen open; her wings turned to rubber.

"That's the Périphérique," Marmot said, with indifference. "The highway that circles the city. We're right under it now."

Audrey continued whispering, not yet convinced that there was no monstrous bear lurking in the darkness. "But the cracks… the rumbling… the…"

"Don't you worry one bit," Marmot laughed. "The cracks are designed to allow the walls to move. If they didn't move, then every vibration from the cars and trucks above would shake the rock-solid walls until they were rubble. We built the walls to give a little, but not to collapse. Now we'll turn right and head for the river. Not far to go now."

Marmot took a sharp right and the party began to walk downhill toward the Seine. The air became cooler, as more moisture now clung to the walls and ceiling. The smell of fish and river mud crept up the tunnel through the darkness. Far ahead, in the ankle-deep fog, a pinprick of light began to widen like a camera shutter. They were nearing the outside world; the end of the tunnel; and the River Seine.

Audrey's anticipation mounted. She was about to learn the secret of how the groundhogs of the Bois de Boulogne forest crossed the wide water; a secret kept hidden from the time of Brother Apius to this very day. As they neared the mouth of the tunnel, Audrey's curiosity got the better of her and she began asking Marmot questions.

"Is this where we'll meet your friend? The one you sent the message to before we left."

"Not here," Marmot replied. "Further on up the river. We won't get there tonight."

Audrey continued fishing for information, trying to get to the questions she wanted to ask without scaring Marmot away.

"Will you cross the river with us? Or should we just fly on ahead without you?"

"I'm staying with you 'til the end. Until we find Esmée."

Marmot started to sense Audrey might be angling for something more. He decided to cut to the heart of the matter.

"Go ahead," he said.

"Go ahead?" Audrey asked, trying on her most convincing look of surprise.

"Ask me," Marmot said with a laugh. "Just go ahead and ask me. I know you're dying to ask."

"Ask what?" Audrey's face flushed and she began shuffling her feet.

Marmot stopped in his tracks at the opening to the tunnel, within sight of the river. Turning to Audrey, he put his hands on his hips and raised one eyebrow.

"You want to know how we do it, that's what. How we cross the river. How the *internet* extends beyond the forest, over the water, and throughout the entire city. You know what? It would have been better if Brother Apius hadn't written anything about it *at all*. Leaving an unanswered question is like putting a wrapped gift in the middle of the room. Nobody can leave it alone. Everybody has to take a guess about what's inside. People just gotta know! So, ask me. Go on."

"Fine," Audrey said, stomping one foot on the ground. "How *do you* get across the river?"

"At last!" Marmot raised his hands in mock relief. "That took far too long, you know. If you'd just asked me in the first place…"

Audrey glared at him with butterfly-sized daggers in her eyes.

"It's easy," the groundhog whispered, thinking it best not to push his luck; then pausing a moment for dramatic effect, he said, "We don't."

"What?!"

"We don't. We can communicate across the water without actually *crossing* the water. You'll see. I promise. But first we need to, well… cross the water."

Marmot relished the irony; and Audrey was now certain she was being made fun of. What was the irritating groundhog talking about?! Audrey liked to *know* things.

She was very serious about learning and discovering. She did not have much patience for riddles or jokes... or for *certain* young groundhogs.

With a roll of her eyes and a flustered "Pfft!" Audrey walked out of the tunnel and right past Marmot, who was beginning to feel a little less popular than usual. Pica hopped on by without a word, hoping to avoid either annoying Audrey further or appearing to take Marmot's side. Pica preferred to remain impartial, always.

Marmot walked over to the water's edge and listened with intensity. It had taken them a few hours to travel through the *network* of tunnels and to the outside world. It was now dusk, and nightfall was fast approaching. All around them, croaking frogs shared news of passing boats and strangers on the shore. The swift flowing river lapped the concrete footings of a nearby bridge, while driftwood -- caught up in eddies of leaves and brown water -- swirled helplessly in the twilight.

"I think it's safe," he said, after a moment. "The city has a million eyes, and not all of them are friendly to butterflies, birds or groundhogs. It's best if we walk across... all of us. This way."

Audrey and Pica kept close to the ground. They didn't know exactly what *eyes* Marmot was referring to; but after their run-in with the bullying crows and Marmot's mention earlier of "untrustworthy barn owls," they decided to take his advice and stay grounded.

The sound of traffic above and water-slapping-concrete below grew louder, as they made their way up the shoreline by the light of a waning moon. Marmot led them to the foot of one of the great pilons that carry the Périphérique highway across the Seine.

Headlights sped across the roadway in both directions, as an endless stream of tires tapped out their rhythm over seams in the pavement. This was as far from the quiet bicycle paths of Saint-Denis as Audrey and Pica had ever travelled. Audrey recalled Marmot's words to her before they left his apartment, how they'd pass the night in a place that would remind her of home. Clearly, he knew nothing of Saint-Denis.

"This is where we cross," Marmot whispered. "Remember, stay close to me and, by all means, resist the temptation to fly out in the open. Come on."

Marmot began to climb up the concrete pillar joining the bridge to the land. Reaching the bottom of the roadway, he swung himself up off the pilon and onto the edge of one of the enormous steel I-beams that ran the full width of the river. Carrying the weight of the road, the pavement, the cars, trucks, motorcycles and scooters above, the steel girders rested on-top of the concrete pilons and formed the structure of the Périphérique bridge fording the river.

He hesitated a moment, waiting for Audrey and Pica to catch up. Once they'd joined him, Marmot led the way across the I-beam. Running as fast as he could, Pica allowed himself to hop, here and there. Audrey rode on the back of her friend, unable to keep up any other way.

Above them, traffic sent shivers down the spine of the bridge, tickling the feet of both bird and groundhog. Below, the river flowed in chaotic motion, swirling around the feet of the bridge that stood in its path. Pica felt dizzy every time he let himself look down. His head was awash in flowing, hopping, and running. It was all just too much movement, even for a magpie.

"When we reach the end, we need to slide down the concrete footing as fast as we can and get under the cover of the bushes nearby. No matter how well the roadway might have concealed us, we still might have been seen. We can't chance it. Get off the bridge and into the thicket quickly."

Marmot stopped at the end of the I-beam and

watched Pica and Audrey hop down and into the overgrowth surrounding the pilon. When he was sure his friends were safe, Marmot slid down the smooth concrete and into the weeds beside them.

"Wait," he whispered, listening to the growing darkness -- his ears standing high on his round head. Marmot sniffed the chill evening air, attentive to their surroundings. Minutes passed, until Marmot finally relaxed his strained senses and spoke at a normal volume.

"Nothing. All clear. Follow me," he said, motioning to Audrey in particular, "I have a promise to keep… two promises, really."

Popping up out of the bushes that had hidden them, Marmot stepped into the clearing not far from the river's edge. He cupped his paws around his mouth, much like Audrey had done with her wings at the tunnel's entrance the day they all met. Whistling out into the darkness, Marmot demonstrated perfect Groundhog 5.1.

All at once, from a patch of yellow wintercress flowers beside the river, the flickering light of a hundred fireflies appeared. As if answering his call, the lightning bugs danced, flittered, and then gathered together in front of Marmot -- who had stopped whistling the moment he saw them.

"Hello, my friends," he said to the playful fireflies. "I have need of your services, yet again."

Turning to Audrey, who sat upon the branch of a forsythia bush, Marmot's face grew serious, solemn even.

"I promised I would share with you the secret of how we groundhogs extend our *interconnected network* across the river. It's a mystery that even the mind of Brother Apius could not unravel. Never before, in the history of the Bois de Boulogne groundhogs, has anyone shared our secret with an outsider. The faith you placed in us – trusting that we could help you in your efforts to find Esmée -- has made you worthy of *our* trust, too. And so," Marmot motioned with both hands in the direction of the wintercress fireflies, "here they are: the secret of how we communicate across the wide waters of the Seine."

Audrey was enchanted by the delicate lights of the sparkling fireflies. But she still didn't understand how they could possibly be *the secret* to how the Bois de Boulogne groundhogs carry their *internet* communications across the boundary of the river; into every corner of Paris; and then back again.

"But how?" she asked. "How do they…"

"I'll show you… and I'll keep my other promise at the same time. Before we left, I told Megalina I would send her a message over the *internet* once we got safely across the river. Now you'll be able to see how it all works."

Marmot turned toward the twinkling constellation of wintercress fireflies gathered in front of him. Whistling once again in perfect Groundhog 5.1, he shared his message to Megalina with them. Once he'd finished speaking, the fireflies flew to the water's edge and began flashing in unison.

Across the river, another group of wintercress fireflies could be seen, flashing a response to their friends back on the other side. In a matter of just a few moments, Marmot's message to Megalina had been communicated *across* the water -- without Marmot actually having to *cross* the water.

The wintercress fireflies on the opposite shore then flew off to the nearest tunnel *access point* to share Marmot's message with a groundhog; who would then deposit it with the nearest *network manager.* The *manager* would then send it out across the *internet;* until it reached the *T1 Server Room,* and Megalina the field mouse.

Even through the dark of night, the *interconnected network* was able to pass messages across any obstacle by means of the flashlight-code of the wintercress fireflies. During the daytime, the fireflies simply flew across the river to share messages in-person with their friends on the other side. All up and down the Seine, wintercress fireflies made themselves available to extend the work of the *internet* wherever and whenever they were needed.

"And now you know our secret: the wintercress fireflies, or Wi-Fi for short. We couldn't do it without them!"

Marmot turned and thanked his tiny friends, who flickered and danced among the flowers of the wintercress patch before settling back into darkness.

"Megalina should receive our message before long," he said to Audrey and Pica. "Only one promise left to keep: it's time to find Esmée."

With that, he turned from the river, headed due east, and led his companions deeper into the city. It had been a very long day and the travelers needed to find someplace to rest and spend the night. Marmot had promised Audrey and Pica that he would take them somewhere that would remind them of the fields of Saint-Denis. Right now, they were so tired that they'd settle for a broken tree limb in the noisiest part of Paris, if only they could rest their wings; but Marmot had something much cozier in mind -- and he would not disappoint.

CHAPTER TWENTY

Parc André-Citroën

The company traveled along the eastern bank (what Parisians call the Left Bank) of the river as fast as they could. Marmot was determined to lead them to their stopping place for the night without delay. He was just as exhausted as the others; but unlike Audrey and Pica, he knew what awaited them. He knew it would be worth the extra distance, and they'd all get a good night's rest.

They soon passed another large highway-bridge over the river -- carrying more cars, trucks, motorcycles and scooters into an already overcrowded city. Up ahead on their right, the city lights gave way to a large, black rectangle of open darkness not far from the river's edge. Buildings and lampposts seemed to be swallowed up as they approached the great empty space. Marmot, who was a few feet in front of the other two, turned his head without slowing his pace and called back to them.

"Do you see it?"

"I see a whole lot of nothing over there," Audrey said, not intending to sound sarcastic.

"That's it!" Marmot replied. "That's where we're heading. Keep going. We're very close."

As they drew near to the mysterious "hole in the city," Pica saw looming shadows standing guard at the borders of the darkened area. Up ahead, the moonlight drew long, skinny shapes across sidewalks; shapes that had huge, round heads atop thin bodies. The closer they got, the more uneasy Audrey and Pica became.

The thought occurred to Pica that Marmot might be leading them into another cemetery. He was quite certain he would not sleep at all if that were the case. In a city of unfamiliar sights where everything looked strange, Pica found fear behind every shape and dread hidden in every shadow. But fear has a way of making common, everyday things look sinister, especially in the dark. If we expect to find monsters, our minds will make monsters appear. This is exactly what was happening to poor Pica.

He saw a pale, wispy ghost sneak up the riverbank and reach its lifeless fingers toward his tailfeathers. He spied mischievous fairies flying among windblown leaves and hiding behind the stalks of toadstools. Worst of all, Pica spotted a ravenous fox as it darted across their path and into the tall grass growing just beyond the last streetlight. There it lay in wait, until the unsuspecting travelers wandered too close to escape its sharp teeth. Pica's eyes widened and his heart beat faster. His whole body turned to stone at the approach of the shadows.

"Did you see that cat?" Marmot asked, from up ahead. "Probably chasing some rat. We'll see a lot of cats in Paris; and only slightly fewer rats." He laughed.

A cat? Was Marmot sure it wasn't a deadly fox? Pica kept shooting glances over toward the shadows; he knew what he saw.

"We're nearing our destination, my friends. Just beyond those tall trees, over there."

Marmot pointed to what Pica was *certain* had been a gang of giants with huge, round heads. There they stood, guarding the entrance to the frightful darkness. Pica rubbed his eyes with his wings, blinking as if trying to hold onto what he *knew* he saw.

Just like when you're putting together a jigsaw puzzle, the moment you find the missing piece the whole picture begins to make sense. As soon as Marmot mentioned the cat and the trees, everything Pica had been seeing – or rather, *mis*-seeing – started to come into focus.

They *were* trees. He could see them now. There was a dense grouping of tall, bushy maples standing on the southwestern edge of a park. They weren't big-headed, slender-bodied giants, after all. Pica chuckled, though not without a hint of nervousness.

Perhaps it was just the fog from the river, instead of a pale, wispy ghost creeping along the ground. He'd been sure they were fingers reaching up to grab hold of his tailfeathers; but then every chill from the night air that he'd ever experienced had begun in his tailfeathers first. Chills always seemed to run *up* Pica's spine, never down.

He took another cautious look at the pile of windblown leaves; and it all looked different. He now saw that the mischievous fairies were just sparkles of moonlight shimmering through the trees and dancing on the toadstools below. Everything made sense now. Pica's pace quickened and he caught up to Marmot and Audrey. His tailfeathers relaxed, and the chill that had run *up* his spine and stopped between his shoulder blades now disappeared entirely.

Marmot was leading them into a park, not an empty hole in the middle of the city. Pica could see that where the buildings and streetlights ended, the park began. Where the darkness started, the bright city lights were not permitted to shine. The park was a haven, a refuge from the noisy, restless city.

Between the branches of the trees, he could now make out open, grassy spaces. He heard the faint sounds of water fountains and the rustle of the wind through the grass. It all appeared much more inviting, and not at all like *another cemetery*. Pica breathed a long sigh of relief.

Threading their way through the trees, they stepped out from under the low branches and into a large, green field. Without buildings to block the moonlight, the whole park was now visible to them -- bathed in silver and smelling of wildflowers.

In the center of the field, a hot air balloon sat tethered to the ground. At first, it was a shock to see such a sight in the middle of a park surrounded by city streets and tall buildings; but then it made perfect sense to Pica. If the craziness of city life got to be too much, he thought, what better way to escape than in a fast-rising balloon? Pica approved of the Parisian's excellent idea and wanted very much to hop onboard and float back to his oak tree in Monsieur Deschamps' pasture.

In fact, this was the *Ballon Generali*. Used to carry tourists to a height of 980 feet (just below the height of the Eiffel Tower). The helium balloon ride follows the river from its home in the Parc André-Citroën, up past the Eiffel Tower, and as far north as Notre-Dame Cathedral. Every day, 30 tourists at a time can see the sights of the City of Lights from the silent calm of the sky.

"Cool, isn't it?" Marmot asked. "But the balloon's *not* our destination. Follow me."

That's exactly what Audrey and Pica had been doing since the day before. Marmot had led them through tunnels; *routers; server rooms*; and a cemetery; before guiding them across an I-beam beneath the Périphérique and through the streets of Paris to this latest marvel.

Following Marmot seemed to be the recipe for excitement. In fact, thanks to Marmot, Audrey learned the greatest secret of her life: how the Bois de Boulogne groundhogs carry their *internet* across the river. Watching the wintercress fireflies signal messages over the Seine was totally unexpected. Now she and Pica stood in the shadow of an enormous helium balloon, parked in the heart of Paris – another unexpected experience. Even though concern for Esmée brought them here, every step of their journey had been filled with wonder

The trio fluttered, scurried and flew across the field; around the balloon; and toward a dense patch of trees on the other side. The grass beneath them was thick and becoming wet in the night air; as the warmth of the day gave way to the chilly moon. Though Marmot always preferred salted catfish to green grass and clover, the scent of fresh salad was mouthwateringly delicious. Dropping his chin as he ran across the open meadow, Marmot was able to scoop up a quick snack which he stored in his puffy cheeks for later.

Reaching the tree line, the travelers pushed their way through the clutter of branches and into a small forest. The moment they stepped into the woods, the noise and light of the city was snuffed out. The difference was remarkable. A moment ago, they could still hear the sounds of the highway. Now, they heard only the chirping of crickets. Rooftops and verandas had surrounded them as they made their way through the city; but now they were sheltered beneath a canopy of twisted leaves and limbs. Then Pica saw it.

In the middle of the forest there was a small clearing, at the center of which stood a large oak tree. It was just like Monsieur Deschamps' oak tree, where Pica always felt most at home. At the base of the tree, a thick meadow of clover and wildflowers swayed in the breeze. The full moon overhead drenched it all in pearl-white light, like a lace tablecloth spread over a banquet table.

"Here we are," Marmot said with satisfaction. "Fields and trees, flowers and breeze… this is as close to the meadows of Saint-Denis as you can get east of the Bois de Boulogne and inside the Périphérique - at least *this* close to the river. Here, we will spend the night."

Pica immediately chose a branch in the oak tree, high above the ground. Stretching his body as if made of rubber, he yawned a comical croaking sound and settled down among the lobe-shaped leaves. Audrey headed straight for the clover patch and took a long drink. Even the flowers hanging from the tree roots in Marmot's apartment couldn't compare to the dew-drenched clover of the Parc André-Citroën in the heart of Paris. Marmot had promised a place to spend the night that was sure to remind them of home; and he'd delivered just that.

"I wouldn't have believed it," Audrey said to Marmot, as he munched on clover buds not far from her. "It's ideal. If I didn't know better, I'd think we were back in the countryside, instead of in the middle of the city. Thank you. This is just what we needed. It's perfectly…"

"We need to take what comfort we can find," Marmot interrupted. "Tomorrow, we have some ground to cover. If we make an early start and press on, we can be in the *Champ de Mars* by afternoon. It's there we'll find Boswell. It was to him that I sent the message before we left. He should be expecting us."

"What do you hope to accomplish with him?" Audrey asked, still sipping from a clover flower.

"Boswell's a badger… no, that's not quite accurate."

Marmot scratched his chin, choosing his words with care.

"Boswell's *the* badger. He's well respected among urban animals; and he generally knows what's going on throughout the city. Not every piece of news reaches the *internet*. The news that *doesn't,* Boswell will know all about it. Like my dad used to say, it's always best to get your news from multiple sources. That way, we're sure to get the whole picture."

Marmot hesitated a moment, wincing as if he'd just stubbed his toe on a rock.

"He's not what you'd call… friendly, though. Even for a badger. But he means well and he's trustworthy. He just takes some getting used to. Anyhow, we'll cross that badger when we get to him," Marmot laughed, enjoying his own joke more than it deserved. "Or rather, we'll *avoid* crossing him… as much as we can. For now, we've earned a good night's sleep."

Audrey chose a branch close to a loudly snoring Pica and nestled down onto a leafy twig. Marmot found a low divot in the ground, filled in by grass clippings and fallen leaves from the previous autumn.

"This will do just fine for me," he said, burying himself in the groundcover. "We'll be quite safe in here. The surrounding city should keep out the foxes and bobcats. Traffic *is* good for *something*! Goodnight, all. Sleep well."

"Goodnight, Marmot," Audrey whispered, as she drifted off to blissful sleep.

Beneath the oak tree, Marmot whistled softly with every breath he exhaled. Among the branches, Pica and Audrey dreamed of fireflies and green meadows. Around them, the park was alive with tree frogs and insects, each singing its own song in the darkness.

Beyond the trees and fields, Paris held the park in its broad arms, spreading out in every direction at the speed of sight. Each available inch of space was employed in useful ways. From the rooftop gutters, holding flowerpots and planters; to the wrought iron terraces upon which laundry was hung to dry; Paris was crammed full of life and purpose.

Away to the north, a slow-moving thunderstorm was on the approach. It had begun midday, and spent all afternoon and evening soaking the Eiffel Tower and the *Champ de Mars*. It was now drenching the *Île aux Cygnes,* which sat midway between where Marmot, Audrey and Pica now slept and their destination: the Tuileries Garden. The storm threatened to make their journey, the next day, a slow and soggy one.

Miles away, back in Saint-Denis, Esmée's best friend, Lisette, still sulked in silence. Her anger at being left behind while her friend embarked on an adventure in Paris without her, had turned to tears on the branch of their milkweed plant. As was always the case with Lisette, those tears turned into anger again, and then soured into something much worse.

Lisette had resolved to wash her hands of Esmée; find a new best friend; and move on with her life. All because of her anger. All because of a misunderstanding. Lisette had a way of reaching the worst possible conclusions -- and making the worst possible decisions -- all because of anger. And this decision was the worst of the worst.

If only she had placed more faith in their friendship. If only she had thought about Esmée instead of herself. If only she had trusted what she knew, instead of the pain she was feeling. If only she had gone to find her friend, instead of leaving their friendship behind. If only. If only. Nothing good ever begins with those two words -- just regret.

Lisette would have more to regret before Esmée's adventure was done. Much more.

CHAPTER TWENTY-ONE

Tragedy by *les Arbres du Souvenir*

The spectacular light show danced upon the face of the Eiffel Tower, much to Esmée's delight. Wrapped in the kind friendship of Pierre's warm wings, she'd never imagined she could be so happy. Below where Esmée and Pierre now sat, the boat's other passengers gazed up at the glowing grandeur of the tower.

Just as suddenly as it had begun, the lights went out and the Eiffel Tower faded into the dark backdrop of the sky once more. It was Wednesday night and -- unknown to Esmée -- just a few miles downriver, Audrey and Pica had just crossed into Paris and were preparing to spend the night in a honeysuckle bush.

Ever since the door of carriage #9 slid closed, trapping her inside the RER B bound for Paris, Esmée had wanted nothing more than to find her way home. The brief distractions offered by the newness all around her had been silenced by her narrow escape from death in the beak of a barn owl.

But then came Pierre…

Even the dangers of tour buses seemed designed only to provide Pierre with opportunities for chivalry. Every word he spoke, every kindness he showed made her feel more at home with him than she had been even in Saint-Denis. It wasn't until the lights went out on the Eiffel Tower and all of Paris was hushed and still that

Esmée realized it: she had fallen in love with Pierre, and she could not imagine a day without him.

Much to her amazement, Esmée couldn't even remember a time before Pierre. Of course, she knew that they'd only spent, perhaps, twelve hours together; but the heart has a way of inserting the ones we love into memories in which they never played a part. It was all very strange to her; and all very perfect. Plus, twelve hours to a butterfly is like a month and a half to a human; it was much longer than it might sound to our ears… long enough to be life-changing.

As they slowly turned and started to head back upriver, the dinner boat's engines rumbled from below, rolling the chalky-tan water into white waves. The passengers returned to the warmth of the dining room below decks, leaving Esmée and Pierre alone up above. The City of Lights blazed in shimmering gold and silver as far as Esmée's eyes could see. The air was alive with light which reflected off white limestone buildings, elegant bridges, and wrought iron. Everywhere one looked, there was something to be seen.

"Are you ready to leave our little boat, *mademoiselle*? Or do you wish to return upstream? The choice, it is yours." Pierre nodded with deference.

"I don't ever want to leave," Esmée said with a wistful sigh. "But, it's late. Is there a tree nearby where we'd be safe for the night?"

Pierre smiled, "*Oui, ma petite*. I know just the place. It is a very short flight. Just to the other side of the river. Allow me to show you."

Standing and extending their wings, Pierre leapt from the flagpole and into the wind. Esmée followed him, riding the fast approaching breeze up from the bow of the boat. Banking to the left, they crossed directly in front of the Eiffel Tower and soon reached the opposite side of the river.

Here, they found an oblong, oval-shaped pool of water, framed on either side by fountains and square sculptures. The numberless fountains cast jets of water high into the air, which descended back to earth as a fine mist. Flanking the reflecting pool, green swathes of grass gave way to groupings of trees on the left and the right.

"You are now in the *Jardins du Trocadéro, mademoiselle.* Just another jewel in the crown of Paris. We will find a safe resting place among the trees, I am certain."

Guiding her past the fountains; over the grass and sidewalk; across the outer lawn and into the trees; Pierre offered Esmée her choice of branches upon which to pass the night hours. Preferring to keep watch from above, Pierre bid Esmée goodnight, then flew up to the very top of the tree in which she now sat. Settling in for the night, Esmée called up to Pierre through the moonlight.

"Thank you, *mon amour.* Today was… unforgettable. I hope you sleep well."

"*Oui, mademoiselle.* Unforgettable. *Bonne nuit.*"

Sleep came quickly for the two butterflies, worn out by a day of sightseeing. Their dreams were filled with images of all they had seen that day. In and around each image, happiness flowed, filling in the spaces. Esmée knew little about Pierre, but what she did know was undeniably true. He was kind and generous. He was brave and attentive to her needs. These characteristics now highlighted every memory of the time they had spent together. Even while sleeping, Esmée was comforted to know that Pierre was near. The night passed in peaceful repose.

The following morning, the sun began its ascent over rooftops and trees and flooded the City of Lights with possibility. To the south of where Esmée now slept, Audrey and Pica had awakened to the sounds of the city. Having spent the night in a honeysuckle bush, they were just then discussing -- from a third story terrace -- Audrey's plan to find a Bois de Boulogne groundhog. It was Thursday and the three friends hadn't been this near to one another since Esmée left Saint-Denis two days prior.

In the *Jardins du Trocadéro*, Pierre woke with the sun and spent a few minutes exploring the gardens and looking for a suitable breakfast for Esmée and himself. As he returned from his mission, Esmée opened her eyes in the early morning light.

"*Bonjour, ma petite,*" Pierre greeted Esmée from a nearby branch. "Did sleep soothe you? Are you rested?"

"*Oui,* Pierre. I slept better than I have in ages. *Merci. Et toi?*"

"*Mais oui, mademoiselle.* The sounds of the river and the gentle moonlight, they are better bedding than the softest dandelion. I slept quite well, indeed. There is a butterfly bush a few yards to the west. It should make for a very pleasant *petit déjeuner*. Please, follow me and I will show you."

Pierre led Esmée to the bush he'd found, and the two butterflies enjoyed a refreshing breakfast of warm nectar. Brushing aside a leaf to reveal a view of the river to the east, Pierre motioned for Esmée to take a look.

There, standing tall and majestic, the Eiffel Tower presented itself against the rising sun. No matter how many times she saw it, the tower always made Esmée's heart thrill. It was both romantic and mysterious and she'd fallen in love with this symbol of all that was noble. Turning to Pierre, she saw the same qualities in him; and her heart was moved to know more about her mysterious new friend.

"Pierre," she began, "tell me your story?"

"My story, *mademoiselle*? What is it that you mean?"

"Tell me… about *you*." Esmée caught Pierre's

eye. "Please?"

"*Mon histoire,* I do not think it would be of interest; but for you I will…"

Pierre took a short sip from a flower bud, then stroked his left wing with one hand. There was sadness in his eyes, and a distant thoughtfulness. With humble reluctance, he began to speak.

"I have not always called Paris my home. *Non, mademoiselle.* For I was born far away from here in Fleur-de-Beynac… in the region of Dordogne. This is a land of great beauty, *oui,* great beauty, indeed. Perhaps not unlike your own home; but for me it is more enchanting than a rose on a summer's eve."

A tear glistened in Pierre's eye. His voice waivered with emotion.

"The Dordogne River, it flows through a landscape of green, rolling hills and gently slanting meadows. There are deep forests and prehistoric caves in cliffs that overlook endless valleys. Valleys which wind their way back through time itself. There is no place like it in all of creation." Pierre stared into emptiness; his eyes were vacant with melancholy.

"It sounds very different from Paris," Esmée said, wondering why anyone would ever choose to leave such a place. Then she remembered how *she* had left just such a place. A hint of homesickness echoed in her heart and she felt Pierre's sadness.

"*Oui, c'est vrai.* The two could not be more different. Even in all of its glory, Paris is no match for Dordogne."

"What made you want to leave your home?" Esmée asked with tenderness.

"I did not want to leave." Pierre paused. "Indeed, nothing could make me. No, I never wanted to leave Fleur-de-Beynac, *mademoiselle.*"

"Then why, Pierre? If it is not too painful, please

tell me. Why did you leave?"

Pierre sat motionless, staring at the branch upon which he sat. The moment of silence which followed Esmée's question seemed to last for an hour or more. Esmée waited with patience, unwilling to press Pierre for a response. The minutes wore on; until at last, he spoke.

"I am not what I appear to be," he said, with caution in his voice. "I am a fraud."

Esmée searched Pierre's eyes for an explanation. What did he mean? Apprehension now stiffened in her chest, as a lump formed in her throat. All her trust was now balanced on the edge of fear. Esmée refused to believe Pierre was anything but truthful and honorable. She held her breath; awaiting the verdict; clinging to her faith in Pierre.

"I am not as happy as I appear, *mademoiselle*," he confessed with shame. "My heart, it is shattered. I have lived in empty misery… and my smile is little more than a lie." Lifting his head, he looked Esmée in the eyes, "A lie, *mademoiselle*. A fraudulent lie."

"Sadness is no shame," Esmée said with conviction, "And *your* smile could *never* be a lie. If you have suffered and are still able to smile, this is great strength. You are no fraud."

She rested one wing on Pierre's shoulder. "Will you share with me what it was that shattered your heart? Share only to heal; but not if the pain is too near."

"It becomes easier to share, with every word," Pierre said, his eyes softening in the morning glow. "I will tell you *my story*, as you say."

"My home, Fleur-de-Beynac, lies in the shadow of the great Château de Beynac. The castle, it controls a sharp bend in the Dordogne River, and from there it commands the entire valley. Have you ever seen the fortress of Beynac, *mademoiselle*?"

"I have not; but you must take me there one day,"

Esmée said, offering hope to her heartbroken friend.

"If only I could," Pierre replied, despair dripping from every word.

"Fleur-de-Beynac, she is a quiet, peaceful place filled with more flowers than townsfolk. In the days of dukes and duchesses, Fleur was the farmland that fed the castle. So rich was the soil of this area, that when the Great Famine of '77 struck, it was the farmers of Fleur who came to the rescue of such places as Nullepart and Bouchevide. *Oui,* ours is a *noble histoire.*

"Little has changed since then; little, except for one thing. Where once all farmland was put to good use; now much of it is left in ruinous neglect. And neglect invites evil."

Pierre's mood now darkened. His eyes fell. He appeared as if draped in a black veil of sorrow. Slowly -- with deliberation -- he plodded on.

"It was out of one of these neglected fields that my sorrow came. *Mais oui,* I remember it well. One evening, in springtime – when I was just a boy – my mother and I were playing among the broom-bush flowers, near *les Arbres du Souvenir.* The leaves on the trees, they were waxy and new with the first green of April. At the foot of the hill, a stream which the local children call *la Dame Errante,* she flowed fat and swollen with the recent rain.

"Surrounded by carefree springtime, my mother and I played a game of hide and seek, until the sun set behind the stalks of an abandoned cornfield. In our joy, we'd lost track of time. Ah *oui,* and we forgot the dangers of dusk. I will forever regret our carelessness on that terrible evening."

Pierre could hold back no longer. Tears now streaked down his cheeks, and emotion flooded his heart, as he remembered every detail.

"I found a hiding place inside the husk of a dried-out ear of corn. There, I concealed myself; and watched as my mother played our game, searching for her little boy. She called to me playfully, '*Pierrot*, I see you!' But still she searched; unwilling to find me too soon; unwilling to spoil my fun.

"She looked everywhere *except* where she knew I was hiding. All the while, *ma mère,* she kept one eye on me -- smiling to let me know she saw me… smiling to let me know… she loved me.

"It was then that I first saw the danger approaching. *Maman*, she saw it, too. But before I could fly to her side, she commanded me to stay where I was and be silent – no matter what.

"And then they came. Dozens of them. In furious flight, they blackened the sky. *Maman*, she flew from where I was hiding; flapping her wings wildly; drawing their attention. The villainous birds followed her, taking no notice of me. Obeying my mother, or maybe just too frightened to do anything else, I remained hidden… safe. My mother, she led the murderous crows far away from me. To protect me from them… and from the memory of what they did to her."

Pierre paused a moment and turned his face away from Esmée, who sat weeping -- overwhelmed by the burden of sorrow she now saw weighing down upon Pierre's shoulders. She had no words; and she was afraid to break the sacred silence. She was helpless, unable to offer Pierre anything but her tears. With slow, aching words, he continued at a whisper.

"I stayed there in that dried-out husk for hours. Trembling. Turned to stone by fear. Afraid that the crows might return and find me alone. I waited. All night, I waited. Hoping she would… but, I knew she would *never* come back. Never.

"I did nothing to save her," Pierre said with bitterness. "My fear kept me from flying to her side. My cowardice."

"Your mother *told* you to stay hidden," Esmée said. "That's what she wanted. What could a little boy do against…"

"I could have been with her," Pierre cut in. "She would not have been alone. She would not have died alone."

Pierre hung his head and cried.

Overhead, the morning clouds had all but disappeared. The sun sailed its steady course through a sea of blue sky; and a healing breeze drifted up from the river, rustling the leaves around them. Through the swaying branches of the surrounding trees, Esmée could see the Eiffel Tower directly opposite where they now sat in the *Jardins du Trocadéro.* Her heart was filled with the memory of the previous evening's dinner cruise on the river. How she wished she could take Pierre back to the joy of those moments, rescuing him from his present sadness.

"So, you see, *mademoiselle,* I *am* a fraud; and what's worse, I am a coward."

"Not so, *mon amour,*" Esmée said, standing and fluttering her wings, "You saved my life at the Arc de Triomphe. Your *bravery* saved me. Let's let *that* speak for you and we shall say no more."

Esmée smiled and extended her hand to Pierre, who stood to accept it. Kissing her hand, he said, "*Merci, mademoiselle.* We shall say no more. I will let your kindness be my guide."

Changing the subject, and hoping to lighten Pierre's spirits, Esmée blurted out, "Do you see it?"

Pointing through the leaves, she spoke in her best Pierre imitation, "*The tower, she plays a game of hide and seek. Just when you've forgotten she's there, she peeks her face out from behind the leaves.*"

Pierre laughed, recognizing his own words in

Esmée's uncanny imitation of him.

"*Oui, mademoiselle,* I see it. But, the tower, she is a prima donna -- ah *oui*, a prima donna, *certainement.*"

Becoming more serious, he proposed, "You have seen her at night, dressed in fine jewels and firelight. But you have not yet seen all that *she* sees. This we must do."

"I was hoping you'd say that," Esmée replied, with a wide grin. "Lead the way, *mon ami!*"

Pierre and Esmée fluttered up out of the butterfly bush in the *Jardins du Trocadéro* and back toward the river. Crossing the wide walkway, they flew over grass and fountains, streets and sidewalks, until they arrived at the edge of the Seine. There in front of them, across the water, the Eiffel Tower stood in the brilliance of a summer day.

The tower's milk chocolate color stood out against a blue Parisian sky. Esmée was surprised by the color, having only seen the Eiffel Tower at night. But, on second thought, she couldn't really say what color she'd expected it would be. She just hadn't thought about it. Upon reflection, milk chocolate seemed to be a very sensible choice.

"Once," Pierre noted, "the tower, she was yellow. Like a great, big banana. She is repainted every seven years or so and seems to prefer milk chocolate to banana."

"Oh yes," Esmée agreed, "banana-yellow does not suit her at all. She's much too elegant for that."

CHAPTER TWENTY-TWO

The Eiffel Tower

Stretching out before them, a wide bridge spanned the Seine in a straight line between the *Jardins du Trocadéro* and the Eiffel Tower. At both ends, a carrousel of painted ponies stood just to the right of the bridge. Like a visitor from ages past, the carrousel turned bobbing horses into timeless memories. Children and adults sat side-by-side, giggling with joy; while accordion music rippled through the air.

Esmée and Pierre crossed the bridge and passed the carrousel, as they made their way into the gardens around the Eiffel Tower. Near the west pillar, Esmée spotted a turret that could easily have been mistaken for a miniature medieval castle. It was made entirely of brick, with toothlike battlements encircling the top. An arch-shaped iron door -- embedded in the side facing the river -- suggested that it could have been a dungeon at some point in its life, if only it were a bit bigger.

"It is the Chimney of the Eiffel Tower, *mademoiselle.* It was built before the tower herself and used in her construction. It is handsome, *non*?"

"*Oui,* it is very pretty, especially hidden as it is among the gardens. I'd like to live in such a place."

"Like a princess in her tower," Pierre mused.

"Every morning, we could have breakfast beneath the Eiffel Tower; and every evening, we could watch the light show. How wonderful.”

“*Oui*, you are, indeed…” Pierre smiled. “We are almost there,” he said, changing the subject.

“Where, Pierre?”

“Why, at our elevator, of course.” Pierre pointed to the massive leg of the tower in front of them.

Rising at a slight angle, a yellow-orange elevator hugged the curve of the leg, then stopped at the first platform. Esmée imagined the people inside tumbling into a jumbled mess of arms and legs, as the elevator tilted toward one corner. There must be a better way to climb the tower, she thought.

“Elevator?” Esmée was sure Pierre was joking. “What do two butterflies need with an elevator?”

“It is all part of the experience, *mademoiselle.* And *the experience* is everything! Come.”

Esmée had no desire to be crushed at the bottom of a pile of tourists inside a cramped elevator. Flying would certainly be safer *and* faster. Who ever heard of a butterfly taking the elevator, anyway?

“Who ever heard of a butterfly taking the *train*?” Pierre asked, reading Esmée’s mind and startling her in the process. “Here we are, *mademoiselle.*”

Down below, a line of people wound its way along a series of ropes; through a security checkpoint; and up to the glass doors leading inside to the elevator. Pierre landed on a tree limb overlooking the whole scene. Straining his neck to see, he scanned the crowd for a few minutes. He seemed to be searching for someone in particular.

“There he is,” Pierre said, recognizing whomever it was he’d been hoping to find.

“Who?” Esmée asked, surprised to learn that Pierre knew someone there.

“The tallest man in the crowd… wearing a hat, of course. That’s an absolute must.”

Now Esmée was truly confused.

"Here we go…"

Pierre led the way straight for the "tallest man in the crowd," as he'd put it; while the group of tourists began to shuffle their way inside toward the elevator. It was easy for Pierre to keep his target in sight, even among the constantly shuffling river of people being pushed along by their common goal.

The man must have been a full six inches taller than anyone else there. Plus, he wore a fedora that sat perched another 4 inches atop his bald head. It was in the crease of his fedora -- like a valley between two small hills -- that Pierre landed. Esmée had no choice but to join him. Both butterflies now rode through the crowd on top of the "tallest man's" black, felt hat.

"This is ideal, *n'est-ce pas?*"

"I'm not sure this is such a good idea," Esmée said, bobbing up and down as the man walked along.

"Ah, but it is the best view from up here. No one can see us, rest assured, *mademoiselle.*"

Walking through the doors to the waiting area, Esmée could see several enormous, yellow cylinders; bigger than the elevator itself and four times as tall. Each cylinder was connected to a thick, steel cable. As an elevator descended, a cylinder would rise up out of the floor and ascend, by means of its cable, up through the shaft.

"Those are the counterweights. They pull the elevator car down, and also allow the elevators to rise up to first-floor platform. Today they must carry two butterflies. I am confident they are up to the task. *N'ayez pas peur.*"

The counterweights rose, the elevator descended, and two doors slid open to allow fifty or so people to cram themselves inside the elevator. The "tallest man in the crowd" chose the center of the elevator car, which seemed to be to Pierre's satisfaction. The doors closed and the elevator began its very smooth and silent ascent.

Pierre pointed directly overhead, *"Regardez, mademoiselle.* This is why we chose to take the elevator."

In the ceiling of the elevator car there was a large window. Esmée could see the elevator shaft as it extended upward in a mesh of steel girders and rivets. They were now traveling up through the heart of the tower; and the window allowed them to see every inch of it fly by. Faster and faster they ascended; it was just like looking out the front window of a spaceship at hyperspeed.

"Whoa!" Everyone inside the elevator car reacted at the same exact moment in the same exact way. Strangers turned to one another and commented about how exhilarating the experience was. Fear and excitement have a way of breaking down barriers and making friends of strangers. Riding the slanted elevator to the first floor of the Eiffel Tower was both amazing and a little bit scary -- just scary enough to make it feel like a great accomplishment of bravery.

Then Esmée realized it; though it should have come as no surprise. The elevator was slanted, traveling up the curved leg of the tower at an angle; but the people inside hadn't all toppled into one corner. The floor remained flat, even as it followed the curve in the elevator shaft. She didn't understand quite how it worked; but she approved of the solution, whatever it was.

The elevator slowed to a stop; the doors slid open; and a somewhat squished glob of tourists all got out in one, great lump. Winding their way through a maze of ropes, the crowd exited the enclosed room -- out into the open air -- and spread itself along railings overlooking the city.

Pierre hesitated a moment, trying to figure out what their chauffeur had in mind. The "tallest man in the crowd" continued walking around the room until he found the line of tourists waiting for the elevator to *le sommet*: the summit or top of the tower. Stepping in line, the man waited his turn.

"*C'est fantastique,*" Pierre exclaimed. "The tallest man in the crowd came complete with a most-convenient hat and *l'esprit d'aventure.* We'll stay right where we are and let him take us to *le sommet.*"

If the ride to the first floor was *both amazing and a little bit scary,* then the ride to *le sommet* was both incredible and a whole lotta terrifying! This elevator was much smaller than the first, not only because it traveled up through the skinniest part of the tower; but, also because (Esmée was convinced) it didn't need to be very big, since only a few people were brave enough to ride to the top.

Inside, there were the elevator operator; the "tallest man in the crowd" (and atop his hat, Esmée and Pierre); two American women in their early twenties; and an elderly French gentleman wearing a newsie hat and carrying a walking stick. Since the tower was much narrower toward the top, there was less structure all around them -- just the four sides of the shaft, with nothing beyond it but the open air; a drop of over 900 feet; and the city of Paris. It felt as if the weight of the elevator might topple the tower over and send them all plummeting into the river, below.

When the doors opened and the cool wind hit them in the face, Esmée realized just how high up they'd traveled. They were now so high that *street-level summertime* felt like *sky-level springtime*. It was noticeably colder at the top.

In all her flying experience, she had never flown so near the face of the sky. Nestling down into the valley between the ridges of the "tallest man in the crowd's" hat, the two little butterflies were protected from the grasp of the gusty wind. Their chauffeur stepped outside; walked to the railing; and stood looking toward the west.

The first thing Esmée noticed was the tremendous shadow of the tower itself. Covering entire city blocks and stretching beyond the river, the Eiffel Tower cast its shadow like a huge sundial. If the sheer size of the structure hadn't sunk in before, it sure did now. Flapping her wings, Esmée looked carefully at the point on the shadow where they now stood, hoping to see her own shadow flapping its wings down below.

"There, *mademoiselle,* do you recognize it?"

At the foot of the tower was a perfectly straight bridge with a carrousel of horses to its left. Across the bridge, Esmée could see two large buildings forming a semicircle, like two arms reaching out for a hug. In the center of the semicircle, an oblong, oval reflecting pool -- flanked by a parade of fountains on either side — reflected the sunlight back toward the sky. Esmée recognized the patch of trees to the left as the place where they'd enjoyed their breakfast that morning.

"*Les Jardins du Trocadéro*! I see it! And the carrousel on either end. *C'est magnifique!* But what is that area over there?" Esmée pointed far out beyond the city to a large forest.

"That is the Bois de Boulogne, *mademoiselle.* Along its paths you will find lakes, gardens and even an amusement park for children. There is also a legend, *oui, un mythe, peut-être.* Some say it is true, but I, *je ne sais pas.*"

"What legend, Pierre? Please, tell me."

"I have heard the myth of the Bois de Boulogne Groundhogs. It is said that they have created a network of tunnels wider and farther-reaching than the Paris Metro. And that they use it to communicate quickly over very large distances. Fascinating, *non*?"

"Yes. In Saint-Denis, the groundhogs are very clever and industrious. They're always popping up, everywhere you look! I believe it."

Esmée found it easy to believe fantastical stories, when she was surrounded by so much that was simply *fantastique.*

"The forest is beautiful," she said. "*Everything* is beautiful from up here."

"Yes, it is," Pierre said, watching Esmée enjoy the view. "Look… just to the right of the forest, but closer-in toward us. Do you see? Look for the hub cap in the middle of the bicycle spokes… the circle where twelve streets meet."

"The Arc de Triomphe! Yes, I see it. It looks so small from here."

Esmée had almost forgotten about her close call with the tourist bus in the roundabout, so distracted was she by her view from the top of the world.

"Like a Monopoly token dropped down in the middle of the city, *oui.* Still, it is majestic. And there, off to the right and on toward the horizon. The high hill. That is Montmartre. Ah, from there you have almost as grand a view as we do now."

Esmée watched Pierre as he spoke. He loved every detail of the city. Most of all, he loved sharing it with Esmée. He knew each place the same way a man might know his best friend; for every corner of the ancient city has its own character. Every landmark, every monument, every café and bakery have a story to tell.

There are tales of ambition and conquest, behind the Arc de Triomphe; tales that ended in failure and defeat for one man, rebirth and renewed greatness for a nation.

There are stories of a faraway land and another age, wrapped up in each engraving on the face of the obelisk in the Place de la Concorde. Even the large crack in the corner of its base has a history all its own to share.

Inside the walls of the Louvre are volumes upon volumes of lives and loves; anguish and achievement;

injustice, injury and eternal truths; all on display for the world to see and contemplate.

From the top of the Eiffel Tower -- itself a symbol of one man's achievement and one city's acceptance of what was once called an *eyesore* (much like the Louvre Pyramid!) -- you can see hundreds of years-worth of history. That history is written across the face of one of the most important cities on earth. You can choose to think about it all with large, sweeping thoughts; or you can choose to use thoughts no bigger than one, single person going about his daily life somewhere among the streets of Paris. Everywhere you look, there is a story unfolding. The story is endless, the actors are infinite.

This is what Pierre saw from the summit of the Eiffel Tower. This is what Esmée could sense reflected in his heart and echoing in his every word. She never wanted it to end. She never wanted to say goodbye to Pierre forever; and she knew he felt the same way about her.

"From that side, *mademoiselle*," Pierre said, motioning over toward the left, "you can look south toward the Parc André-Citroën with its hot air balloon; and beyond toward *La Seine Musicale*. From the other side," he now motioned toward the right, "you can look north past the Louvre, the Pont Neuf, and on toward Notre-Dame. There is so much to take in, *non*?"

The "tallest man in the crowd" now wandered over to the opposite side from where he had been standing. Still hidden in the crease of his hat, Esmée and Pierre now looked out over a large rectangular patch of grass extending eastward from the foot of the tower. Just off to the left and further away from the tower, there stood a single skyscraper. Esmée asked Pierre what it was.

"*C'est la Tour Montparnasse*. An office building. It is tall, *oui*, but we are much taller. To me, it looks out of place. Like a single stalk of corn in a field of small flowers. But it is there and there it must remain."

Further to the left, toward the river, there stood a gold-domed church. Stately and slender, the roof was supported by many graceful columns. Atop the dome, a golden lantern sat crowned by a three-sided obelisk. Beneath the church, in the crypt, is buried the Emperor Napoleon.

"It is the Dome Church of *les Invalides*. The man whose victories inspired the Arc de Triomphe sleeps beneath that dome," Pierre said in a reverent whisper. "His tomb is a work of art in and of itself, *oui*. We must go there someday, *mademoiselle*. We must stand in the presence of Napoleon himself."

The sun had crossed its zenith and was now westering, when their chauffeur finally decided he'd seen enough. The "tallest man in the crowd" reached up to remove his hat, sending his two butterfly stowaways fluttering up to a steel beam overhead. The man wiped his bald head with a handkerchief, then replaced his fedora.

Esmée leaned over and whispered in Pierre's ear, "There's the second shiny dome we've seen today."

Pierre laughed at the comparison of the man's head to the Dome Church, "*Oui, mademoiselle,* and just as pointy as the first."

The "tallest man in the crowd" turned and headed back toward the door leading to the elevator inside.

"Our ride, he is leaving. What would you like to do, *ma petite*?"

"Here's what I think," Esmée rubbed her two upper legs together, savoring the possibilities. "I think we should fly down and eat an early dinner. But before sunset, we should come back up here so we can enjoy the light show up close! What do you think?"

"*C'est une bonne idée*. But it's a long way down and an even longer way back up, *mademoiselle*. Especially if the wind is against us."

"It's all part of the experience," Esmée laughed.

"And *the experience* is everything!"

"Again, you use my own words against me. *Très bien,* tonight the tower, she will be our hostess. But let us hitch a ride down on the hat of our chauffeur before he leaves. Flying back up will be tiring enough."

Just as the "tallest man in the crowd" was getting on the elevator, Esmée and Pierre landed on top of his hat. Laying down on their backs and staring up through the window in the ceiling of the elevator car, they watched as the summit sped up and away into the distance. Talking about all they had seen from the highest point in Paris, they shared their favorite landmarks and most interesting discoveries.

Esmée said that her favorite landmark was the Dome Church of *les Invalides.* It's like a gold coin in a box of buttons: it stands out and shines so brilliantly. Despite her scary experience at the Arc de Triomphe, she said that it was a close second. Nothing gave her a better sense of the height of the Eiffel Tower than the apparent smallness of the truly enormous Arc de Triomphe.

Pierre said the bridges and the river are always his favorite things to see from the Eiffel Tower. Each bridge is unique, and the river always gives you a point of reference by which to find everything else.

"When in doubt, just follow the river," he said.

"When in doubt, just follow the river," she repeated under her breath. "*...because the river will always lead you...* That's what Stéphanie the bee said. Maybe *that's* what she meant."

Esmée looked at Pierre, her eyes popped with sudden realization.

"Maybe she meant that, when we're lost, all we need to do is find a point of reference. But how will the river lead me all the way back to Saint-Denis? The owl moth said it doesn't flow anywhere near there." Esmée sighed. "I guess I still don't understand."

"*Mademoiselle,* if it is home you want, I will do all I can to help you find your way there. I will not be selfish. Although my heart..." Pierre began, then changed his mind, "No matter what, I am at your service. All I want is your happiness."

Esmée looked into Pierre's eyes and, taking his hand in hers, she said, "I no longer miss my home. Not like I did. If going home means leaving you, then I will not go. Everything I want is right here. You have become my home."

Leaning over, she kissed Pierre.

The "tallest man in the crowd" exited the last elevator and walked outside beneath the tower. Stopping a moment, he removed his fedora very carefully. Peering down into the crease of his hat, he thought he saw two butterflies sitting there sharing a kiss beneath the darkening sky; but that would be ridiculous.

Replacing his hat on top of his bald head, he smiled at the thought; then walked off to the east of the tower, in the opposite direction of the river. They were now heading into the *Champ de Mars.*

CHAPTER TWENTY-THREE

The Master of the *Champ de Mars*

Of all the ideal places in Paris to take a walk, ride a bike, or have a picnic, the *Champ de Mars* may be the best. It's not just because it's a wide, sunny space in the heart of the city. It's not just because it has marvelous sidewalks and green, grassy lawns. It's not even because of its curious square-shaped trees. The *Champ de Mars* might very well be the best place in Paris to spend time outside, because of its view of the Eiffel Tower.

Whether you spy the tower as it peeks around buildings or catch it as it pops-up over rooftops and chimneys, you never get tired of saying, "Hey, look! The Eiffel Tower!" From a boat or a bridge, by day or by night, every vantagepoint is new and exciting.

Then you ride the elevators to the top of the tower and step out onto the steel beams and platforms themselves, and you understand all that was required to construct such a wonder. Resting your hand against the bare bones of its skeleton, you feel the tower's heartbeat: throbbing and alive.

Then you begin to explore the city -- not just to discover every hidden jewel of art and history, food and culture – no, you begin to explore the city in order to discover the tower anew. How does the Eiffel Tower look when it's a grey and rainy day? How does it appear against the rising sun? What does it look like from the

Pont Neuf or the Tuileries Garden? Can you capture both the Eiffel Tower and the obelisk of the Place de la Concorde in the same photo? It becomes an obsession, and one that every visitor to the City of Lights has experienced. The tower never gets old; you never tire of finding it; it will always be your favorite.

The "tallest man in the crowd," with his felt fedora and two stowaways, understood this well. That's why he walked from the Eiffel Tower right out into the middle of the *Champ de Mars*: he'd never seen the tower from *there* before. Surely, it would be worth the walk. He was so right.

The sun was now directly behind the Eiffel Tower and setting quickly -- as only a cold, Northern European sun can. From the *Champ de Mars*, the backlit tower appeared black. Rays of light shot out from between steel girders, then hid themselves again, as the world spun into darkness.

Standing in the middle of the great lawn, the "tallest man in the crowd" gazed back at the tower for a while. In a gesture of grateful respect, he removed his hat, tipping it in the direction of *la Belle Dame de Paris*. Esmée and Pierre flew off just in time to avoid the hat-tipping and landed in one of the numerous square trees that line the walkways of the *Champ de Mars*. The man then returned his hat to its place, turned, and walked off into the evening.

"*Merci, mon ami,*" Pierre called out, as the man strolled beneath the boxy trees. "You are very kind."

The man hesitated a moment, cocking his head in Pierre's direction; then nodding with a smile, he continued on his way. Pierre knew it was always best to believe every kindness, so he took the man's head-nod to mean, "*De rien, mes petits papillons.*" Because, you just never know.

The *Champ de Mars* offered plenty of clover buds

for two butterflies to choose from; and so Esmée and Pierre set about sipping their early dinner of nectar. They'd skipped lunch and, though breakfast had been very filling, the excitement of viewing the city from such a height had made their stomachs echo with hunger. There was no hurry; they had no plans, aside from returning to the top of the tower before dark. So, the pair took their time and sampled every flower in the patch.

As the day drew to a close, people in the *Champ de Mars* started to pack up their picnic baskets, collect their children, and head home for the evening. Frisbees and badminton birdies, kites and bocce sets were stowed in bags slung over the shoulders of young and old, Parisians and tourists. It was nearing time for *apéro*: the before-dinner appetizer the French enjoy so well. Before long, Esmée and Pierre were quite alone in the park, still having their dinner in the clover patch.

Out of the long shadows beneath the buzzcut trees on the edge of the park, a large, lumbering figure now appeared. It was wide and squat, as if flattened by a rolling pin; and it walked like a grumpy inchworm in a big hurry. Esmée first spotted the creature from afar and alerted Pierre, who, once he saw it, did not seem to be the least bit concerned.

"You really should be moving on," a gruff voice came from the fast-approaching animal. "I intend to eat every last clover in that patch and, I'm afraid, you'll be left with nothing but stems and roots. Shoo! Shoo, now!"

"*Bonsoir,* friend," Pierre called, from a bud he'd just drained of nectar. "Please, join us!"

"I do *not* like socializing, especially at mealtime. Just keep to yourselves, if you please," the creature huffed.

Esmée looked at Pierre with astonishment at the animal's tone of voice. She was even more astonished to see Pierre chuckling to himself. He still showed no concern at all about the oversized, curmudgeonly creature. Thinking it best to avoid trouble whenever trouble could be avoided, Esmée suggested they let the newcomer to enjoy his dinner – if he was *capable* of enjoyment – and leave him alone and in peace. Pierre obviously had other plans.

Ignoring the request to "keep to himself," Pierre replied in his usual friendly manner, "*Monsieur* badger, you are more than welcome to share this patch with us. The clover is exceptional. I wonder, though, might I have the honor of your name?"

"Badger?" Esmée asked, more than a little bit alarmed. "Aren't badgers dangerous?"

"*Oui, mademoiselle,* they can be." Pierre conceded to her in a whisper, "But this one is more unpleasant than strictly dangerous. I recognize him. His size makes him unmistakable. Fear not, *ma petite,* we are quite safe from harm – as long as we are not too sensitive to his rudeness."

"My dear sir," the badger replied to Pierre's invitation, with a formal though terse impatience, "Small talk is a waste of time, dinner never is. Stay if you must but leave off the chit-chat. And if you expect me to exchange cheek-kisses in the French manner, you'll find me quite resistant to the idea. Yes, quite resistant, indeed. One might fritter-away hours on such nonsense and never see the end of it."

Pierre was very good at ignoring the rougher edges of someone's personality, all the while encouraging their softer qualities. He continued in exactly the same way with the ill-tempered badger, who was now loudly munching his way through wide swathes of the clover patch.

"Am I, *monsieur,* mistaken in assuming I have the pleasure of speaking with the estimable Boswell Badger?"

"You are persistent. I'll give you that." Munch, munch, gulp, swallow, munch, swallow, gulp.

"Assuming is often dangerous, of course. If you assume incorrectly, then everything after your assumption is built on shaky ground. If there is any pleasure to be had in this conversation, I assure you, it is *you* who is having it, not I. Nonetheless, yes, I *am* Boswell Badger of the *Champ de Mars*. In that much, you are correct. I, however, have no interest in learning your name, or that of your silent partner, there. Thank you both very much."

"*C'est vrai, monsieur,* the pleasure *is* all mine, indeed. It is an honor to meet you. Allow me to introduce the lady, Esmée, to you. She is visiting Paris from Saint-Denis. This is her first time in our fair city."

Pierre chose to ignore this latest barrage of impoliteness from the badger. But the moment he'd ignored it, Boswell started right in again.

"Allow you? I hardly had time or opportunity to *prevent* you from introducing her. Very well, then. *Enchanté, mademoiselle.*" Munch, munch, gulp, swallow, munch, swallow, gulp.

"*Enchanté, monsieur* badger," Esmée was careful to avoid annoying the persnickety rodent with chit-chat. She kept her reply short, sweet and to the point.

"And I," Pierre said with some ceremony, switching to French, "*Je suis Pierre Cardui, monsieur. Enchanté.*"

"*Oui, oui,* yes, yes, yes. I suppose you'll be leaving now. *Très bien, bonsoir.*" Munch, gulp, swallow, munch, munch.

"*Oui, monsieur,* we will be enjoying the light show from atop the Eiffel Tower tonight, and we must be on our way. Before we go, though…"

"Oh great, just when I thought it was over…" Munch, gulp, munch.

"*Pardon, monsieur.*" Pierre extended his hand in apology for delaying their departure. "Before we go, I was hoping you might tell us the latest news."

Boswell Badger let out a long, very annoyed sigh, swallowed his mouthful of clover, and responded with great vexation, "There is no news. None. Whatsoever. Sooner or later, everyone asks me that question. It's tiresome. Now, leave me in peace." Munch, munch, munch, grumpy munch, grumpy gulp.

"*Merci, monsieur. Bonne nuit.*"

"Yes, yes, yes," Boswell mumbled through a mouthful of leaves and buds.

Pierre winked at Esmée and the two of them flew as quietly as they could back toward the Eiffel Tower, leaving the antisocial badger alone in his clover patch. Munching, gulping, swallowing until every last clover blossom had been devoured. It must be said that Boswell Badger was not really a mean badger; he was just what you might call… crusty.

He'd always lived alone and the only way he knew *how* to live was… well, alone. He had his ways of doing things; and he was quite certain those were the best ways of doing those particular things. Just like a peanut butter and jelly sandwich left on its own for too long, over time, Boswell got crusty.

Alone, he never had to make conversation with anyone but himself; and even if he did talk to himself, he certainly wouldn't waste his own time with chit-chat, as he called it. Alone, he never had to wait for anyone but himself; or share anything with anyone but himself; or put up with endless, annoying questions from anyone but himself. Alone just seemed to be the best way to be, for Boswell Badger, anyhow.

He'd been born right there in the *Champ de Mars*, so long ago he'd forgotten precisely when. Since he had no close friends to send him birthday wishes, he had no one to remind him of his age -- let alone the exact day upon which he was born. Imagine forgetting your own birthday! That might make anyone a bit grumpy.

He did have two brothers, Brice and Benoit; but it's said they were just as crusty as he was, so they hardly kept in touch with one another. Of the three brothers, Boswell was the oldest, this much was certain. It was also certain that, of the three, Boswell was by far the largest. In fact, of all the badgers in all of Paris, Boswell Badger was the biggest.

He was respected by every animal who knew him; but it wasn't because of his warm, friendly disposition (that's for sure) or even his imposing size. He wasn't well-respected because of his deep, booming voice or even his habit of wearing handsome, tweed waistcoats (unusual for any animal, somewhat less so for a badger).

You might think that an irritable and ill-natured badger such as Boswell would be avoided and disliked by everyone who had the misfortune of meeting him; but this was not the case. The truth is, Boswell was respected for his wisdom.

Like most badgers, Boswell was a keen observer. He kept a close watch on people, animals, things, and events. Unlike most badgers, though, he thought about everything he saw; and he learned from it all. He was like a big, furry, living library. He'd seen it all; he'd drawn his conclusions; he'd learned many lessons. All anyone ever had to do was ask his opinion and, once his annoyance at being disturbed wore off, Boswell could give excellent advice.

Birds would ask Boswell for his opinion on where they should build their nests. Which trees were best? Which locations were safest? Since he was always up-to-date on the news in and around Paris, Boswell knew where the predators were hiding; which trees were scheduled for pruning and trimming; and what parts of the city were the windiest. All of these things were very useful to a new family of birds looking to build their first home.

Squirrels would ask Boswell for advice on where to store their stash of acorns; what streets they should avoid crossing; and which parks were best for finding human food. Boswell constantly received reports of any burglaries around Paris, so he knew which trees had been robbed of their acorns in the past, and likely would be again.

He knew all the busiest streets and traffic circles in the city; so, he could caution squirrels about the dangers of crossing such places as the Arc de Triomphe roundabout or the Place de la Concorde.

Of course, human food was in high demand all around Paris. Parks where people enjoyed picnicking, tourist attractions, and especially restaurant dumpsters were always topics of discussion; and of course, Boswell heard it all. This was very useful information.

Yes, Boswell Badger was well-respected for being "in-the-know" and for giving wise advice; which was absolutely unfortunate for Boswell.

It isn't known for sure if Boswell became so very disagreeable before or after his reputation for wisdom became public knowledge. Some say he was always grumpy, since his brothers are said to be just as surly; but this is difficult to prove, since no one has ever actually met Brice or Benoit.

Some say he became ill-humored *after* word got out about his formidable brain. This seems to make better sense. The more animals who bugged Boswell for advice, the grumpier he got. The more animals who came knocking on his door, the more he wanted to chase them all away.

Like I said before, being respected for his wisdom was very unfortunate for Boswell and his peace, quiet and privacy. So, to make others think twice before asking him for advice or news or even just the time of day, Boswell Badger became the most cross and cantankerous badger southeast of the Bois de Boulogne forest.

Because he was always being badgered for advice, whether he liked it or not (and he did *not*), Boswell had the misfortune of having to speak with dozens of animals every day. The result was that his admirers left wiser than when they arrived; and Boswell collected from *them* all the news from in and around Paris.

Among the flocks and herds of animals trying to pick his brain every day, Boswell also had a small group of business associates who visited him regularly. These three associates came to Boswell, not for advice, but to *exchange* news.

In all of Paris, only two sources could be found for reliable news -- neither of which was *Le Journal*, by the way. The first was Boswell Badger, whose wisdom could sniff-out phony news in a heartbeat. The second source for reliable news was the Bois de Boulogne *interconnected network.*

Every week (more often, when something big was happening), Boswell Badger was visited by a handful of *network managers* from the closest *server rooms* to the *Champ de Mars*. The nearest, of course, is the *CM-TE*. Victor, the *network manager* of the *Champ de Mars – Tour Eiffel server room*, visited Boswell every two or three days, without fail. The badger and the groundhog would share the news from above and below ground over a cup of tea and a buttered croissant. It was always a very brief, matter-of-fact, to-the-point meeting – with no chit-chat, if you please.

Then there was Hugo, the *network manager* for the *JdT server room*, across the river in the *Jardins du Trocadéro*. These weekly meetings often ended in a very irate Boswell showing Hugo the door. It wasn't Hugo's fault. In fact, of all the *network managers* who visited Boswell on a regular basis, it could be argued that Hugo was the most mild-mannered and polite. He was not the type to argue, and rarely allowed himself to get riled up.

Still, the conversation always seemed to go the same way. The tea would be poured; the croissants would be buttered; the latest news would be exchanged; but then, invariably, Boswell would start in on the topic that always ended with an angry, red-faced badger throwing his guest out in a huff.

Hugo tried his best to avoid the inevitable argument; but Boswell always insisted on asking the one question that Hugo simply would not answer: how do the Bois de Boulogne groundhogs extend their *internet* across the river? Poor Hugo, he always dreaded these weekly meetings. Why Boswell never asked Victor this question, Hugo couldn't guess. Most likely, it's because Boswell knew he didn't have a chance with Victor, whereas the kindly Hugo was easier to intimidate.

The third *network manager* to regularly meet and exchange news with the ornery Boswell Badger was from the *T1 server room* just southwest of the Parc André-Citroën and across the river. This *network manager*, though one of the youngest on the *internet*, was as smart as they came. He was descended from a long line of distinguished groundhogs, many of whom had made noteworthy contributions to the development of a more efficient groundhog language.

Despite this particular *network manager's* habit of interrupting others when his brain got ahead of his manners, he was one of the few other living creatures whom Boswell Badger actually liked. Their meetings, though somewhat less frequent than the other groundhogs', always included an element of – dare I say it? – chit-chat. The young groundhog had a way of entertaining the old badger, even to the point of laughter.

If you've ever heard a badger laugh, you know how strange it sounds. Boswell's laugh was stranger, still. The enormous badger's deep, rolling chuckle sounded like a thunderstorm trapped in the cavernous belly of a whale. There's a word that best describes this kind of laugh, but it isn't used very often, nowadays. The word is chortle. The old badger chortled; and only the *network manager* from the *T1 server room* – a groundhog named Marmot (of course) – could make him chortle. No one else ever could.

It was Thursday night, and not far to the south, Audrey and Pica had just fallen asleep in Marmot's apartment -- having barely kept up with the nimble groundhog through the mindboggling maze of tunnels. But here, in the shadow of the Eiffel Tower, Boswell Badger was just finishing off the last blossom in the clover patch.

After his final munch, munch, gulp, and swallow, he turned and waddled his way back to his den beneath the square-shaped trees along the edge of the *Champ de Mars.* Burrowing his way deep underground, he removed his tweed waistcoat -- hanging it carefully on a coat hook-- then pulled a blanket of leaves and discarded bird feathers up around his shoulders. In no time at all, the biggest badger in all of Paris was snoring, rumbling and echoing all throughout his cozy den.

With full bellies and recharged wings, Esmée and Pierre flew over half the length of the *Champ de Mars,* all the way to the foot of the tower. That's when their work really began. It is 1,063 feet to the very tip of the Eiffel Tower, and 906 feet to the uppermost platform. It would take Esmée and Pierre thousands of flaps of their tiny wings to mount to such a height. They were tired after a long day, but the view of the city lights promised to be worth the effort; so, flap, they did. And flap. And flap.

And flap, flap, flap, flap. All the long, windy way to the uppermost observation platform. There, they rested, sitting right down on the floor -- alone atop the Eiffel Tower.

Only the round, bald top of the sun's golden head (the third shiny dome they'd seen that day, Pierre pointed out) now shown above the horizon. The Bois de Boulogne forest was a black eyepatch on the face of the city. Bridges, like strings of Christmas lights, crossed the dark ribbon of the river below. Boats -- some just like the dinner cruise boat Esmée and Pierre had taken the night before -- left v-shaped wrinkles in their wake. As far as Esmée could see, in every direction, buildings and streetlights began to glimmer in gold and silver. Down the *rues* and avenues, diamond-white headlights and ruby-red brake lights pulsed in endless motion, like blood through the city's veins.

The two butterflies sat in silent awe. There wasn't a sound; not even the wind dared to whisper in the presence of such beauty. Though many of the buildings and landmarks were difficult to make out in the dark, some were much easier to find. The Arc de Triomphe and the twelve roads leading into its traffic circle looked like a toppled-over Ferris wheel ablaze with flickering fire. All around the tower, the butterflies moved together: finding something new to look at, then sitting down to enjoy it for long stretches at a time. Still, not a word was spoken

It was now just a few minutes before the hour. During the summertime, the Eiffel Tower light show begins after sunset: on the hour, every hour until 2 a.m. The show lasts for five minutes and then the tower rests until the top of the next hour. In addition to the golden lights which illuminate the entire structure, and the white strobe lights which play upon the surface, great beams shoot up into the night sky from the lighthouse at the summit.

It was this spectacular event that Esmée and Pierre had watched from their boat on the previous night. They would now experience it from the tower, itself. Like fireflies inside a cloud of fireworks, they would be completely surrounded by a five-minute explosion of light.

With the precision of a Swiss watch, right as the second hand crossed the hour the most recognizable symbol of France burst into a scene of sparkling motion. Esmée's eyes widened to take it all in, as her mouth dropped open, speechless with amazement. Watching as the light filtered through her wings, she spread them open like an angel. Down below, all eyes were on the tower. Esmée felt like she did when she was standing on the tip of the *Pyramide du Louvre*: a princess dressed in gold and jewels; a queen bathed in pure light.

Pierre glanced over and saw the look of imagination on Esmée's face. He saw the innocence of her heart and the natural curiosity of her mind. He had never been atop the Eiffel Tower at night; this was a first for him, and he could not imagine sharing this with anyone but Esmée. He wanted to share everything, from this day forward, with her. Before he knew it, the words were on his lips.

"*Mon amour,* will you... be mine," Pierre paused and took Esmée's hand, "...forever?"

"*Pour toujours et à jamais... oui,*" Esmée whispered, "Forever and ever."

Kisses come in many different kinds. Some kisses bring greetings, like the kind of cheek-kisses Boswell Badger despised. There are other kisses that bring healing, like when a child scrapes her knee falling off her bicycle. Then again, a kiss can mark the end of something, like a goodbye kiss. But the best kisses are *beginning kisses*. These kisses mark the start of something wonderful, like the rest of your life. It was that kind of kiss that Esmée and Pierre now shared.

"Last night was so perfect," Esmée whispered, "The cruise, the river, the view of the tower. I couldn't imagine seeing anything more beautiful."

"Tonight, *ma chère*, you have *become* the beauty that you saw. You are a part of this tower; a light in its arms; a star in the night's sky. And I cannot imagine anything more beautiful."

Exactly five minutes after they had first been illuminated, the lights on the Eiffel Tower went out. Only the moon now lent its glow to the darkened sky. In the angled meeting-place of two steel beams, there was an abandoned bird's nest. Not far from it, one of the thousands of well-concealed light fixtures formed a protected nesting place of its own against the face of the tower. Pierre offered the bird's nest to Esmée, to spend the night in comfort. He, himself would take the light fixture. After a kiss on the forehead, Pierre bowed ever-so-slightly to Esmée, and wished her a restful night's sleep.

"*Merci, mon amour,*" she said with a smile. "Today is the first day of the rest of my life with you. We will never be apart again. *Je suis très heureux, oui,* very, very happy. *Bonne nuit.* Sleep well, my love."

The moon rose over the Eiffel Tower, upon which two *butterflies-in-love* now slept. What scene could be more stunning; and what could ever ruin such happiness? Esmée was quite certain that nothing ever would.

Victor

Boswell Badger was not what you might call a "morning person." A "morning person," as you know, is someone who enjoys getting up early and starting their day with bright and cheery optimism. Boswell did not fit this description at all. In fact, not only was he *not* a "morning person," but he could never really be described as bright or cheery at *any* time of the day or night. So, it should come as no surprise to learn that Boswell often slept-in rather late. It was not unusual to find him still asleep at ten or ten-thirty in the morning. It was also not advisable to awaken him. Ever.

Victor, the *network manager* at the *Champ de Mars – Tour Eiffel server room* knew this, of course. Their weekly meetings to exchange news never took place before lunchtime. They were always held during afternoon tea, and only ever *once* a week. The only exception to this rule occurred when there was urgent news to communicate, like there was on this particular Friday morning.

Victor left his hole, located beneath the northeastern foot of the Eiffel Tower, the moment he read Marmot's message, sent the previous evening. This message was important, and someone's safety was at stake. It might just be that this *Esmée's* only hope of ever being found hung upon Victor. Perhaps everything depended upon him spreading the word of her dire situation far and wide.

He only wished that he'd seen the message sooner, but he had gone to bed earlier than usual the night before. He'd felt the beginnings of a "head cold with a sinus infection" and wanted to get rid of it as soon as possible. Anyway, Victor was an early riser (a "morning person," if you will) and knew he could catch up on the night's messages in no time.

First thing that morning, Victor saw the little green label on his *server room* mailbox and went right over to retrieve the folded paper it contained. Dated Thursday night at 8:15 p.m., the message read,

"Priority 1: Urgent!
From: Network Manager, T1 Server Room
To: All Recipients

Alert: Lost butterfly in Paris! Last seen on front page of *Le Journal* posing on top of *la Pyramide du Louvre*. Reference *Le Journal* dated Wednesday last. Butterfly is a *belle dame* named Esmée from Saint-Denis-lès-Chevreuse. According to friends, may be in grave danger. Any information, contact T1 Server Room immediately."

This was the urgent communication Marmot had sent after saying goodnight to Audrey and Pica the night they first arrived at his apartment. And Victor knew just what to do. If anyone outside of the Boulogne *internet* had any information about this unfortunate butterfly, it would be Boswell Badger. Despite the early hour, Boswell needed to be awakened, and Victor was the one to do it.

Clutching the message in one paw, the groundhog

scurried hurriedly through the tunnels connecting the *CM – TE server room* to the outside world. Popping his head out of the *access point* hole, he sniffed the air and scanned the sky for any danger. Satisfied there were no hawks or foxes lurking about, he ran as fast as his four short legs would carry him. Entering the open space of the *Champ de Mars*, Victor hid himself beneath a line of square-cut trees, until he reached the opening to Boswell Badger's den.

Gulping for air and trying to catch his breath, Victor hovered his head over the hole in the ground and called out as loud as he could, "Boswell Badger, I must speak with you immediately. It's an emergency!"

No answer came.

Victor tried a second time, "Boswell Badger, it's Victor. I have news of an emergency. I must speak with you."

Still nothing.

Listening at the entrance to Boswell's den, Victor's ear finally focused on a sound coming from within. It was snoring. Deep, loud, guttural snoring, as if a hippopotamus suffering from a "head cold with a sinus infection" were asleep inside. The badger was out like a light. This called for desperate measures.

Running over to a trash bin near the edge of the park, Victor grabbed the lid from the top of the can. He then picked up the biggest rock he could find, carried the two back over to Boswell's front door, and started banging the rock against the metal lid.

Flocks of pigeons, nesting in the squared-off trees, took to the air in alarm. The morning joggers, sweating their way through the *Champ de Mars,* all stopped mid-jog, listening for the source of the hideous racket. Even a policeman making his early rounds had to rub the disbelief from his eyes when he saw a groundhog beating a rock against the lid of a trashcan. The *gendarme* decided to call-in sick and get some much-needed rest. Surely, he was out of sorts.

If Victor's goal had been to awaken all of Paris, he very nearly succeeded. As it was, there was only one ill-natured badger he meant to rouse; and it appeared he had done just that. Without warning, a paw shot out of the hole in the ground, smacking the trashcan lid and rock out of Victor's hands, and startling the tenacious little groundhog.

"That is *quite* enough!" Boswell pulled himself out of the tight opening with great difficulty. "What is the meaning of this? Have you lost your mind?"

"I received an alert over the *internet*. Here, read it for yourself." Victor handed the message to Boswell, who snatched it out of his hand with a snort.

"Lost?" Boswell's mood softened, as he read the name mentioned in the alert message, "Esmée..." His hand dropped to his side. Still clutching the paper, he turned to Victor with a distant look in his eyes and said, "And she was from Saint-Denis, too. It was her."

"Who?"

"Esmée," Boswell said, piecing it all together. "The two butterflies in the clover patch last night. Pierre. That was him. And he said her name was Esmée and that she was from Saint-Denis. She did not appear to be in 'grave danger,' though. They appeared to be..." the badger scratched his head, "...in love."

"We need to find them," Victor said in haste. "There's a full-scale search and rescue being organized. This message is proof of it. We need to find Esmée and sort it all out. Her friends are obviously worried about her. She needs to know. Oh dear, this is terrible."

"Now relax, young groundhog," Boswell said, patting Victor on the back in an uncharacteristic show of kindness. "I know exactly where they are."

"You do?"

"Of course, I do. They're right there."

Pointing up at the Eiffel Tower behind Victor, Boswell handed the message to him, then walked back over to his hole.

"I'll be right back."

Boswell squeezed himself into his den, while Victor replaced both the trashcan lid and the rock, then waited for Boswell to return. A moment later, Boswell's head reappeared in the hole in the ground, soon followed (though somewhat more slowly) by the rest of him. He had put his handsome, tweed waistcoat back on and brushed his gray hair and silver sideburns. He really was an impressive-looking badger.

"Off we go, then. And do try to keep up."

Boswell lead the way at a surprising pace across the *Champ de Mars.* He paused, only briefly, to grab a mouthful of clover, saying, "We must keep our strength up, mustn't we?"

Victor, of course, was in complete agreement. He, too, grabbed a mouthful of clover, and a couple additional fists-full for the road. Reaching the plaza beneath the Eiffel Tower, the badger and the groundhog ran, full speed, toward the western foot. It was barely 7 a.m. and the crowds of tourists would not arrive for another two hours or so. They still had time. Unfortunately, at this early hour, the tower was closed. That meant no elevators and no stairs.

Neither badgers nor groundhogs like heights. This must be understood. They are not climbers; they're burrowers. Their claws are designed for digging, not for scaling tall objects. In Paris, as you know, there's no object taller than the Eiffel Tower, and these two natural burrowers were just about to climb it.

The concrete base of the Eiffel Tower's western foot has decorative indentations in its face. The indentations look as if someone pushed a star-shaped cookie-cutter into the base when the cement was still wet. Most of all, these divots made excellent toeholds for Boswell and Victor, who wasted no time in running right up the side of the footing and onto the steel beams.

The whole tower is constructed like an enormous rose trellis of mesh of girders. This makes climbing very easy, except for the fact that one can always see right through the steel structure all the way to the ground. For those with a fear of heights (and, indeed, any *sane* person or animal) the very thought of climbing up the outside of the highest structure in Paris would be madness. For Boswell and Victor, it was necessary.

At first, scaling the western leg was rather easy. There was plenty to grab hold of and the pair of climbers was still very near the ground, and so not overly afraid of falling. As they approached the first platform, however, things got trickier. The steal supporting each of the floors has a smooth wall running around it. As a result, when Boswell and Victor got to the bottom of the first floor, there was nothing to hold onto.

After discussing the predicament for a moment, they decided that the best thing to do would be to reach up as far as they could; grab onto the platform; and swing themselves up to the floor's surface. This was risky, since they would have to let go of the tower in mid-swing and fly through the air up to the platform. If they slipped and let go at the wrong moment or missed landing on the floor altogether, they might very well fall all the way back down to the hard pavement below.

Though Boswell Badger was known to be a very large badger, what may not have been widely known was that he was also a very strong badger. Victor, on the other hand, was somewhat short, even for a groundhog. The length of his arms was less than half that of Boswell's; and so, it made sense for Boswell to swing up to the platform first, then reach down and pull Victor up after.

Balancing on the tiptoes of his hind legs, Boswell stood on the ledge just above where the latticework of steel mesh ended and the smooth, solid wall of the platform's supporting beams began. Resting his left paw against the side of the tower, he stretched his right arm up as far as he could reach. Straining and groaning, beads of sweat broke out across Boswell's forehead. He wiggled his fingers, as if trying to make them grow just a bit longer. He bobbed up and down on his toes, hoping the extra spring in his feet would carry him just *that much* closer to the first floor. But, no matter how much he tried, there was still a distance of one or two inches between the tips of his fingers and the first-floor platform. He couldn't reach it.

"This will not do," he said, looking up at his target with annoyance. "This simply will not do."

"I have an idea," Victor spoke up with great reluctance, then stopped short of sharing his idea with Boswell. The groundhog was silent.

"Well, what is it, man?"

Boswell was not a patient badger to begin with. Clinging to the side of the Eiffel Tower 190 feet above the ground made the least amount of patience perfectly impossible.

"We need a ladder," Victor replied, in a whisper.

"Well, yes," Boswell was certain this was the least useful thing Victor could have said, "a ladder would be helpful, but it's a bit late for that; unless you have one in your pocket." Changing his tone from mockery to irritation, he bellowed, "Do try to be useful, Victor."

Undeterred by Boswell's response, Victor clarified his suggestion, "I mean, we need to *be* a ladder. I need to climb up you like a… well, like a ladder. Then, once I'm on the platform, I pull you up. I see no other way."

Boswell paused to consider Victor's idea. He

thought over the situation, talking to himself all the while, "Yes, right, and then… yes, it just might work."

Turning to Victor -- who realized even before suggesting it that he'd end up with the short end of the stick -- Boswell raised one eyebrow, and said, "Are you sure you can pull me up? I'm a bit heavier than you. I'd rather you were sure *now*, than for you to have doubts once I'm dangling from those stubby arms of yours."

Victor just nodded. Again, he saw no other way.

"Right, then. Up you go." Boswell turned to face the tower once more, offering his back to the uneager groundhog.

Victor grabbed hold of Boswell's waistcoat and began climbing, careful not to look down in the process.

"Not the waistcoat!" Boswell complained.

"It's that or the sideburns!"

Victor refused to be picky about what he was going to hold onto. He was much more concerned with not falling than he was about any old waistcoat. Secretly, he always thought it silly that a badger should wear a waistcoat. Now, he was quite certain of it.

"Very well," Boswell grunted, "But I shall hold you responsible for every lost button."

"If you lose any buttons and this blasted waistcoat comes off, I won't be *around* to be held responsible!"

Victor had never spoken so tersely to the *well-respected Boswell Badger* before; but then, he'd never climbed a badger while climbing the Eiffel Tower before either. It was a day of firsts.

"Do be quiet, Boswell. I'm trying to concentrate."

Victor put one foot on Boswell's tail and the other on his hip; one hand on Boswell's shoulder, while the other clung tightly to Boswell's handsome, tweed waistcoat. In this way, he climbed the ill-humored badger.

As soon as he was able to reach the platform with his fingertips, he put one foot on Boswell's shoulder, followed by the other. Victor was now standing stretched out, his hands holding fast to the platform; both feet on the badger's shoulders; his tail wrapped around Boswell's head; and his chin resting on the first floor of the Eiffel Tower. Still, he needed just a few more inches.

"I'm sorry, old friend, but I'm going to have to stand on your head."

"I beg your pardon." Boswell was appalled at the indignity. "I think not."

"There's no time for arguing; just hold still."

Raising his left, hindfoot, Victor placed it on top of Boswell's gray head. A grunt of disapproval came from below.

"Really now… I must object."

"Hush, please," Victor barked. "And thank you."

Lifting his right foot, he placed in on top of the badger's head, beside the left one. He was now chest-level with the first-story floor of the Eiffel Tower, and easily able to pull himself up. Resting both paws on the platform, he hoisted his body onto the steel deck; crawled away from the edge; then stood to take a look around.

"Quite a view from up here," he taunted. "You really should see this."

"If you please, sir!" came the badger's reply.

"Oh, right. Straight away!"

Victor laid down on his belly, his arms dangling over the edge of the floor. Boswell reached up and took hold of Victor's paws. Once he had support from above, Boswell very quickly ran up the side of the tower with his hindlegs and onto the deck beside Victor. Breathing heavily, sweating, and visibly terrified, Boswell lay there collecting himself for quite some time.

"What's the matter, old friend?" Victor couldn't resist. "You look like you've had quite a time of it."

"Not a word," the badger grumbled.

"Take your time," Victor laughed. "I could use a

break, myself."

Still struggling to catch his breath, Boswell muttered, "I'm quite certain… (heh heh heh)… I do *not*… (heh heh)… want to do *that*… (heh) ever again."

"I am trying to understand, *monsieur,* why you would do it even once," a voice said, from above.

Drying their wings in the morning sun, two butterflies sat beside one another on a steel beam, overhead. Victor turned when he heard someone speaking, but Boswell didn't need to look. He recognized the voice. It was the *impertinent* butterfly from the clover patch the night before.

Still without raising his head, the panting badger simply responded, "Because of *you*, sir. We climbed this tower to find *you*, or rather your lost friend there. That's why we did it, thank you very much."

Looking up at last, Boswell motioned toward Esmée. "She's the one in 'grave danger,' after all."

"Grave danger, *monsieur*?" Esmée said, still wary of the big, grumpy badger. "*Je ne suis pas...* I am not in *danger*."

Standing up, Boswell approached the two butterflies with Victor at his side. A kind gentleness now smoothed out his words.

"My dear, your *friends* think you are. They've come to Paris in search of you. They're very worried."

"Oh no. It cannot be. But, how… how did you learn this, *monsieur*?"

Victor stepped forward and raised one paw -- a guilty look on his face -- and took credit for being the bearer of this bad news. Boswell explained.

"Last night, while we were enjoying our dinner in the clover patch, a message was sent from the *T1 server room,* just south of here near the bend in the river."

Victor produced a small piece of paper and handed it to Boswell who read it aloud.

"**Alert:** Lost butterfly in Paris! Last seen on front page of *Le Journal* posing on top of *la Pyramide du Louvre*. Reference *Le Journal* dated Wednesday last. Butterfly is a *belle dame* named Esmée from Saint-Denis-lès-Chevreuse. According to friends, may be in grave danger. Any information, contact T1 Server Room immediately."

Boswell handed the message back to Victor, then turned to Esmée.

"My dear, are you the butterfly referred to in this message? I know your name and your hometown, but are you *le papillon reine du Louvre* from the photo in *Le Journal*?"

"*Oui, monsieur.* I am."

Pierre looked at Esmée in surprise, "You've already seen the glass pyramid, then? Just as you have already met the bees of Notre-Dame?" Pierre laughed, "*La reine*! I am honored to meet you, my lady."

Esmée just shrugged her shoulders in apology. She was too worried about her friends to explain the whole story to Pierre right now.

"What am I to do?" Esmée asked, in desperation. "I must find them. I must let them know I am well, so they do not worry or continue their search for me. But, how?"

Victor spoke up for the first time since meeting the two butterflies.

"I may be able to help with that."

CHAPTER TWENTY-FIVE

The Plan is in Motion

It was nearing 8 a.m. on Friday morning. At that moment, back at Marmot's apartment, Pica was enjoying his very first blueberry-Nutella crêpes. The replies to Marmot's emergency alert, sent after his guests first arrived the night before, had not yet started coming in. Megalina wouldn't arrive for another two hours or so; and no copies of the photo from *Le Journal* had yet been made and distributed.

On the first floor of the Eiffel Tower, Esmée had just learned from Boswell Badger that her friends were in Paris looking for her and fearing for her safety. She was eager to get word to them of her whereabouts, and to let them know she was alright. She had disappeared from Saint-Denis without a word just four days earlier. Since then, she had been trying to make her way back home, until... well, she'd become hopelessly distracted. Worse yet, she'd forgotten about her friends and what they must be going through. Now it all came back to her.

"I have been so selfish," Esmée confessed to Pierre. "At first, I was scared and alone, without anyone to help me. Then I met you, and all my thoughts of home just disappeared. Poor Lisette; I know she must be beside herself with worry. She came all this way to find me. Oh, I'm so sorry."

"How is this selfishness, *mademoiselle*? What

could you have done? *Non, ma petite,* this is not your fault; and soon, all will be put right. But I think you have forgotten something."

"Forgotten? What, Pierre?" Esmée wiped a tear from her eyes.

"You say you have been alone, with no one to help you. But I think you forget. You have not been alone. There was Saint-Michel; then Stéphanie the bee; and the brave owl moth in the Tuileries Garden. No, *mademoiselle,* you have not been alone. And you are not alone now."

Pierre motioned to Boswell and Victor, who stood nearby discussing something between themselves. Seeming to reach a conclusion they could both agree on, Boswell led the way back over to where Esmée and Pierre were talking.

"Victor has an idea, and I think it's a dandy," Boswell said, in his commanding way. "You'd both be well-advised to give him your attention."

The gentle softness had disappeared and Boswell -- the well-respected, intimidating, crusty badger -- was back. Still, Esmée saw more kindness than harshness in him, now that she'd had a better chance to get to know his heart. She was no longer wary of the old grump; in fact, she kind of wanted to give him a hug.

Victor stepped forward.

"Like I said, I may be able to help get word to your friends. The message came from the *T1 server room*; that's Marmot's place. But if I know Marmot, he isn't going to sit around for long. He'll take your friends with him and go looking for you himself. The last place he knew you'd been was the Louvre. To get there, they'd have to pass by the Eiffel Tower on the way. I suggest we do the following…"

Victor drew on the steel floor with his finger, like a football coach diagraming a play.

"Boswell, you should man the *Champ de Mars*. It's your territory. No one knows it better. If they come up the river on this side, you'll certainly know about it.

"I'll man the *CM-TE server room,* in case any more messages come in. I'll also send out a message telling the *network* of Esmée's whereabouts and that she's alright. Just maybe Marmot and your friends will get wind of it.

"But first, I need to see Hugo across the river. I'd say *that's* even *more* urgent than getting a message to Marmot. If they head up the *other* side of the river to the Louvre, that will take them right through the *Jardins du Trocadéro.* That's Hugo's territory. They may be there already, since Marmot's message was sent twelve hours ago. Hugo needs to be alerted immediately to be on the lookout. Since we're already close to the bridge, I'll just run over and see him in person. In-person is always more efficient than by text message. Especially in an emergency.

"That leaves you two," Victor looked directly at Pierre and Esmée. "I'm afraid you have some work ahead of you."

"Anything, *monsieur,*" Esmée assured him. "What do you have in mind?"

"Between Boswell and Hugo, we'll have both sides of the river under watch in case your friends pass nearby. After I get word to Hugo, I'll have all communications covered. But what if they *don't* come up this far? Or what if they can't stay connected to the *network*? We can't just wait for them to come to us.

"It's ironic, really. Up until now, it was you who were lost. It was you everyone was searching for. Now, it's your friends we need to find. You, the lost butterfly from Saint-Denis, need to do the searching. Your friends need to be found and their worries alleviated.

"It won't be easy. There are a thousand different

places they could be; a hundred different routes they could take. But the easiest route to take between Marmot's place and the Louvre is the river. If you stick to the river, it'll be your best bet of finding your friends."

Victor's words were like a cold, bracing wind against Esmée's face, waking her from a long, drowsy sleep. In that moment, she understood what Stéphanie the bee had meant.

"The river will always lead you home again," Esmée said, aloud to herself.

She then repeated Victor's words, under her breath, "If you stick to the river, it'll be your best bet of finding your friends."

Turning to the others, she said, with the excitement of realization, "My friends! My *friends*! *They're* my home! *They* are! Not a place. Not an address. *They* are my home! Wherever the ones I love *are, that's* my home! And my friends are on the river. Right now, somewhere in Paris, my friends are on the river looking for me. The river will lead *them* to *me…* and it will lead *me* to *my friends*. The river will guide me home."

"*Oui, mon amour,* the Notre-Dame honeybee, she knew." Pierre smiled, with reassurance in his eyes.

"You met the *Ignifuge* bees of Notre-Dame?" Boswell Badger was impressed. "I've always wanted to meet the fabled honeybees of Brother Apius. Ah, the wisdom they could share… one day. Perhaps."

"*Oui, monsieur* Badger, I had the honor of meeting them. And I will introduce you, if you'd like."

Esmée was filled with gratitude toward the little bee. She longed to return and thank her in person.

"We haven't time to lose, my friends," Victor cautioned. "We must be on our way."

Turning to Boswell, Victor became very serious. Putting one hand on the badger's shoulder, he said, "Time is of the essence, and there's absolutely no way I'm going to climb back down the face of this tower. I think we need to chance it."

"Chance it?" Boswell didn't follow.

"Take a chance on being seen," Victor replied.

"Right," said the badger, "In this circumstance, I'd have to agree with you."

"Farewell, little friends," Victor said to Pierre and Esmée. "Remember, when in need, find a groundhog. Soon, they will *all* know of your situation. You're not alone; help is always within reach. Just stick to the river and be careful. Good luck."

Boswell walked over to Pierre and Esmée. Holding out one arm, he invited Esmée to land in his paw.

"Yours is the gentlest heart I have ever encountered, my lady. You shall always be *le papillon reine du Louvre* to me… and my dear friend. Until next time we meet…"

With a tear in his eye, the crusty, old badger turned and followed Victor to the locked doors that led to the elevators.

Pierre called out, *"Au revoir, messieurs. À bientôt!"* while Esmée blew a sad and solemn kiss. The two butterflies then flew away downriver.

It was now almost 9 a.m. and the tower would be opening any minute. Doors would soon be unlocked; elevators would begin running; and tourists would be absolutely everywhere. The groundhog and the badger would wait for the perfect opportunity.

"I hope you know what you're doing," Boswell whispered to Victor, as they stood outside the locked doors.

"I know what I'm **not** doing," Victor said, glancing back over his shoulder at the edge of the first-floor platform. "Once is enough for this groundhog."

It was nine o'clock and the Eiffel Tower security guard arrived right on time. He walked over to where

Boswell and Victor were hiding and unlocked the doors which led to the elevators and stairwells.

The moment he opened the doors, two fat, furry, brown creatures sped past his feet at full speed. Rounding the corner, they headed straight for the open elevator. On their way past the control panel, Boswell reached up and hit the button marked "down." The doors slid closed and the elevator began its descent.

Minutes later, they came to a stop on the ground level. The doors slid open; the badger and groundhog bolted out; and a crowd of tourists was sent running in all directions. Screams went up from the hysterical throng: "Rats! Look out!", "Wild dogs!", "Help me! I'm being attacked!" and other such nonsense.

Victor and Boswell ran through the stampede of terrified tourists -- dodging feet as best they could -- as they headed around to the left toward the nearest exit. Following the path which wound back between the tower and the street, neither of them stopped until they reached the Chimney. The tall grass surrounding the brick, medieval-looking battlement was an excellent hiding place to wait until the excitement died down.

Looking at each other – completely disheveled, trying to catch their breath, and sweating in the morning sun -- they both suddenly burst out laughing. Victor rolled around in the grass, holding his belly and wheezing with uncontrollable laughter. Even the big badger, in all his formality, snorted at one point -- before quickly regaining his dignity.

"That… was… great!" Victor said, still laughing. "We've got to share *that* whole experience with the *network*."

"I think not," Boswell insisted, suddenly regaining his composure while rubbing a grass stain from his handsome, tweed waistcoat.

"Yeah, you're probably right," Victor conceded,

coming to his senses. "Not exactly the image you're going for, huh? Ah well."

Victor stood and picked up the message he'd been carrying since early that morning. It seemed to remind him of the urgency of their mission. They had to get moving. It was time for action.

"Best of luck, old chap," Victor said, patting Boswell on the back. "This will be a day for the history books. It's not every day that a badger and a groundhog climb the Eiffel Tower."

Boswell laughed in his oddly characteristic way, "It's not every day that a groundhog climbs a badger either! Good luck to you and to our mission."

The two friends shook hands before heading off in opposite directions: Boswell back to the *Champ de Mars*, and Victor across the bridge to the *Jardins du Trocadéro* to find Hugo, the *JdT network manager*.

Under the cover of tall grass and thick weeds, Boswell scurried away to take up his post on the far side of the tower. Victor, however, had a much more challenging route. He figured, since they'd been successful in simply running through the crowd awaiting entrance to the Eiffel Tower, perhaps the same strategy was in order now.

Running around to the right, Victor approached the sidewalk that lay between the Eiffel Tower and the street. His plan was to wait for a red light; cross the sidewalk and the street; and make it to the nearby carrousel before the stampede of terrified tourists trampled all over him. He watched the traffic lights closely.

The light for cross-traffic turned red; the cars in front of Victor came to a stop; and the light for oncoming traffic turned green; but still he waited.

Watching the signal for the pedestrian crosswalk -- as it counted down before flashing the *no-crossing* hand

-- Victor stood, poised and ready to run. He figured he could make it across the sidewalk and both lanes of traffic in five or six seconds. The street was jammed with cars; the sidewalk was crammed with people. He had to be careful; he had to stay alert.

The crosswalk signal counted down, "Eleven, ten, nine." Victor plotted his course. The front bumpers of the stopped cars were all lined up along the white line. He would run directly along the line, using it as his guide. "Eight, seven;" this was it.

At last, the crossing signal reached, "six," and Victor was off like a shot! Weaving between pedestrians, he crossed the sidewalk and the first lane of traffic in no time. Stopping briefly in the median, he checked the signal just to be safe. All clear!

By now, people were beginning to notice the scurrying, rabid, "vicious rat" who had been terrorizing the city ever since his earlier "attack" at the Eiffel Tower. The intersection erupted in chaos!

Pedestrians hopped up onto the hoods of stopped cars, trying to escape certain death in the teeth of this wild animal. Some people even tried to climb up the nearby lampposts.

Honking horns and panicking pedestrians made even the pigeons run for cover. Meanwhile, Victor took advantage of all the commotion to cross the remaining lane of traffic, just as the crossing signal read, "two, one" then, "no crossing," and the little orange hand started blinking.

Sliding under the carnival carrousel to the left of the bridge, Victor was safely out of sight and out of reach. Here he could rest a moment and formulate his next plan, which would have to carry him all the way across the bridge.

Watching the pedestrians as they walked along the sidewalk from the *Jardins du Trocadéro,* across the river, and to the Eiffel Tower; Victor waited for an opening. What he found, though -- much to his irritation -- was a slobbery mouthful of teeth shoved under the carrousel and barking loudly right in his face.

"Seriously?" he said, shaking his head at the smelly dog blocking his exit. "You gotta be kidding me."

This was danger Victor had no intention of risking. Alone, he might be able to make it across the bridge and into the trees surrounding the *Jardins,* but not with a dog at his heels. He was fast, but the dog would certainly be faster. Still, time was running out, and he had to do something soon.

Looking around beneath the carrousel, Victor spied an electrical outlet. On the ground beside it, a power cord lay unplugged. Attached to the other end of the cord, there was a small box with a big, red button. Crawling over to the other side, Victor kept his head low to the ground.

Beneath the carrousel, discarded trash had piled up; blowing in from the sidewalks all around. It was filthy, and Victor was disgusted by how untidy humans could be. With little choice but to keep going, he pulled himself along through the trash. He was now within reach of the plug at the end of the electrical cord. Taking hold of it, he pulled it over toward the outlet. Pushing the plug into the outlet, he then gathered-up the cord and dragged it toward himself until the box with the red button was within reach.

Just a few feet away, the dog was barking furiously at Victor. Crouched down and pressing itself as far as it could underneath the carrousel, it was quickly approaching where Victor now lay. Taking the box in one hand, the groundhog hovered his other hand over the big, red button. With his face against the ground and his body as flat as he could make it -- well out of reach of the carrousel platform above -- Victor smacked his hand down on the button. A bell rang out, and a split-second later, the carrousel began to turn.

Frightened by the sudden movement -- and knocked for a loop by the spinning of the platform -- the dog exploded out from beneath the carrousel like a sneeze in the wind. Yelping with alarm (and raising a greater fuss than was really warranted), the dog ran off in the direction of the Eiffel Tower to rejoin his master.

Victor chuckled to himself with satisfaction; that was probably more fun than it should have been. He'd never liked dogs, few groundhogs do; but he hadn't hurt the animal. That wasn't Victor's style. Startle it, yes; but hurt it, never! He'd like to think that this particular dog had learned his lesson; but Victor was certain it would be right back to chasing groundhogs the first chance it got.

Victor reached over and unplugged the cord, leaving everything as he'd found it. Looking out from his hiding place, he saw that all eyes were still on the yelping dog. He had to hand it to the dog; it sure made a very useful distraction.

Without hesitation, Victor ran with all his might out from under the carrousel. Galloping down the sidewalk, he nearly lost his footing and skidded off into the river as he rounded the tight corner to the left. There in front of him, the long straightaway of the bridge lay open. Every pedestrian in his path stood looking off to their right across the water toward the Eiffel Tower and the overheated dog. They were all occupied with trying to figure out what could possibly be going on to make a dog act so crazy.

Victor sprinted across the roadway, with the sidewalk's curb to his left. Kicking up dirt and debris as he went, the little *network manager* of the *CM-TE server room* hadn't had this much exercise in quite some time. The adrenaline rush made him feel invincible. This was almost as exciting as climbing the Eiffel Tower, and just as dangerous.

Crossing the far entrance to the bridge, like a marathon runner crossing the finish line, Victor gained traction in the grass and picked up speed. Taking a hard left, he ran up the gentle slope of the hill and into the trees growing beside the reflecting pool of the *Jardins*. The entire journey, from the carrousel to the group of trees on the other side of the river, had taken him just under two minutes. A great burst of energy had carried him a distance of almost a quarter of a mile in record time.

Not one single set of human eyes had seen Victor, thanks to the drama stirred up by the barking dog on the far side of the bridge. Victor had successfully reached the safety of cover. The greatest challenge was over, at least until he had to make it home again; but he didn't want to think about that just yet.

Flopping down in the shade of a maple tree, Victor rested a moment. By now, Esmée and Pierre were making their way downriver in the hope of finding Marmot. Boswell was surely patrolling the *Champs de Mars* behind the Eiffel Tower, keeping his eyes and ears open for any sign of the search party.

It was now Victor's job to find Hugo, the *network manager* for the *JdT server room;* the groundhog in charge of the *Jardins du Trocadéro.* If he could find Hugo and alert him to be on the lookout, they'd have both sides of the river covered. Then, if Marmot and Esmée's friends made it that far north on their way to the Louvre, they'd surely be spotted no matter which side of the river they travelled on.

It was now nearly 11 a.m. It had been 15 hours since Marmot sent the first emergency alert, just before heading to bed the night before. Victor knew that if Marmot had left right away, he could be at the Eiffel Tower or beyond by now. If he hadn't left right away or he'd stopped for the night, then there still might be time to intercept him. First, Victor needed to find the mild-mannered Hugo.

CHAPTER TWENTY-SIX

Hugo

Of course, Victor knew exactly where the *JdT server room* was located. That wasn't the problem at all. The problem was that Hugo -- the *network manager* in charge of that part of the Boulogne *internet* which ran through the *Jardins du Trocadéro* -- was almost never home.

Hugo wasn't lazy, and he didn't neglect his duties. The truth is, the *Jardins du Trocadéro (or JdT) server room* hardly ever received any messages. Not many groundhogs lived in that part of the city, despite its charming trees, shrubs and lawns. The groundhogs who lived nearby preferred the expansive *Champ de Mars* with its close-up view of the Eiffel Tower.

The *JdT* area was also the smallest, and one of the oldest, sections of the Boulogne *internet*. When the *Champs de Mars -Tour Eiffel (CM-TE) server room* was built in 1889, it grew in importance and overshadowed its neighbor, the *JdT*. Without much work to demand his attention, apart from his periodic meetings with Boswell Badger, Hugo had a lot of free time on his paws.

As was said earlier, Hugo was one of the most mild-mannered and polite of all the Bois de Boulogne groundhogs. He had a keen interest in nature, which suited his scholarly personality. In fact, Hugo enjoyed spending all of his free time outside watching, studying, and even sketching everything from leaves, to beetles, to cloud formations. His love of drawing resulted in an underground apartment filled to the ceiling with sketchbooks. He may not have been up-to-date on his current events, but Hugo was an expert on plants and animals.

Though he had very little hope of actually finding Hugo at home, Victor thought he'd better try the *JdT server room* first, just in case. Located beneath a large hydrangea bush beside a rock formation in the front of the gardens, the entrance to the groundhog tunnels was only easy to find for those who knew where to look. Victor, of course, knew where to look.

Pushing aside the branches of the pink, flowering hydrangea, Victor found the hole in the ground he'd been looking for. This was the *JdT access point,* or one of them, anyhow. Sliding into the opening head-first, Victor crouched down and made his body fit the contours of the tunnel walls. Once he squeezed himself into the dark, cramped space, he took off running. If the ground were see-through, it would have looked like a brown, furry clog traveling through a drainpipe at top speed.

Since these tunnels were older and less-often used, there were fewer twists and turns to navigate. His path from the outside world to the *JdT server room* was as straight as you could hope for, with only one *router* (or *intersection*) along the way. Even this intersection offered only two other choices of tunnel to take: one to the south, leading down the river toward Marmot's location; and one to the north, leading up the river toward the Grand Palais.

Along the walls, the same recycled iPads and tablets illuminated the way -- as in Audrey and Pica's experience. The one notable difference was that the *JdT* tunnels had more signs. In the intersection, each of the two tunnels had a sign bearing its name and the distance to the next *router* intersection. Even in the long, straight, main tunnel, there were periodic signs showing the distance to various stops along the way. This included the distance to the *server room*. The signs were probably put up by Hugo, since he spent so little time underground and often forgot his directions.

From the tunnel's entrance at the hydrangea bush to the *server room*, it was 1,208 feet. At Victor's current speed, it would take him about 5 minutes to reach his destination. If Hugo was not, in fact, at home (as Victor suspected he would not be), then only 10 minutes or so would be wasted. He felt it was worth it to eliminate the *server room* from his search for Hugo.

The sign on the tunnel wall read, "Next Left: *Server Room.*" Victor saw the door up ahead. Much like the door to Marmot's place, Hugo's apartment door was round and made out of driftwood from the river.

Victor brushed the dirt from the tunnel floor off his paws and knocked loudly against the *server room* door. He waited; but no answer came from inside.

A moment later, he tried again; this time calling out in a loud voice, "Hugo! Are you home? I say, Hugo!" Victor awaited a response. Still, nothing.

Deciding to try a third and final time, Victor knocked hard and vigorously against the wooden door, calling out as loud as he could, "Hugo! I say, old man, are you home or not?"

"Not," came a small and squirmy reply.

"Who said that?" Victor demanded, somewhat startled.

"Over here," was the answer; still small; still squirmy.

Searching in the glow of the tablets, Victor spotted a little earthworm sticking his head (and, oddly enough, part of his tail) out of the tunnel wall.

"You?" Victor asked, with disbelief.

"Me," the worm said, without the slightest hint of

care.

"Who are *you*?"

"The name's Wormester. Wormester Wormerly, if you're interested. Even if you're not, I suppose."

"And what was it that you said?"

Victor couldn't believe he was talking to a worm. This was a first. In all his years traveling the tunnels, this was the first worm he'd ever heard speak. He didn't even know they *could*.

"Not," Wormester repeated. "I said, not."

"Not...?" Victor was still totally distracted by the worminess of it all.

"You asked if Hugo was home or not. I said... not. For what it's worth."

"So, Hugo's not home?"

"Yup. Not." The worm said, wriggling his tail -- which poked out of the wall not far from his slimy head.

"Do you happen to know where he went?"

"I do," came Wormester's reply.

"Might you *tell* me where he went?" Victor was both amused and a bit annoyed by the worm's lack of interest.

"Fine," Wormester said. "I'll tell you. If you must know."

"I must," Victor said, nodding his head, "I really must."

"Very well. He was talking to himself... he often does, you know."

"I did not know that. Thank you, though. And what was it that he said?" By now, Victor was less amused and somewhat more annoyed.

"Said to whom?" The worm appeared to have a memory roughly as short as his little body.

"To himself," Victor snapped back, letting his annoyance overwhelm any amusement he'd been feeling.

"Oh, right," Wormester didn't seem to notice

Victor's irritation with him. "He was talking to himself, as he often does. And he said, 'Off to sketch the gardenias.' He said that. To himself. He often does."

"The gardenias. There must be a hundred gardenia bushes in the *Jardins*. He might just as well have said he was off to sketch a blade of grass!" Victor was not pleased.

"No. I've never heard him say *that*. A blade of grass? No, never that. How long could *that* possibly take?" Wormester thought the idea of sketching a blade of grass was utter nonsense.

"I mean, he could be anywhere." Victor was now feeling less sarcastic and more hopeless.

"Not *anywhere*," Wormester corrected. "He went to sketch **the** *gardenias*. At the edge of the walkway, near the fountains. If you *must* know."

"At the edge of the walkway?" Victor was reluctant to show any excitement quite yet; he still wasn't sure he could trust a worm.

"Near the fountains," Wormester directed. "Where he always goes. To sketch the gardenias, that is. For what it's worth."

"It's worth quite a lot, if *you* must know," Victor exclaimed with the excitement he'd been holding back. "Well done, little one! Well done. Thank you!"

"Little one?" Wormester objected.

"I beg your pardon," Victor interjected, before the offence had a chance to soak in fully. He wasn't familiar with worm etiquette, having never conversed with a worm before now. "I meant, many thanks, *kind sir*!"

"Ugh," Wormester replied, with a slow and squishy shake of his head. Even among worms, Wormester was a bit touchy and sensitive. Pulling his tail in, his head slowly followed and was swallowed up by the soft earth of the tunnel wall; until nothing remained – not even a hole in the dirt.

"Farewell, my slimy friend," Victor said, with a wave of his paw. "The gardenias. He went to sketch the gardenias. By the walkway. Near the fountains. Right! Off we go!"

Victor turned around in the tunnel and headed back in the direction he'd come. He knew the gardenia bush. He'd passed it many times before, and the perfume from its flowers was heavenly. He could be there in seven or eight minutes. He only hoped Hugo would still be there sketching his flowers.

Trotting along as fast as he could in the cramped tunnel, Victor clutched a dirty scrap of paper in one paw. It was the emergency alert from Marmot, the one he needed to share with Hugo. But there was more to be done. Victor would also need to *respond* to the message; after the plan he and Boswell made on the first floor of the Eiffel Tower was in motion; after he'd spoken with Hugo.

It had only been a hunch of his that Marmot wouldn't sit still for long; that he'd head out with Esmée's friends to look for her. If, by chance, Victor's hunch was wrong and Marmot was waiting in his *server room* for a response to the message, a reply needed to be sent soon. There was no reason to prolong Marmot's waiting. Victor had to be quick.

A flicker of light could now be seen at the end of the tunnel, growing as he approached the opening. A few feet more and Victor popped his head out of the doorway beneath the hydrangea bush to have a look around.

The sky had begun collecting clouds. At first, they were mostly white and fluffy, like lumpy pillows thrown here and there. But, as the morning wore on and noon approached, some of them took on a more menacing slate-blue color. The sun still shown, but it had to elbow its way to the front of a gathering crowd of dark storm clouds.

The few people visiting the *Jardins* that morning were busy packing up their blankets and picnic baskets, in anticipation of the afternoon rain. Since everyone appeared to be occupied, Victor felt it was safe to venture out into the open. He had little choice, anyhow; he had to reach Hugo. Now he was racing against the rain, too.

Hopping up out of the hole, Victor ran straight for the gardenia bush by the corner of the front walkway, some 800 feet away. Stopping often, he hid beneath the cover of every shrub he encountered. It wasn't just human eyes Victor was hoping to avoid. Predators were everywhere. Hawks, foxes, even dogs wouldn't hesitate to attack an unsuspecting groundhog.

Rounding the corner to the left, Victor was now coming to the edge of the tree line. He could see the river down below on his right; and beyond it, the Eiffel Tower. Up ahead, near the front corner of the wide walkway, Victor spotted a large gardenia bush, heavy with white flowers. Two or three feet away, with sketchpad in hand, Hugo the *network manager* of the *JdT server room* was lying on his belly in the grass.

"Hello!" Victor called out, "I say, hello there!"

Hugo raised his head, saw the groundhog walking toward him, and then returned to his detailed drawing of one of the gardenia blossoms. The bloom had not yet fully opened -- it still had a little, torpedo-shaped center – but the petals around it were soft and delicate. Hugo was lost in every fold of the flower's elegance. After a moment or two -- and without taking his eyes off his sketchpad -- Hugo finally responded in a pleasant though distracted voice, "*Bonjour.*"

Victor walked up beside him and looked over Hugo's shoulder at the drawing. Not only was it a perfect likeness of the gardenia flower, but the page had notes written all over it detailing Hugo's scientific observations. It would appear, he was both an excellent artist and a serious scientist.

"Wow," Victor said in surprise, "That's actually *really* good."

Hugo made no reply and showed absolutely no sign of having even heard. He just kept on sketching.

Remembering his urgent errand, Victor took his friend by the shoulder, "Hugo, I need to show you something. It's important!"

Hugo put the final touches on a vein running through a leaf beside the flower, then put down his pencil and turned to recognize Victor for the first time.

"Oh, hi Victor," he said with a smile. "What's up?"

"This!" Victor pushed the scrap of paper into Hugo's hand.

"**Alert:** Lost butterfly in Paris! Last seen on front page of *Le Journal* posing on top of *la Pyramide du Louvre*. Reference *Le Journal* dated Wednesday last. Butterfly is a *belle dame* named Esmée from Saint-Denis-lès-Chevreuse. According to friends, may be in grave danger. Any information, contact T1 Server Room immediately."

"Oh yeah, I saw that edition of *Le Journal*. A couple days ago. Saint-Denis… never heard of it."

Handing the piece of paper back to Victor, Hugo picked up his pencil and continued sketching – still talking, while he did.

"Aside from the photo, I haven't seen her. It's always pretty quiet around here. Not much ever happens." Hugo looked up from his sketchpad and examined the gardenia blossom again. "I kinda like it that way. Peaceful, you know?"

"Well, I *have* seen her. Just this morning. And Boswell and I need your help."

Accidentally snapping his pencil in two, Hugo was alarmed at the mention of the grumpy badger's name.

It was bad enough Hugo had to meet with Boswell regularly to exchange news; but why did Victor have to bring up the badger in conversation and disturb the peacefulness of the *Jardins*, too?

"Boswell? You talked to Boswell? What does he need from *me*? He's not coming here, is he?"

Hugo was fidgeting with the two halves of his broken pencil, anxiously looking over his shoulders. He half-expected Boswell to pop up out of a hole in the ground and start bossing him around.

"Listen," Victor tried to get Hugo's attention. "This is what happened. Boswell met this Esmée -- the missing butterfly -- in the *Champ de Mars* last night; but he didn't know anything about the alert. Not at that time, anyhow. When I received the message this morning, I brought it right over to Boswell before sun-up."

"I bet he didn't care for *that* at all," Hugo chuckled, still fidgeting and looking around. Victor ignored Hugo's comment and continued.

"As luck would have it, Boswell knew that Esmée had gone to the Eiffel Tower after they parted ways. So, we headed there without delay and… well… climbed the tower in search of her…"

"Wait. You *climbed* the tower? What, using the stairs?"

"No, the tower was closed; but that's not important…"

"Hang on, hang on. You and Boswell *climbed* the Eiffel Tower… *without* using the stairs?! How on earth…? And how did the big badger…?"

"Stay focused, Hugo," Victor continued, "So, we found Esmée and her friend, Pierre, on the first floor of the tower. She had no idea that her friends thought she was in danger. She didn't know they were looking for her. We all agreed, they had to be found, and their worries put to rest."

Victor took a long breath, "So… we all made a plan. Knowing Marmot, he and Esmée's friends might already be on their way to the Louvre to look for her, since that's the last place he knew she'd been seen. That means they'd have to come up the river either on Boswell's side or on your side."

Hugo was now paying very close attention to every word Victor was saying. His fear of Boswell had been replaced by something new. In all his time as *network manager* for the *JdT server room*, nothing important had ever happened. In a way, Hugo had been waiting for this moment all his life. He just hadn't realized it. He was beginning to feel a sense of duty.

"Hugo, you have to keep your eyes open. You need to send out sentries. And above all, you have to man your *server room*. If anyone sees or hears anything about Marmot and Esmée's friends, send word out over the *internet*. Do you understand?"

Hugo nodded his head with decision, "Yes! I'm on it! You can count on the *JdT*. I'll spread the word and then head down to the *server room*. We've got this under control!"

"Good man," Victor said, patting Hugo on the shoulder. "I'll go back across the river and take up my position in the *CM-TE server room*. If anything happens on that side, Boswell will let me know and I'll let the *network* know. I knew we could count on you, Hugo."

"Um, well…" Hugo began fidgeting with his pencil stubs again. "Just let Boswell know…"

"Let him know? Let him know what?" Victor asked, noticing Hugo's sheepish embarrassment.

"You know. That you can *count on* me. That I'm *on it*. I know he thinks very little of me."

"Nonsense. That's just his way. He comes off as being a bit grouchy, but he's actually…" Victor searched for the right word to use, while still being honest, "…he's actually… well, he's actually very grouchy; but he has a soft and kindly heart. You may just have to trust me on that," Victor assured Hugo, noticing a look of doubt on his face.

Turning to go, Victor clapped his paws together, "The plan is in motion! Very good. I'll be on my way, then."

Pausing a moment, he looked back in Hugo's direction. "But I'll let the badger know that *you're on it*, just the same."

Hugo breathed a sigh of relief and gratitude, then spun around and headed into the woods, talking to himself (as he often does), "Need to gather the squirrels… need to get organized…"

Victor just shook his head and ran off down the hill toward the river. Overhead, the clouds were beginning to shut out the sunlight. Rain wouldn't be far behind. As Victor neared the bridge, he could see that it was clear; all the tourists had found cover to enjoy a long lunch and wait out the storm. More importantly, they all took their dogs with them!

Victor didn't waste a moment crossing the bridge. Galloping like a racehorse, he ran alongside the wall overlooking the river until he reached the opposite side. Ducking beneath the carrousel, as he had before, he watched the traffic lights and crossing signal -- waiting for his chance.

With all the running around he'd been doing; with all of the danger he'd been careful to avoid, Victor understood why the groundhogs' partnership with the wintercress fireflies was so important. Without *WiFi,* the only ways to ferry messages across the river would be by bridge, boat or swimming. For a groundhog, all three activities were dangerous along the busy Seine. He made a mental note to send out a message of thanks to the wintercress fireflies -- if he was successful in crossing the jammed intersection, that is.

Victor took a look around. There were no pedestrians on the sidewalks. Good. One fewer set of obstacles to run through.

There were no dogs anywhere in sight. Perfect. He didn't need that kind of trouble again.

The light turned yellow, then red. The cars came to a stop. The crossing signal changed to a picture of a little walking-man. That was Victor's cue.

Flying out from underneath the carrousel, Victor catapulted himself across the sidewalk; through the herd of cars; over the sidewalk on the far side; and around toward the Eiffel Tower. The only human who saw him was a little boy in the back seat of a stopped car; but he was too young to tell anyone what he'd seen. It's unlikely they'd believe him, even if he could. You just don't see very many groundhogs in Paris, these days.

There was a tunnel-opening on the other side of the glass wall that surrounds the tower. Once inside the tunnel, Victor could quickly reach his *server room,* located beneath the northeastern foot; it was a straight shot.

Victor wove his way through the grounds over gravel footpaths, successfully eluding Tower Security, and avoiding the few remaining tourists who had not yet found shelter from the coming rain. Taking a right, he passed by the small pond near the northeast foot and entered under the glass wall that encloses the tower. Safely concealed by the tall grass, he was able to slip into his tunnel entrance and disappear from sight.

Back in the intersection, the traffic light turned green and the cars began to move. The little boy waved goodbye from the backseat of his mother's car, as she drove away. Victor had made it across the bridge and back again -- another *first* for the groundhog, on this most exceptional day.

The time was nearing 1 p.m. and Boswell Badger had been busy ever since Victor left to find Hugo. The moment he returned to the *Champ de Mars,* the badger deployed his army of helpers to keep their eyes open and report back to him.

As you know, the Bois de Boulogne groundhogs have the wintercress fireflies to help them send messages across the river. Hugo, the *network manager* of the *JdT server room,* seems to have built a successful friendship even with the over-sensitive and touchy tunnel worms.

Well, the crusty Master of the *Champ de Mars* might not have many friends, but he has literally millions of helpers; and their networks are even bigger than the Boulogne groundhogs' *internet.*

There's a history here, a story worth telling. It's a story of rivalry and missed opportunity; a story of misunderstanding and the wisdom of one badger; a story of the Garden Ants of France.

Of course, ants have been around longer than people. This is true in France as it is everywhere else. Even though groundhogs hate to admit it, ants were around long before they arrived, too. It's an unfortunate fact that groundhogs hate giving ants credit for anything. Instead, they prefer to blame ants (for everything, really), whenever possible. This unfriendly habit dates back almost as far as groundhogs themselves.

It all began with a misunderstanding, as rivalries and grudges often do. When the Bois de Boulogne groundhogs first moved to the forest outside of Paris, they adopted many human customs. At first, it was just the habit of storing food, which gave the groundhogs much more time for other activities. Instead of going out every day to search the fields and forests for nuts, berries, and clovers, groundhogs began collecting more than they needed for one day. Whatever they didn't eat that day, they would store it for the next day and the next day. This was life-changing!

The groundhogs named Wednesday their grocery day. Six days out of the week they would devote to such new and interesting pursuits as sketching flowers or developing more efficient ways of communicating. But on Wednesday, they would spend the day gathering food for the whole week.

Eventually, the groundhogs tried to make their stored food last more than one week. This meant they could gather every *other* Wednesday – giving them even more free time. But, as a result, the groundhogs needed bigger storage pantries. Being fantastic burrowers, this wasn't a problem. They just dug larger rooms out of the earth.

What they hadn't considered, however, was that the more space they took up underground, the less space there was for everyone else around them. Beetles, bugs, worms, and millipedes were forced to find new homes, as the groundhogs expanded their own apartments. Since there was less space, fewer and fewer insects were able to live anywhere near groundhog tunnels; and this was a very sad thing. What's a home without neighbors?

Even though their bigger apartments pushed most other creatures out of the neighborhood, the groundhogs did notice there was one kind of insect that didn't move out. In fact, these insects seemed to multiply in number as the groundhog's pantries grew in size. Groundhogs never had any quarrels with garden ants before, so this didn't really alarm them; until, one day it was discovered just exactly *why* there were so many ants hanging around. One groundhog, in particular, made the discovery.

His name was Geoffrey Glouton and he kept an exceptionally large storehouse of food in his tunnel apartment. Whereas, most other groundhogs were busy putting their free time to good use, Glouton used his mostly to lay around and do nothing at all. One afternoon, while he was busy being lazier than usual, he noticed a long, black line running from his front door to his pantry. Grunting and groaning to haul himself up off the couch, he crawled over to examine the spectacle more closely.

Laying on his belly on the floor, his chin resting on his paws, Geoffrey stared with great interest at the curious line. One after another, a steady stream of garden ants was marching into his pantry, while another line was marching out. There were hundreds of them; thousands, perhaps; and not one of them took any notice of Glouton.

It wasn't so much the line of ants going *into* his pantry that bothered him. It was the line carrying tiny crumbs of food *out* of his pantry that he objected to the most. While it's true that an ant can carry twenty times its own weight (for you, that would mean being able to carry a minivan!), none of these were carrying all that much. In fact, if you collected every crumb carried by every ant in Geoffrey Glouton's apartment that day, the collection of crumbs wouldn't even amount to half a snack for the gluttonous groundhog. But that didn't matter to Geoffrey Glouton.

"Thieves!" he yelled at the top of his voice. "I'm being robbed! Help!"

As with most animals who spend their time doing nothing at all, when something *does* happen, they tend to overreact. If Geoffrey Glouton had more experience doing things, he would have known that having ants in one's pantry is really not surprising. Moreover, his reaction was quite unfair. Like I said before, what was being carried out of Glouton's pantry was not really worth keeping.

Another thing the groundhogs failed to realize was that when you store a lot of food, you need to have a good *food management plan* in place. The newer food should be stored behind the older food, to prevent the older food from sitting around too long and spoiling.

Geoffrey clearly did not have a good *food management plan*. He would shove the newer food in front of the old, never eating what was behind it. His pantry was a mess.

Also, there's just so much a groundhog can eat in a certain amount of time. They hadn't considered that maybe they should only store as much as they could eat *before* the food went bad. The groundhogs overlooked a lot of important things; but the garden ants didn't miss a trick.

They marched right in under Glouton's front door; headed straight to the pantry; collected the leftovers; and carted them right back out again. If Glouton had stopped to think (an activity he had not done for quite some time), he would have realized that the ants were really just cleaning up for him. They were helping him manage his supply. They were preventing spoilage by taking the excess food – the food even Glouton wouldn't be able to eat -- and using it to feed their families. Really, it was the best possible arrangement: free food for the ants' families, in exchange for keeping the groundhog's pantry tidy. But Geoffrey Glouton didn't quite get it.

"Help! Stop! Thieves!" he cried, all the more loudly.

Dragging himself up off the floor, Glouton grabbed a broom and started sweeping the startled little ants all over his living room floor. Flying through the air, tail-spinning across the floor, the garden ants were in a high state of panic. It wasn't long before his neighbors arrived to find Glouton sweeping wildly and yelling at the floor. They were sure that years of doing nothing at all had finally driven him mad.

"Ants!" he screamed. "Ants everywhere! Stealing my food!"

The neighbors just stood there with their mouths open, watching the angry groundhog swing his broomstick. Struggling to avoid the groundhog's wrath, the garden ants ran for the front door and made their escape down the tunnel and up through the hole to the outside world. They decided, then and there, that they'd never again step foot inside a groundhog's tunnel. It simply wasn't worth the trouble.

Down below, news spread rapidly of the army of thieves who ransacked Geoffrey Glouton's pantry. For a groundhog who never did anything noteworthy, this was his moment of fame and he played it for all it was worth.

The story was told and retold by Glouton, growing in every detail, and becoming more and more dramatic as it became less and less accurate. Pretty soon, the story of *The Marauding Garden Ants of Geoffrey Glouton's Pantry* bore no resemblance to the truth whatsoever. As with most stories like this, it was more fun for the groundhog to make it up and pass it on than to get it right. But this is how rumors begin; and rumors are always destructive.

A distrust began to grow between groundhogs and garden ants. The distrust then turned into dislike, which soon became hatred. The groundhogs were certain that the garden ants were thieves. The garden ants were sure that the groundhogs were mad. Dried by the heat of many decades' worth of red-hot anger, the grudge became as stiff and rigid as stone. With the passing of time, neither ants nor groundhogs would remember precisely why it was that they were supposed to hate one another. They just did. Some things you just don't question.

As you know, ants construct tunnels of their own. If you could see underground, you'd see a network of ant chambers and tunnels as large as continents and as numerous as the ant colonies themselves. Compared to the *Garden Ant Network*, even the Bois de Boulogne *internet* looks more like just a few tin cans connected by string.

If only Geoffrey Glouton hadn't overreacted; if

only the groundhogs had tried to learn the truth and understand their little neighbors; then perhaps the two networks could have worked together to form a *World Wide Web* of groundhogs and garden ants. Imagine how fast messages could have been shared across such a global network!

Instead, a rivalry cropped up between the groundhogs and the garden ants. On both sides, ever since that fateful day, there has been an unwillingness to help each other. On both sides, there remains deep distrust.

The groundhogs have always received much more attention, thanks to Brother Apius' research and writings, and this suits the garden ants just fine. They keep to themselves, except when a picnic basket is involved. Most of the time, they prefer to go unnoticed and be left in peace. Perhaps this is why they came to the attention of the most well-respected badger in Paris.

Boswell Badger prefers nothing more than peace and quiet; but even those who love peace and quiet don't always prefer to be alone. This is true of badgers and garden ants. The ants found in Boswell a wise, understanding (although somewhat moody) friend. Boswell found in the ants a million sensible and utterly silent companions. He also saw an opportunity.

The modern-day groundhogs remember little of the *Glouton Affair*. All they know is that, for some reason or other, ants aren't to be trusted. The same is true of modern-day ants. All they know is that groundhogs are known to be overly dramatic, although they couldn't say exactly why. Only Boswell, in his learned wisdom, seemed to remember the ridiculous story of their falling-out. He was of the opinion that the time had come to heal old wounds.

So, when he returned to the *Champ de Mars,* the first thing Boswell did was call his friend, Fourmi, the queen of the garden ants of the *Champ de Mars.* If anyone could help keep an eye out (or two, or two million) for Marmot and crew, it would be her colony of ants. Boswell Badger was in need, and so were the Boulogne groundhogs. It was time for the age-old rivalry to end.

CHAPTER TWENTY-SEVEN

We're On It!

Queen Fourmi was not the kind of queen to sit around on a throne all day and be waited on by servants. She was more of a hands-on kind of queen. So, when Boswell asked one of the millions of garden ants in the *Champ de Mars* to let Fourmi know he'd be grateful for the chance to speak with her, the queen herself showed up on the badger's doorstep within ten minutes.

"What can I do for you, old friend?" she asked with a regal bow.

"My lady, please come in."

Boswell stood aside and waited for the tiny ant queen to enter his den. He then closed the door behind her and led her into his sitting room. Once the queen had made herself comfortable on a throw pillow, the badger continued.

"Your majesty, I'm in need of help from your vast colony," he said, notably less grumpy than usual. He then carefully added, "And not just I, but the groundhogs of the Bois de Boulogne are also in need of your help."

"Oh?" the queen responded with cautious curiosity. "Go on."

"An emergency alert was received over the groundhogs' *network* last night, an alert that was only brought to my attention this morning. A butterfly from Saint-Denis-lès-Chevreuse -- Esmée by name -- was feared lost and in danger. I have, by chance, met her and know that she is well. According to the message, her friends have traveled all the way to Paris in the hope of finding her. It appears they made the acquaintance of a groundhog named Marmot…"

"Yes, I know Marmot well. Continue."

Boswell was surprised by the queen's comment but decided not to ask her how precisely she knew Marmot; not yet, anyway.

"It was Marmot who sent the emergency alert. It is also believed that he may be leading Esmée's friends up the river on a search and rescue mission. Esmée is desperate to find these friends of hers, assure them of her well-being, and put an end to their burdensome mission. She is also, understandably, very worried about them. Even guided by such a worthy groundhog as Marmot, the city can be a dangerous place for butterflies."

"I see," the queen said, deep in thought. "Might this lost butterfly have visited the Louvre a few days ago?"

"You are correct, as always, Your Majesty. She is the same butterfly as the one on the cover of *Le Journal* from a few days ago."

"And you believe Marmot's search party may be on their way to the Louvre to find Esmée. A wise assumption, my friend. That being their goal, they would have to pass *le Champ et les Jardins.* Have you spoken with Hugo already?"

Boswell was again surprised to learn that the Queen of the Garden Ants knew both Marmot and Hugo's by name. He had no idea that she kept track of such things. Being a wise badger, though, he knew very well that he did *not* know everything. He was happy, now, to be reminded of this fact, especially by someone he respected as much as he did the queen.

He went on, "Victor, the *network manager* for

the…"

"*Champ de Mars – Tour Eiffel server room.* Yes, I am acquainted with him, too." the queen interjected.

"Of course, my lady." Boswell paused with respect. "Victor has gone to find Hugo now, to ask for his help. Both sides of the river must be patrolled, if we are going to locate Marmot and Esmée's friends. The search party's errand is an important one, but their fear is unnecessary. For their sake and Esmée's, they must be located. They must be reunited, and all worries set at ease."

"You're right. There are more than enough reasons for fear and concern in the world. We must eliminate the suffering we can and soothe that which we cannot, whenever possible."

Boswell watched the queen as she spoke. There was a commanding kindness about her, a strength of character. He had always been proud of his own wisdom -- too proud, in fact. There before him stood a humble wisdom and a noble humility. The biggest badger in all of Paris felt very small in the presence of the Queen of the Garden Ants.

"Very well said, my lady."

It's funny how some people and animals make all gruff and grouchy grumpiness dissolve away into peaceful awe.

"You will have our help, old friend," the queen decreed. "Moreover, the groundhogs of the Bois de Boulogne shall have the help of the Garden Ants of *le Champ de Mars* and, indeed, all of Paris – wherever and whenever they are in need. It took the actions of one groundhog and the ancient foolishness of *both* our races to start the rip that has torn us apart for ages. It is fitting that a common cause should unite that which was divided, and that one so wise as yourself should bring about the healing."

"My lady, yours is the wisdom that heals. I am your humble servant."

"I have work to do," the queen said, rising from her pillow. "And an army of ants to put on the alert. We shall stay in touch. Farewell, my friend."

Walking to the door, Boswell opened it for the queen, who thanked him and then took her leave. The plan that he and Victor had made on the first floor of the Eiffel Tower that morning was now in place. Both sides of the river were being watched for any sign of Marmot, Audrey and Pica. Esmée and Pierre were on their way downriver to intercept the travelers, if possible. Everything was under control. It seemed that nothing could go wrong.

It was now 2 p.m. on Friday and back at Marmot's apartment, the travelers had just finished copying Esmée's photo from *Le Journal* and were preparing to depart on their journey to the Louvre. Before leaving, Marmot jotted down a quick message addressed to his friend, Boswell Badger, care of the *CM-TE server room.* The message requested a meeting for the following afternoon. Marmot then placed the message in the mailbox; raised the orange "urgent" flag; and departed with Audrey and Pica.

As Marmot led his party through the tunnels toward the Parc André-Citroën where they would spend the night, his urgent message to Boswell Badger was picked up by Otto Oliveri, who was on his way to the river for an afternoon of fishing. Otto carried the message as far as his favorite fishing hole beside the Périphérique bridge.

There, he met Brigitte Lessier, who was on her way to the Parc Sainte-Périne near the Université de Paris. There, her friend, Raquel Apprise, took possession of the message and quickly brought it all the way to the Radio France headquarters. Raquel was part of a groundhog study group doing research at Radio France into alternative methods of long-distance communication. With all the old radios laying around the city in trash cans and recycle bins, the groundhogs wanted to learn the secrets of radio in case they could be put to good use.

From the Radio France building, the message was carried by one of the many *message runners* who work the tunnels between there and the rest of the network. The Radio France *router* is a major hub on the Bois de Boulogne *network*. Most of the messages traveling the *internet* cross over from one tunnel to another at the Radio France *router*. The more urgent messages get picked up by *message runners* who carry them – *non-stop and quickly* – to their final destination.

Since Marmot's message was marked as urgent and addressed to the *Champ de Mars – Tour Eiffel server room*, the *runner,* whose name was Marcel, took it – *non-stop and quickly* – up the river as far as the *Jardins du Trocadéro*. There, at the edge of the river, Marcel began whistling in Groundhog 5.1.

In no time, a little cloud of fireflies rose up out of the wintercress flowers beside the water. Since it was daytime, they wouldn't be able to *flash* their message across the river to their fellow fireflies. Instead, they would have to carry it over by hand… or rather, by feet.

Marcel held the tiny scrap of paper up in the air with one paw. The cloud of wintercress fireflies flew over to the groundhog, circling the message, searching for a foothold. One by one, the little fireflies latched onto the piece of paper using only their feet.

They then carried the message over the river; all working together; all flapping in unison. To passersby, the scrap of paper looked as if it were being blown by the wind, floating on the river breeze. No one knew what was really going on. The fireflies ferried their precious cargo above the passing boats, and at last, into the paws of another groundhog *runner*, named André, who was waiting to take it to its final destination.

Scurrying up the riverbank; across the street; and over the sidewalk, André the message *runner* entered the grounds of the Eiffel Tower. He knew exactly where he was heading, having delivered many messages to Victor's *server room* in the past.

Arriving at the northeastern foot of the tower, André hopped down the tunnel's entrance and ran all the way to Victor's apartment. Urgent messages were usually delivered by hand, rarely just left in one of the 1,250 mailboxes in a *server room's* wall.

A knock came on Victor's door. The groundhog had not been home from his dash across the river for more than 2 minutes and was busy composing a response to the first emergency message received from Marmot earlier that morning. When the knock came, he dropped his pencil and headed for the door in haste.

"Two urgent messages, sir. Origin: *T1 server room.* I'll await your reply."

André knew his business. He was short and to the point, and waited on Victor to read the messages, in case there was an urgent response.

Victor opened the first folded message and read,

"Priority 1: Urgent!
From: Network Manager, T1 Server Room
To: Boswell Badger, c/o CM-TE Server Room

Alert: 2:01 p.m. Friday. Setting out momentarily for the *JdT*, in search of lost butterfly, Esmée (see attached photo). Accompanied by her friends, Audrey and Pica. Will spend the night in the Parc André-Citroën. Hope to be at *CM-TE* by mid-day Saturday. Request a meeting at that time. *T1 server room* being attended by Megalina, field mouse. Replies may be made to her. Gratefully, Marmot.

Attachment: *Le Journal* photo.”

“And the second message, sir.” André handed Victor another piece of paper. “It was sent to every *server room* on the *network*,” he added.

Victor opened the second folded message. It was a copy of the photo from *Le Journal* with the following inscription,

“Priority 1: Urgent!
From: Network Manager, T1 Server Room
To: All Recipients

Alert: The lost butterfly, Esmée. Be on the look-out.”

“Will there be a reply, sir?” André asked.

“Yes,” Victor said in a commanding tone. “Reply: Message received. Esmée last seen at Eiffel Tower, safe and well. On her way south to find you in the company of another butterfly. Boswell will be waiting for your arrival. Signed, Victor, *CM-TE*.”

Looking André in the eye, he emphasized his instructions, “Be sure this message is copied to every *network manager* along the way… *including* Hugo across the river. It’s vital that he sees it, too. Now go!”

André turned and headed back through the short tunnel; up the *access point* hole; through the tall grass; over sidewalks and streets; and down to the river, where a cloud of wintercress fireflies waited to carry Victor’s reply across the swift-flowing water.

By ensuring every *network manager* along the way would be copied on the message, Victor was effectively alerting the entire network – and all of Paris. The message would be delivered to Megalina in the *T1 server room*; but if Marmot happened to be near any of the dozen or so *server rooms* between the *Champ de Mars* and Megalina, he would get the message before she did.

"Right!" Victor said, "Now on to Boswell."

Pulling the door shut behind him, Victor ran in the direction of Boswell's den. Their assumption about Marmot had been correct. He hadn't just sat around waiting for a reply to his first emergency alert. He did the smartest thing he could have possibly done; he employed Megalina to copy the photo from *Le Journal* and sent it to every *server room* on the *network*. Now everyone knew who they were looking for and exactly what she looked like. It was brilliant.

The plan Victor and Boswell had formulated that morning was working well; and now they knew that Marmot was on his way to see Boswell.

The only mistake they'd made was in letting Esmée and Pierre go search for her friends themselves. Had the two butterflies stayed at the Eiffel Tower or in the *Champ de Mars* with Boswell, they would soon be reunited with their friends when Marmot and company arrived the following afternoon. Now, Esmée and Pierre were right back where they had been before meeting the badger: alone and separated from their friends; and possibly, headed into the arms of danger, once again.

After finding Esmée, Boswell and Victor should have held on to her, and not let her go off again into uncertainty. Victor was kicking himself all the way to Boswell's den. This was a terrible mistake, and no one yet knew just how terrible it would end up being.

Across the river in the *Jardins du Trocadéro,* Hugo was busy organizing his own team of helpers. He had briefly considered asking the earthworms for their help patrolling the gardens, but they were much too slow;

too touchy; and far too sensitive. He'd mastered communicating with them, but he hadn't quite mastered worm etiquette, yet. He seemed to always be saying the wrong thing at the wrong time and sending Wormester rolling his eyes and disappearing into the tunnel wall. It was too much trouble dealing with worms.

Hugo needed helpers with energy, intelligence, enthusiasm, and – above all – a tree-level view of *les Jardins*. He needed squirrels, and a lot of them. Luckily, that's precisely what the *Jardins* has in abundance. The problem was that, unlike the Garden Ants, squirrels don't have a queen… or a king… or a leader of any kind. Each squirrel is his or her own leader. Some are very reliable and trustworthy, others are… well, just a little more… squirrelly.

Get the right squirrels on your team, and things get done right and with efficiency. End up with a squirrelly squirrel, and all you have is energetic mischief, chaos, and anarchy. Hugo needed help, but he knew the risks involved in asking squirrels for assistance.

The good news was that squirrels happen to speak a language very similar to Groundhog. Both are rodents; both make high-pitched squeaking and whistling sounds; and both have lived in the same areas together for ages. It should be no surprise, then, that squirrels have borrowed a great deal from *Groundhog* down through the years. On this particular day, Hugo took advantage of this fact like never before.

Running through the trees surrounding *les Jardins du Trocadéro,* Hugo repeated – in *Groundhog 5.1* -- the same message at the top of his lungs, "Help desperately needed. Come to the *server room* for details! Help desperately needed. Come to the *server room* for details!"

Over and over, back and forth, around and around he went, until every squirrel on every tree had heard the message. Satisfied that he'd "gotten the word out," Hugo headed back toward the secret tunnel entrance beneath the hydrangea bush.

When he arrived, he could hardly believe his eyes. A sea of fluffy tails greeted him -- all ruffling in the breeze, all standing around the hydrangea bush waiting for his return. They were eager to learn the "details" of exactly what kind of help was "desperately needed." The chatter of squirrels discussing what the message might mean, was overwhelming. There must have been a thousand or more just standing around the hydrangea bush like a jittery, high-strung group of nutbrown coffee-drinkers.

Hugo knew he had one chance to win the unruly squirrels over to his cause. It wouldn't be easy. The gardenia-sketching, amateur scientist groundhog hopped up on a decorative boulder and addressed the crowd; first gaining everyone's attention.

"Ahem! AHEM! Quiet, now! Quiet! Thank you."

For a groundhog who preferred nothing more than the company of a silent flower bush, Hugo was a surprisingly good public speaker.

"Yes, thank you all for coming. I'll get right to the point."

The groundhog knew how to please his audience: don't lose their attention; don't beat around the bush; and keep the speech short.

"Earlier today, I was informed of an emergency message that had been sent out over the Boulogne *network*. A lost butterfly, possibly in grave danger, was the subject of a desperate search and rescue mission on the part of her friends and one of my fellow groundhogs. The butterfly has since been found; but her friends do not yet know that she's safe. We are now on the look-out for her friends and the groundhog, whom we believe will lead them through either the *Champ de Mars* or *les Jardins* on route upriver."

There was silent attention now from every squirrel in the crowd. All eyes were on Hugo. This was more excitement than any of the squirrels had ever experienced before, except the few who had actually been outside *les Jardins*.

The groundhog continued his speech.

"No one knows *les Jardins* as well as you, my friends. No one else has such an excellent view of the area as you do from the trees. These butterflies and this groundhog *must* be located. Their fears *must* be laid to rest. The dangerous mission they've undertaken *must* be brought to a close before anyone gets hurt. Only you can do what needs to be done! Will you be my eyes and ears?"

A cheer broke out from among the excitable squirrels.

"Will you help patrol our fair gardens?"

Another cheer, louder and more excitable.

"Will you help reunite these friends with their lost butterfly?"

A roar of agreement and thunderous applause.

"Will you lend your support to me…"

Yelling and wild hollering.

"…to Victor, across the river…"

The squirrels erupted in vigorous hoorahs and hooting, jumping and dancing around the rock upon which Hugo stood.

"…and to our worthy friend, Boswell Badger!!"

Silence.

It was as if Hugo had flipped a switch. Even the birds in the trees went quiet, as if waiting to hear the squirrels answer.

"Friends… what is it?" Hugo was losing his audience.

"Boswell Badger is a grump," came a reply, from somewhere in the crowd. "He's bossy and crabby and has no interest in squirrels. Why should we help someone so unpleasant as Boswell Badger?"

An assortment of responses such as, "Yeah! Right! Why should we?" and "Grumpy old badger!" were heard from all throughout the boisterous bunch of squirrels. This was a tough crowd, for sure.

"I understand," Hugo began. "I do understand."

Softening his voice almost to a whisper, Hugo went on.

"I, myself, dread meeting with Boswell. He *is* grumpy, without a doubt. Ill-tempered, crusty, and curmudgeonly. I agree."

More hearty agreement was heard from the squirrel mob. This only seemed to be fueling the fire.

"But…"

Silence again.

Hugo spoke more slowly.

"But… we mustn't forget who we are. Where we live. The noble peace and beauty of *les Jardins*. We made it so. If it weren't for us… for all of you… *les Jardins* would not be as noble and peaceful as it is. In the middle of a city of grumpiness, we made this garden fair and pleasant. We rose above the challenges that surround us."

Hugo was on a roll now. His speech increased in speed and intensity.

"We are small, but we are not weak. We are often forgotten, but we do not hold a grudge. We might not be the *Champ de Mars – Tour Eiffel*… we might not be much more than a garden of squirrels and a sketching groundhog… but this is our moment…"

The crowd began to respond. A murmur of, "Yeah. It's true," and "He really does have a point, there," could be heard among the more sensible, less-squirrelly squirrels.

"This is our time to stand up…"

Agreement went up from the squirrels.

"There are animals in need out there…"

Cheers and applause!

"And we will help them! We will help them, because we are the squirrels and the groundhog of *les Jardins du Trocadéro*! The *JdT!* And we stand together! Who's with me?!"

The crowd went wild with excitement. Squirrels were waving their tails; doing cartwheels across the grass; and jumping in the air. Hugo had won them over and the squirrel army of the *Jardins du Trocadéro* were on the job!

"To the treetops, my friends. If you see a groundhog traveling with a butterfly or two, alert me without delay. Now go! To your posts!"

Chanting, "*JdT, JdT, JdT,*" the *Jardins* echoed with the squeaky sounds of squirrel voices. Like a drop of oil in a pool of water, the squirrels quickly dispersed and disappeared into the treetops and shrubbery scattered throughout the gardens. Hugo had accomplished a great deal: he'd united every squirrel in a common cause, and overcame their uneasiness with Boswell Badger, too. This was no small task.

Heading down the hole beneath the hydrangea bush, Hugo took up his post in the *server room*. From there he would wait to receive word from his squirrel sentries, if any were lucky enough to spot Marmot, Pica and Audrey. Marmot's message had mentioned Esmée's friends; everyone just assumed that meant more than one butterfly. Esmée guessed it was Lisette who had come to Paris in search of her best friend. No one was on the lookout for Marmot, a butterfly and a magpie. Still, it was enough to stay on the alert for a groundhog traveling with at least one butterfly, as such things were rarely seen.

As it turned out, it didn't much matter for Hugo and the squirrels; for, the moment Hugo returned to the *server room,* a message came through from across the river. Victor's reply to the message Marmot sent about meeting with Boswell Badger on Saturday afternoon was copied to every *server room* and *network manager* on the Boulogne *internet*. Hugo now knew that Marmot and Esmée's friends would be heading to the *Champ de Mars* instead of the *Jardins*. Knowing Victor as well as he did, he also suspected that a new task would soon be assigned to him and his squirrels.

Hugo sent Victor a quick response reading, "*JdT server room* and its army of squirrels are standing by," then waited patiently for further instructions. He would not have to wait very long.

On the other side of the river, Victor had just arrived at Boswell Badger's den. Knowing from experience that it's never a good idea to enter a badger's den unannounced, Victor cupped his paws around his mouth and called inside after Boswell.

"Boswell, it's Victor. May I come in? It's urgent."

A muffled grumble came from deep within the den. Victor took this as permission to enter. Once inside, he found the badger at his desk in the study, poring over a map of the city.

"Yes, yes, come in, come in already. What is it?" the old badger said, stroking his silver sideburns by the light of a single candle. He didn't look up at Victor but motioned for him to draw closer.

"We've made a terrible mistake, I fear. Look."

Boswell looked at Victor's face for a moment, trying to read the level of concern in his eyes. He then snatched the two small pieces of paper from Victor's hand and began reading the first message,

"Priority 1: Urgent!
From: Network Manager, T1 Server Room
To: Boswell Badger, c/o CM-TE Server Room

Alert: 2:01 p.m. Friday. Setting out momentarily

for the Louvre in search of lost butterfly, Esmée (see attached photo). Accompanied by her friends Audrey and Pica. Will spend the night in the Parc André-Citroën. Hope to be at *CM-TE* by mid-day Saturday. Request a meeting at that time. *T1 server room* being attended by Megalina, field mouse. Replies may be made to her. Gratefully, Marmot.

Attachment: *Le Journal* photo."

Boswell rubbed his forehead with exhaustion, staring into the flickering flame of the candle. After a moment of consideration, he finally spoke.

"This message was sent within the last two hours. If only we'd received it sooner, we could have stopped them from leaving Marmot's place. What's worse is that we let Esmée go."

The badger now looked Victor straight in the eye.

"We need to find her and Pierre. We need to get them back, before they travel too far."

Victor nodded. They'd made a mistake by letting her go. They had to make it right again. Boswell opened the second piece of paper and saw the copied image of the photo from *Le Journal*.

"Brilliant little field mouse," he said, smiling at the 256MB picture in his hands. "But it's not with a *photo* that we will find Esmée now. We need feet on the streets, and a lot of them. But who?"

Victor snapped his fingers in the air, "We need feet in the trees! And I know just the feet!"

"What do you have in mind, my friend?" the old badger was intrigued

"Hugo!" Victor replied.

"Hugo?" Boswell said, without the slightest hint of confidence in Victor's preposterous suggestion. "That flower-sketching dreamer doesn't even do his job on a reliable basis. And I certainly doubt he can climb a tree."

Victor laughed, "No, old friend. You do him an injustice. Hugo is much more than you give him credit for. At this very moment, he has an '*army of squirrels standing by.*' Any groundhog who can muster an army of undisciplined squirrels *has* to be more than meets the eye. They're our best hope of finding Esmée quickly. It's up to Hugo, now."

"Poor Esmée," the old grump replied. "At least she doesn't know that all her hopes now hang on Hugo. Surely, that would make her despair."

"I'll send the message straight away, then stay in my *server room* to coordinate communications. If all goes well, Marmot will be here to see you tomorrow afternoon. Hopefully, the squirrels will have found Esmée by then. I'm off!"

Victor left Boswell feeling much less hopeful about the whole situation. Hugo had been right when he told Victor that Boswell Badger thought "very little" of him. Boswell didn't really know Hugo, probably because Hugo was nervous and shy around the badger. But also, because Hugo was a quiet, thoughtful kind of person who preferred sketching gardenias and studying insects to just about any other activity he could imagine. If Boswell "thought very little" of Hugo, his opinion was about to change.

Arriving at the *CM-TE server room,* Victor jotted down a brief message, placed it in a letterbox in the *server room* wall, and raised the orange "urgent" flag. In a matter of moments, André the *message runner* picked up the message and flipped the "urgent" flag back down to its normal position. He then took the message down to the river for transmission by *WiFi* to Marcel, the *runner* who waited on the other side. Marcel then ran the message from the river, up the hill to *les Jardins,* and over to the hydrangea bush for immediate delivery to the *JdT server room*. As was his duty, Marcel waited for Hugo to read the message, in case there was an urgent reply. The message read,

> **"Priority 1:** Urgent!
> **From:** Network Manager, CM-TE Server Room
> **To:** Network Manager, JdT Server Room
>
> **Alert:** In light of Marmot's arrival tomorrow in the *Champ de Mars,* the new priority is to find Esmée and her friend, Pierre, who are somewhere downriver looking for Marmot. This is a job for the squirrels of the *JdT*, led by their *network manager*. We're counting on you, Hugo – Boswell and I, both. Keep in touch, my friend. – Victor"

"Will there be a reply, sir?" Marcel asked, realizing this was the first time he'd ever asked Hugo that question. In fact, this may have been the first message he ever delivered to the *JdT server room.*

A look of focus and determination shone brightly from the groundhog's eyes. He had assembled the best team for the job, of this he was certain. Turning to the *message runner,* he said, "Yes. Just three words: *We're on it*!"

CHAPTER TWENTY-EIGHT

The Squirrels of the *JdT*

The storm clouds that had been gathering all morning finally blocked out the afternoon sun. The breeze changed direction, and in its wake, a cold rain now began to fall. At first, the raindrops were oversized and spotty, hitting the pavement in dusty splatters. Thirsty streets and sidewalks soaked up every drop, bathing in the taste of clean water. Then it all turned to grey curtains. Small, stinging droplets – sharp as tacks – left their mark on everything they touched.

A northwesterly wind chased its own tail through side-streets and alleyways, sweeping up discarded scraps of newspaper in a frenzy of swirling air. In the blink of an eye, the City of Lights had become the City of Sogginess. Puddles formed in every dip and pothole. Limestone dripped and wrought iron dribbled, as if every building had suddenly sprung a leak. The air itself was thick and pale; and even the Eiffel Tower searched -- with her head in the clouds -- for any shred of sunlight she might find.

Unannounced, a flash of lightning ripped the sky. Moments later, thunder echoed down the canyons of Parisian buildings, bouncing like a pinball running wild through the city streets. The storm was far away, moving slowly, and promising to take its time. This would not be a quick afternoon shower.

Esmée and Pierre had left the Eiffel Tower that

morning and flown only as far as the long, narrow island that sits in the middle of the Seine. Connected to the right and left banks by three bridges, the *Île aux Cygnes* – or Island of Swans – is a manmade island just south of the Eiffel Tower across from the circular Radio France building. There are no apartments or buildings of any kind on the island, just a long walkway; a lot of trees; and a curious statue at the southern tip.

Three years after the nation of France gave the Statue of Liberty to the United States, a group of Americans living in Paris made a nearly identical gift to the people of the city. A replica of the Statue of Liberty, only one-fourth its size, sits at the southern-most end of the Island of Swans and faces west toward her big sister across the sea. It's both a somewhat moving and a slightly odd statue to find in Paris, especially for an American who has seen the "real thing" towering over New York Harbor.

As the two butterflies left the Eiffel Tower and began their journey downriver, the gathering rain clouds forced them to search for a place to weather the storm. The trees and overhead bridges on the island made it a perfect choice. There were plenty of flowering shrubs here and there to provide nectar in the event the storm lasted longer than expected.

Best of all, the island was right in the middle of the river. From there, they could easily keep an eye on both banks. If Marmot and Esmée's friends were on their way upriver, they would surely be seen from the Island of Swans, no matter which side they travelled on.

Finding an azalea bush beneath the Pont de Grenelle, Esmée and Pierre settled in for a long, refreshing *déjeuner*. Ever since she learned from Boswell and Victor of her friends' worry over her disappearance, Esmée had thought of little else. Now, in a quiet moment, the emotions came flooding into her heart.

"She probably first missed me at *l'arbuste à papillons,*" Esmée whispered.

Looking up from her flower, she continued with a wistful remembrance, "We always shared breakfast together at Madame Legrand's butterfly bush. I'm sure that was when she first realized something was wrong."

"Who, *ma petite*?"

"Lisette," she said, looking at Pierre, with a sadness that would break the heart of even the crustiest of badgers. "My dearest, oldest friend." Esmée didn't feel much like eating anymore.

"Poor Lisette. She must have been frantic trying to find me. And now, her worries have led her far from home, because of me. Who knows what dangers she's faced? But who is with her, I wonder? Who is this *other* friend the groundhog's message mentions?"

"Who, indeed?" Pierre mused. "Surely all of Saint-Denis is concerned for your well-being."

Esmée dropped her head, shaking it slowly; feeling the weight of responsibility for her friends' safety.

"It must be Sylvie. Only she and Lisette would be able to make a trip such as this. Only the two of them are brave enough to risk so much… for me."

Pierre wrapped one wing around Esmée's shoulders.

"We must find them, Pierre. I need to know they're alright. I need to show them I'm safe. And then…" she hesitated. "And then… I must help them get home again."

"*Oui, mademoiselle,* you must, but not alone. Never alone. Never again. I will help you; I will assist you in every way I know how. You will permit me, *non*?"

"*Mon amour, oui… toujours.* But I do not know the way."

"Ah, but that is just it, *mademoiselle*. We find the way together. That is what love means. And that is all I ask of you. *Toujours.*"

Off to the north, storm clouds loomed heavy in the midday sky. It was raining over the Eiffel Tower, and soon it would reach the Island of Swans. The wind was brisk and carried in its hands the scent of distant rain; a wholesome sweetness, uniquely its own. The storm was moving in from the sea, as it often does; and the heavy air from the north was pushing it all downriver.

It was already raining on the den of Boswell Badger, in the *Champ de Mars.* Queen Fourmi had been alerted by the badger that Marmot was on his way. As a result, she instructed her garden ants to "stand down;" which was just as well, since there was little they could do in the pouring rain, anyway. She stayed with Boswell, awaiting the arrival of Marmot and company. Her ants remained on stand-by in case they were needed.

It was also raining on the *CM-TE server room,* beneath the northeastern foot of the tower. Inside, Victor waited patiently for any message from Hugo and his army of squirrels about the whereabouts of Esmée and Pierre. It was up to Victor to bring word to Boswell – and to Marmot, when he finally arrived – putting an end to the desperate search, once and for all.

Across the river from the Eiffel Tower in the *Jardins du Trocadéro,* the rain was falling on a very unusual spectacle. One thousand fluffy-tailed squirrels stood at attention (itself, a peculiar scene), perfectly still and utterly silent (more peculiar, still), hanging on every word of instruction being delivered by a groundhog (to top it all off). This was unheard of. Squirrels never stand still; never keep quiet; and hardly ever listen to anyone, let alone a groundhog. But these were no ordinary squirrels; and this was no ordinary groundhog.

The Squirrels of the *JdT,* under the command of Hugo of the Bois de Boulogne Groundhogs, were exceptional in every way. Unruly, undisciplined, and --

let's face it -- quite squirrelly, they'd found their leader; they'd found their cause; they were ready to venture outside their quiet, peaceful *Jardins* and into the unknowns of the City of Lights and Sogginess. It's amazing what one charismatic leader can accomplish, and Hugo was just such a leader. An artist and scientist at heart, Hugo understood the animals of the *Jardins* better than anyone else. Only *he* could unite and lead them.

"Squirrels of the *JdT*, we have been entrusted with a task of great importance. We must find and return to the safety of the *Champ de Mars* both Esmée and Pierre, the lost *belles dames* butterflies. Are you ready to accept this challenge?"

A wave of applause and cheering swept over the crowd of squirrels gathered in front of Hugo.

"You've been organized into eight squads, under the leadership of eight trustworthy squirrels. Each squad will search and patrol that part of the river which lies north of its home base. The Squirrel Squads are as follows:

"Butternut, you will take your squadron as far south as the Parc Sainte-Périne. From there, you will search and patrol as far north as the next base."

A chubby, yellow-brown squirrel perked up at the mention of his name. Nodding in agreement at every third word, the young squirrel finally said, "Yes, sir! Butternut Squad is ready! Thank you, sir," then returned to eyeing a blackberry bush some two or three feet behind Hugo.

"Sunflower, you will make the Mirabeau metro station your home base, patrolling as far north as Radio France."

The tall, lean, athletic squirrel listened with cool confidence. She then nodded only once, indicating agreement without making a sound.

"Very good. Now, Beaujolais, your squadron's home base will be the Radio France building. This is a major hub of the groundhog *network,* so the butterflies may have headed there to try and make contact with Marmot."

"Will do, sir," came the reply from a young squirrel with a pink bow in her extra-poofy tail. Her fur was beautifully combed and (although Hugo couldn't be sure) she seemed to have much longer (unnaturally so) eyelashes than the other squirrels.

"Yes, uh… thank you. Um… Montgomery Bazillac…"

"Just Baz, sir," the squirrel replied.

"Pardon me?" Hugo was caught off guard.

"Only my mom calls me Montgomery," the squirrel said, looking around to be sure no one was laughing at him. He was a big brute of a squirrel, so that would be unlikely. "Baz will do just fine."

"Right. My mistake. Uh… anyhow, Baz, your base will be the Parc de Passy. There are some shrubs and flowers in that Parc that would certainly attract a butterfly or two. From there, patrol the right bank of the river as far north as the *JdT.* Excellent, then. That should give us good coverage of the entire western side of the river."

"You got it," Baz said, snapping his fingers and pointing at Hugo for emphasis.

"Moving on, now. On the eastern side of the Seine, Baldtail and his squadron will cover the area between the Parc André-Citroën and the next base."

The first thing one noticed about the squirrel called Baldtail was his… well… missing right thumb. He'd lost it in an unfortunate incident with a bobcat some years ago and was rather proud of telling the story.

Coming home one evening after an afternoon spent gathering berries, the squirrel noticed something sticking out of the entrance to his nest in the rotten elm. As he approached, he saw a long, hairy tail attached to the butt of a bobcat who had squeezed himself into Baldtail's tree. There could only be one reason why a bobcat would shove itself inside a hole in a tree, and Baldtail was having none of it. He refused to become dinner for a smelly, old cat.

There's a popular saying that describes a situation in which someone makes a bad decision that isn't easy to change. To say that someone "has a tiger by the tail" means that, after grabbing onto the tiger's tail, it would now be very dangerous for you to let go. Baldtail had obviously never heard this saying before.

Sneaking along as silent as the night, he crept up behind the unsuspecting cat who was still busy wriggling himself deeper into the squirrel's home. Baldtail was tired and grumpy from a day of fruitless gathering; he just wanted to go to bed. His patience had worn thin and taken his reason along with it. Deciding that the best thing to do would be to grab the cat by the tail and yank it out of his den, Baldtail reached out his right paw

The moment the intruder felt the squirrel's fingers wrap around its tail it began squirming backward trying to free itself from the hole in the log. But the angry squirrel held on tight, pulling with all his might, and cursing-up a firestorm. With a sound like that of a cork leaving a bottle of champagne, the cat suddenly popped out. Twisting around to see what creature could possibly be crazy enough to pull on its tail, the bobcat immediately locked its jaws around Baldtail's right hand.

In an instant, all movement stopped. The squirrel stood perfectly still, with his right hand wrapped around the bobcat's tail. The bobcat stood motionless, with its mouth wrapped around the hand that held its tail. The two stared at each other, and no one moved a muscle.

"Bite it off and you'll take half your tail with it," Baldtail said.

"Continue holding onto me in this manner, and you will surely regret it," the bobcat threatened, still holding the squirrel's hand in its mouth.

"I can stand here all day," Baldtail said, with a snort of disdain, "Unless you have a better idea."

The bobcat licked the corners of its lips, its rough, pink tongue brushing up against Baldtail's wrist. The squirrel was disgusted by the slobbery manners of the intruder. He might have teased that he could "stand there all day," but he dearly hoped he wouldn't have to, after all.

"Let go of my tail and I'll let your hand go, too," lied the bobcat through his teeth.

"Oh no, I'm not falling for *that*," the squirrel chuckled. "Cats can't be trusted, this much I know. As long as I hold onto your tail, my hand is safe."

"Then what are we to do?" the cat sneered.

"I suppose you could simply open your mouth, apologize, and be on your way," the squirrel offered.

"Apologize? I think not."

The burglar bobcat felt he had every right to burgle a squirrel's nest. There'd be no agreement on this subject, to be sure.

"Then we count to three, and on three we both let go at the same instant. Fair enough?"

"Very well, but is it *on* three or *after* three that we let go? I wouldn't want to get it wrong and still be holding onto your paw after you've let go of my tail," the bobcat said, with an air of false concern.

"*On* three," Baldtail clarified. "One, two, let go! Got it?"

The squirrel realized that his plan involved trusting the bobcat; and this made him very nervous, to say the least. But, when you have a tiger by the tail, it's always best to make a clean break of it and run with all your might. That's exactly what Baldtail intended to do.

"Very well," the bobcat agreed. "*On* three."

Baldtail wiggled his right wrist, encouraging the

blood to flow back into his hand in preparation for the quick release. Eying the opening to his den, he was ready to put his plan into motion. He started the countdown.

"One…"

The squirrel moved one leg in the direction of the elm tree.

"Two…"

He moved the other leg, ready to sprint.

Out of the corner of his clenched teeth, the bobcat cut the countdown short, saying, "Three!"

Opening his mouth and tilting his head, the bobcat released Baldtail's paw, intending to grab hold of the squirrel's arm, instead. Anticipating some trick or treachery from the bobcat, Baldtail whipped his arm away from his enemy, then turned to bolt inside his home.

Before he could get away, the bobcat caught the squirrel's right thumb in his mouth, biting it clean off. As Baldtail leapt into the rotten log, the bobcat shot out his neck and grabbed the squirrel's fluffy tail between his lips. As the squirrel disappeared deep inside his tree, Baldtail's tail slid between the bobcat's sharp teeth -- which shaved every hair clean off and left him with, you guessed it, a bald tail.

Of course, the squirrel was lucky to have escaped with the rest of his body intact. Bobcats are fast and notoriously clever. It may have been mercy that convinced the cat to let the squirrel go; but it might also have been the smell of a day spent searching for berries in the hot sun. Squirrels are also notorious… notoriously stinky.

Baldtail never tried to conceal his missing thumb, since it wasn't really all that disturbing to see; it just wasn't, well… *there*. Had his thumb *not* had the misfortune to go missing, it would have completed a set of two unusually large paws. For Baldtail was what the squirrels call a "lug nut." He was nuts about working out, and as a result, he was much bigger (and more rectangular in shape) than most squirrels.

It's likely that everyone started calling him Baldtail to take the attention off his thumb… or where his thumb *used* to be. Because, even though it wasn't disturbing to see, the lost thumb was a huge distraction to everyone who met him.

Anyway, Baldtail was a rough-and-tumble squirrel, never afraid to get his hands dirty. After surviving a bobcat attack, everything else looked pretty tame – even if you are one finger short.

He was happy to lead his squad wherever they were sent; so, Baldtail simply grunted his agreement with the proposed plan, and Hugo moved on.

"Pistache, your group will patrol from the Pathé Beaugrenelle Movie Theatre northward."

"Whatever," came the reply.

It mustn't be thought that Pistache was being disrespectful or showing a lack of interest in the importance of his mission. He was a salty squirrel; thick-skinned, although somewhat green and inexperienced. As with most people with salty personalities, Pistache couldn't help but sound like he was giving Hugo attitude – no matter what he said, it always came off sounding exactly the opposite of how he meant it. Hugo knew this about him, and so he interpreted the response of, "Whatever," to mean, "Whatever you say, sir!" which of course *is* roughly what the salty squirrel meant.

"Rupert, the missing butterflies may have been drawn to the trees and flowers of the Mai Garden, especially with a thunderstorm coming. That will be your territory to patrol."

"We'll search every tree, sir; inspect every flower! We won't leave a single leaf unturned, sir! You've sent the best squad in all the *JdT* to do *this* job, I assure you, sir."

Rupert was what you might call gung-ho. His heart was in the right place, he just needed to tone it down a bit.

"Yes, thank you, Rupert." Hugo shook his head once, then moved on down the line.

"Finally, the area running from the Bir-Hakeim metro station all the way north to the *Champ de Mars* will be yours" Hugo said, addressing an unusually tall, skinny and clumsy squirrel. "Can your squad handle it, Kevin?"

Kevin Nutterbush was wondering how he of all squirrels had been picked to lead a squad. When Hugo asked him to be one of the captains, Kevin thought it was a joke and laughed out loud in an explosion of nervous energy. But Hugo wasn't joking.

The thing is, Kevin knew he wasn't brave, or strong, or daring. He knew he wasn't adventurous or even especially clever. Kevin would be the very first to tell you all of these things; and he'd never dream of trying to appear to be anything more than what he really was: just plain, honest, hardworking Kevin Nutterbush. And that's exactly why Hugo chose him. That's why his squad would follow him *anywhere*. Honesty and hard work always lead to success.

"Um, yes… yes, sir," Kevin answered, with a voice crack. "That'll be just fine with us, sir. We're happy to help. Thank you, sir."

"Thank you, Kevin. That takes care of *both* banks of the river. There's one last territory to be patrolled, and that's the Island of Swans. My squad of one-hundred squirrels and I will handle that ourselves. Very good, then. Remember, at the first sign of Esmée and Pierre, send a messenger to the nearest *server room* and get an urgent message out over the entire *network*."

Hugo became quieter, more thoughtful.

"I'm proud of each and every one of you. It's an honor to work with such noble and exceptional squirrels, such as yourselves. Thank you. Thank you all."

Rousing the troops once more, Hugo said, at the top of his voice, "Now let's go find Esmée and bring her home safely. *JdT! JdT!*"

The army of search and rescue squirrels took up the chant, as they scurried off toward their home bases downriver, "*JdT! JdT! JdT! JdT!*"

A huge high-strung tidal wave of squirrels poured out of the *Jardins du Trocadéro*. Hundreds upon hundreds of squirrels flowed down to the river, crossed the bridge, and just kept coming. Thanks to the rain, all the tourists were inside shops and restaurants waiting out the worst of the storm. Had they been outside to witness the mass exodus, they would have thought it was the end of the world.

From third and fourth story windows, the scene must have looked like a flood of brown water rushing through the *rues* of Paris. The energetic army of squirrels squeaked and chattered over street and sidewalk, bridge and quay, until the *Jardins du Trocadéro* had been emptied of all squirrels, except for one.

Devereux Délabré, Esq. had seen more seasons than three-and-a-half squirrels combined. His life stretched back almost as far as Boswell Badger's; and every moment of it had been spent in *les Jardins*.

If the squirrels of the *JdT* ever decided to choose a king, it would surely be Devereux. He was wise, calm, thoughtful and loved by all. On more than one occasion, the squirrels all rallied together to make him their king; but the most they could accomplish was bestowing the title "**Esq.**" on him, for he truly was an **Exceptional Squirrel**. He'd seen it all -- no one would argue with that fact – indeed, he had seen it all, right up until this particular Friday.

Never, in all his experience, had Devereux Délabré witnessed his fellow squirrels so united by one common cause; never had he seen them led by a *groundhog*, either. These were strange times, and Devereux was grateful to live through them. If he had one wish, it would be that he could turn back the clock and become young again. He wished he were in better health and able to join the squirrels of the *JdT* on their mission. Instead, he would stay behind and wait for them to bring back tales of bravery and self-sacrifice in the line of duty.

Down the riverbanks on both sides of the Seine, squirrels swarmed in the streets. Running along sidewalks in herds of fifty or sixty; climbing trees in packs of thirty or forty; balancing on railings; scrambling across bridges, high above the swift waters of the Seine -- squirrels were everywhere!

Fanning out on either side of the river, they left the *Jardins* behind for the first time ever. The further they ventured away from the *Jardins,* the more organized they became; until finally, eight distinct squirrel squads scampered along downriver – four squads to a side. The Squirrels of the *JdT* were on the march.

It was now late afternoon and the storm had become vicious. The clouds were as dark as night, lit only by the occasional flash of lightning. Rain pelted windowpanes and strafed the ground like machinegun fire from an enemy sky. By now, the wind had whipped itself into a panic, shaking the limbs of trees and threatening to tear street signs from their posts. This was perfect weather to justify spending the entire day inside one's den or nest. This was not the sort of weather to be outside searching for a pair of butterflies.

Hugo led his own squadron of one-hundred squirrels down the western bank of the Seine. Their goal was the Pont Rouelle, just north of the Radio France building. There, they would cross over to the Island of Swans.

The Pont Rouelle crosses the island roughly south

of its center point, sweeping in a gentle curve northward after rejoining the eastern bank. Hugo figured it would be best to make landfall in the middle and send half his squadron to search the northern part of the island, while he took the rest of his squirrels to search as far as the southern tip.

The walk from the *JdT* to the Pont Rouelle is roughly half a mile. For a groundhog and his team of squirrels, this could be made in a relatively short amount of time. In the pouring rain, it would take them much longer. Once Hugo saw how slowly they were progressing, he decided they would push on as best they could and weather the storm overnight beneath the overpass of the Pont Rouelle on the Island of Swans. The next day, they would split the party in two and keep to the original plan. It would be enough trouble for one day just to trudge their way to the island. They'd need a good night's rest, before beginning their search the following morning

As Hugo and his squad approached the Island of Swans, further downstream, Marmot, Audrey and Pica were nearing the Parc André-Citroën on the opposite side of the river. There they would spend the night, before continuing their journey northward to the *Champ de Mars* for their meeting with Boswell Badger. The sky looking down on the groundhog and his two companions was beginning to thicken; but a full moon still shown through the gathering clouds. The storm would not arrive until after they had fallen asleep; they'd surely be greeted by rain upon awakening.

Miles away to the west, Lisette Cueilleur could see distant lightning in the darkening sky off to the east. Low rumbles of thunder came long after the lightning's flash. She thought to herself, "There's a storm over Paris tonight. A storm over Esmée." Her mind turned to her friend, lost somewhere beneath those same storm clouds.

Esmée was alone, as far as Lisette knew. She had no idea that Audrey and Pica had gone to Paris in search of Esmée. She had no idea that her best friend had not left Saint-Denis by choice, but rather, that Esmée had been trapped inside the RER B train, all the while desperate to escape. No, Lisette had no idea.

As she watched the thunderstorm play in the night sky like fireworks from afar, Lisette's head at last gave in to her heart. She began to see things more clearly. She didn't know that her friends went to Paris to find Esmée, but her heart should have known they would. She didn't know that her best friend would never willingly leave their home without saying goodbye, but her heart should have known that *that* simply was not possible. Her head didn't know; but her *heart* did. Her heart *always* knew the truth; but her pride and her stubbornness always got in the way.

For the first time in her life, Lisette Cueilleur cried tears of pure sorrow. There was no anger this time. There was only regret and sadness. She'd let her best friend down; not just by failing to follow her to Paris or failing to search for her until she knew Esmée was alright; Lisette had let her best friend down by losing faith in their friendship. Everything else came after this.

It was not enough to be sorry, though. Lisette had to set things right. First thing in the morning, she resolved to go to the churchyard and ask for Audrey Loriot's help -- something Lisette *never* thought she would do.

She would then go to the oak tree in Monsieur Deschamps fallow field and ask Pica for his help, too. Together, just maybe they could brave the dangers and the distance and make their way to Paris. There, they would search for Esmée until she was found. Lisette would set things right, whatever the cost.

Pulling the feathery down of a thistle up around her neck, Lisette cried herself to sleep. Making a change is often painful; making a change inside our own heart is always the most painful. Lisette's heart ached with change; but change for the better is always worth the pain. She knew this was true, but she did not yet know just how much pain it would cost to set everything right.

Back in the rain-soaked streets of Paris, Hugo the groundhog and his squadron of squirrel searchers were nearing the Pont Rouelle. This final leg of their long, wet march was the most dangerous, by far. The Pont Rouelle is a railway bridge, carrying the RER C trainline into the heart of Paris. To cross it and make it to the Island of Swans, Hugo and his squirrels would have to be quick. They had no idea when a train might come screeching down the tracks in their direction.

Hugo decided that the best course of action was to bunch up and cross the bridge in one, big group. That way, they would all make it across at once, rather than risking the safety of one or two slow stragglers. They would need to be cautious, though, and move at the same speed at the same time. Pushing and shoving in close quarters on narrow tracks could be disastrous for everyone.

From the bushes below the bridge's pier, Hugo examined the structure, plotting out the best route up and over. He realized that making their way up the pier would be the easy part. Once they were on the bridge, they would have to jump from sleeper to sleeper (the wooden boards running between the rails every few feet), leaping over the gaps between them without falling through. If they missed a sleeper, they could plummet 20 feet or more into the river below.

As he was making plans to lead his squad over the Seine, a sound -- like the long yawn of a drowsy dragon – came screaming up from behind. Every squirrel in the pack jumped head-first into the tall weeds around the pier. Trembling with dread, Hugo crouched down and stared motionless in the direction of the fast-approaching noise. Then he saw it, the fire from the dragon's mouth. All around, the earth shook with the heavy footfalls of the galloping beast. Their doom drew near, as the squirrels and their leader braced themselves for the worst.

In the skip of a heartbeat, the dragon changed shape and took the form of a commuter train bound for the *Champ de Mars* station upriver. It was the RER C train. Hugo didn't waste a moment. As soon as the train was across the bridge, he called his squad to attention

"This is our chance! There won't be another train along for six or seven minutes; I'm certain of it. Up and over, now! And stay together!"

Hugo led the way, climbing the bridge's concrete foot as fast as his four feet would carry him. Once up top, he hopped along from sleeper to sleeper, jumping the wide gaps between them with great speed. Behind him, a crowd of squirrels moved as one; some choosing to run along the wet and slippery rails; others following their leader and leaping their way across the span.

Below them, boats glided between river and raindrops like undersea divers. On the bridge above, the downpour was so blinding that the squirrels could barely see the train tracks beneath their feet.

Losing his footing on a slippery rail, one terrified squirrel slid right between the sleepers and down toward the brown water. Hugo stretched out one paw and caught the falling squirrel just in time to save him from drowning or being struck by a passing boat. The incident reminded every squirrel on that bridge that their crossing was deadly perilous. Everyone held their breath and watched their step, until the last member of the group was safely over dry land once again

Hugo was the first to reach the middle pier which anchored the bridge to the Island of Swans. Stepping aside to let the squirrels pass, he waited until he'd counted every last one and saw them shimmy down to the ground. Once all squirrels were safe and sound, Hugo ran down the side of the concrete footing and onto solid ground himself.

The bridge's arched overpass appeared to be an excellent shelter from the raging storm. Surrounded by a screen of trees, even the wind was calm beneath the bridge. It would do just fine for the night. Eager to see everyone in out of the rain and wind, Hugo directed the squad of soggy squirrels into the cave-like shelter.

"That's everyone," he said, counting the one-hundredth squirrel. "We made it, each and every one of us. We made it."

An exhausted cheer rose up from among the group. It had been a harrowing day beneath the unfriendly sky, and they missed the familiarity of *les Jardins* very much. Sometimes, all it takes to better appreciate home, is one cold lonely night away from all that we know and love. The squirrels of the *JdT* were all experiencing just that.

Hugo encouraged everyone to eat something and restore their almost entirely spent strength. Opening their sacks and backpacks, the famished squirrels gobbled up a hurried and inadequate dinner of wet nuts and soggy seeds. By now, sleep was more insistent than hunger, and they were all impatient to give in. Still, to an empty and echoing stomach, even a meal such as this tasted better than it deserved.

Thoughts turned to the day's journey. Each squirrel reliving in his or her own mind the challenges and triumphs of what they'd experienced on this day of days. Even the most hardened resolutions feel the gnaw of doubt, from time to time. In its weakness and fatigue, the mind attracts uncertainty like a wounded animal attracts a flock of vultures.

"Why had they left the comfort of their homes in

the *JdT*? This search and rescue mission was not their concern. After all, what did two little butterflies really matter, in all the wide world? Why had they been so quick to follow Hugo on his mad quest?" Questions invaded their thoughts, chipping away at their resolve. And Hugo understood the damage such thoughts could cause.

"The morning will be here soon enough," Hugo said, with sympathetic sleepiness in his voice. "Rest while you can, my friends. Tomorrow we begin scouring the island for two lost butterflies. We remain their best and brightest hope. We will not fail them. Goodnight, brave companions."

The groundhog looked out across the damp, huddled mass of matted-down fur and shivering squirrels. He was proud of them all. They'd made their way all the way south from the *JdT*, without a single complaint and without a single break. If the *JdT server room* had never really been of much importance before, this day certainly made up for it. Squirrels and groundhogs alike would be telling *The Tale of Hugo and His Stouthearted Squad of Squirrels* for years to come.

Only a few yards away in the dark, unknown to Hugo, Esmée and Pierre slept in an azalea bush beneath the Pont de Grenelle. Thinking they had found the best place from which to keep watch over the river for any sign of Marmot and his fellow travelers, the butterflies rested their wings in preparation for whatever tomorrow might bring. Yet, no one can really prepare for such sorrows as they would face in a few short hours.

CHAPTER TWENTY-NINE

Fifteen Bridges

Saturday morning dawned, cold and grey. The rainstorm that had skirted around to the northeast left Saint-Denis untouched. Instead, a light veil of chilly fog lay over the Chevreuse Valley. Off to the east in Paris, it was another story. The rain had begun just north of the city and followed the river south, drenching everything in its path. It was now directly over the Parc André-Citroën where Marmot, Audrey and Pica were just beginning their day.

Back in Saint-Denis, the sun rose without once showing his face. He would have stayed in bed altogether, if he thought it would go unnoticed. Somewhere in the cold morning mist, wrapped in the fuzz of a thistle's mane, Lisette woke with a start. Something had wrenched her out of a deep sleep and back into the world of wakefulness, without the luxury of a yawn or a stretch. The sudden awareness that today was Saturday, and that she had made very important plans for the day, grabbed hold of her and jolted her awake.

Lisette's very first waking thought was an image of Esmée caught in the rain. This was all the motivation she needed to get up and get moving. She'd always been there when Esmée needed her, since their BB-Day and every day thereafter. Every day, that is, until last Wednesday morning when she saw the photo in *Le Journal*. It was this thought that stung her heart and filled her with shame. What made it even worse was the realization that Esmée had always been there for Lisette, too. Always, and without exception. But the time for tears and regret had passed. Now, Lisette had work to do. She was resolved.

Flying off without pausing for even the quickest breakfast, Lisette crossed the foggy field in which she had spent the night. Following the road down toward the center of Saint-Denis, she came to the intersection with the train station directly in front of her. The idea that Esmée could board a train and leave her family, friends and home without so much as a goodbye now seemed utterly ridiculous to Lisette. She was thinking more clearly, now that the fire of her anger had burned out and the smoke had lifted from her heart.

Turning the corner to the left, she passed *l'église* Saint-Denis and entered the churchyard behind the rectory. The fog still hung in the cool of the morning, hiding much of the garden in grey shadow. Lisette knew the churchyard well; she knew where Audrey liked to spend her days. Most importantly, she knew where the only fig tree was located, and that's where Audrey was most likely to be found.

Navigating her way through rose trellises and manicured hedges, Lisette passed a seashell-shaped birdbath where a statue of the Warrior Butterfly stood guard. Pausing a moment, the proud, stubborn Lisette warmed her softening heart with a short request of Saint-Michel. She knew of Esmée's love for Saint-Michel, so her prayer was as much *for* Esmée as it was to *honor* her.

"*Saint-Michel, s'il vous plaît, accompagnez mon amie.* Be with her, Warrior Butterfly. Keep her safe. She is my dearest friend."

Closing her eyes and bowing her head in gratitude, Lisette crossed the broad churchyard in the direction of the fig tree. Landing among its branches, she surveyed every last twig in the hope of finding Audrey. Hopping and fluttering all around, Lisette examined the entire fig tree, calling out for her friend.

"Audrey. Audrey Loriot. Are you here? It's Lisette. I need you."

There was no answer, and Audrey made no appearance.

Calling once more, Lisette said, "Audrey? Please, Audrey. I need to speak with you."

Only the singing birds replied.

Landing a moment, Lisette became aware of the tiniest movement making its way across the branch upon which she now sat. Looking more closely, she saw an inchworm inching along its path -- although it was considerably less than an inch long. Even compared to a butterfly, the inchworm was tiny. Lisette noticed that the little green caterpillar appeared to be exercising; stretching its body out, then bunching up again in slow but jerky motions. She decided that finding Audrey was important enough to interrupt the inchworm's morning workout routine, at least for a moment.

"*Bonjour*," she started. "I'm sorry to interrupt you. My name is Lisette. *Quel est votre nom?*"

The inchworm stopped, stood up on its hind… uh, *end* -- its hind *end*, I suppose – and looked at Lisette with curiosity. Lisette reminded the little inchworm of someone she knew well – a *belle dame* butterfly, like Lisette.

"Chloé," the inchworm said, "*Je m'appelle Chloé.*"

"*Enchantée, mademoiselle Chloé.* I was hoping you could help me."

Chloé wondered how on earth an inchworm could help a butterfly, but she was a pleasant soul and willing to give it a try.

"*Oui,* if I can," came a whisper of a reply.

Bending over to hear her a bit better, Lisette continued.

"I'm looking for my friend, Audrey. Do you know her? She likes to sit in this tree. I thought she'd be here already, but perhaps I'm too early. Have you seen her?"

Chloé inched her way closer to Lisette then stood up on her hind end (yes, that's certainly what it was) and whispered as loudly as she could, "*Oui,* I know Audrey. Everyone in the churchyard knows the butterfly who can read. She's a legend!"

Lisette wrinkled her forehead at the suggestion that Audrey-the-bookworm was actually considered to be a legend. Lisette never thought much of reading. In fact, she thought it made one stuffy and longwinded like Audrey. The idea that reading could be anything more than a waste of time never occurred to Lisette; much like the idea that Audrey could be anything *but* a wordy bore. Lisette's heart may have been softening, but old habits take longer to change than they do to harden.

"A legend? Audrey? Well, maybe to an inchworm…"

"Not just to the inchworms," Chloé interrupted, "Audrey is a legend to every animal in the churchyard… and beyond."

"I can see why a tiny *inchworm* might think that…" which was a fib, "but the other animals? We must have our Audrey's mixed up. I'm sorry to bother you. I'll be leaving now…"

"Audrey Loriot," Chloé said, stopping Lisette cold (and choosing not to be offended by her prejudice against "tiny" inchworms), "*La Belle Dame* of the Churchyard, the reader of Père Lamoine's daily sermons, Audrey the Adventurer. Yes, I know her. *Do you?*"

The question left Lisette with her mouth hanging open, just staring at the little inchworm. Chloé had measured out the length and breadth of Lisette in two tiny words. Did she even know Audrey, or had she always just *thought* she did? Was the Audrey she tried to avoid the real Audrey, or was she really something much more?

Did Lisette know Audrey? Lisette started to think that maybe she really hadn't bothered to get to know Audrey at all. Another stinging thorn in Lisette's heart.

"Audrey Loriot, yes, that's her. The Adventurer? Why do you call her that?"

"Then you haven't heard?" Chloé asked with disbelief. "It's been the topic of discussion among *all* of Audrey's friends."

Lisette was hurt by hearing those words: "*all* of Audrey's *friends*." If Lisette had been among Audrey's friends, she wouldn't have to ask a stranger about her now. The inchworm went on.

"She left with the magpie. I think his name is Pica… in fact, I think *both* of his names are Pica. Hard to tell, really. But they left… Wednesday, I think it was. Headed for Paris, though I can't imagine why."

"I can," Lisette said under her breath, with a sinking feeling in her stomach.

"Well, I'll be on my way, then," Chloé said, dropping back down onto all eights and inching off down the tree limb. "I need to be on that branch over there…" she motioned to a branch just a foot or so away, "…and I need to be there by this afternoon. Must be going! *Bonne journée!*"

"Paris," Lisette thought to herself. "Audrey and Pica, both. And they left on Wednesday. The same day Audrey discovered the picture in *Le Journal.* The same day I…"

A lump came to Lisette's throat at the thought of it.

"The same day I just flew off and left them."

Everything was coming into focus for Lisette, painfully so. While she'd been thinking of herself,

Audrey and Pica thought only of Esmée and took action to help her. While Lisette had been holding onto her anger, her friends – no, she didn't even have the right to call them her friends – *Esmée's* friends had let go of everything except their love and friendship for Esmée.

"Audrey the Adventurer," Lisette thought; then with amazement in her voice, she added, "and Pica the Brave."

Before today, Lisette would have laughed at thoughts such as these; but now… well, now she didn't. Our actions make us who we are, this much she knew; and Audrey and Pica had taken action. If Lisette was going to act, she would need to do so alone; the others already had. It was her turn.

She left the fig tree in the corner of the churchyard and flew back to the rose trellis beside the statue of Saint-Michel. There, she drank rosewater nectar until her hunger was erased and her strength renewed. She would need all that strength for the journey from Saint-Denis to Paris -- a distance of seventeen miles, as the crow flies. And what a terrible thought that was; one Lisette had not yet considered.

For, along the route between Saint-Denis and Paris, a mob of angry crows kept watch; with vengeance rotting away within their black hearts. It hadn't taken them long to figure out that they'd been tricked by the butterfly and her friend the magpie. Once they realized they'd been made fools of, they set about looking for the pair of travelers, to make sure they could never make fools of a crow again.

Lisette turned her face toward Paris, the City of Lights. With a good breeze behind her, she could make the journey in under two hours. It just so happened that Lisette was in luck. Thanks to the wind that had brought rainstorms to Paris the night before, she would be carried along toward the same destination by the very same breeze.

Once there, however, she would face the wet and miserable weather her friends were enduring at that very moment. But first she'd have to cross the open farmland between Saint-Denis and the Seine – and avoid the marauding crows that lay in wait all throughout that open countryside.

Out of anger and spite, Lisette had chosen to be alone when it would have been better for her to be with her friends. Now, in order to once again find her friends, Lisette would have to be more alone than she'd ever wanted to be and face the most difficult journey of her life.

The morning was still young, and the air still thick with fog. Rising on the cold breeze, Lisette fluttered her wings in the silent mist. Toward the east she flew; into a grey sunrise; into a dim hope. But that was more than she needed. She had love for her friends, and love is always enough.

Beneath heavy rainclouds -- drenched and soaked to the skin -- Marmot, Audrey and Pica had just awakened from their night in the Parc André-Citroën. All three of the weary travelers had slept very well, right up until the rain began to fall.

When the first drops dampened their dreaming heads, Audrey and Pica simply moved to a leafier part of the tree in which they'd been sleeping. Marmot, who was sleeping in a shallow divot in the ground, pulled a pile of leaves up over his head and thought no more of it, until the wind started to blow.

Unable to stay dry beneath his wind-blown blanket of scattering leaves, Marmot grumbled like a grumpy badger, then moved to the foot of the tree in which his friends now sat. This turned out to be no better than his leaf-covered hole. As the wind picked up, the branches of the tree blew and bobbed wildly, providing no cover against the rain, and jostling the butterfly and the magpie until sleep became quite impossible for everyone.

Deciding it was best to leave the bare branches of their tree, Audrey and Pica took shelter in a dense hedge of shrubbery not far from the edge of the park. Inside, it was calm and dry, though somewhat cramped for a magpie. When the rainwater started to flow in little rivulets and pool around Marmot's feet, he joined the other two in their hedge. Cramming himself inside the tightly packed branches, he found escape from the wind and rain, but very little comfort.

"So much for happy reminders of home," Marmot said, raising his voice above the howling wind. "I'm sorry, my friends."

"Not at all," Audrey laughed, "This is an *exact reminder* of what Saint-Denis is like when it rains."

"Soggy, soggy," came Pica's discouraged reply.

"You can say that again," said Marmot, not realizing Pica already *had*. "This will slow our progress, for sure. Butterflies don't do too well in a downpour, do they Audrey?"

"With an umbrella, perhaps; but those raindrops are so huge it wouldn't take more than one direct hit to ground me. In this rain, I'm afraid …"

"An umbrella," Marmot said to himself, no longer listening to Audrey. "That's *just* what we need! I wonder if…"

Turning to Pica and Audrey (who was still speaking, despite Marmot's interruption), he said, "You two wait here a while. I'm going to have a look around. Keep dry!"

Bolting out from beneath the hedge, Marmot was

gone.

"*Où? Où?*"

"I haven't a clue," Audrey replied, without the slightest surprise. She'd come to expect the unexpected from Marmot; nothing astonished her anymore where he was concerned.

"I'm sure wherever he went, he won't be gone for long – not in this weather."

The dark clouds passed to the south of the Parc André-Citroën, leaving only white sheets of heavy rain falling from a cheerless sky. Behind the stormfront, frigid air moved in, unchallenged by the sun. Still the wind blew, whipping the furious rain in every direction. Even keeping to the sidewalk and flying beneath the cover of window awnings, the unpredictable wind could soak Audrey in an instant. With wet wings, she'd be unable to fly for hours. She couldn't risk it.

Just when Audrey and Pica had begun to grow concerned about Marmot's whereabouts, a happy, little, brown head poked in through the dense branches of the hedge.

"Miss me?!"

Something about him puzzled Marmot's friends. They couldn't figure out what it was, at first. Then it hit Pica.

"*Pas mouillé! Pas mouillé!*"

"You're right, Pica!" Audrey said with suspicion. Turning to Marmot, she asked, "Why aren't you wet?" Audrey examined Marmot's dry face, demanding an answer. "What did you…"

"I'll show you," Marmot interrupted, "But I'm afraid you'll have to come out *here* to see."

Audrey had no intention of standing in the rain. Even Pica was reluctant to leave the nice, dry hedge and venture outside.

"Come on. Trust me."

Looking at each other with uneasiness, Audrey and Pica waited to see who would follow Marmot's dry head back out into the rain first. For a few moments, neither one budged. Then, bracing himself against the rain, Pica held his breath and hopped out into the open, leaving Audrey in the hedge alone.

Much to his surprise, the rain wasn't falling where he and Marmot now stood. All around them, the deluge battered the muddy ground; but the groundhog and the magpie were as dry as anyone could hope to be in the middle of a raging rainstorm.

"It's alright," Marmot called, encouraging Audrey to join them, "Come on out. It's perfectly safe."

Audrey still didn't understand how this could be; but she could see from inside the hedge that Pica and Marmot were dry, and she was usually willing to trust them both. Marmot held out his paw, inviting Audrey to fly to him. With a flap and a flutter and a leap of faith, Audrey flew out into the downpour and landed in Marmot's open hand. Not one single raindrop dampened her wings.

At first, she thought that maybe she'd somehow managed to fly *between* the drops; but then, examining the area around them, Audrey discovered that the ground upon which they now stood was not being pummeled by the falling rain.

Looking up, she learned the reason why Marmot had left the shelter of the hedge, as well as the cause of their unexplained dryness. She could not have guessed it. Sitting on the ground and arching overtop of them, the see-through canopy from a baby stroller made an excellent and very effective umbrella for a groundhog, a magpie and a butterfly.

"Check this out," Marmot said, placing Audrey on Pica's shoulder. "It's portable!"

Lifting the canopy with no effort at all, Marmot

walked around in circles, while Pica followed him, careful to remain beneath the shelter.

"Pretty cool, huh? It goes where we go and the sides curve down to protect us from the wind. I'd say it was even *better* than an umbrella!" Marmot was rather proud of himself.

"But where did you get it?" Audrey had a sneaking suspicion that somewhere nearby there was a very wet baby.

"From a baby stroller, of course!"

Suspicion confirmed. By the look on Audrey's face, Marmot knew what she was thinking.

"No, no, no," he defended himself, waving one hand in the air, "the baby wasn't still *in* it! There hadn't been a baby in *that* stroller for quite some time. I found it beside a dumpster. Humans throw away the strangest things."

Audrey was relieved, although she continued to eye Marmot for some time, just to be sure he was telling the truth. She wouldn't put it past him to "borrow" anything in a pinch.

"The good news is, now we can make our way upriver to the *Champ de Mars* in time to meet Boswell… and do it without getting soaked."

"And the bad news?" Audrey asked, with apprehension.

"Well, the bad news is, it'll be impossible for us to hide, carrying this thing up the sidewalk. I mean. Humans are pretty distracted by cell phones and the like, but I don't think even pictures of cute kittens on Instagram will be enough to distract them from a walking baby stroller canopy! I do have an idea, though. We may be able to avoid unwanted attention if we stick to the railroad tracks down by the river. It could be dangerous… but… well, what do you think?"

"We have no better option. We'll just have to take

our chances with the tracks and do our best to avoid humans, don't you agree, Pica?"

"*Oui. Oui.*"

"And there's your answer," Audrey said, bringing the topic to a close. "We have somewhere to be; it's best we get going."

"Right! Feel free to flutter around or ride on my back, whichever you prefer. Pica, you'll have to hop along for yourself, I'm afraid."

"*Bien sûr. Bien sûr.*"

"Good man! Off we go, then."

Marmot hoisted the canopy up onto his shoulders, careful to keep everyone inside. Content that Audrey and Pica were sheltered from the pelting rain, Marmot started walking over grass and gravel, mud and puddles until they reached the edge of the Parc. From there, they could see a side street with a small traffic circle. A signpost read, "*Rue Cauchy.*"

Off to the left, toward the river, the *rue* took a gentle turn *à droite* (not *tout droit*, since, as we know, that would mean *straight ahead;* and the Rue Cauchy would end up toppling into the Seine). Instead, the *rue* curved around *to the right*, before continuing upriver.

Immediately to their left, however, the canopied travelers spotted the train tracks. Running alongside the tracks, dense trees and bushes hid the railway from view. Marmot thought the trees and bushes would hide a groundhog, a magpie, and a butterfly quite nicely, too. Giving the canopy a good shake to knock the raindrops off the windshield, Marmot directed the trio toward the tracks.

Standing on the crest of the hill leading down to the gravel bed of the rail line, Marmot tested the ground with his toes. It was squishy and waterlogged, and Marmot had no desire to end up sliding down on his belly. If he was to keep the canopy safely above Audrey's delicate wings, he needed to stay upright.

Inching his way closer to the edge of the slope, Marmot began to lose his footing.

"That won't do at all," he said, backing away. "But it appears to be unavoidable. I'll certainly end up in the mud; I might as well choose which part of me gets muddy."

Turning to Pica, Marmot said, "Up you go. Looks like you two will be riding in style."

Marmot plopped down on his rear-end and motioned for Pica to hop up on his shoulder. Thinking it would be great fun to ride on the shoulder of a groundhog, Pica jumped aboard with delight. On the magpie's back, sat Audrey, like the cherry on a groundhog-and-magpie sundae.

Handing the canopy to Pica to hold over everyone's head, Marmot dug his paws into the soft, wet earth on either side of himself. Sliding back and forth in the mud like an Olympic bobsledder, the groundhog waited for the right amount of forward momentum.

"Hang on tight!" he cried, pushing off with all his might and sending the stack of canopy-covered animals hurtling downhill toward the railroad tracks. In their wake, Marmot left a deep, groundhog-shaped rut in the hillside and a spray of brown mud all over the grass.

Digging his feet into the gravel surrounding the train tracks, Marmot brought the *Groundhog Express* to an abrupt stop.

"That wasn't so bad," he said, picking gravel out from between his toes. "I'm afraid you'll have to walk from here, though, Pica."

The magpie hopped off Marmot's back – having enjoyed the ride and wishing it had been longer -- with Audrey still seated on his shoulder.

"It's a straight shot to the *Champ de Mars* from here, and the tracks stay above ground as far as the Island of Swans. From there, we'll find plenty of cover, so no worries. Let's get moving!"

Audrey, Pica and Marmot looked like an alien astronaut moving up the rail line beneath their transparent dome. Whenever they heard a train approaching, they'd simply move over to the hillside and hunker down until it passed. No one thought anything of the baby stroller canopy on the side of the tracks; it was just another piece of discarded trash in the city.

Following the tracks proved to be an excellent idea, as the travelers were able to move as fast as they liked without the need to hide from human eyes. Of course, they would have made even better time if Pica hadn't spotted a blackberry bush on the side of the hill. He made it quite clear that they needed to stop, which was secretly just fine with both Marmot and Audrey who were hungry, too.

After a very satisfying lunch break, Audrey suggested that they all rest a while beneath a nearby forsythia bush. She was sure Marmot's arms could use a break from holding up that canopy. Marmot agreed.

Overhead, the clouds parted, revealing a hint of blue sky behind the grey. The rain was lessening, and the wind had become a gentle sigh, as the storm moved off toward the southeast. Underneath the forsythia bush, the exhaustion of a long morning took hold, and Audrey, Pica and Marmot all drifted off to sleep. In the sky above them, a single crow now flew, as if spying on the trio.

It was a little past midday. Upriver, on the Island of Swans, Esmée and Pierre had passed the morning under the cover of the Pont de Grenelle, sipping nectar from their azalea flowers and keeping watch over the river. From the tip of the island, they had a commanding view of both sides of the Seine. When the baby stroller canopy containing Audrey, Pica and Marmot approached -- even from down by the train tracks -- it would surely be seen by Esmée and Pierre.

As the rain subsided and the clouds began to dissolve, the sun returned to Paris. The City of Sogginess slowly dried up and became the City of Lights, once more. In the *Champ de Mars,* Boswell Badger and Queen Fourmi emerged from the badger's den to take the sun and stretch their limbs.

Under the northeastern foot of the Eiffel Tower, Victor shoveled mud from the entrance to his tunnel, restoring it to tip-top working order. The rainwater runoff from the pavement beneath the tower always made its way into Victor's tunnel; but it was really the only downside to living so close to the city's most beautiful landmark.

To the west of the city, somewhere between there and Saint-Denis, Lisette Cueilleur fluttered over field and forest, all alone and quite determined. She'd been flying all morning and had just left the sheltering trees of the Meudon Forest, west of the river Seine's southernmost loop below Paris. Lisette was tired and hungry, but the thought of stopping long enough to eat did not appeal to her. Her friends were in Paris searching for Esmée, and she should be there with them. She would not rest until she found them.

Leaving the protection of the forest, Lisette flew over farms and pastureland, as she made her way toward the river. She only had about four or five miles to go before crossing the Seine and entering Paris. All morning, her mind had been awash with emotion and regret. Struggling to push every worry to the background of her thoughts, Lisette tried to stay focused on her goal.

She couldn't stop thinking about her friend and, as a result, she paid very little attention to her surroundings. If she had, she would have noticed something increasingly alarming. The closer she drew to the river, the fewer insects, butterflies, and birds there were to be found. The countryside grew empty, silent, cautious, even. There was danger nearby, and every animal in the area knew it except Lisette.

Fluttering over a cornfield, the strange quiet finally seeped into her awareness. In the hush of a windless sky, beneath the silent face of the sun, Lisette heard a sound like a thousand ships' sails in a gale. Afraid to slow down, she cast her eyes back over her shoulder without missing a beat of her wings. There, not a quarter of a mile behind her and just below the tattered clouds, a murder of crows was approaching at great speed.

Lisette wasn't sure if she'd been seen or not, but she couldn't chance it. She had to find cover or risk the unwanted attention of the crows. Dropping from the sky, she went into a nosedive and landed among the corn. Making her way down a stalk, she hid as close to the ground and as far from the sky as she could manage. There, she waited and listened.

The sound of frantic flight approached. She could hear the cawing of the crows, their wings beating the bruised air. Louder and louder it grew, as the scavengers drew near. The emerald-green glow of sunlight through broad leaves was now blotted out by the dark shadows of a dozen crows in flight. The noise was deafening, and Lisette covered her ears with her wings.

"Wretched creatures," she thought to herself. "Up to no good, I'm sure."

Lisette had no patience for bullies, especially if they were a hundred times bigger than her and came in groups. Back home in Saint-Denis, she'd been known to fight back when picked on by a bullying crow. She'd fly straight for its face and flutter around its eyes until the dazed bird ran away. Lisette's temper was a great deal larger than her body; but she was no match for a dozen deadly crows. This time, she'd lay low, and watch them make their way toward Paris. They were in such a hurry, that it didn't take long for them to recede to a tiny black spot in the sky.

Once Lisette was satisfied that the danger had passed, she crawled back up the stalk and peeked out through the leaves. The first thing she noticed was a barn swallow doing acrobatics through the air. All around her, birds were singing, and grasshoppers were hopping once again. A tiny, white moth flitted past the cornstalk in which Lisette had been hiding. No one appeared to be concerned anymore. It was clear that Lisette was not the only animal who thought it was safe to come out in the open. In the wake of danger, life resumed, and everyone went about their business without fear.

Lisette felt a rush of renewed purpose. The crows reminded her of all the peril at loose in the world, and that her best friend might very well be alone and surrounded by perils of her own. Esmée was far too shy and delicate to defend herself against one crow, let alone a whole flock.

Then Lisette thought about Audrey and Pica. At least Esmée was clever enough to hide from danger; Lisette had no confidence that Pica would do the same. Poor, sweet Pica; the world was too big and complicated for him, by far.

Then there was the bookworm, Audrey. As far as Lisette knew, Audrey had never been anywhere at all, except between the pages of a newspaper or a discarded church bulletin. What could she possibly know about the wide world? She and Pica would be helpless against any challenge they might face. Lisette was certain that she was their only hope; and the sooner she found them, the better.

Taking to the sky again, Lisette flew as fast and as hard as she could. Ahead, she could see the glistening Seine, like a serpent in the sunlight. Its southern loop sagged below the Bois de Boulogne forest, well outside of the city. In the middle of its stream, two crescent-shaped islands sat. This was the same place that Audrey and Pica had crossed into Paris not three days earlier.

Lisette never put much stock in reading or learning of any kind. She was more of a doer than a thinker; which is why she often acted before giving it much thought and, later on, regretted her actions. In this particular case, her lack of interest in learning left her with a dilemma. She'd found Paris with no problem, but where exactly was the Louvre? This was the last place she knew Esmée had visited, and so it made sense that Lisette should begin her search there; but where was it?

This was the same dilemma Audrey and Pica had faced three days before. Audrey's love of reading and learning had helped her make the right decision… quite literally the *right* decision: by deciding to follow the righthand branch of the river. Lisette had no such knowledge to fall back on; yet she faced the same choice.

Having learned her lesson about acting without thinking, Lisette was reluctant to simply choose a direction. The last time she acted rashly, she left her friends behind to search for Esmée and face danger alone. Even though she was in a great hurry, she realized that now was not the moment for quick decisions. She needed to take her time and consider her options. Most of all, she needed help.

Landing on the branch of an apple tree, Lisette took a look around. In front of her, she saw the river with its matching pair of islands, like a saggy basket carrying two croissants. She saw the dense city streets stretching out toward the horizon on her right. On her left, she saw the Bois de Boulogne forest way off in the distance. Neither view offered any guidance as to which route she should take.

Behind her, over sprawling suburbs and through the Meudon Forest all the way back to Saint-Denis, the path was known. She was confident she could find her way home again. But here, far from home, she was more alone than she'd ever been. Every face she saw seemed unfriendly. Every place in which she found herself was unfamiliar.

She imagined that this is how Esmée must have felt, this is what Audrey and Pica had experienced. Her heart ached with sadness at the thought of her friends' loneliness. She blamed herself. If she hadn't been so selfish, they would not have made the journey alone. Just like them, alone and with no one to help her, Lisette had to make her decision. She had to do this on her own.

Leaving the apple tree, Lisette began flying upriver toward the right. A few yards upstream, doubt began to spill the wind from her wings, and she turned back. Rounding the loop in the river, she headed up the left side toward the Bois de Boulogne. Flying only a dozen yards or so, she once again felt fearful doubt about her choice of direction. Confused and uncertain, Lisette turned back and returned to the apple tree. She had no idea which way to go.

She was frustrated and becoming desperate. For the first time ever, when so much depended on her ability to make the right decision, Lisette felt paralyzed with doubt. Boiling up out of her heart like black, bubbling tar, the wretched fears and worries that made her a prisoner now burst forth in tears. It was hopeless, she was done. Her friends would have to fend for themselves. She would not have the chance to undo her terrible decision to just be selfish and abandon her friends. Her opportunity to fix what she had broken was slipping away.

"Bonjour, mademoiselle!" Like the chiming of a tiny bell, a pleasant voice rang out in the summer breeze. *"Ça va bien?* Are you alright?"

On a branch of the apple tree, just in front of where Lisette sat crying, there stood a butterfly. Her wings were purple and orange with flecks of white and speckles of black. Her body was brown velvet. Atop her sweet and intelligent head, two antennae branched out, each one ending in a tiny dot of gold like a princess' tiara. She stood beside a pink apple blossom, fanning her wings slowly -- her head titled to one side with concern.

Looking up from her tears and dejection, Lisette saw the butterfly standing nearby. She wiped her eyes, sniffed and replied, "I'm a little lost, I think." Then correcting herself, she said, "I'm a lot lost. No doubt about it."

"Maybe I can help. My name is Jenna. *Quel est votre nom?*"

"Lisette. *Enchantée, mademoiselle.*" There was no pleasantry in Lisette's voice, only despair and loneliness.

Wrapped up in her sadness, Lisette had missed Jenna's offer to help. Right now, all Lisette wanted was for someone to make everything alright; make all her troubles go away. She just wanted to be home surrounded by her friends. The thought of having to make a decision or search for her friends; or even the thought of having to make the journey back home again, was all too much for her to bear. She didn't want to *go* home, she just wanted to *be* home.

Noticing Lisette's sadness, Jenna tried again to help.

"Where are you from, *mademoiselle*?"

"Saint-Denis."

"Ah *oui*, Saint-Denis. It is beautiful, *non*? And where do you travel to?"

"I'm looking for my friends. They're in Paris."

"*Oui*, Paris. It is my home. You are almost there, *mademoiselle*. It is just across the river, there. Do not lose heart."

"But... I don't know which way. Which side to

choose, I mean. *À droite ou à gauche*. To the right or to the left."

"That all depends on *where* in Paris you are meeting your friends. Either way, the river is an excellent guide. It will take you to many wonderful places. Where are your friends awaiting you, *mademoiselle*?"

"That's just it," Lisette said, beginning to cry again, "they're not waiting for me. They didn't wait for me. They went without me, but it's my fault. It's all my fault."

Lisette broke down sobbing, her face buried in her knees and her wings hanging loose about her body. She felt utterly defeated. Jenna flew over and draped one wing around Lisette's shoulders.

"I am sorry, *mademoiselle*. I am very sorry. I did not mean to remind you of painful things. I wish only to help if I can. Your friends, they love you, *non*?"

Between sobs, Lisette was able to respond, softly and with some hesitation.

"I think so."

"I think you *know so, mademoiselle. Oui,* of course you do. Your friends, they love you, and so they will *always* wait for you. *Oui,* they wait for you even now. And so," Jenna said, rising to her feet and inviting Lisette to stand up, too. "And so, you mustn't keep your friends waiting any longer. What is your destination, *mademoiselle*? Where do you go today?"

Lisette looked up at the beautiful, purple and gold butterfly. There was such kindness in her eyes that, for a moment, Lisette felt like a fresh, spring breeze was blowing through her heart – clearing out the fumes of black, bubbling fear and the weariness of worry. In that moment, Lisette wanted only to find her friends and remain by their side wherever that might lead her. There was no home behind her; home could be found only where her friends were.

Standing, Lisette replied, "The Louvre. I need to find the Louvre."

"*Oui,*" Jenna said with a smile, "That's easy! The Louvre is to the right. Fifteen bridges up and on your left. It is not as far as it sounds, *mademoiselle.* In Paris, there is a bridge every few meters, and each one is its own universe."

"To the right, then?" Lisette felt hope awaken in her heart once again.

"*À droite. Oui, mademoiselle!*"

"Then fifteen bridges?"

"*Oui, quinze.*"

"*Merci, merci beaucoup, mon amie!* I can't thank you enough! You have no idea how much you've done for me today."

"But I *do* know, *mademoiselle.* I see it, for you are no longer crying." Jenna's eyes lit up with the joy of having brought healing hope to Lisette. "*Au revoir,* new friend; until we meet again."

The elegant, purple butterfly flew from her place beside the apple blossom, crossed the river, and alighted in a little garden at the heart of one of the crescent-shaped islands. Lisette watched her fly away with a new more positive opinion of "seemingly unfriendly faces and unfamiliar places."

It was now Lisette's turn to cross the river. She knew both her destination and her route, she had only to take it and count the bridges along the way. The stories Esmée's mother used to tell them about the treasures of the Louvre now came back to her memory. The sculpture of Cupid giving a rose to the young butterfly was especially dear to her. She'd always wanted to see the Louvre. Now, at last, she just might; but for the deadly danger that lay in her path.

CHAPTER THIRTY

The Battle of the *Pont de Grenelle*

The forests and fields flew by, unappreciated, in a blur of sickly green. If it had been food they were searching for, the crows would have had plenty from which to choose; there was no need to fly so far. But it wasn't hunger that drove them on; at least not a hunger in their stomachs. Theirs was an altogether unhealthy hunger: a ravenous craving for revenge.

Three days earlier, while stalking a *belle dame* butterfly, they'd run up against a repetitious magpie, as well. As you know, crows will eat anything, and often kill small animals and other birds; but it wasn't for food that they began mobbing the magpie. It was purely for fun. This particular magpie was too much of a target for the crows to pass up. This magpie liked to repeat himself, and the cruel crows found him irresistible.

In the middle of harassing the magpie -- somewhere over the Meudon Forest -- a hawk screeched its bloodcurdling call from above, sending the crows scrambling for cover as fast as they could find it. Hidden among the leaves and branches of a sycamore tree, they kept watch on the sky above the forest; but the hawk never appeared.

All day, the crows watched and waited, certain that the cry they'd heard belonged to their old enemy; but still, no hawk was seen. A suspicion began to form itself like a cancerous growth in the mind of their leader. As the days crept by, his suspicion became a wicked resolution. He'd been fooled by the devious butterfly and her repetitive friend, he was certain; and the crows would make them pay. They would have their revenge and enjoy every moment of it; and when they were done, there'd be no trace of either butterfly or bird.

Rousing his companions, the crow-leader led his murderous flock along the same path they'd taken three days earlier. They were determined to follow the trail as far as it led, even if that meant crossing the great river.

Sending out his scouts to scour the countryside, the lead crow gathered information on the butterfly and her magpie friend. Wider and wider they flew, patrolling more of the area between the Meudon Forest and the heart of Paris itself. Until finally, that Friday, word returned to the leader that the pair had been spotted in the company of a groundhog travelling north toward the Parc André-Citroën.

The foul weather delayed them for only a few hours; but that Saturday morning, the crows set out in haste for the city. By the time they flew overhead and overtook Lisette in the cornfield, their scouts had pinpointed Audrey and Pica. They knew exactly where they were. They also knew that the *belle dame* butterfly they'd spotted nosediving from the sky into the cornfield was *not* their prey. Lisette had hidden from the crows among the stalks of corn, but she had not gone unseen.

Crossing the river at the same spot where Audrey and Pica had crossed, the crows were now a good hour ahead of Lisette and moving fast. Receiving continual updates from his scouts, the lead crow kept a lock on Audrey and Pica's location. Soon, the predators would reach their prey; and no baby stroller canopy would conceal them from the vengeful eyes of the crows.

Marmot, Audrey and Pica had been napping

beneath the tree for an hour or so and were now awakened by a new sensation: sunlight was streaming through the transparent windshield of the canopy under which they hid from the rain. The warmth awakened them so gently that it took minutes for them to even realize they'd fallen asleep.

"Looks like we won't be needing this anymore," Marmot said, tossing the canopy to one side. "I'll bring it up to the top of the hill and leave it beside the trash can. Silly humans, they'll just cart it away when clearly it has many uses left in it."

Marmot breathed deeply and spread his arms to embrace the sunlight. Audrey had grown accustomed to the cover of the canopy; being beneath the bare sky again made her feel exposed and considerably less safe. Pica was just glad to be able to open his wings. Being a creature of the air, he did not care for confinement of any kind.

The moment the canopy was gone, the travelers heard a disconcerting sound that made their blood freeze. The cawing of a distant crow fell on their ears like the clanging of a cymbal. Looking up, Marmot saw the source of the noise high above them and flying off toward the south.

"Whew! It's just a single crow, and look, he's flying away." Marmot was relieved. "We'll have no trouble from him today."

Trudging over muddy ground and course gravel, the travelers made their way up the rail line toward their meeting with Boswell Badger in the *Champ de Mars*. Marmot had planned it all perfectly, they were right on time to arrive by mid-afternoon. As they neared the small garden area between the Pont de Grenelle and Beaugrenelle Mall, all three stopped dead in their tracks.

Only a short distance downriver, approaching with hatred in their wings, a murder of a dozen crows bore down on the trio. There was no time to hesitate; Marmot took the lead.

"Follow me!" he cried, scurrying up the side of the hill from the train tracks.

Marmot ran full tilt toward a patch of trees located in a small park situated in front of the Beaugrenelle Mall's parking garage. Audrey and Pica followed. Crossing the road, they made their way to the base of one of the trees and hid right up against its trunk. They all could have wished for better cover, but it was the best they were able to find in such short and sudden notice.

The sound of the approaching crows sent shivers down Audrey's spine. She remembered well how she and Pica had barely escaped death at the beaks of the crows only three days ago. Pica was paralyzed with terror. Unable to stand, he leaned up against the tree muttering over and over to himself, *"Corbeaux, corbeaux."*

Marmot had little to fear from a flock of birds, except for the annoyance of being mobbed and perhaps some pecks and scratches. They couldn't kill a groundhog, but they could drive one crazy with their flapping and cawing. His concern was for Audrey, most of all; and for Pica, too. Marmot saw his role as that of protector, and he was already tired from a poor night's sleep that had been interrupted by the rain. He'd spent the day carrying a canopy over his head for miles; his arms were sore, and he was in no mood for crows.

The city echoed with the caws of what sounded like a thousand angry birds. Swirling overhead like a black hole in space, the flock rained down spite and vengeance in a storm of black feathers. There was no question as to why they were there.

"You two stay close to me," Marmot yelled above the noise. "We can't outrun them; we have to beat them at their game. Bullies only understand strength, and we have to push back on them. Their behavior is not ok, and

I intend to let them know it!"

The crows now landed in the tree limbs above Marmot, Audrey and Pica's heads. With half of them remaining in the branches, the leader took the other half down to the ground around the foot of the tree. Marmot, Audrey and Pica were now surrounded by crows, above and below. The lead crow hopped forward, standing in front of the huddled travelers, and began to taunt them.

"Clever little butterfly. Chasing away a mighty murder of crows with your trick. Well done. Yes, very well done."

The big crow shot out his neck with every word he spoke, much as he had done days ago when picking on Pica; just as he had done while poking and piercing Pica's chest and forehead with his sharp beak. Each word stung Pica to the heart with the reminder of it all. He began to tremble.

"And look who we have here. The brave magpie. How's your forehead, stupid bird?"

Marmot stood up and put his hands on his hips, "Now wait one minute. That might be how you talk in the country, but this is Paris; we're a bit more sophisticated around here."

Marmot thought that maybe a little humor might defuse the ticking timebomb and cool the hotheads a bit.

"If you've come all this way, you might as well see the sights while you're in town. I'll even give you a metro ticket I found on the street. There's a 50/50 chance it's still good. Whatd'ya say?"

The lead crow hopped over to Marmot and stared him straight in the eye. The bird was not amused. Even standing up on his hind legs, Marmot was only an inch or two taller than the enormous crow. The six or so other crows standing around the base of the tree now closed the circle, tightening the noose around the three friends. Up above, the remaining crows hopped down to the lowest branches of the tree. The overall effect was that Audrey, Pica and Marmot now felt absolutely drowned in dangerous crows, all of whom were bent on having their way with the travelers.

The leader shot out his head, pecking Marmot on the chest, "Sit down, whistle pig. I wasn't talking to you."

Startled by the attack and taken aback by the crow's aggressive behavior, Marmot fell backwards, landing on his rear-end next to Pica.

"Enough!" came a commanding voice. "This is foolishness. We are on an errand of mercy of great importance. You'd be wise to let us pass."

Audrey was fed up. The clock was ticking, and they were scheduled to meet with Boswell within the hour. They had no time for such nonsense.

"We'd be wise?" the evil old crow cawed. "And what will happen if we don't let you pass? What will you do, little fly?"

The crows standing around the foot of the tree were now pressing in against their captives. The leader had turned his attention to Audrey: the one who had fooled him; the one who had slipped through his talons before and dared to stand up to him now. With a band of murderous bullies to outnumber and intimidate the groundhog and magpie, the lead crow made no attempt to hide his intention of eating Audrey -- of being rid of her, once and for all. Revenge crippled his mind and gave strength to his hatred.

"I almost feel sorry for you..." the vile crow croaked, "...little fly."

At once, the crows in the branches above dropped down on Marmot and Pica, landing on their heads and pecking mercilessly at their faces. Blinded by their attackers, the groundhog and magpie fought to free themselves and come to Audrey's aid. Out of the corner of his eye, even with a flailing crow in his face, Pica could see the leader clamp his foot across Audrey's body.

"Non, non!" Pica fought to be rid of his attacker. *"Non, non, Audrey! Audrey!"*

Turning his head in the direction of the magpie, the fiendish leader said with mock sympathy, "Poor thing. But you're too late." He then snapped his beak across Audrey's waist.

A sharp, high-pitched whistle went up from within the crowd of crows, magpie and groundhog. The pitch was deafening and nearly shattered the eardrums of everyone within a hundred yards of that tree. Marmot had struggled to his feet and was busy fighting off the pecks and blows of three wretched crows, when he let out a second loud whistle that would not soon be forgotten by anyone who heard it. It was the Bois de Boulogne Groundhog Emergency Alert, reserved for special times of need; times such as this.

The sound was so jarring that the lead crow dropped Audrey from his beak, then covered his ears with his wings. Unfortunately, he was not so distracted that he forgot to pin her to the ground with his foot. Audrey lay against the muddy earth, writhing to break free of the leader's sharp toes. Marmot let out a third whistle, just as alarming as the first two; but it was cut short by a sharp beak to the forehead, delivered by one of his three attackers.

"The next time you make such a hideous sound," the lead crow threatened, "will be your last. Keep him busy, boys!"

At their leader's command, the three crows began pecking and pummeling Marmot until he was quite overwhelmed. Pica was huddled up against the tree trunk, sobbing more from his inability to help Audrey than from the beating he was receiving.

"I've had enough of your groundhog," the lead crow said, tightening his grip on Audrey, "your magpie," lowering his beak to within striking distance, "and you!" He caught Audrey up in his beak once more. This time would be the last.

Across the river, on the Island of Swans, Esmée and Pierre had been keeping watch over the river since morning. Though they hadn't seen Marmot and company -- thanks to the hillside, shrubs and trees which hid the low rail line -- they could not now miss the sound of the cacophonous crows. They knew something was up, and it couldn't be good. It didn't take long for Esmée to guess what or who might be the target of the crows' attention. She'd been expecting Marmot and her friends to make their way up past the Island of Swans; it looked as if the crows had been expecting it, too.

Turning to Pierre, she didn't have to say a word. He said it for her.

"*Oui, mon amour,* we must go *now.*"

Pierre reached the same conclusion: someone was in dire need and it might just be Esmée's friends. Leaping into the wind rising up from the river, the two butterflies flew straight across the Seine and crossed the road on the other side.

Thinking it best to first assess the situation before flying headlong into danger, Pierre led the way to the top of the parking garage of the Beaugrenelle Mall. Behind them, the unique structure of the shopping mall stretched back away from the river. On its uppermost roof, a field of grass, shrubs and wildflowers grew above the city streets. Under any other circumstances, the rooftop gardens of the Beaugrenelle Mall would be a wonderful place for a butterfly to spend her day; but today, beside the Pont de Grenelle, terrible deeds were afoot.

Pierre and Esmée landed on top of the parking garage and looked down into the little park between them and the street. Scattered throughout the lower branches of a small tree, half a dozen crows screeched and cawed like demons.

Beneath them, Esmée could see perhaps half a dozen more crows occupied in harassing three unfortunate creatures. The first was a groundhog who appeared to be holding his own against three vicious ruffians who were busy battering and pecking away at him. The second was also a bird, although in the blur of black feathers it was impossible to tell what sort of bird it might be.

At the center of the circle of attackers; under tree limbs thick with the wretched birds; and clutched tight in the talons of one exceptionally large crow; a butterfly flapped and fluttered for dear life. Amid the commotion, Esmée heard the raucous taunting of cruel beaks; but she also heard something that froze her heart.

"Non, non! Non, non! Audrey! Audrey!"

"Pica! Oh no, Pierre! And Audrey, too! But, Lisette? Where? We must help them! We must help them now!"

Jumping down from the high roof of the parking garage, Esmée was halfway to her friends before Pierre realized what she had done. Hurling himself after her, Pierre flapped with singular purpose, intent on reaching the crows before Esmée did.

Her target was the lead crow, who looked up just in time to see the two butterflies approaching. Without an opportunity to remove himself from their flight path, the evil crow was struck directly in the face, first by Pierre and then by Esmée.

The shock of the blows caused him to loosen his grip just long enough for Audrey to escape. Pierre didn't wait for the crow to recover, but immediately flew straight for its eyes. Fluttering his wings and kicking with all his might, Pierre meant to blind the old sinner; but with a savage smack from his sooty wing, the lead crow sent Pierre spiraling into a nearby rosebush.

Meanwhile, Esmée had flown down to Audrey's side. Panting with terror, Audrey looked up to see the face of her long-lost friend. She threw her wings around Esmée's neck and began to cry.

"It's you!" she sobbed. "We found you, we found you at last."

"My dear friend, what worries I must have put you through. I'm so sorry, so very, very sorry. And now *this*." Esmée pulled Audrey closer to the foot of the tree, out of the way of thrashing wings and stomping feet.

"They're here for me," Audrey confessed. "They're here for revenge. Too many of them, just too many."

From the rosebush, Pierre saw his chance. Prying a thorn free from the stem of a rose, he held it tightly in his feet. Then -- flapping his wings to gain momentum -- he threw himself, feet-first, in the direction of the lead crow. Just as the wicked bird was bending his neck to grab both Audrey and Esmée in one final bite, Pierre landed his thorny dart squarely in the crow's right eye.

"Caaaaaahhhhwwwww!!" came the hideous scream from the stricken leader.

In a rage of agony, the old bird flopped and flailed all around the foot of the tree. Above, half a dozen crows cried out in anger. Marmot made good on Pierre's attack by kicking all three of his assailants into the same rosebush from which Pierre had made his move. Tangled up in thorny branches, the crows screeched and howled as they tried to free themselves.

"Come on," Marmot yelled, grabbing hold of Pica and pulling him out from under his attacker. "Follow me! There's an *access point* near here."

Marmot led his companions down toward the riverbank, all the while searching among the weeds for the *access point*.

"A what?" Esmée asked, having no experience of

groundhog tunnels.

"A hole in the ground. An entry to one of our tunnels. Stay close, now!"

Three butterflies, a magpie and one groundhog -- no matter how brave -- are no match for a dozen enraged crows. The commotion caused by Pierre's direct hit was simply not enough to buy them the time they needed to find an opening to the groundhog tunnel. Daring escapes are often purchased more dearly than this; far more dearly.

The one-eyed crow now led his band of marauders down to the riverbank. This time, their plan would be different. Rather than wasting their energy attacking each animal separately, they would focus all their hatred on just two: the one who had blinded their leader, and the one who had fooled them all. Pierre and Audrey were the sole targets of their enemies' venomous rage.

Marmot searched with desperation in the riverbank beneath the Pont de Grenelle bridge, but he could not locate the tunnel opening. It mattered very little, anyhow. The crows were upon them once again. Turning to meet them head-on, Marmot raised his paws in defense; but the lead crow passed right by him, much to Marmot's surprise.

Instead, the one-eyed leader took hold of Pierre in both his talons. Carrying him high above the pavement, the crow threw Pierre onto the deck of the bridge with heartless malice. Unable to right himself, Pierre struck the bridge without once flapping his wings.

Below the bridge, the other crows were clawing toward Audrey in a fierce attack. Marmot had picked up a piece of driftwood from the shore and was swinging it around, knocking crows from the air and sending others tumbling into the river.

At the same time, Pica had placed himself between the butterflies and their vicious attackers. When one got too near, the magpie would jump at it, feet-first, gripping and gouging whatever he could grab hold of. Still deathly afraid, Pica had found the secret of bravery. Courage, he found, is not a lack of fear; it's simply the motivation to ignore fear and fight on anyway. Pica's love for Audrey and Esmée was all the motivation he needed

Unable to escape the hoard of crows beneath the bridge, no one knew what Pierre was facing up above. After being flung down upon the bridge's concrete roadway, Pierre was dazed and paralyzed with shock. The one-eyed crow took advantage of the situation by landing, full force, upon Pierre's wings – pinning him to the ground. Pierre barely had time to open his eyes, before the crow moved to take hold of the butterfly's body in his sharp beak.

At that very moment, a high-pitched whistle shattered the sky above everyone's head. The lead crow paused, cocking his head to listen. Below the bridge, every attacker stopped and waited, unsure of exactly what was happening. Even Pica and the butterflies were startled and held their breath, not knowing the source of the whistle. But Marmot knew.

The minutes during which they'd been under attack by the crows had felt like hours. In reality, it had been less than three minutes since Marmot had sounded the Groundhog Emergency Alert. What they now heard was an answer to his call for help. What they then witnessed was completely unexpected.

Pouring over the side of the bridge, down the concrete pilon, and across the riverbank was a sea of fluffy tails. Dozens and dozens of squirrels swarmed over the scene, and the most unlikely groundhog led their charge.

Hugo had spent the morning organizing his Squirrel Squad into search parties: one to search the upper half of the island, one to search the lower. When

Marmot's Groundhog Emergency Alert was heard, all plans were scrapped.

Instead, Hugo rallied his troops for an all-out invasion. They wasted no time in crossing the length of the island, scurrying up the midway point of the Pont de Grenelle, and running down the roadway toward danger.

Seeing the most concentrated attack taking place below the bridge, Hugo ordered his squirrels into the fray. Once he knew the counterattack was well in-hand, Hugo himself turned his attention to the one-eyed crow on the bridge's deck.

Carrying an old umbrella that he'd picked up from a trash can along the way, Hugo ran straight for the lead crow. The groundhog began flapping his umbrella -- opened and closed – hoping to scare away the attacker. When he saw that the old villain was not so easily frightened, Hugo turned the umbrella to better use.

Wielding it like an expert swordsman, Hugo landed several blows on the lead crow's back, distracting it from biting Pierre. The crow now turned his attention to Hugo, flying right at the groundhog with claws open and pointy beak aimed straight for his forehead. Hugo jumped out of the way, moments before impact, sending his attacker tumbling down the bridge's roadway. Leaping into flight, the crow leader grazed the groundhog's face as he flew past Hugo in a fit of rage. While the two continued to fight their deadly duel, Pierre lay a few yards away, trying to regain his strength.

Below, the squad of one-hundred squirrels had their paws full. Thanks to Hugo's direction, they were all working together as a team rather than fighting off the crows one by one. While half the squirrels helped Pica and Marmot defend the butterflies from certain death, the other half mobbed one crow at a time. Trampled beneath a hundred tiny feet, the crows were soon overwhelmed. Bruised and knocked about, their feathers matted down in river mud, it was impossible for the crows to make their escape by air.

Instead, one defeated bird after another hopped, limped and hopped again; until they had all hopped so far into the maze of city streets and alleyways that they were soon hopelessly lost. They'd never find their way back to the river or out of the city again. The crow population of Paris increased by precisely *eleven* black-eyed crows, that day; and *only* eleven.

Once Marmot had verified that Audrey and Esmée were alright, he led them, Pica and one-hundred *tired-but-exhilarated* squirrels up the concrete pilon and onto the bridge's roadway. There, they saw something that would enter groundhog folklore, myth and legend for generations to come.

Standing in the middle of the roadway, umbrella in hand, Hugo – artist, nature-lover and *network manager* of the *JdT server room* -- was single-handedly defeating the enormous, one-eyed leader of the gang of crows.

Holding the old devil at arms-length, Hugo avoided every attempt the crow made at pecking the groundhog's eyes out. Marmot stood nearby, dumbfounded, and unable to believe what he was witnessing. Clearly, Hugo had matters well under control.

The crow was noticeably weakened and growing tired of Hugo's attempts to drive him off. Half-blind and completely exhausted, his strategy now changed. Much to Hugo's surprise, the crow broke off his attack and took to the air.

Certain that he'd finally won the battle, and dripping with fatigue, Hugo dropped his umbrella on the pavement and turned to attend to Pierre.

But the old liar was not running away at all. He had one last deceit left in him.

Swinging back around in midair, the one-eyed crow flew straight for Hugo's head. Hugo thought this was a renewed attack and quickly ducked to avoid being struck; but no attack came. Instead, the lead crow passed the groundhog and, reaching down with his talons, scooped Pierre up off the pavement.

Reeling back toward the river, the crow once again flew in the direction of Hugo's head, intending to scare him. But the old fool's pride and arrogance would be his downfall; for, just as he drew near the groundhog, Hugo jumped up into the air and landed on top of the big crow's back.

Fumbling for a moment, it looked as if the one-eyed marauder would plummet back to earth; but Hugo was a very small groundhog and the crow was exceptionally large. He regained his command of the air, and off the villainous crow flew, clutching Pierre in his claws with Hugo clinging to his back.

Marmot ran after his friend, but it was no use. The crow flew at great speed over the bridge and downriver; and very soon they were out of sight. Marmot turned to one of the squirrels standing with him and shouted a command, "Go!" Taking six of his companions, the squirrel ran off across the bridge and down the island in the direction the treacherous crow had flown.

Everyone stood by with their mouths open and their hearts heavy. A loud cry of defeat went up from the Squirrel Squadron. They'd won the battle, but it appeared that they'd lost the war. Their captain had been carried off by the enemy; and Pierre was lost, too.

Esmée broke down in tears as she watched the love of her life being carried downriver in the grimy talons of her foe. Pierre had fought bravely, facing the lead crow all alone and drawing him away from the group. The butterfly from Dordogne was a hero, not the coward he'd insisted to Esmée he was.

Then something occurred to her; and her heart broke with the realization: Pierre had done for Esmée and

Audrey exactly what *his* mother had done for him. He'd led their attacker away, bearing the full brunt of its wickedness himself. Just like his mother, Pierre sacrificed himself to save others. Esmée's tears now flowed like the river beneath her feet.

"We have to go after them," she said between her tears.

"We will, *mademoiselle,*" Marmot assured her, "but first we must tend to your friends' wounds."

"What?" Esmée was reminded of Audrey and Pica and the part they'd played in the Battle of the Pont de Grenelle. Turning around, she scanned the bridge for them, asking, "Where are they?"

"Below," was all Marmot said, then turned and led them all back down the side of the bridge.

Esmée's heart was torn in two. Away to the south, one half of her heart was being carried toward certain death. Under the bridge, her two best friends were wounded and in need of attention.

"*Two* best friends," she thought to herself, as she followed Marmot down the riverbank. "But where was *Lisette?*"

CHAPTER THIRTY-ONE

The Island of Sacrifice

Pica lay on the riverbank beneath the Pont de Grenelle. In the middle of his forehead, a gash about an inch long shown -- red and raw -- through a bald spot where black feathers used to grow. His left eye was bruised and swollen, and he looked very much like a boxer who had lost his match.

Leaning up against him, Audrey Loriot sat motionless in the mud. She'd been the target of the crows' rage, and she owed her life to her friends.

Pica and Marmot had fought to protect her, drawing the flock of crows' attention away from Audrey and Esmée.

The squirrels had arrived just in time, driving the wicked birds deep into the heart of the city, never to be heard from again.

Pierre had attacked the lead crow, making it impossible for him to direct the movements of his minions; and Hugo had fought valiantly to defeat their leader, once and for all. The butterflies were alive because of their friends.

However, both Pica *and* Audrey had suffered wounds during the battle. Pica's forehead and eye would heal, and his feathers would grow back again; but Audrey's wound would never heal; her loss would never grow back. It would forever be a reminder of this day.

As Marmot led the way back down to the river from atop the bridge, Esmée caught sight of her friends and flew to them in haste.

"We must bandage his forehead," she said to Marmot, inspecting Pica's wound. "What can we use?"

"Will this do?" one of the squirrels asked, producing a roll of surgical gauze and some medical tape from the pack he had slung across his back.

"Clever squirrel," Marmot said, taking the gauze and tape and setting to work on Pica's forehead. "You guys thought of everything!"

"It was Hugo's idea," the squirrel said. "He made sure we were well prepared."

At the mention of Hugo's name, everyone fell silent. Their hearts ached for their friend, and for the prisoner, Pierre.

"He's a most excellent groundhog," Marmot said, finishing with Pica's forehead. "And a good friend."

Looking the squirrel directly in the eye, with a look of rock-solid resolve, Marmot added, "On my honor, we *will* see them again."

While Marmot attended to Pica, Esmée sat beside Audrey, cradling her in her wings. The battered butterfly was drifting in and out of consciousness. Exhaustion would have carried her off to sleep, if it hadn't been for the severe pain she was feeling.

The prodding, snapping beaks of a dozen vicious crows had tried and tried to catch the helpless butterfly in their grasp. Thanks to the efforts of her friends, none had been able to reach her; except one.

In the heat of battle, when both Pica and Marmot had been occupied with their own desperate struggles, one crow had succeeded in landing a blow on Audrey. Catching her left antenna in his sharp beak, the murderous crow broke it in two, leaving only a stump behind. The pain of having her antenna bitten off shot through her body like an electric shock. Audrey felt as if she might faint and reeled in agony; until she fell back against the riverbank and out of reach of her attacker. Laying there in the mud, she finally passed out.

When Pica and Marmot saw what had happened, they redoubled their efforts to protect her. The sight of one-hundred squirrels was more wonderful than anything the magpie and groundhog had ever seen before; but it had come too late to save Audrey from injury. Ever since leaving Saint-Denis, Audrey had been a truer friend to Pica than any he'd ever known. All along their journey, she'd been a wise and decisive leader. If it hadn't been for Audrey Loriot, the bookworm, they would never have made it this far.

Esmée caressed her friend's face.

"Audrey," she whispered. "Dear Audrey, can you hear me?"

A faint moan escaped the lips of the stricken butterfly.

"Sweet friend, I'm so sorry. So very sorry…" Esmée sat on the brink of desperation.

"Don't be," came a soft and anguished voice, "Finding you was worth an antenna." Opening her eyes, Audrey looked up at Esmée and asked, "Who needs *two*, anyway?"

Esmée buried her face in Audrey's neck and wept; holding her tightly, unwilling ever to let her go again.

"Are you able to fly, my friend?" Marmot asked Pica.

"*Oui… oui…*" he answered, somewhat unconvincingly.

"I think it's best if you take Audrey up to the *Champ de Mars*. You'll both be able to rest and recover in the den of Boswell Badger. And I'm sure everyone will be happier knowing *you're* there, too, *mademoiselle*."

Marmot said, turning to Esmée. "Please go with them and leave this one last crow to me."

"But… Pierre. I can't just leave him."

"You aren't leaving him. You're accompanying the wounded back to safety. Pica and Audrey need your help, too. Please, *mademoiselle.* Go with them to the badger's den. I will find Pierre and Hugo. I will bring them home."

Esmée couldn't bear the thought of leaving Pierre behind, but Marmot was right. Her wounded friends needed her help, and there was little she could do for Pierre or Hugo. She was the reason her friends had undertaken the dangerous journey to Paris. She was the reason the groundhogs, squirrels and badger had organized their search and rescue mission. She owed it to everyone to grant success to their efforts by going somewhere safe. Otherwise, who knows what else might happen or who else might get hurt? Through no fault of her own, Esmée was the cause of it all. It was time to do what she could to put an end to it.

"I'll ask half the squirrels to guide you safely to Boswell and Victor. They'll guard you from any further dangers."

Marmot turned and addressed the squirrel standing beside him.

"I need someone to get a message to the nearest Boulogne *network server room.* Any volunteers?"

The squirrel replied, "For such an important task, I volunteer myself."

"Excellent," Marmot said with an approving nod of his head. "And your name is?"

"Reginald," said the squirrel, "Reginald Renault. Call me Reggie."

"I'm afraid I have nothing to write with, Reggie, so you'll have to remember the message…"

"Here you go, sir," said the same squirrel who had

produced medical supplies from his backpack, earlier.

Handing a sheet of paper and a newly sharpened pencil to Marmot, the squirrel closed his backpack, then stepped back into line.

"Impressive." Marmot shook his head with amazement. "Prepared for anything, indeed. Anyhow, strike that, Reg. No need to memorize anything."

Scribbling on the piece of paper, Marmot jotted down the following message:

"**Priority 1:** Urgent!
From: Marmot, in the field
To: All Recipients

Alert: Lost butterfly, Esmée, found! En route to *CM-TE* in the company of injured friends, Pica and Audrey; under the protection of the *JdT* Squirrels, formerly under the command of Hugo. Remaining half of the squad and I will be pursuing crow captain in an effort to free Hugo and butterfly, Pierre, and defeat their captor. Will return to *CM-TE* upon completion of mission."

Folding the paper, Marmot handed it to Reggie, saying, "The Pathé Beaugrenelle Movie Theatre is a few blocks in that direction. That's the closest *server room*. The *network manager's* name is Gus. He'll know what to do. Once this message is delivered, start recalling the *JdT* squirrels back to the *Champ de Mars*. We'll meet-up there when I'm done with the one-eyed crow. Be swift, Reg. And thank you!"

The little squirrel took the message and immediately bolted inland from the river. Crossing busy streets and rounding buildings in his path, Reginald Renault made his way toward the Beaugrenelle *server room*.

Of all the *access points* on the Boulogne *network,* the Beaugrenelle *server room* was the most unique. Located in a rooftop garden high above the city streets, the Beaugrenelle was not easy to get to. Finding the building upon which the *server room* was located, wasn't the problem. Getting up high enough to find Gus, was; unless you're a squirrel.

Reginald stood in front of the theatre, forming his plan. His eyes moved from ground level, up the side of the building, and all the way to the rooftop garden; this would be his path. From ground to trees, then trees to windows, the squirrel pictured himself scurrying across window frames along the front of the building, until he finally reached the ledge surrounding the roof. He had to be sure there would be a foothold at every step along the way. After minutes spent carefully observing, he could tell that there were plenty of footholds to keep a squirrel from falling. He was ready to go.

Reggie ran up the trunk of a short tree in front of the movie theatre. Swinging from branch to branch, higher and higher within the leafy limbs he climbed. Reaching the uppermost branch of the tree, he took a running leap and landed on the face of the building. His tiny claws and agile feet found enough of a lip around each window frame to allow him to scale the building like Spiderman.

Inside the theatre, people pointed and stared with surprise, as the fluffy-tailed squirrel put on a show of aerial acrobatics with steady nerves. He was undoubtedly much better entertainment than the movies they had paid to see.

Reggie reached the top, and swung himself up and over the ledge, landing on the cushy green grass carpeting the rooftop garden. He wasted no time in locating the *server room access point* which, anywhere else along the *network* would have been a hole in the ground. Up here, however, the *access point* was Gus the groundhog himself. Find the groundhog and you've found your way onto the Boulogne *internet*.

On this particular day, finding Gus was as easy as simply showing up. The groundhog had heard Marmot's Emergency Alert whistle; Hugo's reply; and then the noise of battle, even from high atop the movie theatre. Most of all, he'd heard the terrible cry of the lead crow the moment Pierre put its eye out. Gus already had a good idea what was going on down below.

Running up to the groundhog who was standing not far from the ledge, Reggie the squirrel delivered his message.

"From Marmot, sir."

"I've been expecting this," the groundhog said, opening the sheet of paper and reading the message to himself. "Right," he said, looking up from the paper. "I'll send it straight away."

"I'll be off, then, sir," Reggie replied. "I have to round up my friends and meet up with everyone at the *Champ de Mars – Tour Eiffel* when I'm done."

"I can help there, too," the groundhog said. "After I send Marmot's message out over the *network,* I'll send one asking all *network managers* along the Seine to pass the word to the squirrel squads. They'll do the work for you and you can head straight to the *CM-TE.*"

"Thank you, sir!" Reggie said, with grateful relief. It had been a long and tiresome day.

"My pleasure, friend. And the name's Gus. No need for the 'sir'."

The groundhog smiled, then turned and headed for a small clump of flowering bushes in the middle of the garden. There, he whistled the way Marmot had by the side of the river the day he shared the secret of WiFi with Audrey.

Immediately, the air was alive with fireflies. The

groundhog passed his message along to the fireflies who carried it, not with flashes of light from their tails, but by word-of-mouth to every *message runner* nearby. The *runners* then carried the message to the many *server rooms* along the Seine where it was sent out over the Boulogne *internet.*

Far away to the south in the *T1 server room,* Megalina the field mouse was roused from her afternoon tea by the tinkling of a bell. Getting up from her place in front of the open-hearth fire, she entered the *server room* and searched the wall for a green label indicating a new message. She'd been waiting impatiently for news from Marmot ever since receiving the message he'd sent after crossing the river. Finding the mailbox with the green label, she pulled out the message and began reading.

"**Priority 1:** Urgent!
From: Marmot, in the field
To: All Recipients

Alert: Lost butterfly, Esmée, found! En route to *CM-TE* in the company of injured friends, Pica and Audrey; under the protection of the *JdT* Squirrels, formerly under the command of Hugo. Remaining half of the squad and I will be pursuing crow captain in an effort to free Hugo and butterfly, Pierre, and defeat their captor. Will return to *CM-TE* upon completion of mission."

Megalina dropped the message on the floor at her feet, and stared into the empty air, stunned. "Injured friends," it said. "Free Hugo and the butterfly, Pierre…"

For the first time since she'd learned of the situation, Megalina understood the full depth of just how serious it really was. Animals were being injured and captured. Battles were being fought. Now, Marmot was heading into a dangerous fight with the leader of the crows.

Megalina felt helpless. She wanted to run out and join the fray; but despite her big, talented teeth, she was only a tiny field mouse. What could she possibly do to help?

"Wicked crow*th*," Megalina thought to herself. "*Th*omeone need*th* to teach them a le*th*on."

As a field mouse, Megalina knew how dangerous a murder of crows could be. She shuddered to think about her friend locked in combat with their leader. Marmot was exceptional, even by groundhog standards, but was he any match for the enormous captain of the crows? She just didn't know.

The *server room* bell began to ring again, and a second green label appeared on the letterbox wall. Megalina quickly located and retrieved the message, eager to know more about what was going on upriver.

> "**Priority 2:** Important
> **From:** Gus, *Beaugrenelle Server Room*
> **To:** All Recipients
>
> **Alert:** All members of the *JdT* Squirrel Squads are directed to return to the *Champ de Mars* as soon as possible, in light of the finding of the lost butterfly, Esmée. Further instructions will be given upon your arrival, by Reginald Renault, squirrel."

Megalina folded the message, then stood there in the *server room* trying to make sense of it all.

"Why are the *th*quirrels being recalled? Why would they no longer be needed? I*th* the captain of the crow*th* alone? What'*th* going on?"

The uncertainty was more than she could take.

She had to know what was happening out there and why Marmot felt he could handle the crow leader without any help from the squirrel squads. But Megalina had promised to stay behind and man the *T1 server room* in Marmot's absence. She had to stay put in case any important messages came through.

Still, she felt useless; helpless; of no real service. She'd copied the photograph from *Le Journal*; that was all. It now looked as if that was the *only* meaningful contribution she'd be allowed to make.

Frustrated and more than a little tired of being cooped up in Marmot's apartment, she decided to run up to the surface just long enough to get some fresh air. Scrambling up through one of the many narrow ventilation shafts leading from the tunnels up to the surface, Megalina reached the world above ground in a matter of moments.

The sun was high, and the sky was blue, with only a few clouds left behind after the storms. Megalina sat down in a spongey patch of moss; turned her face toward the sun; and let the summer breeze sweep the stress from her thoughts.

In an apple tree just a few feet from where she sat sunning herself, Megalina spotted a familiar face. In reality, it was the bright purple and gold of her wings that first drew Megalina's attention to Jenna the butterfly.

"*Bonjour,* Jenna. How'*th* the nectar today?"

"*Ah, bonjour, mon amie.* It is very (slurp!) delicious, indeed. Are you having a restful day?"

"Re*th*tful, *non,*" said the field mouse. "There'*th* trouble upriver, and it appear*th* that Marmot'*th* in the middle of it."

The butterfly's interest was piqued. Flying down, she landed on the moss beside Megalina in the hope of hearing more.

"What kind of trouble," she asked.

Megalina proceeded to recount the whole story to Jenna. She told her how Esmée had gone missing from Saint-Denis and that her friends had crossed the Meudon Forest in search of her. She said that Marmot had found them and sent out an emergency message across the Boulogne *internet* with a copy of the photo from *Le Journal.*

"I saw that picture. She was… at the Louvre," Jenna said, hesitating as the echo of a memory sounded in her mind.

Megalina went on to tell her about how Marmot led Audrey and Pica upriver to meet with Boswell Badger, in the hope of gaining his help in locating Esmée. Finally, she told the little butterfly about the messages Megalina had received that day concerning a battle.

"All I know i*th* that *Ethmée* ha*th* been found and that she and her injured friend*th* are on their way to the *Champ de Marth.* And Marmot… he'*th* going after the leader of the crow*th*, to free Hugo the groundhog and a butterfly named Pierre. *Th*o, no, thi*th* i*th* not a re*th*tful day."

"Saint-Denis…" Jenna said, piecing it all together in her mind. "The butterfly from the photo taken at the Louvre…"

She remembered that Lisette had told her she was traveling from Saint-Denis to meet her friends who had gone ahead without her; and that her destination was the Louvre Museum. These *had* to be the same butterflies Megalina was talking about. It all made sense.

"I met one of them earlier today, I think. Just outside the city. Her name was Lisette. She said she was looking for her friends, and that she was bound for the Louvre. She was in great distress. It *must* be the same friends… the ones you're telling me about and the one's she's trying to find."

"But they aren't at the Louvre anymore. And

E*th*mée ha*th* been found. If we don't find thi*th* Li*th*ette, we'll have another lo*th*t butterfly on our hand*th*!"

"I know where she is," Jenna said, "Or at least where she'll be. She's coming up this branch of the river. I know because I gave her directions. She can't be far behind me."

"We have to keep watch," Megalina replied, with resolve. "We have to catch her before she pa*theth* u*th* and end*th* up *lotht* and alone at the Louvre. Come on!"

Jumping to her feet, the toothy field mouse and the elegant, purple butterfly set off for the river. They were determined to do all they could to intercept Lisette and head-off another disastrous misadventure of *A Butterfly in Paris*. Their chances of finding Lisette were no worse than Lisette's chances had been of finding Esmée. In fact, Lisette's only chance of finding her best friend now lay in the vigilant hands of Megalina and Jenna.

After sending Reginald Renault on his way, Marmot saw to it that Pica, Audrey and Esmée had an escort of fifty squirrels to accompany them safely to the *Champ de Mars*. Although Pica had bravely agreed to fly all the way, the squirrels wouldn't hear of it. Instead, they constructed a stretcher out of sticks tied together with vines and made the magpie as comfortable as they could. They would carry him on the stretcher -- and Audrey and Esmée along with him.

With words of encouragement, Marmot waved goodbye to the *JdT* squirrels and their precious cargo of two butterflies and one magpie. The sooner they arrived at the den of Boswell Badger, the better. Thanks to Marmot's message, sent by Gus the *network manager* of the Beaugrenelle *server room,* Victor and Boswell would be awaiting the injured travelers. All would be well, Marmot was certain.

The groundhog now turned his attention to the task of freeing Hugo and Pierre. The moment the old crow had flown off with the butterfly in his claws and Hugo on his back, Marmot had sent seven squirrels to follow them. His quick thinking ensured that he'd know exactly where the wicked bird had taken its captives.

As they ran along in pursuit of the crow leader, each of the seven squirrels had stopped at a different spot along the way. They now had a chain of squirrels that reached from the Pont de Grenelle at the midway point of the Island of Swans, all the way down the long narrow island to its southernmost tip.

Each of the seven squirrels could see and hear the others from a distance. That way, they could pass along the exact location of Hugo and Pierre by means of their own high-pitched, squeaky language. Marmot had only to cross the bridge running from the eastern bank of the river to the Island of Swans, then follow his chain of squirrels.

"Follow me!" he said to the forty or so remaining squirrels. "It's time to set things right."

Leaping up onto the deck of the bridge, the flood of fluffy soldiers, led by their fearless groundhog captain, swept across to the Island of Swans. From there, they crawled down the concrete pilon and onto the island where they met the first of the seven squirrels who had been sent to keep an eye on their friends' location.

"They're on the small island off the southern tip, sir," the sentry reported to Marmot.

"Well done, my friend," Marmot said, patting the squirrel on the shoulder. Turning to his squad, the groundhog addressed them all in a whisper.

"We must approach carefully," he began. "From what I've just been told, there's a small island off the southern tip of this one. Somehow, we will need to quietly cross the water in between. We'll figure that out when we arrive. From here on, we must have absolute silence. Any sound might alert the old crow of our approach and cause things to go very badly for our friends. On we go."

Marmot took up the lead position, walking on all fours. Concealed by the weeds and bushes lining the sides of the island, the groundhog and his squadron of squirrels were well hidden. It was slow going; but their advantage was not in speed, but rather, in stealth. They must not be seen until the attack was under way.

Crawling along ahead of the others, Marmot reached the southern shore of the island first. Hiding behind the tall statue at the island's tip, Marmot was able to survey the situation. Across a gap of water of maybe forty feet, Marmot could see a small, round island. On it, he saw the figure of a black-feathered bird. The crow seemed to be holding something in his talons. Off to one side, Marmot could barely make out the shape of a groundhog who appeared to be sleeping.

Washed by the river's current and caught against the stone prow of the island, driftwood swirled in the tide. Marmot had an idea; but it would require squirrels and groundhog to go against every instinct of their nature. For neither groundhogs nor squirrels care for water; and yet, there was no better solution within sight.

Marmot crawled back to speak with his squirrel companions.

"Friends, we haven't much time. Across the way, our friends are in dire need. The only way over to them is by swimming. We must be silent as a piece of driftwood, and camouflage ourselves to look like one, too. If we crawl down the stone wall that extends into the river, we'll find an assortment of floating wood. Grab hold of a piece and paddle your feet behind you. Quietly. Always quietly. I'll lead the way."

Marmot turned and crept to the edge of the water.

Slipping down into the brown water, he took hold of a piece of driftwood. Using it as a life preserver, he floated out into the Seine. As many pieces of wood as could be found, that's how many squirrels followed Marmot into the river and across to the other shore. The rest remained on the Island of Swans, watching from the weeds.

The current was against them as they paddled in silence across to the island on which their friends were being held. Keeping his eyes fixed on his enemy, Marmot watched for any sign that the crow sensed their approach.

As he and the squirrels landed on the rocky shore, they spread out and kept themselves covered. With great care, they crawled up out of the water. The squirrels all looked like drowned rats; their tails had completely lost all fluffiness. Dripping and shivering with cold, they kept coming; until, at last, they were all safely across. Marmot took a quick count to see how many had been able to find a piece of wood and make the short journey. Ten, he counted, plus himself. It would have to be enough.

In a whisper, beneath the hush of the river breeze, Marmot gave instructions to his team.

"You four, head over to Hugo and make sure he's alright. Stay with him. If he survived the journey, he still won't be in any shape to put up a fight."

Turning to the remaining six squirrels, he said, "You come with me. The moment we get close enough to the one-eyed crow, the four of you jump right in his face."

Speaking to the fifth squirrel, he instructed, "That'll buy you time to grab Pierre and run."

To the last squirrel, Marmot spoke with grave humor.

"And you… stay with me. We get to have the *most* fun. Are we ready, team?"

The squirrels nodded in agreement, then fixed their eyes on their individual goals.

"Right, then. For Hugo and Pierre. Here we go."

Taking a deep breath, Marmot leapt to his feet and ran as fast as he could. At his heels, ten squirrels pulled up the rear. The tall grass opened up in front of them, as Marmot swept it aside with his stick of driftwood. The invaders now began to widen their area, spreading out and splitting up into their designated teams.

The four assigned to Hugo veered off to the right. The five assigned to distract the crow and grab Pierre held to a straight line. The last squirrel, who would be accompanying Marmot, veered to the left, staying directly behind the groundhog all the way.

Marmot began yelling at the top of his lungs, startling the old crow and drawing his attention away from Hugo's rescuers.

"Fool," the menacing bird spat with disdain. "You've come to join your friends, I see."

"I've come for you," Marmot replied, holding his enemy's focus. "And I won't be leaving without you."

"Oh, you're right about that, whistle pig. You won't be leaving this island at all."

The four squirrels reached Hugo and immediately determined that he was still alive. They began to drag him as best they could, until they'd succeeded in moving the groundhog out of the clearing and into the dense bushes by the water's edge.

There they worked to revive him, keeping Hugo silent and perfectly hidden the whole while. Hugo had been dropped from a great height by the crow who'd intended the fall to knock the groundhog out for a very long time. He was bruised and bloodied but becoming more aware by the minute. The squirrels were relieved to see that if they made it off the island at all Hugo would surely be alright.

While Marmot and his squirrel-rearguard approached from the left, the five squirrels assigned to rescue Pierre remained in the one-eyed crow's blind spot.

Just as Marmot drew close enough for the crow to strike, the five rescuers arrived. Flailing around in the wicked leader's face, they caught him completely off guard. The one squirrel entrusted with the task of snatching Pierre from between the sharp claws of his captor swooped in from the side, took hold of Pierre, and was gone again before the crow knew what had happened.

Distracted by the *furious four*, the crow had forgotten about Marmot altogether. Marmot took advantage of the situation and ran straight up to the overwhelmed bird, striking him with a piece of driftwood right across his beak. Staggering backwards, the crow dangled over the side of the island above the swift-running Seine.

Feeling his strength now return to his wings, Pierre saw his opportunity to put an end to their common enemy.

As the crow struggled to regain his balance after being struck by Marmot, Pierre took to flight and headed straight for the waterline. Blinded in one eye; confused by the squirrel attack; and teetering on the edge of the shore; the murderous leader of the gang of marauders never saw it coming. The brave Pierre flew with full force and purpose directly into the crow's one good eye, causing him to lose his balance, and casting him down to the deep waters below.

Carried by his own momentum, Pierre fell over the side, along with the crow. At that very moment, a fast-moving barge came steaming upriver toward the tiny island. Unable to fly out of its way in time, the crow was struck by the bow of the boat and tumbled into the white water in its wake, with Pierre close behind.

From the shore, Marmot, the squirrels and Hugo gasped. With unblinking eyes, they waited for any sign of Pierre or the crow to emerge from the swirling river. The boat passed, and the white water grew calm. The familiar flow of the Seine returned. Brown and steady, it made its way downstream to *la Manche* and, from there, to the open sea where all memory is eternal. There was no question; their friend was gone.

For nearly an hour they stood there on the shore, motionless and speechless. There was nothing they could do; there was no hope to be found; and there was nothing anyone dared to say. At that moment, they were the only ones in all the universe to know that they now lived in a world without Pierre. This was terrible knowledge; too terrible to share; too crushing to hold inside.

Why would they choose to leave this place, when leaving meant spreading the word that their friend was gone? Why would they leave, when it meant going back to those who awaited Pierre's return? But he would not return. Where could they go to find him; and, finding him, how could they bring him home again? Like a sword through the heart, the truth was piercing and ice cold: their friend was gone.

Marmot found the courage at last to look the others in the eye. Without a word, he met their blank stares. One by one, he gazed at each face. Then, with no explanation and no emotion, he walked over to the water's edge where they had landed. There was a rosebush there beside the waters of the Seine. Picking one red rose, he held it in his teeth. Then, taking his stick of driftwood, he entered the water and began swimming back to the *Île aux Cygnes;* the Island of Swans.

CHAPTER THIRTY-TWO

A Single Red Rose

Fifty squirrels are a formidable force. Few would dare trifle with such an army. To small animals, fifty squirrels are overwhelming. To large animals, they're maddening. To humans, they're just plain alarming. So, while the fifty squirrels of Hugo's squadron guarded the stretcher carrying Pica, Audrey and Esmée -- guiding it north toward the *Champ de Mars* -- no one troubled them at all.

The little stretcher made of twigs fastened together by vines, was just big enough to hold the magpie. Upon his belly, there sat two butterflies... or rather, one sat, the other lay down; for Audrey was still in great pain and her spirits were low.

She felt the loss of her left antenna acutely. Not only the pain of it, but the permanence of the loss weighed heavily upon her. She'd never be as she once was, and not a day would go by when she wouldn't be reminded of the Battle of the Pont de Grenelle. It would forever haunt her memory.

Four squirrels bore the stretcher on their shoulders, running alongside the river toward the Eiffel Tower and the badger's den. Around them, nearly fifty squirrels formed a vanguard, a rearguard and several flanking guards; without the slightest concern for being seen by human or animal eyes. They were in a hurry and they were strong enough that such concerns were really no concern at all. Let the crows come back; they'd be taught a lesson they wouldn't soon forget. Let the humans see them; the squad of squirrels would run up their pantlegs and down their backs, until the nightly news reported mass hysteria among the squirrel population of Paris. Bring it on!

The squirrels belonging to the squad of the brave and intrepid Hugo of the *JdT* were fearless and focused on one goal and one goal alone: delivering their precious cargo to Boswell Badger before sunset. They were well on their way. It was coming on evening and they were just passing the Stade Emile Anthoine athletic field at the foot of the Eiffel Tower. They'd arrive at their destination in a matter of minutes.

Having received the message Marmot sent to "All Recipients" along the Boulogne *internet*, Victor forwarded it (with the help of Queen Fourmi's garden ants) to Boswell Badger in the *Champ de Mars*. Kept underground by the recent rainstorms, the vast army of garden ants had been, well… antsy to help. Utilizing their many ant tunnels, they formed a hotline from the *CM-TE server room* all the way over to the badger's den beneath the *Champ de Mars* where their queen and Boswell Badger awaited word of Esmée and Marmot.

When Boswell received Marmot's update, he was gravely concerned. Though relieved to hear of the imminent arrival of Esmée, the fact that she was accompanied by two injured friends was deeply troubling. Equally disturbing, was the news of Marmot's mission to free Hugo and Pierre by facing the king of the crows virtually alone. Boswell, it's true, had little confidence in Hugo; so, he put even less confidence in the *JdT* squirrels who would be fighting alongside Marmot. In Boswell's mind, the blundering squirrels were more likely to get Marmot killed than they were to be of any help to him.

By now, though, Marmot's attempt to rescue both Hugo and Pierre had played out. There was nothing Boswell or Queen Fourmi could have done to help Marmot or to change the outcome, even if they had been there or known what was happening. Pierre was gone, and Marmot, Hugo and their squad of squirrels faced a long, sad march upriver to the *Champ de Mars*. Once they arrived, they would need to share their burden of grief with everyone, including Esmée.

Not long after five o'clock, the half-squadron and their cargo of magpie and butterflies arrived at the Eiffel Tower. The grounds were packed with tourists; some waiting in line to ascend the tower; some wandering around taking photos. At the same time, Reggie, the squirrel who had delivered Marmot's message to Gus at the Beaugrenelle movie theatre, also arrived. Meeting-up with the half-squadron in the gardens surrounding the tower, Reggie conferred with the stretcher-bearers.

As the squirrels discussed the best way to cross the plaza beneath the Eiffel Tower without being seen, groups of squirrels began arriving. They'd received Gus's message directing them to assemble in the *Champ de Mars* and hurried along to their destination.

The first to arrive was Baldtail, whose base was the nearby Bir-Hakeim metro station. His squirrel scouts had seen the stretcher-bearers making their way north along the river. As a precaution, Baldtail directed the entire squad to follow them closely, in case there was any trouble. From a distance, he and his squirrels made sure Pica, Audrey and Esmée made it to the Eiffel Tower safely.

"Welcome!" Reggie said to his old friend, Baldtail. "You got the message, then?"

"We did, and so did everyone else. The other squads should be arriving any minute. What can we do to help, now that we're here?"

"Now that the butterflies have been found, I think someone should take a message to Devereux, back at the *JdT*. He's been waiting for news and I'd hate to be the one who failed to get it to him."

Reggie was thinking of Devereux Délabré, Esq., the venerable, old squirrel from across the river. Too old to leave the *Jardins du Trocadéro,* Devereux's adventurous nature hadn't aged with his body. He was impatient to hear how the squirrels' mission was progressing.

"I'm happy to take my squad back to the *JdT* and inform Devereux; but someone should stay here and let the other squads know to go home, too.

"You're right, Baldtail," Reggie said. "I'll station a squirrel at every entrance to the Tower and the *Champs de Mars* to let everyone know it's ok to head home. I, myself, should go see Victor. Someone needs to tell him everything that happened."

Before they'd finished speaking, the rest of the squirrel squadrons began streaming in. First, Beaujolais, with her pink bow and stylish fur, followed by the athletic Sunflower and decidedly *un*athletic Butternut. Bazillac came in next, and then Rupert who was still "yes, sir-ing" and "no, sir-ing" with enthusiastic vigor.

The salty Pistache arrived, walked right up to Reggie and said, "The Beaugrenelle Movie Theatre was *my* territory. I had it under control. Humph… Go ahead with your 'further instructions.'"

He just couldn't help but sound annoyed all the time. It was hard to tell when he was really upset and when he was just being Pistache; but in this case it was safe to assume he was offended about being left out of the battle that took place in front of the movie theatre. It *was* his territory, after all; but he'd been patrolling north of the bridge and hadn't heard Marmot's Emergency Groundhog Alert. Still, he'd done his duty, and this was nothing to be ashamed of.

The last squad to wander into the area around the Eiffel Tower had traveled the farthest. Led by the young (and most unlikely leader) Kevin, this group of squirrels had been put in charge of the Parc André-Citroën where Audrey, Pica and Marmot had spent the previous night.

They'd received numerous reports from animals in and around the Parc about a groundhog, a magpie and a butterfly who were traveling together. In fact, Kevin was the first of the searchers to realize that it wasn't a group of butterflies they were looking for at all; but rather, a magpie and only one butterfly. By the time he arrived at the nearest *server room* intending to share his discovery with the *network,* the battle was over, and the squirrels had been recalled. The young squirrel captain had done well; but he and his troops were very happy to hear they could go home.

"We'll leave a few sentries posted around the various entrances to the *Champ de Mars,* just in case we get some stragglers; but you guys did excellent work. Head home and get some rest. I'm proud to be a *JdT* squirrel, today!"

Reggie waved goodbye to nearly one thousand of his friends, then watched them stream across the bridge and into the *Jardins du Trocadéro.* They'd marched all over that city in the past 24 hours without much concern for being seen by human eyes. Now that they were exhausted and finally able to go home again, they just walked right past tourists and Parisians, alike. Disrupting traffic and causing pedestrians to run for cover, the fluffy-tailed mob of squirrels had earned the *right of way,* as Audrey's driver's manual would have called it.

While all the squirrel squads had been checking in with Reggie, the stretcher-bearers had taken the wounded Pica and Audrey, along with Esmée, safely around in the direction of the *Champ de Mars.* Keeping to the gardens that surround the tower, the party remained hidden by grass, shrubs and trees. Rounding the northeastern foot, they headed straight into the immense rectangular field that stretches out away from the Eiffel Tower. The squirrels knew the area well, and before long, they located the hidden entrance to the badger's den.

All around the hole leading down to Boswell's home, garden ants patrolled. Forming unbroken lines that circled the area, then ran down deep into the badger's den, Queen Fourmi's ants kept a lookout for the arrival of the stretcher-bearers. Once they saw them approaching, the ants sent a message down the line to their Queen, who waited with the badger, below.

As soon as the news reached them, Fourmi and Boswell ran up to the surface to receive the wounded. It was a heartbreaking scene, watching the four stretcher-bearers carry Pica and Audrey across the field. It would not be the last heartbreak of the day. Recognizing the badger at a distance, Esmée flew to meet him.

"I am very glad to see you, *mademoiselle.* I received news of your companions from Marmot. We are ready to nurse them back to health."

"*Merci, monsieur* Badger," Esmée replied, landing on a bush in front of Boswell. "My friend, Audrey, is in greatest need, for the crows were merciless."

Stepping forward to examine Audrey and Pica, Queen Fourmi assessed their situation, then turned to speak with the nearby garden ants.

"Go now and collect *yarrow, ginseng,* and *aloe* from my storeroom. Bring them quickly, my children."

Speaking with the stretcher-bearers, she instructed them, "Carry the stretcher into the den where our guests can rest in safety. I will attend them there."

The stretcher was brought down the entrance through a short tunnel and into Boswell's cozy home. The squirrels then lifted Audrey with great care and placed her on a cushion, where she would be more comfortable. Pica sat in the old badger's rocking chair, close to a small pot-bellied stove. The sun was setting, and all the *Champ de Mars* grew chilly. Boswell brought a blanket from his closet and draped it across the magpie's lap.

As soon as Audrey and Pica had been made comfortable, the garden ants arrived, carrying the plants their queen had requested. Directing her helpers to attend to Pica, Fourmi tended to Audrey herself.

The garden ants appeared to possess great skill with healing-herbs. With Boswell's help, they applied *yarrow* powder to Pica's wounds, which immediately stopped bleeding. Next, they rubbed *aloe* on his bruises and scrapes. The badger then changed the magpie's bandage, while the ants went over to join their queen.

Fourmi stemmed the bleeding in Audrey's antenna, first. She then cleaned the wound and soothed it with *aloe*. Tying a tiny bandage to the tip of what was left of Audrey's antenna, the queen asked that tea be brewed using the *ginseng*. Sitting beside Audrey, she helped her sip the tea, then stroked her forehead until the butterfly fell asleep.

Esmée looked on with painful concern. She thought about all the events that had taken place over the past few days, events that had led to this moment. It all began with a bouquet of flowers too beautiful to resist. If only she had resisted… oh, if only.

When the doors of the RER B train slid closed, trapping her inside, Esmée could not have imagined that she'd be standing here watching her friends suffer. None of it felt real. It all seemed out of proportion.

Back home in Saint-Denis, she had family and friends; she had the splendor of nature all around. She'd never wanted to go searching for anything more anywhere else. She was sure that there *was* nothing more.

How could there be?

Then the world opened up before her at the speed of a commuter train. Beauties beyond count, wonders beyond imagination presented themselves to her; and danger, too. There was always danger, from the moment her train left the station. There was ugliness and there was cruelty, but none of it was *more* or *bigger* or *stronger* than the good things she had found.

In fact, some of the greatest kindness she'd encountered came in distressing packages. The rescuer who looked like a barn owl, but who was really an owl moth; the badger who was gruff and crusty, but was really grandfatherly; and now the noble queen who was no bigger than an ant; they had all shown greater self-sacrifice and kindness than she had ever thought possible outside of Saint-Denis.

Then her thoughts came to rest on Pierre, the butterfly who saved her life at the Arc de Triomphe and had told her he was just a coward. At the Pont de Grenelle, Pierre drew the wrath of the lead crow away from her and her friends; he'd been taken captive to set them free. Pierre had shown her all of Paris; until she fell in love with the City of Lights and the charming butterfly who had introduced her to it all.

As she stood there watching the garden ants nurse her friends back to health, Esmée desperately wanted to see Pierre; to know that he was alright; to hear his voice once more. His bravery and gentleness had given her the strength and courage to open her eyes to the beauty all around her, even if she was far from home. In Esmée's heart and mind, Pierre *meant* home; and she wanted to go home.

Pica had been bandaged, given a bowl of blueberries and some fresh water, and was now asleep in his rocking chair beside the woodstove. Audrey had finished her *ginseng* tea and then fell asleep beneath the loving caresses of the Queen of the Garden Ants. Audrey now slept in peaceful comfort on a cushion from Boswell's armchair. Everything that could be done for her friends had been done. Esmée now returned to the surface and sat in the lengthening shadows of twilight.

Fireflies flashed and played beneath the trees of the *Champ de Mars*. To the west, the sun had just hidden itself behind the grouping of tall buildings called *La Défense,* just beyond the city limits. A perfect likeness of the Eiffel Tower spread out in thin shadows across the rectangular field to its east. Nighttime was upon them, and still there was no sign of Marmot, Hugo, Pierre and the half-squadron of squirrels.

Boswell Badger sat on the stump of a tree, smoking his pipe and leaning on a walking stick. Beside him, at the tip of a tree branch, Fourmi rested her legs and watched the southwestern horizon. Reggie the squirrel had stopped off at the *CM-TE server room* to inform Victor of all that had happened. Thanking him, the groundhog encouraged his friend to return to the *JdT* and get some rest. He would be notified as soon as Marmot returned. Victor then walked the short distance over to Boswell's place, finding him and Fourmi outside when he arrived.

"You keep vigil, I see," Victor said, as he approached his friends.

"We do," replied the badger, "with hope in our hearts. What news from the *CM-TE?*"

"I spoke at length with Reggie the squirrel. He told me the details of all that took place at the Pont de Grenelle. I'll share it with you, my friends, but you will need to hold on tight to this faint hope of yours. The story of their battle brings little hope of its own."

Victor sat down in front of Boswell and Fourmi -- Esmée by her side -- and recounted the events leading up to the Battle of the Pont de Grenelle. He told of how

Marmot, Audrey and Pica had been set upon by a dozen crows bent on revenge for having been tricked a few days earlier by Audrey's imitation of a hawk. When the attack became overwhelming, Marmot sent up the Groundhog Emergency Alert whistle, then held off the marauders until Hugo arrived to answer the alert call.

Victor told the story of Hugo and his squad of squirrels pouring over the side of the bridge and sending the crow minions running for cover deep within the heart of the city. Esmée added to the tale and spoke about Marmot and Pica's brave defense of the butterflies and how Pica had received his wounds at the point of a half dozen sharp beaks. She went on to tell about the blow which cost Audrey her antenna.

Then she came to Pierre.

With great difficulty and raw emotions, Esmée spoke of Pierre's courage in drawing the villainous leader away from his army of crows. She talked about the cruel way in which the wretched creature threw Pierre to the ground, then stood on his wings, pinning him down. When she found herself unable to continue, Victor picked up the story.

He spent a long time telling every detail about Hugo and his wrathful umbrella, and how he beat the lead crow into submission. Victor then recounted how the wicked bird pretended to fly away, only to turn and swept down to kidnap Pierre before making his escape.

"And then…" Victor said, shaking his head with disbelief. "Reggie says that Hugo leapt upon the back of the enormous crow, and all three flew off downriver together."

Boswell sat forward on his stump.

"Hugo? Did what?" the badger said with surprise.

"He refused to let the scoundrel get away," Esmée said, staring down at her feet.

"Reggie said that Marmot immediately

dispatched seven squirrels to follow the crow and his captives; so, it's likely he knows exactly where they are."

Boswell sat motionless, trying to take it all in. He would not have expected such bravery from Hugo. Marmot, of course; but Hugo? Never. The badger understood exactly how much danger Pierre and Hugo were in; he understood what Marmot was walking into. Victor was right, the story of the Battle of the Pont de Grenelle brought little hope of its own.

"I will keep watch with you," Victor whispered, "There's little else that can be done now."

Evening darkened beneath the rising moon. The minute hand reached the top of the hour, and the lights of the Eiffel Tower sprung to life. In the warmth of its gold and silver glow, Fourmi, Boswell and Victor almost forgot their sadness and worries.

Not so with Esmée, though. She remembered the last time she watched the light show, when she and Pierre had been a part of the beauty shining all around them. The pain of that memory stole her breath and pierced her heart. She began to cry, hiding her tears from the others.

Against the backlit horizon, the silhouettes of two groundhogs now appeared, and grew in size and as they neared the badger's den. Victor strained his eyes in the dark.

"It's them!" he said, "It's Marmot!"

Jumping to his feet, the groundhog ran to meet his friends. Boswell stood and peered with sharp eyes at the approaching figures. Then, looking down at Fourmi, he shook his head slowly.

Victor met the two groundhogs, twenty feet or so away from where he had been sitting.

"Marmot! Hugo! You're alright! But the squirrels?"

Hugo spoke in barely more than a whisper, "We sent them home... to the *JdT*."

"And Pierre?" Victor asked, as a terrible feeling of dread soaked into his heart.

Marmot just turned and looked into Victor's eyes. His face was a blank page; his mouth was drawn up tight. He betrayed no emotion, only defeat. Nothing needed to be said. Victor understood. Together, the three groundhogs walked slowly back to where Esmée, Fourmi and Boswell were waiting.

"Pierre?" Esmée asked, with desperation in her trembling voice.

Stopping in front of her, Marmot stooped down and placed a single red rose on the ground in front of Esmée -- the rose he had picked before leaving the island. Esmée melted in a flow of warm tears, which escaped through the cracks in her broken heart. Marmot stood up then turned to face Boswell with a look on his face to extinguish all hope.

CHAPTER THIRTY-THREE

Cupid and the Butterfly

Boswell Badger walked over to where Esmée sat crying. He bent over and stroked her folded wing with the back of his fingers. Without a word, he cupped his paws around the butterfly and lifted her to his heart. It was the closest a badger could come to hugging a butterfly.

Walking to the opening leading down to his den, he entered, carrying Esmée inside. Once there, the badger gently placed Esmée on the cushion beside Audrey, then turned to stoke the woodfire.

Audrey sat up, walked over, and wrapped her wings around her friend. From the woodstove, Pica watched the scene unfold. The pain in his forehead and the soreness in his body was replaced by anguish at Esmée's heartache. He went over to the cushion and held it and his truest, dearest friends in his arms.

The garden ants attended to Hugo's injuries much as they had done with Pica and Audrey's. They worked to bandage his wounds, applying the healing herbs according to their queen's instructions.

When the ants had finished, Hugo rolled up next to the fire, and waited for sleep to bring him healing from the heartbreak of the day. Hiding his face, he cried himself to sleep that night. His was the heart of an artist, not a warrior; and the most sensitive hearts break too easily.

After tending to the fire, Boswell returned to the surface where Esmée would not be able to hear them speak. He needed to talk to Marmot. The ant queen and Victor were bandaging Marmot's wounds, when Boswell reemerged from his den.

"How are you, old friend?" the badger asked of Marmot.

"I'll be alright. It was Hugo who bore the brunt of it, I'm afraid. But he's doing better than when we found him. He and his squad of squirrels saved our lives."

"What unexpected strength he showed. I've been wrong about him," Boswell admitted, "and the squirrels, too."

Pausing a moment, trying to find the right words, Boswell whispered, "Tell me what happened. All of it. Please."

Taking a cup of hot tea in his paws, Marmot held it close to his face, inhaling deeply. He was exhausted and his heart and body ached. All he wanted was to curl up somewhere, alone, and sleep; then maybe he would awaken in the morning to find it had all been just a bad dream. Reliving the events of the day was painful, but he owed it to his friends – those present and those who could not be. He meant to honor them by telling their story.

"The squirrels I'd sent to keep track of the captives led me to the tip of the Island of Swans. From the bushes, I could see another small island -- little more than a pile of boulders in the river. I spied our enemy holding Pierre in his claws; and Hugo, laying on the ground off to one side. I couldn't tell what condition they were in; but we had to find a way to reach them quickly."

Marmot took a sip of tea, which bathed every cell in his body in warmth and renewed strength. He continued recounting the events of that day.

"We decided to use pieces of driftwood to float across the gap between the two islands. Once we'd made it to the other shore, we formed our plan. A few of us would go straight to Hugo and move him to safety. A few would fly directly into the crow's face, distracting him long enough to free Pierre from the crow's claws; while I and my companion would approach loudly, holding the crow's attention and delivering a blow, once Pierre had been rescued."

Victor looked up and caught Boswell's eye. They'd always known their friend was brave and daring, and they never tired of admiring him for these qualities.

"The plan worked well enough. Hugo was dragged to cover, and Pierre was snatched out of the villain's talons and carried to safety. The blow I struck knocked the old crow off balance and, as he was teetering on the edge of the shoreline overlooking the Seine, Pierre flew headlong into him, knocking our enemy into the path of a passing boat."

Marmot stopped here, sipped his tea once more, then looked directly at Boswell. The badger reached into his waistcoat pocket and took out a handkerchief. Blowing his nose, he replaced it and cleared his throat.

"His was the final sacrifice, then," Boswell said, his voice wavering.

"And the rose," Victor said, at last understanding its significance, "you brought back the rose as a reminder of the thorn Pierre used to blind the crow during the Battle of the Pont de Grenelle."

"I brought back the rose for Esmée…" Marmot said, to make clear the meaning, "as a symbol of Pierre's sacrifice. I promised her I'd bring *him* home again; instead, all I could bring her was a flower… a rose picked from the island where her love sacrificed everything for his friends. *L'île du Sacrifice. L'île du Papillon.*"

Finishing his tea, Marmot stood and bowed to Queen Fourmi. He rested one hand on Victor's shoulder, paused a moment, then walked over to where the badger was sitting. Boswell struggled to his feet and took the groundhog by the hand. Marmot simply nodded, then walked off down the *Champ de Mars* to find a place where he could be alone and sleep until sunrise, when the day would be young and new hopes might be born.

Victor bid his friends a restful night -- though he knew heavy hearts rarely find sleep -- then stood and turned back toward the *CM-TE*. Walking home alone, Victor looked up at the night sky in time to see a shooting star pass behind the Eiffel Tower.

Thinking of the fallen butterfly, he smiled with sad remembrance. He wondered why it is that we can smile when we're sad, but we can never be sad when we smile. How he hoped Esmée would be able to smile again soon. Today had been a day of lost hopes, and even the stars wept for Pierre.

Before going to bed, Victor sent the following message out across the *network,*

> **"Priority 2:** Important
> **From:** Network Manager, CM-TE Server Room
> **To:** All Recipients
>
> **Alert:** Today we remember our friend, Pierre, who sacrificed himself for others, defeating our common enemy, the captain of the marauding crows. We are thankful for the safe return of Esmée, Audrey, Pica, Hugo, Marmot and all the brave squirrels of the *JdT.* All searchers: stand down. Farewell to our friend."

The moon rose over the *Champ de Mars,* as the long, bleak night wore on. Below, in the badger's den, Pica slept beside the woodstove. Boswell sat in his rocking chair, unable to sleep and unwilling to leave Esmée and her friends alone. Audrey had fallen asleep on her cushion; but Esmée just sat there next to her, staring at the rose.

Her heart ached with a cold numbness. Her brain had given up on ever making any sense of her loss. There is no reason that can be given in the face of such sorrow. When Pierre fell, Esmée's whole world fell, too. She was certain she could never love again. The thought of it was impossible, like 0 + 1 equaling 2. It could never be. In silence she sat; lonely to her soul, but not alone. The queen sat close to Esmée, offering only her presence, when words had nothing to say.

Beneath a flower bush, not far from the badger's den, Marmot found a warm, secluded place where he could unpack the emotions of the day. More than anything, he just needed to sleep. He couldn't bear to see Esmée or Audrey; the two he most wanted to protect. He felt like he'd failed them. Sleep would set right everything that was out of place inside his heart. The morning would bring a new perspective; he was counting on it. It *had* to.

Far to the south, past the Island of Swans, beyond the Parc André-Citroën, Megalina the field mouse sat in the *T1 server room,* writing out the following message.

> "**Priority 1:** Urgent!
> **From:** Acting Network Manager, T1 Server Room
> **To:** Boswell Badger, c/o the CM-TE Server Room
>
> **Alert:** Jenna the butterfly departed this afternoon, bound for the *Champ de Mars* in the company of Esmée's friend, Lisette. Estimated arrival by midnight tonight."

Folding the message and placing it in a letterbox,

Megalina raised the orange, "urgent" flag, saying, "God*th*peed, little butterflie*th*." She then snuggled down into the embrace of a bird's nest in Marmot's enormous tree root wall and went straight to sleep.

By the time Victor was awakened by his *server room* bell, Jenna and Lisette were just leaving the river; passing the carrousel on the street corner; and flying underneath the Eiffel Tower. They'd been traveling all afternoon and evening, ever since Megalina and Jenna caught sight of Lisette coming up the river near the *T1 server room.* Happy to see the little purple butterfly again, Lisette was happier still to hear news of her friends. She was eager to find them, but unsure of the way. Always willing to help, Jenna offered to guide the butterfly north to the *Champ de Mars,* while Megalina held down the fort, as she'd promised Marmot she would.

When Lisette encountered Megalina and Jenna, the last messages they'd received had said that Esmée was accompanying her injured friends to the *Champ de Mars.* Rumors of a great battle met Lisette and Jenna from everyone they met along their way north. Lisette received just enough information to set her mind awash with worries. What would she find when, finally, they arrived at the badger's den? She feared the worst.

Once again, aware of her companion's distress, Jenna tried to encourage Lisette. When that failed to distract her, Jenna then started pointing out landmarks and places of interest as they flew through Paris. As they approached the Eiffel Tower, before leaving the river that had been their guide, Jenna said, "Five!"

"Five?" Lisette asked.

"From the *T1 server room* to the Eiffel Tower, there are five bridges! You can always navigate the river by counting bridges. I always do, and I always get where I'm going!"

It was now nighttime, and the two butterflies

arrived at the Eiffel Tower at the bottom of the hour when the lights were extinguished. Lisette was in awe over the size and noble grandeur of the structure; and, indeed, of the magnificent city around her. Something in her heart wanted very much for her to lose herself in Paris. There's no better way to discover wonders than by letting yourself get lost in and among them.

"One day," she thought to herself, "maybe, one day."

While Victor was just receiving and reading the message Megalina had sent a few hours earlier, not far away in the *Champ de Mars,* Jenna and Lisette landed in a squared-off tree above the entrance to the badger's den. Though the Groundhog *network* may have been running a bit slow that evening (everyone was exhausted by the day's excitement), the Garden Ant Hotline running between Victor's apartment beneath the northeastern leg of the tower and Boswell's den underneath the square-shaped trees was as fast and efficient as ever.

The moment he read the message from Megalina, Victor sent it over to the badger by way of Queen Fourmi's hotline ants. The unbroken line of ants passed the message along in a matter of seconds. In fact, when the last ant in line finished sharing the message with the queen and Boswell (who were down below in the badger's den), the garden ants who were patrolling the area around the Boswell's home reported two butterflies in the tree just outside.

Boswell and Fourmi headed straight up to ground level, eager to greet the visitors. Popping up out of the hole, they found Jenna and Lisette discussing who would be the first to venture into the badger's den in search of Esmée, Audrey and Pica.

"Welcome, *mesdemoiselles,*" Boswell said, peering up into the tree limbs. "We just received the message from your friend the field mouse. You've come to the right place."

"*Enchantée, monsieur* Badger. My name is Jenna, and this is Esmée's friend, Lisette. She flew all the way from Saint-Denis alone. I have guided her here from where Megalina and I found her."

"Well done, *mademoiselle*," the badger said.

Jenna smiled and curtsied. Turning to Lisette, Boswell addressed her directly.

"I'm sure you're eager to see your friends, *mademoiselle*. Let me assure you that they are all going to be just fine, despite what might greet your eyes. They've been at the center of the Battle of the Pont de Grenelle today, and they sustained many injuries."

Lisette listened with attention, her worries now confirmed.

"But the most painful injury they received was the loss of their friend. Indeed, to Esmée he was much more than a friend. Pierre was the focus of her heart. Go gently with her, for the body forgets its wounds, but the heart never does."

Lisette felt like she was living in a strange dream; nothing made sense. Her friends were seriously injured? Esmée had been in love? And now, a butterfly Lisette had never met -- a butterfly who had captured her best friend's heart -- was gone. She felt as if she and Esmée had been out of touch for years; so much had changed.

Turning to Lisette, Jenna said, "Remember what I told you at the river when we first met. Your friends *love* you and they are waiting for you. They wait for you now; and no matter what, they will always love you. Go to them and set all things right. *Au revoir*, new friend."

Giving Lisette no time to say goodbye, the little purple butterfly smiled then immediately flew off in the direction of the *Champ de Mars*, away from the tower. There was always so much to do, and Jenna never seemed to slow down for long. As she left, she caught sight of a bruised and bandaged groundhog sleeping beneath a flower bush. Dipping down just above his head, she whispered, "Wake up, noble groundhog; your friends await *you*, too." Jenna then fluttered her purple wings and continued on her way. She was by far the most beautiful butterfly in all of Paris – best of all, she was beautiful, inside and out.

Marmot awoke from a deep sleep, certain that he'd heard the voice of an angel; though he never could say if he'd heard it with his waking ears or his dreaming ears. Either way, he immediately began making his way back to the badger's den. Something was up, and he needed to go see for himself.

When Jenna left, Lisette felt very much alone, even though she was with Fourmi and Boswell and only a few feet away from seeing Esmée, Audrey and Pica again. She was surprised to find that she was not at all eager to enter the badger's den and meet her friends. She was afraid; and Lisette Cueilleur was *never* afraid. But the things she never feared before were the things that she could always conquer -- like a single bullying crow, or an ornery hornet. Her feelings of regret, shame and sadness were much harder to conquer.

"Follow me, little one," Boswell said, motioning toward the entrance. "Jenna was right, your friends are waiting for you."

Lisette took a deep breath, then fluttered down from the tree and into the badger's den. She'd never flown underground before. Between the darkness, the chill and the uncertainty of what awaited her inside, she found the experience altogether disagreeable. Turning a gentle corner to the right, the air in the tunnel became warm and a soft orange glow could now be seen. Following the badger, with the queen ant by her side, Lisette entered Boswell's living room.

"Lisette, Lisette!"

Pica was the first to spot his old friend, even before Lisette's eyes had adjusted to the light. For a moment, all she could see was a big, black, feathered figure with something white wrapped around its head. Then her eyes narrowed, and focus was restored. Standing in front of her was a bandaged Pica, smiling so wide he could have swallowed his ears. The magpie threw his wings around Lisette and held onto her far longer than Lisette was really comfortable being hugged by *anyone*.

"I missed you, too, Pica," she said, this time meaning every word of it.

Audrey woke up the minute Pica announced Lisette's arrival. Feeling much better, thanks to the medical care of the garden ants, she flew over and landed in front of Lisette. Audrey was never as affectionate as Pica (few animals are), and even less so with Lisette. She knew she wasn't Lisette's favorite person, so she was always wary of the hot-tempered butterfly. Audrey just stood there with the stump of her antenna bandaged -- sore and groggy, but happy to see a familiar face.

"What brings you to Paris?" Audrey asked, with a hint of humor in her question.

Lisette took a few steps forward, then wrapped her wings around the startled butterfly. Audrey could not remember having ever been hugged by Lisette before, but she'd never forget this one. There was something different about Lisette; something had changed. When, at last, she let go and stepped back, there was a tear in Lisette's eye. And she didn't even try to hide it.

With barely restrained emotion, Lisette asked for her best friend, "Esmée?"

After sitting in absolute shocked silence and staring into emptiness for most of the evening with the ant queen by her side, Esmée had finally fallen asleep. Not even Pica's voice could rouse her now; it had been a long and trying day.

Stepping aside and motioning toward the cushion, Audrey revealed the sleeping butterfly. When Lisette saw her -- after days of worry; after doubt and fear and anger; after miles traveled alone -- she broke down in tears. There were moments when she thought she'd never see her best friend again; now, there she was. A flood of every emotion Lisette had been holding back and trying to control flowed freely through the badger's den.

"I'm certain Esmée would want us to wake her up for this," Audrey said; and no one disagreed.

"Lisette, Lisette," Pica said again, voicing his choice.

"Yes, I think so, too, Pica. You do it, Lisette," Audrey said. "You should awaken Esmée. She'd be very happy to see your face first."

Lisette looked at her friends; and it occurred to her that Audrey and Pica had become more perfectly themselves than they had ever been. The kind and helpful Pica had become fiercely loving and brave. The intelligent and wordy Audrey had become strong, confident and decisive. The qualities they'd once had in seed form had now blossomed and grown. They were *more* than before, even missing half an antenna and a whole lot of feathers. Maybe it was because of what they'd suffered that they were now so much more. Maybe it was because of how they had loved their friends without a thought for themselves. Either way, it was undeniable.

Lisette flew over to the cushion upon which Esmée was sleeping. Landing ever so lightly beside her best friend, she tip-toed closer. Esmée looked so serene, her golden orange wings draped around her body like a comforter. There wasn't a scratch on her; she'd been well protected by her companions. As she breathed, her two antennae fluttered with the rise and fall of her head as it rested upon her chest. To Lisette, who had begun to think she'd never see her again, being able to stand in front of

Esmée was the renewal of all her hopes.

At that moment, another familiar face greeted Pica and Audrey at the door to the badger's living room. Marmot had arrived and snuck in so as not to disturb the others. Turning around, Pica opened his mouth to greet the groundhog; but Marmot simply raised one finger to his lips, then pointed to Lisette. Pica understood and smiled his greeting in silence.

Lisette reached out one hand to touch Esmée's forehead. When her fingers caressed her best friend's face, Lisette began weeping. Struggling through her tears, she whispered, "Esmée."

All eyes were on the two friends. Boswell and Fourmi stood beside the woodstove. Pica and Audrey waited near the entrance of the living room, close to Marmot. Even the members of the Garden Ant Hotline stood by, their eyes glued to the two butterflies.

Lisette continued to stroke Esmée's forehead, whispering once more, "Esmée, it's me. Lisette."

At the sound of Lisette's voice, and at the mention of her name, Esmée began to stir. Opening her eyes, she found herself looking into the face of her best friend. They hadn't spent a day apart since their BB-Day, and the last five days were enough to make them never want to do so again.

"Lisette… you came. You're here. At last, you're here."

Esmée sat up and wrapped her arms around Lisette, their tears mixing in streams of relief and joy. Nearby, the ever-tender Pica added his own blubbering tears to those of the two butterflies. Most surprisingly, perhaps, was the unabashed sobbing coming from Boswell Badger. Nudging Audrey, and speaking loud enough for the badger to hear, Marmot joked, "I didn't even know badgers *had* tears."

"I heard that," the grumpy badger complained,

then quickly changed the subject. "I know it's late or early, however you want to look at it; but who will join me in the lounge for a late-night snack? I'm sure Esmée and Lisette have some catching-up to do."

"Count me in," Marmot said, without hesitation.

"Me, too," Hugo called, waking up at the mention of food. The fireplace nap had done him good; it was time to see what eating something might do for him.

"*Myrtilles, myrtilles*?" Pica asked, hoping the badger had some blueberries left.

"Of course, my good man. Follow me."

Boswell led Marmot, Hugo, Pica, Audrey and Fourmi into the lounge, leaving Esmée alone with Lisette. The room was now silent, except for the crackling of embers in the woodstove. Lisette at last began to feel less like she was living in a strange dream and more like things ought to be; she was with her best friend, and this felt as natural as it had always been.

"I know about Pierre," Lisette began. "I've heard about his bravery. *Monsieur* Badger told me. I'm so sorry, Esmée."

"He was wonderful, Lisette. He showed me Paris. He showed me so very much. So many beautiful things. I thought I'd never want to leave; I knew I'd never want to leave *him*. But now… everything is just… emptiness. This morning, he was my future; now, there is only the past; and the memories are too painful to hold near."

Lisette glanced at the rose; its bloom, still red; its petals, still firm. Esmée noticed Lisette looking at it and longed to tell her so much.

"Marmot brought it back from the island where Pierre…" Esmée couldn't say it. Not yet.

"It's beautiful. It reminds me," Lisette said, becoming thoughtful, "It reminds me of the sculpture. The one in the Louvre your mother used to tell us about. Do you remember what she said?"

"Yes," Esmée replied. "I remember every word. She said that the young Cupid gave the butterfly the gift of a rose. I always dreamed of seeing it. I thought it was so romantic."

"Do you remember what the sculpture *means*, though?"

Esmée was puzzled. She thought the sculpture was a symbol of love. Cupid was the Greek god of love, after all. Why would Lisette question her about this, when it had been such a big part of both their childhoods? Of course, she knew what the sculpture was all about.

"It's about love," Esmée said, with uncertainty starting to grow.

"No, Esmée. It wasn't about love. Not *just* about love, anyway. Think. Remember why she told us about the sculpture in the first place." Lisette paused a moment. "She told us as a warning."

"A warning…"

All of a sudden, Esmée remembered. She *had* forgotten, Lisette was right. She'd always focused on the kindness the sculpture showed; the young Cupid giving a rose to the butterfly as a gift. But that wasn't the whole story.

Lisette explained, refreshing her friend's memory as she did.

"The butterfly was drawn to the beauty of the flower; and when she drew too near, Cupid captured her. He's holding the butterfly by the wings. Don't you remember?"

"Yes, but…" Esmée was confused.

"The *rose* symbolizes love. But, once the butterfly is lured by the rose and captured by Cupid, she can't break free. Instead of joy, all she feels are the *pains* of love. That's why your mother told us the story, to warn us not to be too easily tempted by the beauty of flowers; not to let ourselves be captured or caged; and that even love has its pains. Even love has its thorns."

"Caged…" Esmée repeated. "Tempted by the beauty of flowers and caged… but… that's what happened," she said, looking up at Lisette.

"That's what happened to *me*. I saw the bouquet of flowers on the train. The young woman was holding them. When I got on to drink from them, the doors closed. I was trapped… caged… Oh Lisette, and *now* look. All because… I forgot. *All* of it, because I forgot."

Esmée hung her head and started to weep without restraint. This time, her tears were tears of regret. She felt as if everything bad that had happened was her fault. Lisette held Esmée close, comforting her as best she could.

"It was *never* about love or butterflies or roses, then." Esmée said, her sorrow now mixed with the bitterness of anger. "It wasn't just a beautiful statue. It was a warning and I missed it because of my stupid, romantic heart. I've been a fool and now Pierre is…"

"It was *always* about love." Lisette stopped her mid-sentence. "Everything beautiful is *always* about love; that includes your romantic heart, sweet friend. But now I see… it also includes my *practical* heart. There's a reason we're best friends… we'd be a wreck without each other. You with your squishy heart and me with my stony one. We were made for each other." Lisette smiled, comforting Esmée with her eyes.

"But you're still forgetting," Lisette went on. "The butterfly triumphs in the end. Don't you remember how? How does the butterfly break free and return to its friends?"

Lisette watched her friend's face closely, awaiting the realization. She then revealed the answer, "The captive butterfly is *set* free… by the bees."

"By the bees… the bees who stung Cupid until he let go of the butterfly's wings," Esmée said, finally recalling the whole story. "The honeybees," she continued, "freed the butterfly and helped it find its way home again."

Lisette was relieved, "You *do* remember!"

"*The river will always lead you home again,* she said."

"Who said that?" It was Lisette's turn to be confused.

"The honeybee." Esmée said, still marveling at the fact.

"And she was right," Marmot interjected, walking back into the living room from the lounge.

"She was right," he said again, "You followed the river and it led you back to your friends. You now have your friends, dear one; so, you're home." Marmot leaned over and kissed Esmée on the tip of her wing.

"And I must be going home, too. I've done all I can and neglected my *server room* for too long. If I don't get back soon, Megalina will steal my job! So, I must say farewell, sweet Esmée, and may happiness be yours again. I *know* that it will be one day."

Turning to Lisette, Marmot said, "It was a pleasure to meet you, *mademoiselle.* I see now that you are the truest of friends."

Marmot smiled, then slowly crossed the room to say his goodbyes to the others. He was in no hurry to take leave of them. His heart was heavy and the road before him was long.

Bowing low before Queen Fourmi of the Garden Ants, he said, "Your majesty, thank you for your healing care. I hope that the healing you gave to me and my fellow groundhogs will bind up the ancient wounds between our peoples. I gave you my promise long ago, and I renew it now. I will always honor our friendship and do all I can to bring Garden Ants and Groundhogs together."

"I'm confident those wounds will soon be

forgotten," the queen replied, lowering her eyes with gracious respect for the groundhog.

Looking up at the badger and taking Boswell's hand in his, Marmot smacked him on the shoulder with his other paw.

"I won't tell a soul," Marmot laughed. "Your reputation as a certified grump is safe with me, old friend."

That reputation may have been crumbling right there in front of everyone's eyes, for Boswell Badger – the biggest and most ill-tempered badger in Paris – broke down in tears yet again and hugged Marmot for far longer than Marmot was comfortable being hugged by a badger. There was a lot of that sort of thing going around today.

Pica didn't wait for Marmot to reach him, but met Marmot halfway, throwing his wings around the groundhog's neck and weeping like a baby. Marmot thought back to the time he first met Pica -- when the groundhog dropped back in line just to ask Audrey what was up with her friend's repetitive manner of speaking. He had to admit, at that time, he thought Pica was a bit odd. Truth be told, he still did; but Marmot saw the kindhearted bird behind the repetitions and was proud to be his friend.

"Steady on, Pica," Marmot joked, stepping back from the magpie's hug.

"*Nous serons toujours amis. Nous serons...*" Pica began, before being interrupted by Marmot.

"You're right, my friend," the groundhog said, rubbing the magpie's shoulder, "Some things don't need repeating; they're true enough the first time."

Marmot took a deep breath, then walked over to the rocking chair where Audrey waited atop the armrest. The two natural leaders looked at each other. They'd both succeeded in their missions: Audrey to find Esmée, and Marmot to help her do so. They felt admiration, one for the other; and they knew neither of them could have succeeded without the other's help.

"Shouldn't you be somewhere reading a book or something?" Marmot said, with a wink.

"There may be more to life than just books," Audrey replied, "But books are *much* safer."

She flew over and landed on Marmot's shoulder. Resting her head against his face, she fluttered her wings, tickling Marmot's cheek.

"A butterfly kiss," she said, "for Marmot the Magnificent."

"Audrey the Adventurer... I will never forget you."

The butterfly sighed, then fluttered back to the fireplace to be alone for a while. Audrey hated goodbyes -- saying goodbye to Marmot, most of all.

Marmot wiped his eyes with the back of his paws, then turned and faced Hugo.

"Are you ready, my friend?"

"I am," the flower-sketching, nature-loving groundhog said, more than ready to cross the bridge and go home to his beloved *JdT* again.

Boswell Badger walked over to Hugo and stood right in front of the groundhog. Despite everything Hugo had faced that day, the badger still intimidated him. Immediately, Hugo's face turned red and his ears felt warm. He was terrified of Boswell.

"May I have the honor," Boswell began, "of shaking the hand of *The Hero of the Battle of the Pont de Grenelle?*"

Hugo's mouth dropped open. Boswell had never spoken to him that way before. In fact, he rarely spoke to Hugo without shouting. Indeed, this *was* a day of firsts. A wave of courage broke over the groundhog.

"If it means I may have the honor of shaking the hand of the most well-respected badger in all of Paris, I'd be delighted."

Boswell took Hugo by the hand, then drew him in for a very big and very alarming badger hug. When Hugo pulled himself back from the embrace, his eyes were as big as dinner plates and all color had drained from his face. He stood there like a block of wood.

"Then we'll be off," Marmot said, taking Hugo by the arm and uprooting him from the floor.

He could see that Hugo was in shock. Guiding him out of the tunnel (so he wouldn't get lost) and up to ground level, Marmot made sure his friend got home safely – laughing all the way at how red-faced Hugo had been when the badger was talking to him; and how pale-faced he became when Boswell hugged him.

"Really, old boy, Boswell's just a big softy. And I'd say with absolute certainty that he thinks very highly of you now."

Hugo agreed; and there was no finer feeling in all the world.

As soon as the groundhogs had left, Boswell suggested that everyone try to get some sleep. It was well past midnight. Sleep had been hard to come by lately; and not nearly as refreshing as it should have been. It was time everyone tried again.

Pica took up his place by the woodstove. The butterflies all nestled down atop the same cushion. Lisette sat next to Esmée, trying to console her with her presence. As soon as they'd snuggled into their comfy spots, most everyone fell fast asleep. Esmée, however, found it impossible to quiet her mind. She simply sat on the cushion with her arms around her knees. Without sleep, the few remaining hours of the night would be endless.

Boswell walked Queen Fourmi to the entrance to his den. Bidding the garden ants farewell and thanking them for their service as members of the hotline between Victor's *server room* and his own home, Boswell paused to speak with the queen.

"Thank you for all of your help, Your Majesty. Your assistance with fast communication between here and Victor's was essential; but your healing of the wounded was valuable beyond measure."

"I'm glad that we were able to help," the queen replied. "Before going home, I will drop in on Victor. Despite the late hour, I have a job for him to consider. Until next time, my friend."

The queen bowed in her usual way, then turned and walked off toward the Eiffel Tower and Victor's *server room.* Boswell waited until she was out of sight (which was really only a few feet away), then returned to the warmth of his den and went to bed for the night.

The city was silent, and the lights of the tower were cold. Word of Pierre's sacrifice had spread throughout the animal world. In the hush of the early hours, all Paris seemed to hold vigil for the life of one butterfly. Esmée still sat upright, her eyelids heavy with fatigue. Her last thought, before finally drifting off to sleep, was how much she wanted to put this horrible day behind her. She hoped tomorrow would at least bring the sunshine. Everyone could use a hopeful sky. For now, all was darkness.

CHAPTER THIRTY-FOUR

Hugo *du Trocadéro*, O.D.U.

The next day was Sunday, and, from the first glow of daybreak over the white limestone landscape of the city, it looked as if the day might live up to its name. The sky was cloudless and blue; and even the murky waters of the Seine wore sparkles of sunlight like a spray of diamonds.

Across the river from the Eiffel Tower, the *Jardins du Trocadéro* were alive with pleasant activity. Birds were singing in the trees, while honeybees moved from flower to flower gathering the first nectar of the day.

Every squirrel seemed to be out and about, already busy -- not with the day's work of gathering nuts and berries -- but rather, busy with a whole lot of chatting.

There were groups of squirrels gathered around elegant statues. There were groups of squirrels gathered near glorious fountains. In fact, everywhere one looked, groups of squirrels could be seen hanging about; and they were all talking with one another about the events of the previous day.

"He was magnificent," some said.

"Fearless! Not the least bit concerned with his own safety," others remarked.

"Leapt right onto its wicked ol' back," many exclaimed. "Right on its back, I tell ya! Then went for a ride! Never heard anything like it!"

Word was spreading like gossip, beginning with

the squirrels who had "been honored to serve beside him," all the way to the squirrels who had not taken part in the Battle of the Pont de Grenelle. Hugo, the *network manager* of the *JdT server room*, was being heralded as a hero.

Even Devereux Délabré, Esq. – the **E**xceptional **Sq**uirrel who was, regrettably, too old to take part in the previous day's events – was beginning to think that the squirrels of the *JdT* had someone *more* exceptional among them than even himself.

Beneath it all, still sleeping-off the aches and pains of the previous day, Hugo lay in bed in his underground apartment. Walking home from the badger's den the previous night, he commented to Marmot that the one thing he'd like to do that next day would be to take his sketchpad and find a new tree or flower to draw. He hoped the weather would be nice so that he could sit in the sun and let the day soothe his injuries. Hero or no, Hugo was happiest with a pencil in his hand and the sun on his face.

While he was still asleep, a knock came on his apartment door. Maybe he dreamed it. Surely, it was *much* too early for visitors. Rolling over and pulling the covers over his head, Hugo went back to sleep. Then it came again. This time, he was disappointedly certain he had *not* dreamt it.

"Who could it be, at this hour?" he huffed, checking the clock on his bedside table.

Knock! Knock! Knock! Knock! Knock!

"Pfft… this is intolerable," Hugo complained, as he got out of bed and headed for the front door, ready to give whomever he found there an earful.

Swinging the door open with annoyance, Hugo was greeted by three squirrels. He immediately recognized them as Montgomery Bazillac (or Baz, to his friends), Butternut, and Sunflower; all of whom had led a squad of squirrels the previous day. Since they had all served in the Great Event (as it would come to be called), Hugo was less inclined to "give them an earful" and more willing to hear them out.

Calming his irritation, he put on his "best squirrel" behavior, and forced a smile to his lips through somewhat clenched teeth.

"Good morning. Aren't we up early?" he said, still smiling; still clenching his teeth. "Won't you come in?"

Sunflower spoke-up, all business, as usual.

"Thank you, no," she said. "We're here to deliver an invitation."

"An invitation?" Hugo rubbed the sleep from his eyes. "To what?"

Sunflower cast a sideways glance at her companions, then answered with a smile.

"Be at the Cloven Oak Tree in one hour and you will find out."

With that, the three messenger squirrels turned and abruptly left. Hugo was left still holding the doorknob, having expected them to come in for breakfast or at least tea. This was all very mysterious and out of the ordinary. Squirrels are many things, but mysterious is not usually one of them.

"The Cloven Oak Tree," Hugo said to himself. "That's Devereux's place. What could he want with me? Oh… I'm in *no* mood for surprises today."

Then he was sure he'd figured it out, "An account of the Battle of the Pont de Grenelle, of course. But couldn't he wait until a more reasonable hour? Who does he think he is, the king? But if I'm up, I'm up, and I might as well go."

Hugo returned to his bedroom long enough to make his bed. He then ate an all-too-speedy breakfast, brushed his teeth, combed his hair, and prepared to meet with the Exceptional Squirrel himself. It all felt very much like a summons; but Hugo revered the old squirrel as much as everyone else in the *JdT* did, so he really didn't mind too much. He was just a little out of sorts for having been awakened prematurely.

Devereux Délabré, Esq. lived in the hollow of an ancient oak that had been struck by lightning at some point in its long history. The experience had left a wide gash in the trunk of the mighty tree, cleaving it in two. The gash was just deep enough for a small animal to make a very comfortable home inside. Since Devereux's limb-climbing days were behind him, the "ground level" accommodations made an excellent apartment for the venerable old squirrel.

Devereux spent most of his day sitting outside the front door of his oaken home, chatting with the younger squirrels. Older than Boswell Badger by far, Devereux was a living legend; and everyone knew it, except the humble Devereux.

On this particular day, when Hugo arrived at the Cloven Oak, the wise, old squirrel was outside in his usual place; but it wasn't for the purpose of chatting with the younger squirrels. He was there for another reason altogether.

Seeing Hugo approach, Devereux struggled to his feet, helped by a few of the several hundred squirrels who surrounded him. In fact, when Hugo reached the top of the hill and saw the vast crowd of squirrels, he stopped dead in his tracks. He couldn't imagine what might be going on.

"Here he is!"

The cry went up from among the throng and was immediately greeted with loud and excited cheering and applause.

Hugo stood dumbfounded, his eyes wide and brows wrinkled in cautious suspicion. "What on *earth* is going on around here," he thought. He would have turned right around and gone back home to bed, if it were not for the presence of Devereux. Without him there, Hugo would have been quick to believe the whole thing was just a practical joke put on by the mischievous *JdT* squirrels.

"Please, come closer," the old squirrel said, with a slight motion of his right paw.

Hugo walked up the hill and stood beneath the Cloven Oak in front of Devereux, who was leaning heavy on his cane.

"Thank you, my friend," the squirrel said, always gracious and kind.

"What can I do for you, sir?" Hugo asked, with respect.

"You've already done it," Devereux said, shifting his weight (he was not used to standing for any length of time). "I would be grateful to rest these old bones of mine, though."

"Of course," Hugo replied, as he helped the aged squirrel into his chair.

"Thank you. I beg your pardon for the early hour. I wanted to catch everyone before they began their daily rounds through the gardens. Forgive me for awakening you."

"Not at all," Hugo said, with a surprising degree of forgiveness for having been roused from his sleep.

"I'm sure you're wondering why I've asked you to come see me this morning."

"I thought perhaps you wanted an account of the battle yesterday. I'm happy to give you a full report."

"No, my good groundhog, I have already received a full report and *that* is the reason why I wanted to see you."

Hugo didn't quite follow. Devereux went on to clarify.

"I have heard many things about the great battle; stories about our enemy's wrath, and tales of bravery, too.

Mostly, I have heard about one warrior in particular who demonstrated the heart of a lion… in the body of a most unlikely groundhog. You, my friend."

"We *all* did our duty," Hugo was truly modest; a simple artist and devoted nature-lover at heart.

"Yes, that I know. And all did their duty under the leadership and inspiration of their captain. Without you, there would have been no victory. You led *all* to victory. For that reason, the squirrels of the *JdT* have voted unanimously to bestow upon you an honor befitting your noble heart and brave deeds."

One of the squirrels standing at his side handed Devereux a small box. Opening the lid, the old squirrel pulled out a red ribbon upon which hung what appeared to be the J-shaped, wooden handle of an old umbrella. Devereux held the ribbon in both hands, and asked Hugo to approach. Placing the ribbon around Hugo's neck, Devereux spoke these words with great formality.

"For your mighty deeds at the Battle of the Pont de Grenelle where you wielded your fierce umbrella and defeated the vile leader of the crows, and by unanimous acclamation, I hereby confer upon you the Order of the Dread Umbrella. All hail, Hugo du Trocadéro, O.D.U."

Hugo received the ribbon around his neck, then stood up straight, only to be greeted by the sight of leaping squirrels turning somersaults in the air. The *Jardins* had erupted into one, big, jubilant party — everyone celebrating the groundhog who had led them so valiantly into battle and on to victory. Hugo was speechless.

"We know the desires of your heart, dear friend," Devereux spoke softly to the stunned groundhog. "We know you have no wish to be honored, only to be left in quiet contemplation with pencil in hand. This honor was given more for our sake than for yours. We thank you for letting us celebrate you this day."

The wise, old squirrel turned to address the crowd gathered around him.

"One last cheer for our hero! Hip hip…"

"HOORAY!"

"Hip hip…"

"HOORAY!!"

"Hip hip…"

"HUGO!!!"

The squirrels all began scurrying away to their favorite trees and berry bushes, each one singing and dancing along the way. Devereux stood, leaning on his walking stick, and bowed low to the groundhog. He then shuffled off to his home inside the Cloven Oak.

Hugo du Trocadéro, O.D.U. stood there holding his award in his paw, looking at it with wide wonder. In a matter of just a few days, he'd gone from being certain that Boswell Badger "thought very little of him" to receiving the Order of the Dread Umbrella.

He was glad for the award; not so much because of the honor the squirrels had shown him, but because, on that ribbon the handle of the umbrella he had used to fight off the wicked crow now hung. It would forever be a reminder to him of that fateful day: the day upon which Hugo the groundhog learned something about himself. And, like most people in such situations, he was surprised by what he had learned. Hugo learned he was much more than what others had thought he was; and that felt pretty good.

Across the river in the *CM-TE server room,* Victor was busy drafting a message. Early that morning, long before sunrise, Queen Fourmi of the Garden Ants had stopped in on her way home from Boswell's den. She had a job offer for him, a task of great importance. The events of the day, and the emotion of that evening, made it difficult for the groundhog to calm his thoughts; so, when the knock came on his door, he was still very much awake.

Opening the door, he was surprised to find the queen asking for a moment of his time. Inviting her in, the two sat in Victor's living room; and the queen got right to the point, as was her way.

"The time has come," she said, "to heal the old wounds between Groundhogs and Garden Ants; wounds dating back to well before our own memories began. I have tried to build a friendship with Hugo, Marmot and yourself, to this end. We have proven that it can be done; friendship *is* possible."

"I can speak for the others, my lady, when I say that it has been an honor being your friend and enjoying the friendship of all of your fellow garden ants."

"I feel the same. Prejudice and hatred grow out of fear, and fear takes root where we don't understand one another. These things are always destructive and should never be allowed to stand. But when they live longer than the memory of how they began, they take on a life of their own. Your friends and my garden ants have ignored such ancient foolishness; and by getting to know each other all fear has slipped away. So, it is time."

The queen moved from her seat across from Victor and sat beside him.

"Will you help me spread the word? Will you use your network, as I will use mine, to communicate only that which will promote understanding and put an end to prejudice and hatred? I asked the same of Marmot and Hugo, and they have agreed. If you lend your voice to the cause, it will only strengthen it and guarantee our success."

Victor stood, turned, then dropped to one knee in front of the ant queen.

"My lady, since I was not able to fight in the Battle of the Pont de Grenelle, I will gladly fight alongside you and my friends for this worthy cause."

"Thank you, noble groundhog. Then my efforts have not been wasted. I knew that you, Hugo and Marmot were the ones best suited to help bring this about. The *network manager* of the most influential and important *server room* on the Boulogne *network*; the widely respected, sensitive and thoughtful artist, scientist and hero; and Marmot, the clever groundhog-of-action. And so, I will take no more of your time."

Standing, the queen walked over to the front door, then stopped to address Victor once again.

"It has been a long and painful day. Tomorrow, the sun will shine. Goodnight, my friend."

"Goodnight, my lady."

Victor closed the door behind her, then went to his desk to draft the message that would herald the dawn of a new day for garden ants and groundhogs alike.

"**Priority 2:** Important
From: Victor, *CM-TE Server Room*
To: All Recipients

Alert: The Groundhogs of the Bois de Boulogne would like to thank Queen Fourmi and her army of garden ants for their essential work in nursing back to health all those injured in the Battle of the Pont de Grenelle. The Garden Ants of France join the squirrels of the *JdT* and the illustrious Boswell Badger on the list of our most valued allies and friends. Here's to the promise of a new tomorrow."

Placing the message in a letterbox on the *server room* wall, Victor paused a moment before blowing out the candle on his desk. This was the first time in nearly a week that no green labels were showing on the mailboxes; there were no new messages waiting to be read. All of

Paris was silent and still. Victor sighed with relief.

His role was clear to him now: to use the *internet* to spread only what was good, true and beautiful; to heal all that was broken. Though he had not seen battle, he had witnessed its effects on his friends; and he never wanted to see them suffer again. He was sure that friendship between all the animals of Paris would mean an end to war, an end to unnecessary suffering.

This first message of healing and friendship between groundhogs and garden ants was a simple one: just a thank you note. But often, healing and friendship, happiness and peace depend upon small things like a thank you. Victor was wise enough to know that life is made up of a billion little things such as this; and great change would begin with this one little message. Leaving the *server room,* he pulled the door closed behind him and headed to bed. His work was done, and it had also only just begun.

CHAPTER THIRTY-FIVE

A Journey Upriver

The next morning, while Hugo was being awarded the Order of the Dread Umbrella across the river, everyone who had spent the night in Boswell's den was just waking up. The first one awake was Audrey, of course. Though her antenna still ached, she was feeling much better than she had the previous night.

Hoping to find a scrap of newspaper or old discarded sermon to read, she flew up the tunnel and outside into the *Champ de Mars* in search of breakfast and the news of the day. What she found was a clear blue sky and the gradual warmth of a rising sun. It was going to be a delightful day.

Landing among the flowers of a nearby azalea bush, Audrey sipped a slow, serene *petit déjeuner* while surveying the surrounding area for a trash can. A few feet away, the can which Victor had employed in waking Boswell up a few days earlier sat overflowing with newspapers. Audrey was in luck! She now knew exactly how she'd be spending her day. A little breakfast, followed by warming her face in the morning sun, and finally, hours of uninterrupted reading – there was no more perfect agenda, in Audrey's opinion.

Pica was the next one up, and he was very eager to be aboveground and outside beneath the limitless sky. He'd had quite enough of holes, dens, tunnels, and baby stroller canopies to last a lifetime. His first priority was also breakfast. Wild berry bushes were easy to find, for a seasoned gatherer such as Pica. All he had to do was take to the air.

A short flight over the garden beds of the *Champ de Mars* led him to an assortment of berry bushes from which to choose. Pica picked, gulped and swallowed until half a bush was bare. His breakfasts were always much faster and less serene than Audrey's. Pica was more interested in the quantity and speed of his meals than he was in observing any formal table manners. Once he'd eaten his fill of blackberries, he turned his attention to his second priority: dessert.

Pica belonged to a growing group of animals and, indeed humans, who believe dessert should not be limited to dinner alone. Every meal was accompanied by a drink; so, every meal should also be accompanied by a dessert. It just made sense.

It took Pica no time at all to find a chestnut tree heavy with nuts, which would do just fine for his dessert. The magpie plucked chestnuts from the tree like the greediest squirrel, storing them away in his *belly* for the winter. Full and satisfied, he decided to stretch his wings a bit and fly over to the river for a long drink.

The morning air was clean and sweet, and the gentlest breeze rustled the leaves on the trees. Pica breathed deeply and let the new day fill his heart with new hope. Flying high above the *Champ de Mars,* Pica approached the Eiffel Tower. It was too early for tourists, so the bandaged magpie landed on the railing encircling the first-floor platform without any concern for being seen. From his perch, he could look downriver as far as the Island of Swans and, beyond that, to the *Île du Papillon.*

He sat there a moment, remembering the events of the previous day. The clouds of exhaustion had cleared, and in their place, Pica was left alone with sadness. He had not really known Pierre, but Esmée's heartbreak wore heavy on her friends -- the sensitive Pica most of all. Sitting there deep in thought, Pica was sure that the best thing for Esmée to do today would be to stay busy. It was not good for her to sit idle and alone in sadness. They needed an activity for the day, something to occupy her mind. What they needed, he was sure, was a mini adventure.

Returning from his drink in the Seine, Pica found Audrey sitting in the sunshine reading a scrap of *Le Journal*. She was occupied in her favorite way, perfectly content and at peace… until Pica arrived.

"Audrey! Audrey!"

She remained absorbed in her reading and made no answer. Perhaps he would give up and go away.

"Audrey! Audrey! Audrey! Aud…"

"Yes, Pica!" she interrupted, rather than being forced to listen to her name repeated over and over again. "What is it?!"

Audrey's eyes never left her newspaper. She was desperately holding on to her threadbare hope of enjoying a day of *uninterrupted* reading. Her ears were all Pica's, but her eyes and most of her brain belonged entirely to *Le Journal*.

"J'ai une idée! J'ai une idée!"

Without looking up from her reading, and with a growing degree of annoyance, Audrey said, "Like I asked… What. *Is*. It?"

"Nous avons besoin d'une aventure! No..von…soin…d'une aventure!"

Audrey was pretty sure Pica was so excited that he actually found a way to talk *overtop* of himself. His repetition came out sounding like oatmeal being squished through a magpie's toes. Putting her newspaper down and sighing loud enough for Pica to understand he was greatly annoying her, Audrey looked him in the eye.

"An adventure? You think we need an adventure? Didn't we just *have* an adventure? Didn't we just barely *survive* that adventure? Wasn't that adventure enough for quite some time? Don't tell me you've become some sort of adrenaline junkie or something. That just leads to burnout, my friend," she said, returning to her newspaper. "Burnout, I tell you."

Pica saw that he was making no progress with Audrey; she was too busy with her reading and determined to stay at it all day. He decided to take his case to a higher authority than even Audrey Loriot. Flying back toward the badger's den, Pica saw Boswell emerging from the entrance.

Boswell was up much earlier than usual; and that always meant a much grumpier than usual Boswell. But, if anyone could come up with a good "adventure" to keep Esmée occupied, it would be the wise and persuasive badger. Pica flew right up to Boswell and landed on the ground in front of him.

"What is it, Pica?" He growled; indeed, much grumpier than usual.

"Esmée, Esmée."

"She's still sleeping, thankfully. What about her?"

"*Aventure! Aventure!*"

"An *adventure*? For Esmée? What on earth for? The poor girl needs her rest. Now, leave me in peace."

"*Aventure pour* Esmée! *Pour* Esmée! *Une distraction, une distraction!*"

The badger stopped short -- in mid-stretch, his arms held high above his head. The magpie might just be onto something.

"A distraction, you say. An adventure to distract her… hmm, you never cease to amaze me, young sir. And I may have *just* the thing for her. Go collect the bookworm, then both of you join me downstairs."

Pica flew back to where Audrey had been *trying* to enjoy her morning *alone*. Had she flown across the river and joined Hugo – who had already received his award and was now beginning a day of drawing -- she would have had much better luck.

"Yes. Pica." She made no attempt to hide her irritation, greeting him with less of a question and more of a warning.

"Boswell. Boswell. *Maintenant, maintenant!*"

"Seriously?" It was clear that the badger was now in on it, too. "Fine! Ugh! I'll never have a moment of peace in this city. Where does one go to read in Paris?!"

With begrudging reluctance, Audrey followed Pica back to the badger's den; down the entrance; through the short tunnel; and into his living room. There, they found Boswell in his favorite rocking chair speaking with a groggy Lisette, while Esmée lay sleeping on her cushion.

"Sorry to pull you away, Audrey," the badger said, noticing their arrival and her obvious annoyance. "Pica had a fine idea and I wanted to discuss it with everyone. Come in."

Audrey gave Pica a look dripping with sarcasm, as if to say, "Thanks a lot." The magpie just hopped up and down, shrugging his shoulders. Boswell began his explanation.

"Lisette and I were just talking about it, and we're both in agreement. Pica is absolutely right; what Esmée needs right now is activity, or else she'll just stew in her own sorrow. When Pica told me his idea, something Esmée said to me popped back into my mind. Before she and Pierre left to search for Marmot downriver, she made me a promise. I think we could put that promise to good use for us now. Esmée will certainly keep her word, and by keeping it, we will be able to take her mind off her sorrows."

Audrey looked at Lisette, who nodded with assurance. Pica was just excited that the grumpy old badger liked his idea.

Boswell got up and walked over to the cushion where Esmée lay sleeping.

"*Mademoiselle… mademoiselle…*"

Esmée stirred, then slowly opened her eyes. When she saw that everyone was standing there looking at her, she wrapped her wings around herself and sat up in alarm.

"Is everything alright, *monsieur* Badger?"

"*Oui, mademoiselle,* everything is as it was last night; though, I daresay, somewhat better for the sleep."

"What can I do for you, *monsieur*?" Esmée blinked the bleariness from her eyes.

"I wanted to ask a favor of you, my dear," he said, with as much gentleness as a badger could muster -- and perhaps just a bit more. "You made me a promise sometime back. Do you remember?"

"A promise, *monsieur*?"

"Yes. You promised that you would take me to meet the bees of Notre-Dame."

"*Oui, monsieur, je me souviens.* I remember."

"Will you take me today?"

"Today?"

The thought was almost too much for Esmée to consider. The forgetfulness of sleep had worn off, and dark emptiness was returning to her heart. She didn't feel like doing anything at all; she wanted only to sleep and forget.

"Yes, little one, today. The sky is blue, the sun is shining, and your friends need something to do."

Audrey shot a glance at the badger. *She* didn't "need something to do." She *had* something to do; but she was not being allowed to *do it*.

Esmée pulled her wings tightly around her shoulders. The desire to go back to sleep and let her mind drift off into forgetfulness ached in her heart. She felt like crying; but she also loved the old badger. He was like a curmudgeonly old grandfather, and she knew he only wanted to help. What else could she do?

"*Oui, monsieur,*" she struggled to reply, "I will take you today, if you like."

"Thank you, dear one. I know we will *all* be better off for it."

Audrey was still annoyed. She was tempted just to say, "Have a nice adventure! I'll be here *reading* all day," but her better nature prevailed. She huffed one last time, then readjusted her expectations *and* her plans for the day. She'd go along with everyone else, for Esmée's sake.

"We will leave in fifteen minutes," Boswell decreed, eager to be underway just in case Esmée's resolve started to weaken. "Have some breakfast, while Pica and I ready some supplies of berries and nectar."

As soon as he heard "berries," Pica got right to work. They mustn't forget the necessities. An adventure, no matter how small, was serious business -- as were berries. The two began packing a small magpie-sized backpack.

While Pica and Boswell worked, Lisette and Audrey tried to encourage Esmée to eat a little breakfast. Try as they might, one or two tiny sips were all Esmée could force down. Her friends may have been able to distract her thoughts for a while, but her heart never stopped feeling Pierre's absence -- and the stomach always follows heart.

It was barely eight o'clock in the morning, and the trip upriver to the *Île de la Cité* and Notre-Dame would take them only about an hour or two, depending upon how fast Boswell felt like walking. Pica and the butterflies could cover the mile and a half distance in a matter of minutes, but the badger moved considerably slower. With any luck, they'd arrive in the cathedral's rose garden around eleven o'clock.

Lisette was worried about her best friend. Esmée was not at all herself. She showed no interest in anything; she'd lost the spark that once fired her sweet personality. If she was going back to Notre-Dame, it was only to keep her promise to the badger. Everything she saw around her was a reminder of what she'd lost; of whom she'd lost. The *Champ de Mars* wasn't any more painful a reminder than anywhere else in the city; for, she carried the memory of each place she and Pierre had seen, as well as heartbreak for the places they'd never be able to see together. Everything was pain.

Taking her friend aside, Lisette caressed Esmée's face, "Are you sure you're up for this?"

"I have a promise to keep," Esmée said, without emotion.

"Yes, but if you can't do it, just say the word. I'll stay here with you, and they can go on by themselves."

"It doesn't matter," Esmée sighed.

Her response frightened Lisette.

"I'll be with you. All the way," Lisette assured her; but Esmée appeared not to have heard her at all.

Lisette leaned over and hugged Esmée, with deep concern in her heart. She then caught Boswell's eye and gave a nod to indicate they were ready.

Even though Esmée was the only one in the company to have actually visited Notre-Dame, she didn't know the way. She and Pierre had taken a detour to the Arc de Triomphe then traveled by boat as far as the Eiffel Tower. A straight line is always easier to remember than a twisty one.

Luckily, even though he'd never met the *Ignifuge* bees before, Boswell knew the way to Notre-Dame. The badger took up the lead position, guiding them out of the *Champ de Mars,* under the Eiffel Tower, and down toward the river.

"Will we follow the river all the way there?" Audrey asked, having had some experience with such methods of navigation.

"We'll do better than that," the badger replied. "We won't just follow the river -- we shall ride it. It's safer and faster, at least for a badger. That's why we brought berries and nectar with us. We'll be far from both shores."

Before leaving the area near the medieval-looking Chimney of the Eiffel Tower, Boswell stopped the group.

"Stay here a moment," he instructed, then began walking around in wide, wandering circles. Between the street-side walkway and the tower, in among the grass and bushes, Boswell was searching for *something* with great care. He didn't seem to remember precisely where *whatever-it-was* had last been seen; but he covered the area thoroughly and soon found success.

"Ah ha! Here it is. Come along, now. Follow me."

Ducking behind a decorative rock formation partially hidden by forsythia bushes, Boswell removed a metal grate, then led the group down a tight hole in the ground. This was completely unlike the groundhog or even the badger tunnels they'd already experienced.

The hole in which they now found themselves was perfectly round; and the walls, floor and ceiling formed a hard, circular, metal enclosure. The tunnel was not muddy like the groundhog tunnels would be this close to the river. That was a plus. But the floor sloped so steeply toward the river, that Pica reckoned he could simply sit down, give himself a good shove, and slide all the way downhill.

"What *is* this we're in?" Lisette asked, having only been inside the badger's underground den before.

"It's a drainage pipe for rainwater. It will carry us beneath the sidewalk and the road, and then deposit us next to the boat docks on the river. To my knowledge, only I ever use it. I don't think even Victor knows about its existence."

"Is it safe?" Lisette was somewhat alarmed. Clearly, she would not have done well inside the tunnels of the Boulogne *network.*

"For a badger, a magpie and three butterflies, yes. For anyone bigger than me, no, it would *not* be safe."

Lisette couldn't imagine anyone bigger than Boswell Badger.

"Almost there. Watch your step, Pica. The floor gets slippery sometimes."

The moment Boswell said that, the magpie – who had been hopping along behind the three fluttering butterflies – lost his footing on the slick floor of the drainage pipe. Both feet went out from under his body, and he landed hard on his rear-end.

Since the pipe was slanted at such an angle, Pica began to slide forward, building speed as he went and scooping-up all three butterflies along the way. Slamming hard into the back end of the badger, Pica came to a very sudden and uncomfortable stop. It was a five-car pile-up, Pica style. Between the magpie's front end and the badger's rear-end, three butterflies with crumpled antennae and wrinkled wings found themselves jumbled up on top of one another.

"Do be careful, Pica!" Boswell complained.

The magpie pushed himself against the badger's bottom, struggling to get back up onto his feet.

"Easy now! I say!"

Boswell was *not* amused to be used in such a way. It was well below his dignity, much like letting Victor climb up his back on the side of the Eiffel Tower. This whole week had been one long insult to the proper, dignified badger.

Beneath his feathers of black and white, the poor

embarrassed magpie blushed a bright pink. Pica was brave and valiant, but still just as clumsy as ever.

"We're nearing the mouth of the pipe. Everyone wait here a moment. That includes *you,* Pica"

The badger eased his head out the end of the drainage pipe and took a look around. He now saw that the pipe exited the stone wall about six inches above the sidewalk. Directly in front of him, a broad walkway led over to the water's edge. Eighteen to twenty feet overhead, the busy roadway bustled with morning commuter traffic; but there was no sound of cars down below. It was a peaceful oasis in the middle of the noisy city.

Moored to a large, iron ring attached to the stone wall, a tour boat sat bobbing in the water. That was their goal. All they needed to do was cross the stone walkway, board the boat, and let it carry them upriver to their destination. As far as Boswell could see, there were no humans around. This was their chance.

"The coast is clear. As soon as we exit the pipe, make your way onboard the boat and up to the top deck. I'll lead the way. Stay close, now. Did you hear me, Pica?"

The magpie had, in fact, *not* heard the badger, since he hadn't really been paying attention. His mind was on the blueberries packed away in the bag strapped to his back.

"Pica! Did you hear me?" Boswell demanded.

"*Oui, oui!*"

"That's better." Boswell shook his head with exasperation. "Let's go, then."

The badger squeezed himself out of the end of the drainage pipe, then scurried across the stone pavement, up the ramp, and onto the lower deck of the boat. Right behind him, three butterflies and one, clumsy, distracted magpie followed. Once all were aboard, Boswell led them up the ladder and onto the upper deck.

Their first order of business was to find a place to hide in case the boat filled up with tourists. Boswell spotted a box of lifejackets in the stern and headed over to check it out.

"This will do fine for me, unless the boat sinks and everyone needs a lifejacket. Of course, then they won't mind having a badger on board. Pica, you might want to find the highest place to sit. People won't take much notice of a magpie. Same for you, ladies. The higher the better, especially if there are children aboard. It shouldn't be long now."

Around eight-forty-five, the boat started to fill up with tourists. Most people seemed interested in riding on the lower deck in the bow of the boat; no one came upstairs. Still, the badger stayed hidden, in case anyone changed their mind. He had no interest in being discovered, chased by the crew and thrown overboard into the Seine.

Nine o'clock arrived and the ship's hands removed the ramp joining the deck of the boat to the stone quay. Bow lines were cast off and the captain started the engine. Churning up the brown water, the boat slowly made its way into the river and away from shore. From his perch atop a radio antenna, Pica enjoyed the sensation of flying without the need to flap his wings. The wind in his face and the sun on his back felt perfectly glorious.

The three butterflies remained on the port side handrailing, shielded from the wind by the boat's wheelhouse. Lisette and Audrey watched with great interest. Esmée sat quietly.

Boswell was less interested in enjoying the view than he was in catching a few more minutes of sleep. The past week had been very light on sleep and the mornings had come much too early for his liking. He felt more like a cat taking a nap than the most well-respected badger in all of Paris, as the boat road the back of the river toward the *Île de la Cité.*

Pica, Audrey and Lisette had done most of their sightseeing, up to that point, during the nighttime. Now that they were able to see so much of the City of Lights by day, they were enchanted. White limestone buildings, marble sculptures, and bridge after bridge went by. It was a parade of the glories of Paris, and the three of them were enjoying it very much.

For Esmée, though, the boat ride was a reminder of the dinner cruise she'd shared with Pierre. Paris held no enjoyment for her anymore; only painful memories of happy moments lost forever. Even the waters of the Seine were an eerie echo of Pierre's final sacrifice. She kept thinking she might see him, carried along by the tragic hands of the river. The thought made her shudder.

Lisette spent her time counting bridges like Jenna had taught her the night before. She knew there were fourteen bridges between the Eiffel Tower and Notre-Dame. Thanks to Jenna, she could even name them all.

There was the Pont d'Iéna, connecting the *Jardins du Trocadéro* to the Eiffel Tower and, behind it, the *Champ de Mars.* Then there was the Passerelle Debilly pedestrian bridge. Followed by the Pont des Invalides, the Pont de l'Alma, the Pont Alexandre III and the Pont de la Concorde.

Next came the Passerelle Léopold-Sédar-Senghor (a name she had a hard time remembering, so she just called it Leo's bridge), the Pont Royal, and the Pont du Carrousel.

Between the Pont des Arts and the beautiful Pont Neuf, was Jenna's favorite place to sit and think. A small rise in the stone sidewalk on the western bank of the river offered a park bench and a breathtaking view of the Pont Neuf (the city's oldest bridge), as well as the leading point of the *Île de la Cité.*

On the left (eastern) bank of the river, connecting the *Île* to the mainland, there was the Pont Saint-Michel, the Petit Pont and finally, the Pont au Double -- the bridge nearest to Notre-Dame Cathedral.

Over and over, all along their route to Boswell's place, Jenna repeated, "Iéna, Debilly, Invalides, Alma, Alex, Concorde, Leo, Royal, Carrousel, Arts, Neuf, Michel, Petit, and Double," until Lisette was sure she'd go mad.

If that wasn't enough, Jenna then taught her a little trick for remembering the bridges in order from the Eiffel Tower all the way up to Notre-Dame.

Jenna said, "**If Dogs Invaded And Ate Cats' Lunches, Rats Could All Now Sleep Peaceful Dreams.**"

Lisette was now sure it was *Jenna* who'd gone mad, until the purple butterfly explained.

"The first letter of each word is the first letter of each bridge. **I**éna, **D**ebilly, **I**nvalides, **A**lma, **A**lex, **C**oncorde, **L**eo, **R**oyal, **C**arrousel, **Arts,** **N**euf, **M**ichel, **P**etit, and **D**ouble. Now you'll never forget!"

And Lisette never would.

This morning, as Lisette and her friends floated upriver, she checked off the names in her mind as each of the bridges passed overhead. She smiled, as she thought about Jenna and her pack of invading dogs who allowed the poor rats to get a good night's sleep by keeping the hungry cats busy! Lisette didn't quite know why, but she was fascinated by *les ponts de Paris*; she loved each one.

Pica was also interested in the bridges of Paris. Though the carved faces (or *mascarons*) on many of their façades frightened him, there was something mysterious about the unique character of each bridge. He wanted very much to explore all thirty-seven of *les ponts de Paris;* flying over and under each one; discovering new and hidden wonders. Perhaps Pica *had* become an adrenaline junkie, like Audrey suggested he had; that would suit him just fine, if it meant finding new and exciting things to see and eating blueberries along the way.

Passing beneath the Pont des Arts, Audrey saw a domed building rising up on the eastern bank of the river.

"What is *that*?" she asked, to no one in particular.

Poking his head up from among the lifejackets, Boswell looked off the starboard side in the direction of the dome.

"That's the Bibliothèque Mazarine. It's the oldest public library in France," he said.

"Public library? You mean, anyone can go in and read… *anything*!?"

"That *is* the function of a *public* library," the badger replied, grumpy for having had the misfortune of waking up without enough sleep twice in one day.

"It's huge! Much bigger than Père Lamoine's library back in Saint-Denis! Imagine all the books."

"Not just books," Boswell added, "but *everything* printed. Newspapers, manuscripts, plays, reference materials… you could spend the rest of your life in there and never read one tenth of what it contains."

A sudden sense of urgency filled Audrey's heart. If she could spend the rest of her life inside and only read one tenth of the books, she had better get busy. So much to do, so little time.

The ancient waters of the Seine flowed beneath them as they rapidly made their way upriver. The captain could be heard on the loudspeaker pointing out tourist attractions to the small, early-Sunday-morning group of passengers seated on the lower deck. Above, not a single cloud could be found to mar the spotless blue of the summer sky. Surrounded by the most beautiful city on earth, it was easy for Audrey, Lisette and Pica to forget their soreness and sorrows.

But if *they* could forget, Esmée could not; for, she

carried enough sadness for them all. Boswell watched her closely. He was worried about her and had begun to think that even Pica's great idea wouldn't be enough to distract her sorrow for a while. It might take a miracle to bring Esmée some relief from her troubles; but miracles are few and far between.

Having left her friends on the handrailing, Esmée flew down to the floor of the upper deck. There she sat in her usual position -- her wings draped around her back, her chin resting on her updrawn knees. Closing her eyes, she remained motionless for the rest of the boat ride.

Around nine-thirty, the boat crossed underneath the fourteenth and final bridge: the Pont au Double. Drifting out of the center lane of the river, the boat drew up alongside a pier on the island's eastern shore. Dockhands tossed heavy bowlines to the ship's crew, who tied them securely to the boat. The ramp was let out, the engine went silent, and the little group of tourists disembarked for a day of sightseeing.

Once everyone had gone and the crew was occupied with cleaning the lower deck, Boswell collected his own little group and led them down the ladder, across the ramp, and into the bushes not far from the water's edge. There, among the leafy branches, they discussed their next move.

"Look!" Lisette flew to the top of the bush they were all hiding in, to get a better view.

Just behind the trees, Notre-Dame Cathedral crouched, with its leg-like buttresses poised to leap toward heaven itself. It looked like the bare skeleton of a sailing ship, stripped of its outer boards. But it was the two, rectangular towers of stone and colored glass that first caught Lisette's attention. Of all the stone bridges she'd seen today, this one – a bridge between heaven and earth – was by far the most unique. It was magnificent.

"Not much farther now," the badger said; then

turning to Esmée he added, "But I'm afraid you'll have to guide us from here, my dear."

"*Oui, monsieur.* I know the way."

Esmée flew to the highest branch on one of the nearby trees, to get her bearings.

"I can see the rose garden. We will find the honeybees at work inside."

"We'll follow you, *mademoiselle.*"

Boswell smiled to show his confidence in her. He knew she had no energy for such things today. Still, he was hopeful that seeing the bees would bring her some happiness.

It was a very short distance from the river to the rose garden behind the cathedral. As they crossed over into the Square Jean-XXIII, the bells chimed the hour: ten o'clock. Strolling around the grounds of the great church, tourists and Sunday worshippers mixed, forming a stream of awestruck admirers.

The flowers in the garden beds looked like dabs of bright paint against a canvas of green; everywhere was color, contrast and perfect composition. The trees were atwitter with birds of all kinds. Jays, cardinals, even other magpies could be seen (and heard!) picking elderberries and munching on seeds.

Grasshoppers popped up like spring-loaded toys hidden to startle unsuspecting tourists. From the high rooftop of the cathedral, an unbroken line of honeybees traveled back and forth between the flowers below and a row of beehives above. These were the fabled *Ignifuge* bees, brought over from Glowermouth-on-Dart by Brother Apius many years before. As you know, their story had long since become myth among Parisians and Glowermouthians, alike.

"There, *monsieur,*" Esmée said, pointing in the directing of the honeybees, "those are the bees you wish to meet."

Boswell Badger stood still among the hedges and flowerbeds of the Square Jean-XXIII, watching the bees move with precision and efficiency. He knew their story well. He'd studied the science behind Brother Apius' discovery and marveled at the brilliance of it all. Boswell had read about their perilous crossing of *la Manche* and how the cardinal-archbishop of Paris struck a deal with Brother Apius -- a deal that the bees, the cardinal, and the poor of the city still benefit from to this very day.

All his life, he hoped to travel upriver and enjoy the company of the *Ignifuge* bees of Notre-Dame; to ask them questions and learn from them all the secrets that only bees could share. A dream was planted in his heart from the earliest days of his youth, when first he learned about these amazing creatures; and now, there they were. Boswell could see the myth become reality before his own eyes.

"I will introduce you, *monsieur.*"

Esmée fluttered over to the same rosebush in which she had first encountered Stéphanie, the honeybee. Lisette, Audrey and Pica landed nearby, in the same immense bush; while Boswell trudged along behind them.

Careful to stay outside of the bees' flight pattern, Esmée inched closer to the restless traffic, waving her wings in the air in the hope of gaining someone's attention.

"*Excusez-moi, s'il vous plaît,*" she called out to a passing bee.

"*Oui, mademoizelle?*"

"Oh, yes, thank you. I was hoping you could help me. I'm looking for Stéphanie, please."

"*Ah, oui,* Ztéphanie, she iz here zomewhere. I will put out zhe word for her. Wait here, pleaze, *mademoizelle.*"

The bee turned, then flew a zig-zag pattern

between the *approaching* and *returning* lanes of honeybee traffic. It was clear she was passing along a message to both lanes. The butterflies, magpie and badger watched as the bee was swallowed up in a cloud of her fellow workers which surrounded the rooftop hives.

Waiting for any sign that their message had been received, the travelers weren't sure what to make of it all. After a few minutes spent waiting, they began to wonder if maybe they'd been forgotten. It wouldn't have surprised them one bit, since everyone appeared to be so very busy.

"Maybe we should try again… with another bee," Audrey suggested, and Lisette agreed.

Pica just shrugged his shoulders. He had no idea what to do but was enjoying watching the bees at work.

"I think we should wait," Boswell said, unwilling to risk irritating the honeybees with impatience, which was totally out of character for the usually impatient badger. "Let's see what happens."

Boswell was living in the moment; eating up every observation, every buzz and hover going on around him. This is what he'd longed for all his life, and he was in no hurry at all.

He noticed how the bees communicated by dancing on the petals of a flower. He watched as they all traveled along the exact same flight paths through the air. He marveled at the methodical way they went about their business, never missing a bud.

If bees were allowed to rule the world, he thought, what an orderly world it would be! No one would go hungry; no one's talents would go unused; and we'd all experience the care of a motherly queen. Indeed, Notre-Dame Cathedral might very well have been dedicated to *both* of the royal mothers of Paris: she, who became a mother on the first Noël; and she, who was the queen mother of the *Ignifuge* bees.

As they all searched the sky for any sign of Stéphanie, the travelers saw that, among the swarm of honeybees flying down from the rooftop, one bee had broken away from the crowd and was heading straight toward them.

"*Elle est là.* There she is," said Esmée, confirming what everyone had suspected.

"*Bonjour, mon amie! Bienvenue! Zzz... zzz... zzz...*"

Flying right up to Esmée, Stéphanie kissed her on both cheeks; first her right, then her left; as is the French custom.

"*Bonjour, madamez et mezzieurz.* Welcome to you all. I have been hoping to zee you again, my friend; but I am alzo delighted to meet your freindz."

"Thank you, Stéphanie. It is good to see you. Let me introduce you to everyone."

Gesturing with her wing, Esmée began the introductions.

"This is my best friend, Lisette Cueilleur."

"*Enchantée, mademoizelle,*" Stéphanie said, with a slight nod of her fuzzy head.

"And this is Audrey Loriot and Pica, the magpie."

"*Enchantée, mademoizelle* Audrey. *Enchantée, monzieur* Pica."

Pica liked being called *monsieur or* even *monzieur.* It never happened back home in Saint-Denis. Stéphanie was clearly enjoying the opportunity to meet so many new friends. It wasn't every day a honeybee got to meet a magpie or a badger, for that matter. In truth, she was most interested in who this badger might be. She already had a hunch.

"And this is the illustrious Boswell Badger; very famous among the animals of Paris."

"*Enchantée, monzieur* Badger. Your name iz known to uz here, too. We have long hoped to meet you."

"M-m-me?"

Boswell stammered, surprised that the subjects of his lifelong admiration would know anything *at all* about him. It might not have been his most eloquent moment, but it certainly was his most sincere.

"*Oui, vous, monzieur.* You are widely-known and well-rezpected for your wizdom, even among zhe zimple beez of Notre-Dame."

"Well, I'm… that is to say, you're very kind."

The badger was very nearly speechless. Of course, it might have been better if he had remained speechless altogether. He was afraid that he wasn't making as dignified a first impression as he'd hoped.

Esmée came to Boswell's rescue.

"He has wanted to meet you all for a very long time."

"Az we have wanted to meet him," the gracious honeybee replied. "Like I zaid, I have been hoping to zee you again, my friend. I have a gift for you."

Esmée was taken by surprise. She hardly expected Stéphanie to remember her, let alone *have* a *gift* for her. What could it possibly be?

"A gift? *Mon amie,* it is not necessary."

"*Oui,* but it iz. Quite nezezzary, indeed. I muzt take you zhere now, if you will allow me. We will take a badger-friendly path. Pleaze, follow me."

The little honeybee flew over to the foot of a nearby buttress. Waiting for everyone else to catch up, she then gave instructions to the whole group.

"We muzt follow zhe buttrezz to zhe rooftop hivez."

"The rooftop?" Boswell wasn't sure he'd heard her right.

Stéphanie overlooked his question and continued with her instructions.

"Thoze of uz who can fly, will ztay cloze to our

good friend, *monzieur* Badger. Do not be afraid, *monzieur,* zhe concrete it iz eazy to grab hold of wizh your clawz. Zhe hard part will come clozer to zhe roof. Zere, you muzt jump from zhe buttrezz to zhe gutter. It will be fun, *non?*"

Jumping from the top of the buttress to the gutter two-hundred feet above the ground was not Boswell's idea of fun. He thought his climbing days were over, after the excitement of scaling the Eiffel Tower. But this was a once in a lifetime opportunity. The *Ignifuge* bees of Notre-Dame Cathedral had invited him to visit their rooftop hives. He couldn't pass up this chance, even if it meant risking a fall to his death.

Stéphanie took the lead, walking along the top of the buttress, while Esmée, Lisette, Audrey and Pica flew overhead. Behind the honeybee, Boswell Badger scrambled up the side of the enormous leg of the cathedral. Digging in with his claws, the badger climbed the stone face like a mountaineer -- only without the benefit of a safety rope.

He kept his eyes fixed on the honeybee in front of him, unwilling to look down to the garden floor below. Imagining he was climbing over a short wall, Boswell succeeded in convincing himself it was actually true.

That was all the distraction and confidence he needed to make it up the most difficult part of the climb. At last, rounding the buttress's knee, Boswell now had more stone beneath his feet than he did in front of his face. He was moving more horizontally than vertically; and that was a very encouraging change.

The thoughtful honeybee stayed with the badger the whole way, glancing back often to be sure he was alright. Huffing and panting, sweaty and exhausted, Boswell finally made it to where the leg joined the wall of the ancient church.

Looking up, he could see the gutter running just

below the roof's edge. It was maybe three and a half feet above the surface upon which he now stood. A leap of a few inches would allow him to grab onto the gutter and pull himself up to the rooftop. At worst, he'd miss and slide all the way down the buttress on his rear-end, more embarrassed than injured.

Stéphanie sat on the gutter just above Boswell's head. Around her, the others now congregated like a group of cheerleaders.

"You can do it, *monzieur* Badger. You will not mizz."

Boswell wasn't quite as confident as the honeybee seemed to be. But he was willing to take his chances, if only to sit a while among the rooftop hives and chat with Brother Apius' legendary bees.

Reaching and stretching with both paws, the illustrious badger hopped straight up as high as he could and grabbed hold of the edge of the gutter. He then started swinging his legs back and forth, back and forth, faster and faster. Once he'd built up enough momentum to carry him – *allez hop!* – over the edge he went. The biggest badger in all of Paris landed flat on his back -- staring straight up at the sky – on the slanted roof of Notre-Dame Cathedral.

The claws of both paws and feet were dug in tight -- clutching the shingles of the roof -- as he lay there trying to find the courage to let go. White terror paled his face to the color of his silver sideburns.

In the epic leap from buttress to roof, the badger had caught one of the buttons of his handsome, tweed waistcoat on the gutter, sending it sailing *no-one-knows-where*. With sincerest sympathies, Stéphanie now pointed out this great loss to Boswell.

"*Monzieur* Badger, you have lozt a button, I'm afraid."

Between gasps for air, the badger assured her,

"That's fine. No problem. Quite alright. Easily replaced."

He would have much rather sent one button sailing *no-one-knows-where* than to end up there himself. It was a small price to pay for the honor of being able to sit where he now sat.

"Zhe road iz much eazier from here."

The little bee now led her tour group around the corner to the left, in the opposite direction of the gardens below. As the only one walking, Boswell had to carefully navigate the slanted roof -- holding onto the slate shingles with all the strength left in his fingernails. After a brief but harrowing trip (for the badger, anyway), they arrived at a point where a flat area, a few feet below the slanted roof, joined the main part of the cathedral.

This was the sacristy roof, and it was here that Brother Apius first placed his precious cargo of beehives so many years ago. Since that day, the hives have grown and flourished, until now over 200,000 honeybees call the simple wooden rooftop boxes their home.

Jumping down onto the flat roof of the sacristy, Boswell found himself in a place he never dreamed he'd be. The terrors of the climb and the irritation of one lost button faded from memory. He was standing in a mythical place: the legendary home of the *Ignifuge* bees.

Examining the hives more closely, he saw that each individual bee, when she returned from the flowers in the Square Jean-XXIII, touched down gently on the narrow ledge that ran along the front of the hive. She would then wait for her turn to enter through a small, square hole in the hive body. He imagined the wonders he would find if he, like the bees, could walk inside that tiny entrance. Oh, how he wished he were a little honeybee, instead of the biggest badger in all of Paris.

Surrounding the beehives, there were several long wooden workbenches. Each bench had been drilled with dozens of round openings. Held upright in these openings, rows of terra cotta vases, each containing an assortment of fresh flowers, sat upright in the summer sun.

"Zheze are zhe flowerz uzed for zhe altar and ozher plazez of honor in zhe cazhedral. Zhey keep zhem here zo zhey will be fresh when zhey are needed inzide. Zhey are alzo a kind of treat for uz beez. We can collect zheir pollen wizhout having to fly zo far. It iz juzt anozher happy arrangement between zhe cardinal-archbishop and zhe *Ignifuge* beez of Notre-Dame Cazhedral."

Stéphanie flew over and landed on the edge of one of the wooden workbenches, inviting Esmée, Lisette, Audrey, Pica, and Boswell to join her.

"I told you I have a gift for you," she said, smiling at Esmée with sweet sympathy in her kindly eyes. "And here it iz."

In the middle of the workbench there was a greenhouse, constructed of clear plastic walls supported by a wooden frame. Inside, the caretakers sheltered the flowers that were too delicate to be kept in terra cotta vases beneath an open sky. Occurring every few inches along the front of the greenhouse, hinged doors allowed access to the flowers inside. One of these doors lay open, and it was to this opening that Stéphanie now flew.

Once the others had gathered around, Stéphanie asked them to wait a moment while she went inside the warm, humid enclosure. Everyone else stood-by outside, overflowing with expectation, wondering what kind of exotic flower their friend was going in to retrieve. A moment later, the honeybee emerged with a more unexpectedly wonderful gift than any of them could have hoped to receive.

CHAPTER THIRTY-SIX

The *Île du Papillon*

Stéphanie stood in the doorway of the greenhouse; her black and yellow fuzz covered in tiny droplets of water from the moist air inside. As soon as she crossed the threshold, she suddenly began beating her four, little wings as if she had flipped-on an electric motor. Rising from the workbench surface, she flew over to where Boswell stood and landed on his shoulder.

All eyes turned to the honeybee, in confusion. Everyone had expected her to return from inside the greenhouse with some sort of gift for Esmée, as she said she would. Now, the star of the show had decided to join the audience. No one understood why.

Pointing to the door, Stéphanie once again drew everyone's attention away from herself and back to whatever was inside the greenhouse. She had, indeed, joined the audience of onlookers; and she didn't want anyone to miss what was about to happen – herself included.

"Look," she said, "Zhere iz your gift, *mon amie.*"

Esmée cast her eyes back to the door of the greenhouse. What she saw, she did not believe. A wave of conflicting emotion swept over her, engulfing her bruised and saddened heart. She burst into tears. There, in the open doorway of the greenhouse enclosure -- beyond all hope and expectation -- stood Pierre.

"*Ma petite,*" he said to Esmée, "your heart, it is broken. I have returned to heal it, and it will never break again."

Flying over to where she stood, Pierre dropped to one knee in front of Esmée, as she struggled to make sense of the dream in which she found herself living.

"Forgive me, *mademoiselle.* I did not mean to cause you distress. The last 18 hours have been a fog of pain and fitful sleep; and I owe my life to these noble bees. Without their kindness, your darkest fears would certainly have come true."

Lisette drew her friend close, cradling Esmée in her arms. Esmée stood with a look of despair on her face. This was a cruel joke, an imposter, a ghost sent to torment her broken heart; and now her mind had begun to crack. She felt herself slipping into madness. How could any of this be real?

Audrey and Pica stood by in silent disbelief. Pierre was dead. Marmot, Hugo and half a dozen squirrels had seen him fall off the edge of the island along with the villainous crow. They were both struck by the bow of a passing boat. They'd been pulled beneath the waters of the Seine, lost forever. This was not possible. It simply could not be true.

Boswell stepped forward, in an effort to make sense of the situation. He saw Esmée struggling within herself, and he wanted to bring her relief.

"Please," he said to Pierre, "tell us what happened. We need to understand. We need you to make sense of it all for us. Please."

"*Oui,* of course, *monsieur.* I will tell you how it is that I came to be standing here before you today. But, where do I begin?" Pierre said to himself, struggling to find both the right moment to pick up the story and the courage to relive it.

"When I saw Marmot strike the evil crow and

cause him to lose his balance, I knew what must be done. If only I could hit him before he had a chance to regain his footing, I just might be able to coax our foe clean off that island, over the edge and into a watery grave.

"My time to act was upon me. I leapt into the air and made straight for his right eye – his one remaining *good* eye. Hitting my target as hard as I could, it proved to be enough. The befuddled old fool was cast, screeching for dear life, directly into the path of the oncoming boat.

"But I'd flown with such force that I was unable to stop in midair. Instead, I followed my enemy over the side of the island and down toward the swirling waters of the Seine. But this is where chance decided our separate fates.

"Since the vile crow had fallen first, he arrived in harm's way before me, and was struck by the bow of the boat. From behind, I saw him go under the white water -- and he never came up again.

"But, carried by my own speed, I followed him a split second behind – just long enough of a delay so that, instead of hitting the bow of the boat and being dragged beneath the waves, I landed on the boat's deck and was carried upriver and out of sight.

"When Marmot – desperate to save me -- reached the edge of the shore, the back of the boat had passed his position. He never saw the bow, so he could only assume the worst; and, but for a split second of good luck, his assumption would have been correct."

Pierre rubbed his forehead. Remembering the events of his final battle brought the full weight of them back to his mind. He was tired. Still, there was more to be told.

"I passed out, either from the force of hitting the deck of the boat or from my own exhaustion. Then next thing I remember was waking up and realizing that the boat had stopped moving. We were moored beside the

Pont au Double, very near here. I saw men carrying boxes off the boat and up the ramp to the quay. I knew I had to get up off the deck or risk being stepped on.

"Looking around, I saw several terra cotta vases filled with flowers. This, I thought, would be a good place for a butterfly to hide; and hide I must, for the men were drawing closer to where I lay. I waited until their backs were turned, then flew into a bunch of flowers, hiding deep among the blooms.

"My head was spinning, throbbing with pain. The crow's grip had been merciless, and every part of my body burned in agony. I was hungry and thirsty and desperate for sleep. My hiding place, it provided the nectar I needed to stay alert; for, I could not yet sleep.

"The crates carrying the vases were unloaded from the boat and placed in the back of a refrigerated truck. When the back door of the truck was pulled shut, I thought I would die in cold darkness – never to feel the warmth of summer again.

"The truck ride lasted only a few minutes, though; just long enough to reach the cathedral. This was an unexpected mercy among a riot of dangers. The door of the truck was raised, and the men unloaded their cargo of flowers onto handcarts. With a splitting headache, made worse by the numbing chill of the truck's cargo compartment, every bump and vibration of the handcart over paving stones was excruciating.

"At last, the men reached the cathedral's service entrance. There, the crates were carried by hand to a hidden elevator just inside the cathedral walls. The doors closed and, when they opened again, I saw what you now see all around us: the sacristy rooftop and the hives of the fabled *Ignifuge* bees of Notre-Dame. Hope was once more kindled in my heart."

Everyone listening to Pierre speak was rivetted to his story. Boswell watched Esmée carefully, as her face betrayed signs of utter disbelief at first. As Pierre spoke, the familiar warmth of his voice soothed her heart, and she began to realize that the pain and desperation of the past 18 hours were just an illusion. He had survived. He had come back to her. Boswell hoped that by keeping her promise to introduce him to the *Ignifuge* bees Esmée would find some relief from her sorrows. He was now satisfied that no better relief could have been found.

As the pieces of the puzzle fell into place, Pica became *nearly* certain that Pierre was, in fact, real and not just the ghost of a butterfly. When Pierre first appeared in the open door of the greenhouse, Pica thought it was an apparition. No other explanation could possibly make sense. He'd been tempted to go up and peck-at it with his beak, to prove to himself and everyone else that it was not really Pierre. He was now feeling rather relieved that he hadn't given in to that temptation.

"I do not remember what happened after I arrived here. I've had to rely on the reports of others to fill in those blanks for me. The bees, they found me among the flowers, and carried me into the warmth of the greenhouse. There, I spent the long, cold night – safe from anything that might harm me.

"All through the night, the bees, they worked on me. Cleaning and salving my injuries until, feeling my strength return, I finally awoke. My first thought was of you, *ma petite*. I knew how worried you would be, and how all hope had surely been driven from your tender heart. I wished only to fly to your side or send word to you assuring you I was still alive.

"My heart was breaking, and darkness invaded my thoughts. Desperate to get word to you, despair over my weakness and injuries began to take root within me. It was then that the bees administered their most effective medicine. Seeing that the only wounds I had left to be cured of were those in my heart and mind, one drop of their mythical honey was brought to me for my breakfast.

"Of course, I knew the story of Brother Apius, and the people of Glowermouth-on-Dart who had been cursed by the wicked *fromager*. I knew well the tale of the *Ignifuge* bees and their Miraculous Miel; but I must say, I was not sure if these tales were true. I can assure you now, my friends, they are all true. Yesterday, my whole body was aflame with excruciating pain. Today, I feel only… well, the slightest amount of fatigue. But, more importantly, my heart knew hope again, the moment I tasted their honey.

"That hope was soon confirmed. After I had my breakfast, I intended to leave this life-giving place and go in search of you, my love. But word arrived, saying that you and your good friends were already here, below in the gardens. You… came for *me*."

Esmée drew near to Pierre. Resting her head on his shoulder, she said, "But I did not know you were here. How would I have ever found you?"

"Do you not remember, *mademoizelle?*" Stéphanie interrupted. "All you had to do waz follow zhe river. She will alwayz lead you home again. Haz zhiz not been true?"

"*Oui, mon amie,* it has *always* been true. You were right, and I thank you for giving me the hope I needed when I needed it. It led me to my friends; it also led them to me. Now it has brought Pierre to this place; and guided me back to him… though I did not know it."

"You did not need to know, *mademoizelle.* You only needed to believe and follow."

Esmée threw her wings around Pierre. In love, he had sacrificed everything -- even risking his own life to save her and her friends. Now, he had been set free from the sorrows of love; set free and restored to life.

"Just like in the sculpture," Esmée said, turning suddenly to Lisette, who stood looking on. "Just like in the *sculpture*," she repeated in a whisper.

Lisette understood, when no one else around them did.

"The captive butterfly is set free… by the bees," she said, then paused a moment. "And so, he was."

Everyone had been caught off guard by the discovery that Pierre had survived his fall. They'd all spent the last 18 hours struggling to come to grips with their "new normal:" a world without Pierre.

Now, here they were, cast back into the world as it should be. How would they move forward, when so much had changed -- then changed back again -- in so little time? They needed to find their paths again.

They needed to realize that they had all changed; they had all learned things about themselves; and they could rely on their new strengths as well as their new friends -- as they had always relied on their friends.

It was now up to the badger to lead them out of this dream they'd wandered into -- and back into the real world.

"Word of this must be sent out across the *network*, immediately," Boswell declared, shattering the silence that had descended upon everyone.

"We would be happy to carry a mezzage to Barthélemy Courrier at zhe *Notre-Dame zerver room*. We beez know him well," Stéphanie offered.

"Thank you, Stéphanie." Turning to Pica, Boswell asked for a piece of paper and a pencil from the bag the magpie had strapped to his back. Taking the pencil in hand, the badger began writing.

"We would be very grateful, dear friend," he spoke to Stéphanie, "if the following message could be sent out:"

"Priority 1: Urgent!
From: Network Manager, Notre-Dame Server

Room
To: All Recipients

Alert: Pierre lives! I repeat, the Hero of *L'île du Sacrifice* lives! Safe and sound and reunited with his friends at Notre-Dame Cathedral. Heartfelt thanks to the *Ignifuge* bees for nursing him back to health. A happy day, indeed!"

Handing the pencil back to Pica, Boswell folded the message, adding, "Many hearts will be lightened by this good news."

"I will zpeak to my friendz right away, and zhey will carry your mezzage to Barthélemy Courrier. Zzz… zzz… zzz…"

Picking up the scrap of paper in her legs, Stéphanie flew off without another word, eager to pass along the message of Pierre's good fortune to the Boulogne *network*.

Beside the greenhouse, Esmée sat with Pierre, their wings sheltering them in a cocoon of their own making. They talked about everything that had happened, and everything they had felt; and their hearts grew whole again.

Over the course of a few short days since their first meeting, the two butterflies had begun to build their future upon the foundation of their newfound love. Returning to that foundation was like returning to solid ground after trying to walk on shifting sands. They might have only spent a few days together, but a few days are like months to a butterfly. They had been changed forever.

Pica and Lisette held their own private conversation, seated upon a ledge overlooking the river below. They, too, appeared to be making plans of some kind; though no one could hear what they were talking about. A week ago, Lisette would never have chosen to spend time with Pica; and Pica would not have enjoyed time spent with the hot-tempered Lisette. Now, the two found they had something in common. A common interest, a shared passion was about to take them on an adventure of their own.

Off to one side, Audrey sat by herself as she often did and always preferred. She gazed downriver in the direction of the Bibliothèque Mazarine. Ever since passing it earlier that day, her imagination had been running wild beneath the dome of the largest public library in France.

Sitting in the churchyard in Saint-Denis, she was always at the mercy of the wind and the parishioners. Whatever the breeze blew in or the churchgoers threw out, Audrey would pick up and read. As a result, she knew a great deal about *Who's Who in Ancient Church History*, right up until page 28. She was an expert on *Attenborough's Guide to the Birds of Northern Europe*, at least until page 42; and she was well versed in the rules of the road, having read *le Code de la Route* as far as page 73. How she longed to read a real book all the way through from cover to cover.

Lost in his own thoughts, Boswell Badger stood examining the row of beehives. If Audrey's imagination found its home within the walls of an enormous library, Boswell's imagination was equally at home within the walls of a small, wooden hive. He longed to know its secrets. He had been just as overwhelmed by the miracle of Pierre's survival and discovery as everyone else, and he knew that his friends needed to find their way back to everyday life; but he wasn't ready to leave this magical place just yet. He wondered if he ever would be.

Boswell had spent years reading and researching, studying and seeking; and now, there he was standing face to face with the reality of everything *wonderful* he'd ever *wondered* about.

All he'd ever known were the streets and alleyways of Paris, the tunnels and drainage pipes of the *Champ de Mars*; but now, he'd finally reached the rooftops and stood in the presence of some of the oldest and most fascinating legends in France. Why go back, when he'd already learned everything the old city had to teach him? Perhaps it was time for a change.

"The time has come, dear friends," the badger spoke. "The day awaits you. Everything is as it should be. It would appear that Pica's idea was a good one, after all. We set out this morning in the hope of finding something to distract Esmée from her sorrows. She now appears to be thoroughly distracted. Bravo, Pica."

Esmée smiled, then turned her eyes back to Pierre. Pica hopped up and down with proud excitement. He'd done something right, and the badger had noticed. This was surely the high point of the magpie's young life.

Boswell walked over to the two butterflies, crouching down to speak with Esmée.

"Only five days ago, you were lost and alone in the wide world. See how that world came together to find you and set things right again? You made so many friends along the way. And, although you have not yet returned home, your home has come to you."

"*Mais oui, monsieur* Badger," Esmée said, facing Pierre, "I am already home."

At that moment, Stéphanie the bee returned from her errand, "Your mezzage haz been zent, *monzieur*. Zoon, all zhe *network* will know of your good fortune."

"Thank you, my friend. I'm comforted to hear that Victor, Hugo, Marmot, Megalina, the squirrels of the *JdT*, and Queen Fourmi will all learn that their efforts and sacrifices had not been in vain. Esmée has been found and restored to her loved ones; the enemy has been defeated, and Pierre lives. I'm encouraged to see what can be accomplished when all work together."

Audrey stood up and flew over to the top of the greenhouse at the center of the group. She had an announcement to make.

"This morning, my plan was to spend all day in uninterrupted reading. At that time, the best I could manage was a scrap of newsprint. Now that I've seen the Bibliothèque Mazarine, I'd like to change my plans for the rest of the day."

Walking over to Boswell, Audrey had a few questions she needed answered.

"So, just to get this right, you're saying they have *whole* books in there. Books that have *all* their pages. And I can read as *many* as I like?"

Boswell chuckled, "That's what I'm saying."

"And reference books, on *any* topic I can imagine?"

"Those, too."

"And… there are flowers nearby? With nectar?"

"My dear, Audrey, this is Paris. There are *always* flowers nearby."

"Then I think I'd like to spend more than just the rest of the day at the Bibliothèque Mazarine. Much more, in fact. If anyone needs me, that's where I'll be. But, please," Audrey said, directing her eyes at the magpie, "don't need me *too* often."

Pica hopped over and engulfed the little butterfly in a great, feathery hug. He hated goodbyes. Audrey had been the first person ever to ask Pica his opinion. She'd been the first person ever to listen to what he had to say. She was his best friend, and she always would be. No, Pica didn't like goodbyes; and goodbyes to his best friend... well, those goodbyes were not good at all.

"This isn't goodbye, silly magpie," she assured him. "It's just *à bientôt.*"

Fluttering into flight, Audrey kissed Pica on the

forehead, then smiled at everyone else. With a wave of her hand, the bookworm-butterfly turned and flew off downriver toward the Bibliothèque Mazarine.

Every morning, from that day forward, Audrey Loriot would awaken with the first rays of the rising sun, much as she had in Penelope Porcher's lilac bush back in Saint-Denis. After a *petit déjeuner* of nectar from whatever flowers the library had used that day to decorate their tables and statues, she would lose herself within worlds of written words for hours on end -- without ever being interrupted.

"Alright, Pica," Lisette said, breaking in on his sadness at seeing Audrey go, "It's time. Are you with me?"

"*Oui, oui,*" he replied, with a sigh and a heavy heart.

"There are thirty-seven bridges out there waiting to be explored. We need to get going!"

No one had really been surprised to see Audrey leave. She always preferred solitude and the company of a good book, newspaper or sermon. But Pica? With Lisette? No one saw *that* one coming. Esmée, least of all. She knew them well, and she knew they had always tried to avoid one another.

"*We*?" Esmée asked, with disbelief. "The two of you, *together*?"

"Crazy, isn't it?" Lisette said, in her carefree way. "Pica and I both agreed, these bridges are something else! We want to take a closer look. Right, Pica?"

Lisette was obviously trying to cheer up the magpie, and it appeared to be working. She had successfully reminded him of all the beautiful bridges, and their conversation from earlier. It was then that they had decided to go off on an adventure of their own and explore every single one of *les ponts de Paris*.

"*C'est vrai, c'est vrai!*" Pica said with growing

excitement.

"Right! So, where do you think we should begin?"

Pica drew his head up at attention. What did Lisette just say? Did she ask Pica what he thought? This was unprecedented. This was completely unlike the bossy butterfly he'd always known. Maybe she'd learned from Audrey. Maybe things *were* changing between them.

Lisette barely gave Pica a chance to respond, before continuing, "I say we start with the Pont au Double, since we're already here."

Well, at least she asked him what he thought, even if she did answer the question for him. It was a start, and Pica would take it.

"That little trick Jenna taught me to remember the names and order of the bridges will still work. Just backwards: **D**reams **P**eaceful **S**leep **N**ow **A**ll **C**ould **R**ats **L**unches **C**ats' **A**te **A**nd **I**nvaded **D**ogs **I**f. See? It works great!"

Pica wasn't so sure.

"Anyway, *you two* don't need us hanging around," Lisette said, turning to Esmée.

Fluttering over to Lisette, Esmée landed in front of her, then paused before hugging her tight.

Esmée never asked Lisette why she hadn't gone with Audrey and Pica when they'd first set out on their search and rescue mission. Esmée knew her friend well enough that she didn't really need to ask. She was just glad Lisette was there now.

Holding her close, Esmée turned and whispered in Lisette's ear, "Thank you. My truest friend…"

Stepping back, the two friends held onto one another's hands for a moment. This would be the last time they'd see each other -- for a while, anyway – and they both knew it.

With a smile, Lisette finally drew herself away, then walked over and threw her wings around Pierre, saying, "Take care of her. She's everything to me."

Lisette wiped a tear from her eye, then flew over to where Pica was standing. The magpie had removed his backpack and placed it on the workbench next to the greenhouse. Looking somewhat reluctant to leave it behind, Pica kept glancing over at Boswell.

"You may *take* the backpack, Pica," the badger said, as if reading the magpie's mind. "It belongs with the adventurers -- and that would be you and Lisette. You'll have need of it."

Pica's face immediately lit up. He really didn't want to part with the blueberries.

"Just leave the rose, please" Boswell added.

Taking Esmée's rose from the backpack, Pica laid it on the workbench, then slung the bag back over his shoulder and rejoined Lisette.

"*Allons!*" she said. "The bridges *must* be explored. *À bientôt!*"

Lisette took to the wing, with Pica close behind. As they flew away toward the river, Boswell Badger called out to them both, "Farewell, Lisette Cueilleur! And farewell to you, Pica the magpie!"

From the sky, a voice was heard correcting the badger, "*Je ne suis pas la magpie! Je suis Pica Pica!*"

Boswell laughed and shook his head. At last everyone now knew Pica's last name; and like Marmot said before, some things don't need repeating -- they're true enough the first time. There never was a truer magpie than Pica.

Esmée saw the rose lying on the table, and immediately recognized it as the one Marmot had brought back to her from the *Île du Sacrifice.*

"You had Pica bring my rose," she said to Boswell.

"I thought you might want it," the badger replied, with kindness in his eyes.

Flying over to where Boswell stood beside the beehives, Stéphanie asked, "And what planz do you have, *monzieur* Badger?"

"Mine are not really plans, dear friend. They're only wishes."

"Zhen what are your wishez, *mon ami?*"

"I wish more than anything to remain here awhile. I'd like to get to know all of you and learn whatever you're willing to teach me."

"But what can zhe beez of Notre-Dame Cazhedral teach zhe illuztriouz Bozwell Badger?"

Boswell hesitated, taking a moment to consider his answer.

"The secrets of your hives; the secrets of your way of life; perhaps, the secret of happiness. I've grown tired of being wise; I want to be a student again."

"You are welcome to remain wizh uz for az long az you dezire, *monzieur*. We will share wizh you our honey, and you will find happinezz. If zhiz iz what you wish, zhen it will be zo."

The honeybee lifted off the workbench, like the tiniest black and gold helicopter.

"I will go now and tell my people zhe newz. Zhey will be zurprized, for zhere iz nozhing more out of plaze than a badger on a rooftop, *non? Zzz… zzz… zzz…*"

Stéphanie laughed at the thought, then flew off to spread the word that Boswell would be staying with the *Ignifuge* bees for as long as he liked. It was all much more than just a dream for the badger; it was a dream come true.

"It's funny," Boswell said to Esmée and Pierre, "there may not be 'anything more out of place than a badger on a rooftop', but I've never felt more at home *anywhere* as I do right here."

Walking over to one of the beehives, Boswell knelt down in front of its tiny square entrance. Bending over, he rested his chin on the thin ledge that ran just below the opening. Closing one eye, he peeked inside the beehive with the other.

A wide smile spread like daybreak across the badger's face, as he whispered to himself, "Simply magnificent..."

Boswell Badger had always been well-respected among the animals of Paris, but it wasn't because of his size or his bearing. It wasn't because of his serious, and often grumpy personality. It wasn't even for his handsome, tweed waistcoat that he'd always had such a reputation.

Boswell Badger was well-respected because he had the wisdom to become a student once more, and the courage to climb-up to where he'd stick out; appear different; be out of place -- just to learn something new.

Esmée and Pierre watched their friend marveling over the world he'd found inside the beehive. It was like watching a child discover a new toy. There was no doubt in their minds, Boswell would be quite happy with the *Ignifuge* bees of Notre-Dame. For the butterflies, though, it was time to go.

Esmée and Pierre flew over to the workbench where Marmot's rose lay. From the moment she received it, the rose was all she had of Pierre; a reminder of his love for her and the place where he gave his all for others. Now, the rose —and even its tiny thorns -- reminded her of much more.

Flying over to the flower, Esmée tore one petal off and held it in her feet.

"The rest will remain here," she said to Pierre, "because it was here that you returned to me."

"And this petal?" he asked.

Esmée just smiled.

Fluttering above the slanted rooftop of Notre-Dame Cathedral, Esmée led Pierre down toward the Square Jean-XXIII. Crossing the green gardens with their flower beds and rosebushes, a voice called out from above.

"Enjoy your time in *Paree, mademoizelle et monzieur*! *À bientôt! Zzz… zzz… zzz…*"

"*Au revoir,* Stéphanie!"

The two butterflies flew down toward the Pont au Double, where Lisette and Pica had just arrived. The magpie insisted they have lunch before exploring the first of their thirty-seven bridges. As Esmée and Pierre passed overhead, Lisette waved, while Pica called out, "*Myrtilles, myrtilles!*"

"*Profitez de vos aventures!*" Esmée said, then turned south.

Following the path of the Seine, Esmée could see a domed building off to the east. She imagined Audrey fluttering merrily down aisles and over bookshelves stacked with every book, play, newspaper and encyclopedia the bookworm-butterfly could ever want to read. The thought made Esmée's heart happy.

Turning west at the Pont des Arts across from the Bibliothèque Mazarine, Esmée and Pierre entered a vast, stone courtyard. The courtyard was held in the embrace of two enormous arms comprised of palatial buildings. At the center of the plaza, an enormous, glass pyramid stood directly in the way (much to the Parisians' annoyance) of an unbroken line of sight extending all the way down to the Arc de Triomphe.

On the westerly side of the pyramid, a large sign hung overtop a set of doors. The sign simply read, "*Mus*ée *du Louvre.*" Above it, much smaller and barely noticeable by the crowds of tourists, another notice read, *"Pas de Mâcheurs!"* Certain that it couldn't be directed at her, Esmée ignored the small, printed warning altogether, and led Pierre inside.

Flying in wide spirals down the staircase, the butterflies soon reached the bottom level where an identical glass pyramid stood upside down on its point. Between the pyramid's point and the floor, a small stone pyramid sat -- the tips of both nearly touched, but for a few inches of space between them.

Esmée paused a moment, reading the signs which marked out the various wings of the museum.

"Richelieu," she said, "Over there."

Without explanation, she was off again. Flying with the rose petal still clutched in her feet, Esmée entered the ground-floor level in search of the Chaudet exhibit.

The moment he realized they were visiting the museum, Pierre was delighted. He loved the Louvre, and he wanted to share every painting, sculpture and artifact with Esmée. He'd always envisioned the two of them taking their time; discussing everything they saw; and being able to see only a tiny fraction of its treasures in one day.

What he never envisioned, however, was flying down hallways and around corners at top speed in search of *heaven-knows-what,* ignoring everything they passed along the way. And that's exactly what they were now doing. Esmée was laser-focused on finding whatever it was she was searching for. Pierre didn't dare break her concentration, but simply tried to keep up as best he could.

"Here it is," she said, after minutes of silent searching. "Room 225."

The moment she entered the room, a change came over Esmée. All the frantic energy of their flight through the museum dissolved. In its place, a hushed awe descended across the butterfly's face like a wedding veil. It was as if she'd entered the sacred space of Notre-Dame Cathedral or Sainte-Chapelle. She felt... a presence.

In front of one of the glassless windows looking out onto the mezzanine, there stood a white, marble sculpture. Three figures composed the scene: a young boy, a butterfly and a rose. The figures were life-sized, and so very *lifelike* that one might expect them to breathe.

In his cheeks and limbs, the young boy -- a god, really – still wore the full, round, baby fat of youth. His hair fell in heavy locks around his handsome face. With one knee bent, he delicately held the stem of a rose pinched in the fingers of his left hand. Between the fingers of his right hand, he held captive the wings of a butterfly.

Esmée landed on the stone pedestal just in front of the statue. With a heart overflowing with emotion, she stood in silence. Remembering, feeling, thinking back on everything this sculpture had always meant to her, Esmée's eyes came to rest upon the marble rose. Pierre stood beside her, watching.

After a long while spent examining every detail, Esmée began repeating the words Lisette had spoken in the badger's den the night before.

"'*The rose symbolizes love. Once the butterfly is captured by Cupid, she can't break free. Instead of joy, all she feels are the pains of love – the pains of captivity.*' That's why my mother told Lisette and me the story; to warn us not to be too easily tempted by the beauty of flowers; not to let ourselves be captured or caged; and that even love has its pains. Even love has its thorns…"

Turning to Pierre, she whispered, "And that's what happened to me… to *both* of us."

Esmée flew over and landed beside the sculpted flower. Laying the red rose petal down upon the white petals of the sculpture, she smiled, then returned to Pierre's side.

"This statue was *lifelike*, but still lifeless. Until *we* brought it to life… we lived this scene. We lived it all… the story of this sculpture… our sculpture. Your sacrifice, my heartbreak, it brought life to it … like a living, red rose petal laid on cold, white stone."

Esmée looked one last time at the petal she'd left behind. A sense of fulfillment dawned in her heart. It was enough. The time had come.

"Let's go home," she said to Pierre.

"Home? But where *is* home, *ma petite?*"

Esmée laughed, then fluttered into the air, hovering in front of the sculpture of Cupid and the butterfly.

"*Au revoir, petit papillon,*" she said to the marble butterfly.

Leaving the exhibit salon, Esmée led Pierre out into the marble mezzanine beneath the immense skylight-ceiling. She waited until he'd caught up to her, then turned and said, "*Allons!*"

Without warning, she was off like a shot.

Calling back to him, from up ahead, Esmée taunted Pierre to "catch me, if you can." Down the wide hallways of the Richelieu wing, she wove in, out, and between the hats and heads of a thousand startled tourists. Had there been a photographer from *Le Journal* at the Louvre that day, Esmée surely would have made it on the front page again. Reaching the doors in the front of the glass pyramid before Pierre did, Esmée declared herself the winner of the race, before leading Pierre outside into the courtyard.

The two *belle dame* butterflies flew south along the river, riding the afternoon breeze without effort. Past the Tuileries Garden, the Grand Palais, and the Pont Alexandre III, all of Paris lay beneath them. The scent of fresh-baked, buttery croissants rose from *boulangeries* and street-side cafes. The sound of a dozen different languages mingled with the music of *La Vie En Rose*, played to provide the tourists with an "authentic Paris experience." All the city was alive, filled with the whisperings of history and the demands of the present day.

Rounding a gentle curve in the Seine, the Eiffel Tower vaulted up toward the blue sky, as the *Champ de Mars* spread out behind. From a short distance, they could now see the *Île aux Cygnes,* or Island of Swans, like a needle floating on the surface of the water. At its southern tip, a small, circular island lay empty and alone. On its shore, rosebushes heavy with nectar grew untouched by any hand except one.

Still leading the way, Esmée floated on a current of warm air, until she came to rest among the rosebuds on the shore of the *Île du Sacrifice.* The butterflies took a sip of nectar, quenching their thirst after their long flight from the Louvre. From their place in the rosebush, Esmée and Pierre looked around at the tiny island.

The shore was made-up of large boulders with tall grass sprouting out of every crack and crevice. In the center of the island, thick shrubs provided many places for a butterfly to nest. Wildflowers sprung up wherever roots could take hold. It was a safe, secluded place, too small to be of any interest to humans or predators.

"Are the memories painful?" Esmée asked, with some hesitation.

"*Mais non, ma petite,* they are not painful. For it was here that I found my courage; something I had long thought I did not possess. When I saw the wicked crow teetering on the edge there, I thought of you, *mon amour. Oui,* of you… but also of my mother. It was the anger of a child helpless to save his mother that made me fly with fierce purpose into the eye of danger itself. No, my sweet Esmée, the memories of this place are not painful at all. They feel more like the freedom of forgiveness -- hard won and overflowing with new life."

"Then we shall live here," she said, with resolve. "The Island of Sacrifice will be our home: *L'île du Papillon,* The Island of the Butterfly."

Pierre wrapped his wings around Esmée's

shoulders, pulling her close to his heart. On a little island of stones in the middle of the Seine -- within sight of the Eiffel Tower -- he kissed her, whispering, *"L'île des Papillons, ma petite.* The Island of Butterflies."

- THE END -

Afterword

Over the years, as time and tide etched away at the islands that stand in the swift waters of the Seine, many things have been lost. Once, a collection of boulders lay off the southern tip of the *Île aux Cygnes*; now, not a trace remains. Today, the Island of the Butterfly lies below the waterline, hidden from view and nearly forgotten.

Esmée and Pierre's children, grandchildren, and great-great-many-times-over-children nibbled the leaves of milkweed plants and emerged from their chrysalises to set out on adventures of their own. Generations of *belles dames* began their lives on the Island of the Butterfly; but, with the passage of time, fewer and fewer recalled exactly why it bore that name.

Recent generations have chosen the less windy, more sheltered spaces of such parks as *les Jardins du Trocadéro*, the Tuileries Garden, the *Champ de Mars,* or the *Parc André-Citroën,* without knowing anything about the roles such places played in the lives and love of their two ancestors. Since the *Île du Papillon* has been left empty and abandoned, few have returned to visit the site of the final struggle in the Battle of the Pont de Grenelle.

One, however, did return.

By the time the old badger had aged a decade, ten generations of Esmée and Pierre's children had come and gone. Though Boswell was still widely regarded as the most well-respected badger in all of Paris, he had long since been replaced as the source of all wisdom. Marmot, Victor, and *Hugo du Trocadéro, O.D.U.* took over as the three groundhogs most sought after (and least likely to be left in peace) by those needing advice or guidance.

Having spent much of the previous ten years in the company of the *Ignifuge* bees of Notre-Dame Cathedral, Boswell hadn't stepped foot in the *Champ de Mars* since departing by boat with Esmée, Audrey, Lisette and Pica. The honeybees and their *Magnificent Miel* had kept him quite occupied and exceedingly happy during those years. He saw no reason to return to his old den or visit the *Île du Papillon*, until news reached him from the *CM-TE server room*.

A message arrived from Victor, one afternoon, addressed to Boswell Badger, care of the *Ignifuge* bees. As with all messages of an urgent nature, this one was hand-delivered. Barthélemy Courrier, the *network manager* of the *Notre-Dame server room*, saw to it that the important message made it into the badger's hands.

The previous few days had seen thunderstorms and flooding -- the likes of which, few could recall – wreaking havoc all throughout the ancient city. The Seine had swelled to such a height that it overflowed its banks, spilling onto stone walkways and reaching up to splash against the bottoms of bridges in its path.

The entrances to many tunnels along the Boulogne *network* were entirely washed away, as the river pushed inland in great surges of mud and water. Whole islands were swallowed up by the rising tide; and when the flood waters finally receded, not all of these islands resurfaced from the depths. It was about this that Victor's message now spoke.

"Priority 2: Important
From: Network Manager, CM-TE Server Room
To: Boswell Badger, c/o Ignifuge bees, Notre-Dame

Alert: *Île du Papillon* lost in the flood. Thought you'd want to know. -Victor"

The news struck Boswell to the heart. He always held Esmée in high regard; and, of course, everyone who had lived through the events surrounding the Battle of the Pont de Grenelle remembered Pierre's final sacrifice. Had it not been for the butterfly's bravery and selflessness, the wicked leader of the crows would still be terrorizing every animal who attempted to traverse the open fields and woodlands between Saint-Denis and Paris.

The badger determined, then and there, to visit the site of the *Île du Papillon,* where Esmée and Pierre had made their home, and pay his final respects to the memory of his dear friends. In fact, he wanted to do just a little more than that.

During his time spent living among the gardens of Notre-Dame Cathedral, Boswell Badger had made the acquaintance of the cardinal-archbishop. A shared love of learning, and a deep appreciation for the *Miraculous Miel* of the rooftop honeybees, blossomed into a strong friendship between the badger and the archbishop. Boswell now intended to cash-in on their relationship and ask his friend for a favor.

Requesting an audience with the archbishop, the badger stated his case.

"Your Eminence, thank you for seeing me," Boswell began.

"*Monsieur* Badger, it's always a pleasure. How may I be of service?" the cardinal replied, with great esteem for his most well-respected friend.

"We have spent many years working together, distributing honey to the poor of the city – human and animal, alike. I've been honored to play a small role in this worthy charity; and I thank you for it." Boswell was at his most formal and diplomatic.

"You have been an example to all who know you," the cardinal said, resting one hand on the badger's shoulder. "I can't imagine a more noble creature in all of Paris."

"That's why I've asked to speak with you," Boswell said, humbly lowering his white-whiskered face, with sincere modesty. "For there *is* a more noble creature in Paris, or rather, there *was*. It is he whom I hope to honor, with your help."

"I will help you in any way that I can," the cardinal promised. "Please, tell me more."

Boswell then proceeded to recount the entire story of Esmée's unwilling journey to Paris; the search and rescue mission that followed; and the Battle of the Pont de Grenelle, during which Pierre made the ultimate sacrifice to save his friends.

The badger spoke of how the *Ignifuge* bees found and nursed Pierre back to health, at last restoring him to Esmée. Finally, Boswell told the cardinal-archbishop about the *Île du Sacrifice* -- the *Île du Papillon* -- and how it was claimed by the floodwaters during the dreadful storms of the past few days.

"Though the island has been lost," the badger continued, "I would like to honor the memory of both Esmée and Pierre with a small sculpture marking the site where so much was sacrificed for so many. Of course, we cannot erect anything that would be visible to humans, as they would neither understand its meaning nor allow it to remain in place. So, the sculpture I have in mind would need to be sent below the surface of the water, to live on the sunken island as a perpetual memorial to these two noble hearts."

Pausing a moment and sensing that the cardinal would surely agree to his request, Boswell asked the question he'd been leading up to.

"Your Eminence, would you help me by ordering that such a sculpture be made by the skilled artisans who work in the service of the cathedral? I lack the means to pay for such a commission, but I assure you it is a worthy endeavor. If you are able to help, once the sculpture is finished, I will carry it to the *Île du Papillon* myself."

"It shall be as you wish, my friend; for, no request of yours could exceed the value of our friendship. Leave your plans with me, and I will commission the sculpture. In three days-time, return to see me and I will deliver it into your worthy hands along with my blessing."

"Thank you, Your Eminence," Boswell said, with a low bow. "You have my gratitude and the gratitude of every animal in Paris."

Boswell took leave of the cardinal and returned to his home in the Square Jean XXIII. Once there, he immediately sent a reply to Victor's message via Barthélemy Courrier, the *network manager* of the *Notre-Dame server room.*

"**Priority 2:** Important
From: Boswell Badger, c/o Ignifuge bees, Notre-Dame
To: Victor, *Network Manager, CM-TE Server Room*

Alert: Message received. Indeed, I *did* want to know of the loss of the Island of the Butterfly. Meet me at the southern tip of the *Île aux Cygnes* in four days -- on March 6th at 2:00 p.m. At that time, we shall honor our friends and the tragic loss of their home. -Boswell Badger"

The next three days were spent in preparation for Boswell's trip south. It was time for him to leave the Square Jean XXIII for good and return to his home in the *Champ de Mars.* He'd been away for nearly ten years, and he'd learned everything the *Ignifuge* bees had to teach him. Lasting friendships had been forged with the bees and the cardinal-archbishop. Now Boswell needed to return to his den and restore his friendship with the groundhogs, squirrels and garden ants.

Packing his few belongings – some notebooks he'd kept over the years, detailing things he'd learned; a beeswax candle he'd been given by the archbishop as a thank you for his work delivering honey to the needy animals of the city; and the fragile remnants of a single pressed and brittle rose – Boswell said his goodbyes to the *Ignifuge* bees, then awaited the appointed time to return to the cardinal's quarters.

On the third day, true to his word, the cardinal-archbishop of Notre-Dame Cathedral presented Boswell Badger with a little, iron sculpture in the shape of a butterfly. It was exactly what the badger had requested, down to the smallest detail. Twice the size of a badger's paw, the sculpture would just barely cover the open palm of a grown man's hand. It was perfect.

"You and your friends will always have a home among the gardens of Notre-Dame, my friend," the archbishop assured Boswell. "I hope to have your help every year, when the time for distributing honey comes around. It will give us a chance to catch up. I will look for you next summer. Until then, go with my blessing and may the memory of Esmée and Pierre be eternal."

"Thank you, Your Eminence. If these tired, old legs of mine can carry me here next summer, you will have my help. My friendship will always be yours."

With that, the old badger placed the butterfly

sculpture inside the bag containing his belongings, then turned and headed toward the river.

After ten years spent in and around Notre-Dame Cathedral, the boatmen of the area were well acquainted with Boswell Badger. The most well-respected badger in Paris no longer had to stowaway aboard whatever boat he could find. He no longer needed to try and remain unseen or worry about being thrown overboard if he *were* discovered. Boswell could now choose from any number of boats, and ride in comfort as a welcomed guest.

It was now around 11:00 a.m. on Friday, March 6th. Boswell had plenty of time to get to the southern tip of the Island of Swans by 2:00 p.m. Since this was his first boat ride all the way back down the Seine in nearly a decade, he wanted to take his time and enjoy every sight, sound and memory along the way. Sitting on a *chaise lounge* beneath an umbrella on the upper deck of a tourist boat belonging to his friend, Captain Dérive, Boswell looked out over the port-side railing. Slowly, they left the dock, entered the main current of the river, and began their journey downstream.

So many memories drifted by. He saw Audrey's library, off to the left; and *les Ponts de Paris* -- each and every one of which had been visited by Lisette and Pica's team of exploration. Everywhere he looked, something looked back at him and reminded him of his friends. How he missed them all.

As Captain Dérive piloted the boat around a curve in the river, a familiar sight came into view: *le Champ de Mars;* the location of his old den. Across the river on the right he saw *les Jardins du Trocadéro;* and dead ahead, the Eiffel Tower. He'd forgotten how much he loved this particular corner of the world. Each landmark was like a kindly smile welcoming him home.

Passing the tower, Boswell now crossed beneath the first of three bridges connecting the *Île aux Cygnes* to both banks of the river. Motoring down the length of the narrow strip of land, the second bridge soon glided overhead. A few moments later, the Pont de Grenelle became visible, at the far end of the island.

As they approached the southern tip of the *Île aux Cygnes*, Boswell saw a group of tourists standing around the water's edge. He was concerned that they might pose a problem to what he had in mind; but it was just as likely that they'd all run away at the sight of a badger. He intended to do everything in his power to make them do just that.

The captain guided the boat up alongside the island, where a ramp was let out from the deck just for Boswell's use. Thanking the crew, the badger walked down the gangplank and onto the dry land of the Island of Swans. The boat then continued on its way downriver.

Carrying the iron sculpture of a butterfly in his bag of belongings, Boswell Badger walked down the wide, central sidewalk until he reached a covered area sheltering a playground and some workout equipment. As he drew closer to the mini-Statue of Liberty's pedestal, he now recognized the faces of those whom he had earlier mistaken for tourists. They were not tourists at all, but old friends.

Victor was the first to notice Boswell's arrival. The groundhog walked over and, without saying a word, clasped the badger's paw in his own. After Victor, Hugo was the next to welcome his friend. No longer afraid or intimidated, the Hero of the Battle of the Pont de Grenelle hugged the once-grumpy Boswell Badger, who was becoming visibly emotional with each new greeting.

Next, came the *network manager* of the *T1 server room*.

"It's been a while," Marmot said, as he patted Boswell on the back. "Still as weepy as ever, I see." Marmot laughed, noticing a tear in the badger's eye.

"More so, old friend," Boswell said, without the

slightest hint of shame. "Much more so, I'm afraid. But who can blame me? I never expected…"

"You never expected to see all of *us*," Marmot interrupted (some things never change), "but we *all* needed to be here. We loved Esmée; and I, for one, will never forget Pierre. I'll never forget what happened here."

A look of painful remembrance darkened Marmot's face, as he turned toward the waters that lay off the tip of the island. All the events of that fateful day came rushing back to him: how he had led a team of squirrels across the Seine, and into danger. The encounter with the leader of the crows played out in slow motion in his memory. Dragging Hugo to safety; freeing Pierre from the hateful grip of murderous talons; the blow Marmot delivered to the old bird's beak; it was all still too near, as if it had happened only yesterday.

Boswell reached into his bag and pulled out the cast iron sculpture of a butterfly. The three groundhogs gathered around the badger, who slowly began to speak.

"Many times, over the last few years, I'd thought to visit this place. I wanted to leave some token of respect for our friends and for the heroic acts that took place here. When Victor's message arrived, I thought it may be too late. The island had been reclaimed by the river, just as time had begun to reclaim remembrance. But it's never too late to honor those we love.

"And so," Boswell held the butterfly sculpture in his hand, high enough for everyone to see, "We stand here within reach of the Island of Sacrifice. Though it is hidden beneath the waves, we know it's there. The same will now be true of this memorial-butterfly. Though hidden, it will never be forgotten -- just like Esmée and Pierre will always be remembered, hidden in our hearts."

Boswell tossed the sculpture out over the water where it broke the surface of the Seine, sank out of sight, and finally came to rest on the *Île du Papillon*.

Everyone stood in silence, gazing at the river, remembering.

The badger recalled the time when he first met Esmée and Pierre in the clover patch near his den.

Victor remembered climbing up Boswell's back on the side of the Eiffel Tower and being greeted by the butterflies on the first floor.

Hugo thought about the feeling of helplessness he experienced as he watched the crow swoop down and scoop Pierre up in its claws. The groundhog barely had time to think, before jumping on its back.

Marmot just stared into the water. He had no desire to relive the events of that awful day, not even in his mind.

After a few moments, Boswell Badger once again reached into his bag and pulled out the pressed and withered remains of a rose. Turning to Marmot, he asked, "Do you recognize it, my friend?"

"Is it…"

"It is," the badger assured him. "Picked by your own hand from the *Île du Sacrifice* and given to Esmée that very same night."

Walking over to the river's edge, Boswell bent over and placed the rose in the water. Victor, Hugo and Marmot drew near.

"I kept it all these years, just to bring it here. And so, now I have," Boswell said, as the waves carried the rose out over the place where the iron butterfly now rested.

Standing once again, the badger whispered in the direction of the rose, "You're home."

Then turning to the three groundhogs, he said with a smile, "… *for the river will always lead you home again.*"

Postscript

Even today, if you were able to look beneath the surface of the Seine off the southern tip of the *Île aux Cygnes*, you would find a small, cast iron butterfly marking the location of the *Île du Papillon*; for, wonder can always be found where fiction and reality meet.

Cupid Playing with a Butterfly

Sculpture in marble by Antoine-Denis Chaudet.
Louvre Museum, Paris.

Glossary of French Phrases

À bientôt (Ah be-en-toe). See you later.

À droite (Ah dwah-t). To the right.

À droite ou à gauche (Ah dwah-t ooh ah goash). To the right or to the left.

À la gare (Ah la gair). At the train station.

Allons (Ah-lon). Let's go!

Apéro (A-pair-oh). A time for enjoying appetizers before dinner.

Après toi (Ah-pray twah). After you.

Arc de Triomphe (Arc duh Tree-ohmf). The Arch of Triumph built in honor of Napoleon's victories.

Attention à la marche en descendant du train (Ah-ton-see-own a la marsh on da-sahn-da do tren). Watch your step when getting off the train.

Au revoir (Oh rev-wah). Goodbye.

Audrey Loriot (Audrey Lor-ree-oh). The butterfly who loves to read and leads the search for Esmèe, along with Pica.

Avec toi (Ah-vek twah). With you.

Aventure (Ah-ven-two-er). Adventure.

Ballon Generali (Bah-lone Gener-ah-lee). The helium ballon located in the Parc André-Citroën in the middle of Paris.

Beaugrenelle Mall (Bo-gren-nell Mall). The shopping mall located near where the Battle of the Pont de Grenelle takes place. The mall has a rooftop garden complete with grass and trees.

Belle dame (Bell dahm). Beautiful lady; the species of butterfly Esmée, Audrey, and Pierre belong to. Also called a painted lady butterfly.

Bibliothèque Mazarine (Biblio-tech Maz-ah-reen). The largest library in France, located in Paris.

Bien (Be-en). Well.

Bien sûr (Be-en soor). Of course.

Bir-Hakeim (Beer Ha-keem). The metro station near the Eiffel Tower.

Bois de Boulogne (Bwah duh Boo-lone). The large forest just outside Paris where the Bois de Boulogne groundhogs come from.

Bonjour (Bone-jshoor). Hello.

Bonne journée (Bone jshoor-nay). Good day.

Bonne nuit (Bone new-ee). Good night.

Bonsoir (Bone-swar). Good evening.

Boucherie (Boo-sherry). Butcher shop.

Boulangerie (Boo-lohn-jsher-ee). Bakery.

Brigitte Lessier (Bree-jsheet Less-ee-ay). One of the groundhogs who carry messages along the Bois de Boulogne network.

Brother Apius (Brother Ay-pee-yiss). Discovered the cure to Grumpy Pucker Face, befriended the Ignifuge bees and brought them to Notre-Dame Cathedral.

Brother Zephyrinus (Brother Zeffer-eye-niss). Friend to Brother Apius who helped him escape with the Ignifuge bees under the cover of darkness.

Bures-sur-Yvette (Boor-sir-Eevette). A stop along the RER B train line.

C'est ici (Say-t ee-see). It's here.

C'est magnifique (Say mah-nee-feek). It's magnificent.

C'est toi (Say twah). It's you.

C'est une bonne idée (Say-t oon bone ee-deh). It's a good idea.

C'est une longue histoire (Say-t oon long east-wahr). It's a long story.

C'est vrai (Say vray). It's true.

Ça va bien (Sah vah be-en). Are you well?

Certainement (Sair-ten-mohn). Certainly.

Champ de Mars (Shawm duh Mars). The park behind the Eiffel Tower where Boswell Badger lives.

Champs-Élysées (Shawm Eh-lees-ay). The broad, tree-lined avenue running between the Arc de Triomphe and the Place de la Concorde.

Château de Beynac (Sha-toe duh Bay-nack). The Beynac Castle in the French region of Dordogne.

Chaudet (Show-day). The sculpter who created the statue of Cupid presenting a rose to the butterfly, called "Cupid Playing with a Butterfly."

Chèvre (Shev). Goat.

Chloé (Kloe-ee). The inchworm who tells Lisette about Audrey and Pica's quest to find Esmée.

Cité Universitaire (See-tee Oon-nee-vair-see-tay). A stop along the RER B train line.

Cochon (Ko-shaw). Pig.

Comment (Ko-mo). How.

Comment ça va (Ko-mo sah vah). How are you doing?

Comment vas-tu aujourd'hui (Ko-mo vah-two oh-jshor-dwee). How are you doing today?

Corbeaux (Kor-boh). Crows.

Courcelle-sur-Yvette (Coor-sell-sir-Ee-vette). A stop along the RER B train line.

Crêpes (Krepp). Like a pancake, but thinner and filled with anything from fruit and whipped cream to ham and cheese.

Crique de Rouen (Creek duh Roo-ahn). The mouth of the Seine River, where it meets the English Channel in the north of France.

Croissant (Kwa-sun). Crescent-shaped flaky pastry that is sometimes baked with chocolate chips -- very light and delicious!

Denfert-Rochereau (Den-fair-Ro-shrow). A stop along the

RER B train line.

Devereux Délabré, Esq. (Dev-er-oh Dell-ah-bray, Esquire). A venerable old squirrel who was honored with the title Esq. which means Exceptional Squirrel.

Dordogne (Door-don). A region in the southwest of France known for its beautiful forests, rolling hills, castles and prehistoric caves.

Église (Ay-gleez). Church.

Enchanté (On-shon-tay). Nice to meet you.

Esmée Délancourt (Ez-may Dell-on-coor). A Butterfly in Paris! Esmée gets trapped on a commuter train and must find her way back to her friends.

Et toi (Ay twah). And you.

Et, non madame (Ay, no madam). And, no madam.

Étretat (Ay-tray-tah). Beautiful cliffs in Normandy, France - overlooking the English Channel, one of which is shaped like an elephant.

Fantastique (Fon-tah-steek). Fantastic.

Fleur-de-Beynac (Fler duh Bay-nack). Flower of Beynac - fictional town in the region of Dordogne in the southwest of France.

Foie Gras (Fwah grah). A delicacy made from duck liver and fat. It doesn't sound very delicious, but it is.

Fontaine-Michalon (Fon-tane-Mee-sha-lo). A stop along the RER B train line.

Fourmi (Four-me). The Queen of the Garden Ants of France, and friend of Boswell Badger.

Frére Apius (Frair Ay-pee-us). Brother Apius. In French, brother is frére.

Fromager (Fro-majsh-ay). Cheesemaker.

Fromagerie (Fro-majsh-air-ee). Cheese factory or store.

Gare du Nord (Gair-doo-Nor). Enormous train station in the North of Paris.

Gâteau (Gah-toe). Cake.

Gato (Gah-toe). Spanish word for Cat.

Gendarme (Jshon-darm). Policeman.

Gendarmerie (Jshon-darm-air-ee). The Police.

Gentille (Jshon-tee). Kind, nice.

Geoffrey Glouton (Geeyoff-ray Glue-toh). Groundhog whose pantry was raided by ants. He overreacts and causes distrust to ruin the relationship between groundhogs and ants for many years.

Gif-sur-Yvette (Jsheef-sir-Ee-vette). A stop along the RER B train line.

Grand Palais (Grahnd Pal-ay). Grand Palace, museum in the heart of Paris.

Grande maison (Grahnd May-zoe). Big house.

Honfleur (Ohn-fler). A seaside fishing village on the English Channel.

Hourra (Ooh-rah). Hooray!

Ignifuge (Eeg-nee-foo-jsh). The mythical bees of Notre-Dame, their name means fireproof.

Île aux Cygnes (Eel oh Seen). Island of Swans.

Île de la Cité (Eel duh la See-tay). City Island, the most ancient part of Paris, it is where Notre-Dame is located.

Impeccable (Ahm-pay-cobb-leh). Spotless, flawless, perfect.

J'ai une idée (Jshy oon ee-day-eu). I have an idea.

J'y vais (Jshee vay). I go, I'm going!

Jardins du Trocadéro (Jshar-don doo Tro-kah-dair-oh). The gardens across the river from the Eiffel Tower, home of Hugo the groundhog and a thousand squirrels.

Je m'appelle (Jsheu ma-pell). My name is.

Je me souviens (Jsheu meh soo-vee-en). I remember.

Je ne sais pas (Jsheu neh say pah). I don't know.

Je ne savais pas (Jsheu neh sah-vah pah). I didn't know.

Je ne suis pas la magpie! Je suis Pica Pica (Jsheu neh swee pah lah magpie! Jsheu swee Peeka Peeka.). I'm not the magpie. I'm Pica Pica.

Je pensais que tu étais Esmée (Jsheu pon-say keh two ay-tay Ez-may). I thought you were Esmée.

Je suis content d'attendre (Jsheu swee con-ton da-tohnd). I am happy to wait.

Je suis de Saint-Denis (Jsheu swee duh Sahn Den-ee). I am from Saint-Denis.

Je suis désolée (Jsheu swee deh-so-lay). I'm sorry.

Je suis très heureux (Jsheu swee tray her-er). I am very happy.

Jouy-en-Josas (Jsheu-wee own Jshow-sass). A town between Saint-Denis and Paris.

L'île du Papillon (L-eel doo Pap-ee-yone). The Island of the Butterfly.

L'île du Sacrifice (L-eel doo Sack-ree-feese). The Island of Sacrifice.

L'âme Perdue (Lahm Pair-doo). The Lost Soul.

L'arbuste à papillons (Lar-boost ah pap-ee-yone). The butterfly bush in Madame Legrand's backyard.

L'esprit d'aventure (Lay-spree d'ah-vuhn-toor). The Spirit of Adventure.

L'Yvette (Lee-vette). The Yvette River which runs from Rambouillet through Saint-Denis.

La Croix de Berny (La Cwah duh Bare-nee). A stop along the RER B train line.

La Dame Errante (La Dahm Air-ron). The Wandering Lady.

La Ferme Deschamps (La Fairm Day-shawm). The Deschamps Farm.

La gare (La Gair). The train station.

La Hacquinière (La Ah-keen-yair). A stop along the RER B train line.

La Manche (La Mawnsh). French name for the English Channel.

La Seine Musicale (La Sen Muse-ee-cahl). An orchestra house located in the south of Paris on an island in the middle of the Seine.

La Vie en Rose (La Vee on Rose). Famous French song often played only for the sake of tourists.

Le bon père (Le bon pair). The good father (priest).

Le Code de la Route (Le code de la root). The Rules of the Road, Driver's Manual.

Le duc de Nullepart (Le duke de Nool-par). The Duke of Nullpart (fictional town meaning Nowhere).

Le Faune Sautant (Le phon so-taunt). The Leaping Faun.

Le fleuve (Le floove). The River (indicates a very large river).

Le Guichet (Le Gee-shay). A stop along the RER B train line.

Le Havre (Le-ahv-ruh). A town in the north of France, on the English Channel.

Le Journal (Le Joor-nahl). Literally, the newspaper.

Le métro (Le may-troe). The metro.

Le métro n'est pas loin (Le may-troe nay pah loo-wahn). The metro isn't far.

Le Musée du Louvre (Le Moo-say doo Loov-ra). The Louvre Museum.

Le Palais du Louvre (Le Pal-ay doo Loov-ra). The Louvre Palace, another name for the Louvre Museum.

Le papillon reine du Louvre (Le pap-ee-yone ren doo Loov-ra). The Butterfly Queen of the Louvre, a nickname given to Esmée by the people who saw her on top of the Pyramide.

Le sommet (Le so-may). The summit, pinnacle, top.

Le Temps des Chèvres (Le toe day Shev). The Goat Times, or Time of the Goat.

Les Arbres du Souvenir (Lays Ar-bra day Soo-ven-eer). The Trees of Remembrance near where a young Pierre played hide and seek with his mother.

Les Invalides (Lays On-va-leed). The Disabled, a place in Paris containing museums, monuments and a hospital for war veterans.

Les papillons (Lay pap-ee-yone). The butterflies.

Les ponts de Paris (Lay Pon duh Pair-ee). The Bridges of Paris.

Les Yvelines (Lays Ee-vah-leen). A region of France just outside of Paris in which Saint-Denis is located.

Lisette Cueilleur (Lees-ette Coo-yair). Esmèe's best friend, they share a BB-Day and are rarely apart from one another.

Louvre (Loov-ra). The world's largest museum, located in Paris, famous for housing the Mona Lisa among many other treasures. The Louvre used to be a palace, and it is so large it's impossible to visit every exhibit in one day.

Lozère (Lo-zair). A stop along the RER B train line.

Luxembourg (Loox-ahm-boor). A stop along the RER B train line.

Ma chère (Mah shair). My dear.

Ma maison (Mah may-zone). My home, my house.

Ma petite (Mah pet-eet). My little one.

Madame Legrand (Mah-dom Le-groh). She owns the butterfly bush in which dozens of butterflies meet to enjoy their breakfast every day.

Mademoiselle (Mad-mwoh-zell). Miss. An unmarried, young woman.

Maintenant (Ment-no). Now.

Mais le faucon (May le fo-cone). But, the falcon.

Mais oui (May wee). But, yes - of course.

Malevolum pokerfacie (Mal-lev-oh-lum poker-fatch-ee). Poker face, a fictional sickness.

Malevolum puckerfacie (mal-ev-o-lum pucker-fatch-ee). Grumpy Pucker Face a fictional
sickness afflicting the people of Glowermouth-on-Dart in England who were poisoned by a wicked fromager.

Maman (Mama). Mommy.

Mardi: Fermé (Mar-dee: Fair-may). Tuesday: Closed.

Marmot (Mar-mut). Groundhog and Network Manager of the T1 server room who accompanies Audrey and Pica north to meet Boswell Badger.

Mascarons (Mask-are-own). Faces, masks carved into bridges along the Seine in Paris.

Massy-Palaiseau (Mass-see-Pal-ay-zoh). A stop along the RER B train line.

Méchant's Fromage de Chèvre (May-shownt Froh-mah-jsh duh Chev). Méchant's Goat Cheese.

Megalina (Mega-leena). The field mouse who can copy pictures using her teeth.

Merci (Mair-see). Thank you.

Merci à toi (Mair-see ah twah). Thanks to you.

Merci beaucoup (Mair-see bo-coo). Thank you very much.

Merci, gentille dame (Mair-see jshahn-tee dom, mair-see).

Thank you, kind lady.

Merci, mon amie! Profitez de votre miel (Mair-see mone ah-mee! Pro-fee-tay duh vote mee-el). Thank you, my friend. Enjoy your honey.

Messieurs (Mess-yer). Plural form of monsieur. Sirs.

Meudon Forest (Meh-doh Forest). The forest located between Saint-Denis and Paris.

Michel (Mee-shell). Michael.

Miel (Mee-yell). Honey.

Moi (Mwah). Me.

Moi aussi (Mwah oh-see). Me, too.

Mon ami (Moan ah-mee). My friend.

Mon amour (Moan ah-more). My love.

Mon histoire (Moan ee-stwah). My story.

Monsieur (Miss-yer). Sir.

Monsieur, vous êtes merveilleux (Miss-yer, voos et mair-vay-yer). Sir, you are marvelous.

Montgomery Bazillac (Moan-goam-ree Bahz-zee-yack). One of the squirrels who leads a squad in search of Esmée and Pierre.

Montmartre (Moan-mart). The high hill in Paris upon which sits Sacré-Cœur Basillica. The view from Montmartre is spectacular.

Musée d'Orsay (Moo-say Dorsay). Museum in Paris famous for its Impressionist paintings.

Myrtilles (Meer-teel). Blueberries.

N'ayez pas peur (Nay-yay pah per). Do not be afraid.

N'est-ce pas (Ness-pah). Isn't it?

Nicolas Méchant (Nee-ko-lah May-shaw). Wicked cheesemaker who poisons the people of Glowermouth-on-Dart and strikes an evil deal with the Wizard of the Valley.

Noble histoire (Nobe-leh ee-stwah). Noble history.

Non (No). No.

Nous avons besoin d'une aventure (Noos av-on beh-swan doon ah-vuhn-tyure). We need an adventure.

Nous serons toujours amis (Noos air-on two-jshoors ah-mee). We will always be friends.

Nullepart (Nool-par). Fictional town in the Dordogne region of southwest France.

Orsay-Ville (Or-say Vee). A stop along the RER B train line.

Oui (Wee). Yes.

Oui monsieur, un peu (Wee miss-yer, on per). Yes, sir, a little.

Palaiseau-Villebon (Pal-lay-so-Veel-bon). A stop along the RER B train line.

Parc André-Citroën (Park Ahn-dray See-trow-en). A park in Paris, famous for its helium balloon.

Parc de Passy (Park duh Pass-see). One of many small parks in Paris.

Parc de Sceaux (Park duh Scoh). A stop along the RER B train line.

Parc Sainte-Périne (Park Saunt Pair-een). Another one of many parks in Paris.

Pardon (Par-doan). Excuse me, pardon me.

Parfumier (Par-foom-ee-yay). Perfume manufacturer.

Pas de Mâcheurs (Pah day Mah-share). No Chewers!

Pas exactement (Pahs ay-zact-uh-moan). Not exactly.

Pas mouillé (Pah moo-yay). Not wet.

Passerelle Léopold-Sédar-Senghor (Just call it the "Pon Lee-o" - it's too hard to say!). Léopold-Sédar-Senghor footbridge crossing the Seine in Paris. The name is so long and hard to pronounce, Lisette and Jenna just call it the Pont Leo.

Pathé Beaugrenelle Movie Theatre (Pat-tay Bo-gren-nell Movie Theater). Movie theater in Paris, located near the Beaugrenelle Mall and the Pont de Grenelle.

Penelope Porcher (Pen-nay-loap Por-shay). Own the lilac bush in which Audrey lives in Saint-Denis.

Père Lamoine (Pair Lah-mwahn). Priest at the Church of Saint-Denis, not a very good public speaker.

Périphérique (Pair-ee-fair-eek). The highway that encircles Paris.

Petit (Peh-tee). Small, little.

Petit déjeuner (Peh-tee day-jshah-nay). Breakfast, literally "little lunch."

Pica Pica (Peeka Peeka). The repetitive magpie who goes on a search and rescue mission with Audrey Loriot.

Pierre Cardui (Pee-air Car-doo-wee). Esmèe's boyfriend who shows her around Paris and fights in the Battle of the Pont de Grenelle.

Pistache (Pee-stahsh). One of the Squirrel Squad leaders.

Place de la Concorde (Plahs duh la Con-core). Enormous plaza and traffic circle in Paris, in the middle of which stands the Egyptian obelisk.

Place Saint-Michel (Plahss Saun Mee-shell). Plaza in Paris where the statue of St. Michael is located.

Pont Alexandre III (Pon Alex-ah-nder twah). The Alexander the Third bridge over the Seine River in Paris.

Pont d'Iéna (Pon Dee-nah). Bridge of Iéna crossing the Seine in Paris.

Pont de Grenelle (Pon duh Gren-nell). Bridge where the Battle of the Pont de Grenelle takes place, located near the small Statue of Liberty on the Island of Swans.

Pont de l'Alma (Pon duh l-Al-ma). The Alma bridge over the Seine in Paris.

Pont de la Concorde (Pon duh lah Con-core). The Concorde bridge which crosses the Seine near the Place de la Concorde.

Pont Debilly (Pon Deh-bee-yee). The Debilly bridge crossing the Seine in Paris.

Pont des Arts (Pon days Art). The bridge of Arts over the Seine in Paris.

Pont des Invalides (Pon days Ahn-va-leed). Bridge of the Invalides crossing the Seine in Paris.

Pont Double (Pon Doo-ble). The Double bridge crossing the Seine in Paris.

Pont du Carrousel (Pon doo Carousel). The bridge of the carousel which crosses the Seine near the Arc du Carrousel.

Pont Neuf (Pon Neouf). The most famous and oldest bridge in Paris, crossing the Seine at the Île de la Cité.

Pont Rouelle (Pon Roo-ell). Rouelle Bridge crossing the Seine in Paris.

Port-Royal (Port-Roy-yahl). A stop along the RER B train line.

Pour (Poor). For.

Pour Gare du Nord Paris (Poor Gair doo Nor Pair-ee). For the Gare du Nord Station in Paris.

Pour toujours et à jamais (Poor two-jshoors ate a jshah-may). Forever and ever.

Pourquoi (Poor-qwah). Why?

Prêt (Pray). Ready!

Prima donna (Preema doan-ah). Someone who is a bit conceited and likes to act more important than they really are. A term used by Pierre to describe the Eiffel Tower.

Profitez de vos aventures (Pro-feet-tay duh vose ah-ven-two-er). Enjoy your adventures.

Puis-je (Pee-jsh). May I?

Pyramide du Louvre (Peer-ah-meed doo Loov-ra). The Louvre Pyramid which is made of glass and located in the outer courtyard of plaza between the two arms of the Palais du Louvre.

Qu'ils mangent du gato (Keel mawnjsh doo gat-toe). Let them eat cat.

Que le geôlier soit emprisonné (Keh le jo-lee-yay swat ahm-pree-soan-ay). Let the jailer be imprisoned!

Quel est votre nom (Kell ay votrah nohm). What is your name?

Quel oiseau pénible (Kell wah-so pen-nee-blah). What a painful bird, what an annoying bird!

Qui est là (Key ay lah). Who is it? Who's here?

Qui êtes vous (Key et voo). Who are you?

Quinze (Cahns). Fifteen.

Quoi (Kwah). What?

Rambouillet (Rahm-boo-yay). A town not far from Saint-Denis, where the Yvette River begins.

Raquel Apprise (Rock-kell Ah-preez). One of the groundhogs who carry messages along the network.

Regarde le papillon (Ray-guard le pap-ee-yon). Look at the butterfly!

Regardez (Ray-guard-ay). Look!

Reginald Renault (Reginald Ren-know). The squirrel who carries a message from Marmot to the network manager of the Beaugrenelle server room, Gus.

Richelieu (Ree-shell-you). The name of one of the wings or sections of the Louvre Museum, in which the statue of Cupid giving a rose to the butterfly is located.

Rien, pour le moment (Ree-yen, poor le mo-mo). Nothing, at the moment.

Rond-point (Roan-pwan). Roundabout, traffic circle.

Roquefort cheese (Roak-four cheese). Delicious blue cheese, St. Augur is the best, in my opinion!

Rue François Chesneau (Roo Frahn-swah Shay-no). Fictional street in Saint-Denis on which Lisette lives.

Rues and routes (Roos and routes). Streets and roads.

S'il vous plait (See voo play). Please.

Saint-Denis-lès-Chevreuse (Saun Den-nee lay Shev-reuse). Fictional town in France, based on the real town named Saint-Remy-lès-Chevreuse.

Saint-Michel (Saun Mee-shell). Saint Michael.

Saint-Michel-Notre-Dame (Saun Mee-shell-No-trah-Dom). A stop along the RER B train line.

Saint-Michel, s'il vous plaît, accompagnez mon amie (Saun Mee-shell, see voo play, ah-comb-pah-nay moan ah-mee.). Saint Michael, please be with my friend.

Sainte-Chapelle (Saun Shah-pell). A chapel in Paris famous for its beautiful stained-glass windows.

Seine (Sen). The large river that runs through Paris all the way to the English Channel in the north.

Square Jean-XXIII (Skwair Jshawn Ven-twah). The gardens located behind Notre-Dame Cathedral.

Sylvie de Clément (Sill-vee duh Clem-mo). Another butterfly from Saint-Denis who discovers the secret of the hidden barrier (windows).

Toujours (Two-jshoor). Always.

Tour Montparnasse (Two-er Moan-par-nass). Tall office building in Paris.

Tous les jours (Two lay jshoor). Every day.

'Tout droit' and 'à droite' (Two dwah -and- ah dwaht). Straight ahead -and- to the right.

Très bien (Tray be-en). Very well.

Très loin (Tray loo-wah). Very near.

Tu es très gentil (Two ay tray jshawn-tee). You are very kind.

Tu vas bien (Two vah be-en). Are you well? Are you ok?

Tuileries Garden (Twill-er-ees Garden). Large gardens located between the Louvre Museum and the Place de la Concorde.

Un mythe, peut-être (On meeth, poo-tet-ra). A myth, maybe.

Un petit papillon (On pet-tee pap-ee-yon). A little butterfly.

Une distraction (Oon dee-stract-see-yoan). A distraction.

Université de Paris (Oon-nee-vair-see-tay duh Pair-ee). University of Paris.

Votre arbre (Vote-ra arb). Your tree.

About the Author & Illustrator

Matt Pelicano was born and raised in Upstate New York, the youngest of eight kids.

From his youth, Matt has always loved the poetry of E.E. Cummings, Shel Silverstein, TS Eliot, Walt Whitman, Robert Frost, and William Shakespeare.

His literary heroes include JRR Tolkien, CS Lewis, Oscar Wilde, Agatha Christie and David McCullough. At age 10, he pulled an old guitar out of the trash, taught himself to play, and soon began writing lyrics, songs, poetry, short stories and books.

A widower, Matt has three children, Andy, Joey and Megan, and lives in Greenville, SC with his family of three people, five cats and one dog.

Don Cornue, Artist, Illustrator and Graphic Designer has lived and worked in Central New York for over 50 years. He was employed as an art director for a leading manufacturing firm, retiring after 36 years. He has since been working on his own, specializing in graphic and logo design as well as architectural illustration and portraiture in various mediums. Examples of his work can be seen at **www.DonCornue.com**.

Visit Matt online at:
www.MattPelicano.com

Facebook.com/MattPelicanoWriter
Instagram.com/MattPelicano

CPSIA information can be obtained
at www.ICGtesting.com
Printed in the USA
FSHW021840210520
70347FS